IT SEEMED LIKE A *Good Idea*

LAUREN BLAKELY

COSMO READS

Copyright © 2025 by Lauren Blakely
Cover and internal design © 2025 by Sourcebooks
Cover design by Nicole Lecht/Sourcebooks
Cover art by Yordanka Poleganova

Sourcebooks and the colophon are registered trademarks of Sourcebooks.

All rights reserved. No part of this book may be reproduced in any form or by any electronic or mechanical means including information storage and retrieval systems—except in the case of brief quotations embodied in critical articles or reviews—without permission in writing from its publisher, Sourcebooks.

No part of this book may be used or reproduced in any manner for the purpose of training artificial intelligence technologies or systems.

The characters and events portrayed in this book are fictitious or are used fictitiously. Any similarity to real persons, living or dead, is purely coincidental and not intended by the author.

All brand names and product names used in this book are trademarks, registered trademarks, or trade names of their respective holders. Sourcebooks is not associated with any product or vendor in this book.

Published by Cosmo Reads, an imprint of Sourcebooks.
P.O. Box 4410, Naperville, Illinois 60567-4410
(630) 961-3900
sourcebooks.com

Cataloging-in-Publication Data is on file with the Library of Congress.

Printed and bound in the United States of America.
WOZ 10 9 8 7 6 5 4 3 2 1

This book is dedicated to anyone who ever dreamed of falling in love in a field of flowers, with a really hot man who wants to protect you. ☺

CHAPTER 1
ORIGAMI MAN
RIPLEY

"You can't just leave after dropping news like that on me."

Seriously. My sister can't take off yet. Not when I need to make the list of all lists. Hands parked on hips, I stare, slack-jawed, as she zips up her peach suitcase, the color matching her personality.

"You've got this, Ripley," she says breezily as she springs up from the plush carpet, pops the handle of the suitcase some luggage company gave her, and nods to the door, a sign she's heading off to catch her flight.

I briefly consider flinging myself against the hotel room door and forcing her to stay in this suite till we've covered every single detail of the things I'll have to do in less than thirty days, but when my sister wants something, not even a human shield can stop her.

"But there's not enough time. Can't we have more time?" I ask since I'm still flabbergasted at the impossible assignment she wants me to make possible, and I need to process my flabbergast with her.

"Who else but you can take care of things this quickly?" Haven says.

"Quickly?" I know time isn't Haven's favorite thing, but *quickly* is the mother of all euphemisms. She's asking me to hustle at the speed of a time-lapse video. "I have to get our farm ready to host a film crew in one month? I'm good at doing all the things. Very good, mind you. But I am not *that* good."

She stops on the way to the door of the suite she'd booked for this sisters' getaway weekend and gives me a *don't be ridiculous* look. "Yes, you are. This is what you do. All this"—she waves a hand—"kind of stuff."

"*This kind of stuff?*" I flick through the memories of, oh, say, my entire life, but nope, not once did I fix up our small-town lavender farm in twenty-eight days for the benefit of a Hollywood film company.

Haven gives me one of those magic smiles that's impossible to look away from. A smile I can't even try to mimic when she begs me at get-togethers to do my impression of her—*the sweet sister*. "You know what I mean," she says. "Like how you drove me to the audition for that perfume commercial when my car broke down."

"I didn't fix your car," I grumble, remembering that wild day when she said she was so stressed about being late that she was going to pee her pants but at the same time was so excited that she was also going to pee her pants.

Spoiler alert: she did not pee her pants.

But she did get the gig.

She drops her suitcase handle and reaches for my hands. "You fixed *me*. I wouldn't be here without you." She holds my gaze for a weighty beat, and we're not talking about the car anymore.

Darker memories flash in my mind, and I blink them back. There's no time for those today—not when I have a farm to whip into shape. The film financing for *Someone Else's Ring*—a project she'd been waiting to get the green light on—has officially been finalized. Seems our little farm, more than an hour from the big city, is going to be her co-star, so to speak, as long as I can get her into shape.

"You're leaving me when I need to figure out this whole thing."

She squeezes me harder. "You'll make money on *this whole thing*, I'm sure. It'll be exactly what Lavender Bliss Farms needs to show off its rustic charm," she says, grabbing the handle of her suitcase with a certain finality.

"Oh. It's definitely rustic. So rustic that I'll get sued for everything I'm worth if a cameraman's foot goes through a rotten board."

"They have, you know, insurance and stuff."

"Insurance doesn't prevent you from getting sued. It pays for—" There's no point in explaining damages. Haven doesn't need to worry about behind-the-scenes details of running a family flower farm that needs a fork-ton of work.

"It pays for dreams," Haven says, eyes wide and imploring. "And you know this is a dream come true."

My hardened heart softens, like it always does for her. "I know. And of course I'll do it." We both know I was always going to say yes the second the financing came through. In this case, about, you know, ten minutes ago.

Haven had been biting her nails for weeks, waiting for word on this film, her first big starring role. *Someone Else's Ring*, based on the runaway bestseller of the same name, just so happens to be set in a small town, so her agent had pitched the producers on shooting some key scenes on my lavender farm. My little desperately-in-need-of-a-new-coat-of-paint lavender farm.

But I'll make it happen. That's what I do. "Like I can turn you down."

"Yay! I told my agent a few minutes ago not to worry since you're the best older sister in the world."

"I'm hardly older," I point out, but we both know I might as well be five years older instead of the five minutes that separate us.

"Details," she says with the brightest smile.

I step back and take a look at the woman in front of me with the straight nose, high cheekbones, and sleek, shiny blond hair, twisted up in an ever-so-casual bun. Then, the artful mascara sweeping across her eyelashes, the polished peach nails, and the fair complexion.

She's a mirror of me, minus the nails. I never polish mine if I can help it. Plus, I'm a little tanner from working outside, and a lot more covered in ink, since, well, why have naked skin when you can have art? I have an armful of ink, while Haven has one tiny bird tattoo on her shoulder to match my flock.

But she insisted I have my nails done when she dragged me to the spa earlier today for facials and mani-pedis. Haven picked the color—a bright, girly pink, like a gumball. I can't wait to take it off when I get home.

Haven glances apologetically at the time on her phone, then gives me one last hug. "Sorry to cut our weekend short. The suite is booked for one more night, so use it. Take a bubble bath and order champagne, on me."

I snort. Bubble baths are her thing. "I don't have time for that. But go." I shoo her out. "Get out of here. The security line at SFO will be ridiculous. Tell the Lyft driver to take Nineteenth Avenue, not 101."

"I know, I know. Always take Nineteenth Avenue," she says as she heads off.

As the door creaks shut behind her, I turn around, ready to work. I brought my laptop, so I can do some research and look up everything I'll need to tidy the farm before I meet with her producers next week on site.

But the bed is strewn with camis and yoga pants, jammies and my *Bees Do It Better* T-shirt. There are books too, and a water bottle with the farm logo on it. I can't think straight in this room. It makes my brain messy and cluttered. The lobby bar is arctic, so I grab a white hoodie and my phone. Snagging my clutch purse, I head downstairs, stuffing my arms into the hoodie as I go, following the soft hum of jazz melodies and the glow of pendant lights.

I can do this. I'm a glass-half-full kind of woman, so at the bar, I order a glass of rosé, and as soon as the bartender pours it for me, I thank him, then start brainstorming ways to fix up the farm on a budget.

I grab a napkin, start searching on my phone, and begin mathing.

How much more money will Lavender Bliss be able to make with this kind of exposure? On the flip side, how much of the meager savings will we have to spend to get the place ready for a film crew?

Maybe I needed a stiffer drink than rosé.

I scan the mirrored shelves of liquor, briefly considering an upgrade to bourbon. But the bartender's busy mixing margaritas on the other side of the U-shaped bar.

A few stools away from me is a slick blond dude wearing one of those business shirts with a different-colored collar—blue stripes against white, like the kind the douchey boss wears in a movie. A few stools away from him, a pair of women are huddled close together, lifting pink drinks and sharing secrets. Over there, on the other side of them, is a hulk of a man with dark eyes and broad shoulders that tell me he probably juggles refrigerators for fun. He's got an amber drink set neatly next to a tablet, and he's making… what *is* he making?

I try to stare without being too obvious, and I'm pretty sure he's doing origami. Maybe a butterfly.

Which reminds me. The butterfly lavender essential oils we sell in the little shop attached to the farm—the shop that's become the most dependable part of the business—will I be able to sell them in the shop with a film crew there? And where will the crew stay? Does Bridget have room at The BookHouse for everyone? There's The Ladybug Inn too, which adds eight or so rooms. Are there enough Airbnbs in town? How big is a film crew? A dozen people? A hundred?

As I'm writing details down on my napkin, there's a scratch of metal against the concrete floor, then footsteps, then a cleared throat next to me.

"Don't I know you from somewhere?"

The voice is fratty. Bet it belongs to douchey boss. And as far as opening lines go, it's pretty demanding.

I barely look up. "No, you don't."

"I do though," he says, grabbing a stool and sitting too close to me. The scent of patchouli and sandalwood clings to him. I thought we left body spray back in the last decade. I guess I was wrong. "Did you go to Brown?"

Great. It's one of those lines that's supposed to be a compliment. *Like, I'm not going to start with your eyes, but your brain, babe.*

"Nope."

"Well, let me buy you a drink, and we'll figure it out."

It's best to be direct in these situations, so I turn, and no surprise, it's douchey boss, and I meet his gaze head-on. "No, thanks."

He makes no move to go though. He leers, his slick eyes roaming from my face to my chest, then back up. A smirk forms, victorious and irritating. In no time, I'm cycling through my self-defense moves, picturing the throw I'd use to take this creep down in a parking lot when he snaps his fingers, highlighting a tan line where a wedding ring once belonged. "Wait. *Wait.* I've seen you in a movie."

Oh.

For a few seconds, I'm disarmed. This is a first for me. This never happens in Darling Springs since everyone there knows Haven and me. And while my identical twin sister isn't a household name *yet*, she's well on her way. She finished two successful seasons on the streaming ensemble hit *The Dating Games*, and she had a supporting part in a breakout Webflix movie, *Top-Notch Boyfriend*.

Still, I don't want to be rude in case he tells people I *am* Haven, so I toss him a bone, managing a small smile as I start to say, "Actually, that's—"

"The one where you, you flashed your…" His hands cup imaginary melons at pecs-level.

My sister has never done a nude scene, you jackass.

But I bite back that comeback since he's just not worth it. I stare pointedly at the stool douchey boss is occupying. "Excuse me. I'm meeting someone," I say, hoping he finally gets the message to go back to Creepville now.

"Someone who couldn't be bothered to show up on time?" he asks as the sound of footsteps growing closer registers.

"How do you know he's late?"

"He's not here. I am. Don't you want a man who shows up?"

He's officially ruined my rosé. I open my purse so I can pay the tip and get the hell out when the footsteps stop. The origami man wedges himself between us, looming over the other guy but turning to me. "Hi, honey, sorry I'm late. But I got us a great table to make up for it. Did you want to join me, or do you still need to make that phone call to your aunt?"

In his dark-brown eyes, I see the offer. *I'm here to whisk you away if you need me to.*

I also see the out. *I'll cover for you while you walk away from this asshole.*

I flash a *see you later* smile at the asshole, then a real one at my temporary hero as I push back in the stool, ready to leave. "Thanks, sweetie. A table sounds great."

But douchey boss harrumphs faster, then pushes back in his stool, the grating sound of metal against metal screeching in my ears. With an aggravated sigh, he tosses a dollar on the bar. Nice tip. He heads off, his tail tucked between his legs.

The towering man tracks him the whole way, eyes like a hawk's, till the man's out of sight.

That's just…hot.

When he turns back to me, he's mostly, but not quite, all business-y as he says, "He's gone. Do you need anything else?"

That's a good question, and I should say no given the length of my to-do list. But there's a hint of something more in his voice that I like. I'm revved up from the way he got rid of that jerk. Does he think I'm Haven too? No idea, but if it comes down to it, I'll make sure *this guy* knows I'm *not* my sister.

Because his moves have got me a little hot under the hoodie. Looking back, I might blame the adrenaline for the words forming on my tongue as I impulsively say, "Yes. Can I buy you a drink?"

CHAPTER 2
READ THE ROOM
BANKS

Do I always pretend to date random women in bars?

No, I don't.

But the way that sleazeball crowded her, leered at her, and spoke to her when she clearly told him she wasn't interested fired me the hell up. If anyone did anything like that to my little sister... My shoulders tighten with tension. I wouldn't stand for it.

And while I didn't hear everything he said, it didn't take a body language expert to know she was telling him to get lost. Sure, I could have just physically shown the man the door—eight years as a Marine means I'm no slouch in the *shifting unwanted types along* department—but I don't like to make a scene.

In fact, I'm excellent at *not* making scenes. Hence the offer to pretend to be her dude for the night.

But something I'm even better at than not making a mountain out of a molehill? Spotting opportunities.

I take the one this gorgeous woman with the long blond hair is offering me. "Yes, you can," I say, meeting her captivating crystal-blue gaze at last, now that I'm done sending death rays at that guy. With him in the rearview, I pause, like we need a reset to move past that part of the night and into *this* part before I add, "On one condition."

"What's your condition?"

"That you let me buy it for you."

A soft laugh falls from her glossy lips. Such a better expression than the tight, tense look on her face moments ago. Now her shoulders are relaxed, her eyes inviting. "Chivalry is not dead."

"Not with me, that's for damn sure."

With a *well then* expression, she gestures to the stool next to her. I take it, placing the tablet I've been holding on the bar top. Time to set my business plans aside, along with the proposal I've been working on since my early evening meeting here in this hotel. I'll send this proposal to Dean tonight to review. Get his feedback. Make sure it's airtight and confident before I fire it off to a huge potential client. A kernel of hope rushes through me. This gig could be huge for our recently launched firm.

But for now, a drink. I nod toward her empty glass. "Rosé?"

She lifts a brow. "You noticed what I was drinking?"

"I notice lots of things." But I don't want her to think I'm just as bad as that guy, like I've been stalking her in a whole new way, so I widen the aperture. "Like, I noticed the women over there traded lipsticks before they shot selfies while drinking cosmos, and the guy who hit on you removed his wedding band."

My companion's lips part. "He did? I noticed a tan line, but not that he'd taken it off."

"About fifteen seconds before he moved next to you. And the bartender didn't come over because he was working on a big order for a dozen blueberry margaritas."

"Are you an anthropologist studying bar behavior? A secret shopper who observes hotel lobbies? Or a superhero who saves the day when a gal needs a temporary boyfriend to ward off creepers?"

I laugh. "The latter sounds like a good gig. But no, I'm just observant." I offer my hand. "Banks. I'm in town for the night from Los Angeles."

For a brief second, she appears taken aback when I say Los Angeles, but then clears her expression and says, "Ripley." Like it's important to her to say her name. "Like *Ripley's Believe It or Not!*"

"Or Ripley from *Alien*," I add.

"Or *The Talented Mr. Ripley*. I'm in the city from—" She must think the better of supplying that detail because, with barely a pause, she finishes, "A little town by the coast." She holds my hand for a beat longer than most do, and I definitely don't mind the extended shake or the way she holds back where she's from. That's just smart for a woman these days.

She lets go of my hand as the bartender comes our way.

I raise a finger to get his attention, and he stops in front of us.

"Sorry for the wait. Had a big order." His smile is apologetic. "Thanks for your patience. What can I get you?"

Ripley shoots me a look that says she's impressed. I like it—the cute smirk, the twinkle in her irises. "No worries, Duke," I tell the bartender, reading his name tag. "A rosé for the lady."

"Actually, a whiskey sour for me," she says, keeping me on my toes.

"I stand corrected," I say.

Then, she continues to keep me on my toes, tilting her head toward my glass. "And what was it you were drinking? Bourbon?"

I let out a low, appreciative whistle as I reach for the credit card in my pocket and slap it down. "Yes, I was. But I'll have the same as my…*girlfriend*."

She rolls her lips, sealing up some satisfied laughter.

"Two whiskey sours coming right up," Duke says.

When he leaves, I turn to Ripley. "And so are you—observant, that is."

She shakes her head, dismissing the compliment. "I was actually admiring your butterfly when I noticed the drink. I'm more of a gambler. I took a guess it was bourbon."

"Gut instinct," I say with an approving nod. My job, my whole business, is fueled by gut instinct. "That's a good thing."

She gives me a grateful smile. "Seriously though. I appreciate what you did."

"It's no problem," I reply.

"And guys wonder why we think dating is rough. But I'm glad you decided to fake date me tonight." She pauses a moment, teasing me with a smile. "And I'm extra glad you decided to be my *boyfriend*, not just someone meeting me for a first date."

"You don't like first dates?" I ask. But who does?

She gives a faux shudder. "First dates are horrible. It's like a review of your dating CV. All that talk about what you do for a living, where you see yourself in a few years, how many pet goldfish you have, and so on."

"I don't have any pet goldfish," I say dryly.

"Good." She crosses her legs. I try not to check her out too blatantly but damn, she's not only beautiful—those eyes are impossibly captivating—she's also seriously fucking hot in jeans and a cropped white hoodie that slopes down her shoulder, revealing more of her neckline. I want to roam my eyes up and down her long legs and her athletic frame, enjoying the view, but staring would make me no better than that guy I nearly tossed in the trash.

"I don't think you can find out if someone's right for you by asking those staid, boring questions," she goes on.

"How *do* you find out then?"

She gives a hopeful shrug. "By asking if they blast music while they drive, or if they've ever bungee jumped, or what was the last thing they googled."

The bartender returns with our drinks. We thank him, and then she lifts a glass to toast. "To noticing things," she says. "And to very smooth saves. The phone call *and* the table? That was well played, Banks."

As she sips, her gaze strays around the bar to some of the booths in the corner, a little more private. I like to think I can read the room. Read a woman too. "Want that table?"

She pauses, but not like she's reluctant. More like she's weighing my offer, writing a pros and cons list in her head. I'd love to know what's in each column, but mostly I want her yes.

It comes seconds later as she says, "You know what? I do."

Yep, that business proposal can wait a little longer.

I take our drinks, tucking my tablet under my arm and grabbing my paper butterfly from where I left it when I got up. As we weave through the tables, I stay very, *very* close to her. Just in case. But I give myself a long enough leash to drink in the view of her as we go. The fall of her shiny blond hair over her shoulders, the sway of her hips, the slap of her flip-flops against the concrete floor. She holds a small clutch purse. A sliver of a farmer's tan peeks out by the strap of the cami under that hoodie, while a few freckles dot her nose. She's right that dates shouldn't be about CVs, but I'm still curious who she is. She doesn't have the polished reserve of a banker or a lawyer. She's not a city girl either, by her own admission. Bet she runs a store, maybe a café, possibly a bar.

When we reach the booth, she meets my eyes straight on. "You're a very good boyfriend tonight."

Tonight.

A reminder that what we do doesn't matter. This is a one-night-only kind of thing, and that's fine by me. "I blast music in my car," I tell her. "So loud it shakes."

Her smile spreads deliciously. Playfully. "And does everyone know you're coming from the Mozart sonata?"

That image is too much. And scarily *almost* accurate. "You know, Ripley? I bet they can." Then I slide a little closer because, yes, I can read the room, and I fucking like what it says.

An hour later, we switch to water—her idea, since she says she has a two-drink limit. "So, yes, I did, in fact, bungee jump for the first time when I was twenty-five." She sets down her water with a defiant clink. "It was my friend Chloe's idea. Since then, I've gone surfing, white-water rafting, and also, Black Friday shopping at six a.m."

"Don't tell me it was a Walmart."

"It was," she says, sitting straighter, then holding up her hands in defense. "Look, they were having a fantastic sale on mulch. I couldn't pass it up."

My brow creases. "Mulch? Was that a holiday gift for someone?" I don't bother to hide how much I don't want mulch as a gift.

"No, but it's the way to *my* heart," she says. I note that detail—she's an outdoorsy girl through and through. Maybe a gardener. "I bought it for myself. Besides, it was half off. I love deals," Ripley confesses. "But now that you know my answers," she begins, and yup, I've learned that rather than a goldfish, she has a summa dog—some of this, some of that—named Hudson and she likes music she can sing along to. She's also direct, confident, and a little tough, in a good way. She gives me a fierce look and says, "I want to know something about you that's not on the list."

If she asks, after all, what I do for a living, I'm not sure I'll tell her. It opens up too many questions. But I do like her tenaciousness, and I'm a little taken with her already, so I gamble. "Sure. Try me."

"What's with the origami?" She looks down at the butterfly I was making earlier.

Ah, that's easier to answer. "Oh, this thing?"

She rolls her eyes. *"Oh, this? Why yes, that was just a little play I wrote one afternoon. Had no idea anyone would be into that dude named Romeo and his lady, Juliet. Just that thing."*

I smile, smugly. "You think my origami is Shakespeare-level? Why, thank you."

"It's…well, an unusual hobby for…" She looks me up and down, perhaps not wanting to say *a guy* because it would sound sexist.

And I think I'll have a little fun with her. "For a temporary boyfriend?" I ask, like I'm a little confused.

"You know what I mean."

"For a whiskey sour drinker?"

"C'mon, Banks!"

"For a Mozart aficionado?"

"For a guy," she says with a huff.

"Ah, *that*." I lift my glass of water and take a sip. She watches me with avid eyes, and the flicker of heat in her irises does not go unnoticed.

Or unwanted.

"My little sister taught me," I say. I don't tell her that I find it calming, that I need to keep my hands busy, that if I don't, my mind veers in frustrating directions.

"What else can you make?"

I gaze at her face, then down her neck to the collarbone, where her hoodie has slipped, exposing some of her right shoulder and skin that looks soft, tender, and thoroughly kissable. A sparrow peeks out from the fabric, spreading its wings.

I meet her eyes. A charge zaps between us. "Something pretty," I say, without looking away from her.

Her smile is just south of shy, and I want to kiss it off. Instead, I open my tablet case and take out a crisp sheet of white paper. I fold it in half on the diagonal, then unfold it at the crease. Quickly but methodically, I flip the paper over, up, down, until a minute later, I present her with a bird.

She takes it, clutches it gently. "I love it. And I needed this tonight." It's said like a confession, and I don't think she's talking about the paper bird. "I just got some wild news."

I straighten my spine, dropping the flirty tone like that. "Everything okay?" Translation: *Who do I need to hurt?*

"Yes. It's all good. I didn't mean to alarm you. It's a huge project. So it's good, but overwhelming, like *how can I possibly get everything done in that amount of time* overwhelming. It's a lot of pressure, even though it's good pressure."

"I hear you. But I bet you'll get it done early."

She laughs. "You have a lot of faith in me."

"You're tough. You're strong. You know how to get things done."

"You can tell all that in one hour of meeting me?"

No doubt about it. "I sure can. You're the kind of person who doesn't back down from a challenge."

Her smile magnifies. "And are you the same?"

"I am. So I get what you're saying, because I know that feeling too. That *how the hell will I get this done* feeling, but then you do it. I'm waiting to find out if my firm just got a new gig."

She pauses, seeming to absorb that little nugget. "Sounds like you have a lot of tension," she muses, her eyes sparking with possibilities of the after-dark variety.

And I like it. A lot. "Sounds like we both do," I say, as she takes her time and sets a hand on my leg, and damn, that feels good. It also feels like a new direction for the night. "What are we going to do with all this tension then?"

She glances toward the lobby, then the hallway beyond, and maybe, just maybe, to the elevators and where they lead. *A hotel room.*

The way things started with us tonight, I don't want to push her. But I do want to kick open the door. "Ripley," I say, my husky tone making my meaning clear—*say the word, and we're out of here.*

"Banks..." She draws a deep breath, holds it, then *fuck it* flashes in her eyes. "Should we take this to my room?"

A bolt of lust slams into me. "Yes." But just because it's a good idea to check, I add, "If you're sure you want that?"

Her teeth slide over her bottom lip, then she whispers, "Well, it is our third date, after all."

I take that opportunity and run with it. "We've probably had our first kiss already."

She smiles, seductive and inviting. "Did we? I can't recall."

I lift a hand and slide my fingers through her hair, savoring the way she trembles as I touch her. "Sweetheart, when I kiss you, you will definitely recall it."

She lifts her chin. "Why don't you refresh my memory?"

CHAPTER 3
POUNCE ON ME
RIPLEY

This *never* happens to me in Darling Springs. I don't meet men like Banks in my hometown. An interesting, flirty man built like a Mack truck who *maybe* listens to Mozart?

Nope.

I hardly meet men there because that's where I grew up. I know everyone already. Like William, the Irish guy who runs the local bookshop that his Brazilian grandmother gave to him. Or Fox, who moved to Darling Springs from Montreal and now owns the bar and commiserates with me over a game of pool about the price of things.

But meeting a man at a bar and having this kind of zingy chemistry is like being in college all over again.

And the best part of college was sex.

That's what I want tonight. I want this man to relieve some of the pressure I'm facing by relieving *another* pressure. He's like an answered prayer, this tattooed hottie. The sleeves of his button-down shirt are rolled up, revealing muscular forearms with ink coasting up his fair skin, geometric shapes that have me staring at the art and the muscles. How do you even get muscles in your forearms? I squirm a little at the thought of him throwing me around with those strong arms. What do the rest of them look like? How far up does the art go under that button-down shirt I want to rip off?

Soon, you'll find out soon.

I meet his gaze again. His eyes are intense, but thoughtful too. The look in them—both soulful and filthy—makes my pulse kick up.

Under the low light in this corner booth, anticipation threads through me, spooling through my cells as I wait for him to make the next move. He lifts a big hand and I think he's going to cup my cheek, but instead, he covers my shoulder, curling his palm over me. Powerfully.

Making me shudder.

He pushes down my hoodie another inch, then slides his thumb along my collarbone.

And that's…shivery.

I tremble head to toe, then lean into his hand, mesmerized by the way he travels along my skin. Taking his time, he changes direction, coasting his fingers back then up the side of my neck.

I let out a shuddery breath.

This is…outrageously sexy.

He's touching me in some kind of slo-mo seduction. His fingers move to my jawline, the pads grazing along my face, then coming to a stop at my chin where he holds me. Roams his thumb right under my lower lip. Breathes out hard, full of wanting.

I am done.

"Just kiss me," I whisper, already begging.

His lips curve up in the pleased grin of a man who holds the cards. "Patience," he says, voice deep and in charge.

"I'm not feeling very patient," I murmur.

"Good," he says, a lion toying with his prey.

Pounce on me.

I'm caught in his tease. In his talented hands. In his dark eyes. They're the deepest brown I've ever seen. A tempest of colors, like dark chocolate and black coffee. His hair is dark, wavy, the perfect length to hold on to. His nose strong and Roman. His jaw square. His lips full, lush, and confident.

And so damn close.

As he gazes down at my mouth, he raises his other hand, then holds my face in both his palms. He hasn't even kissed me yet, and somehow this warm-up exercise is the hottest moment I've experienced in some time. I can't wait to drag him back to my room. He can take my mind off anything he wants, and he can do it all night long.

If he just kisses me.

But he doesn't. He looks. He studies. He parts his lips.

And still, I wait.

Until I can't. Until I'm squirming.

"Dammit, just kiss me," I plead, since I can't stand this.

He tsks me, shaking his head. "Say please."

I pout. "Fucker," I mutter.

He laughs devilishly. In charge. "Try again," he says, amusement and arousal in his tone.

Two can play. "Please...*fucker*," I taunt.

Another chuckle.

"Much better, Ripley," he says, and it sounds like my name on his lips tastes good to him. So good that I close my eyes.

The world is dark for a few delicious seconds, and I'm sure he's going to kiss me the way he touched me—with slow, tantalizing, barely-there kisses. But the second his lips touch mine, I hurtle into new terrain.

He crushes my mouth with his, and I gasp in surprise. He swallows the sound in a bruising kiss that knocks me off-balance, even though I'm sitting. His hand curls tight around my head. He kisses with a hunger I've never experienced before. With a passion that's all new to me.

It's hot, deep, a little rough.

It's the kind of kiss where you haul a woman up against the kitchen counter and bend her over. It's a kiss that says we're both grown-ass adults who need to blow off steam.

But when he breaks the kiss, his eyes flash with guilt, maybe. Or is that concern? "Shit, was that too rough?"

He says it like he's legit worried. Like he thinks I might not like his rugged kiss. "No, it wasn't," I say, breathy and surprised.

He breathes out hard, perhaps grateful. "Good," he says, then purses his lips, like he's holding something back. Maybe that he likes it a little rough?

Maybe I like being rough too.

I grab the collar of his shirt, jerking this big man a little closer. "Just to be sure though…do it again."

"Yeah?" It's asked with a wild kind of delight.

"Yeah," I answer the same damn way.

In no time, he seals his mouth to mine, curls one hand around my hip, and ropes the other through my hair. He gives a tug, and I yelp softly into his mouth, but he doesn't break the kiss.

He amps it up. Hard. Fierce. Certain. His hand lets go of the hold on my hip, climbing higher to my waist.

I angle closer, letting him know with my body that I want his touch. Need it. He slides his hand under my shirt, splaying his fingers across my stomach, spreading them over my skin, then wrenching away a few seconds later.

"Fuck, you're soft," he says, kind of mesmerized. His eyes look hazy. Then he blinks. "I'd like to get you naked really fucking soon. Think that'll work for you?"

I furrow my brow. "Was it not clear?"

"I just like to ask."

He's an unusual mix of gentleman and caveman. I want to feel him above me, under me, and over me.

God, that image sends a wicked thrill through me, a hot ache in my core.

But then I picture the suite, and the hot mess I left it in flashes before my eyes. The laptop, my *Bees Do It Better* T-shirt—all the reminders of the farm. Reminders I don't need right now when I want to *not think* about every single thing I need to do in the next twenty-eight days.

"Can you give me ten minutes?" I ask.

"Yeah, I…" He stops, then a hint of shyness flickers in his eyes. "Need to get a condom anyway." He scratches his jaw, then shrugs. "Sometimes at hotels, the fitness center has them in a vending machine, or the front desk does. If you ask, that is."

My heart gets a little fluttery for a few seconds. I don't know why I love that he's not carrying one, but I do. "Like an *if you know, you know*."

"Exactly."

"Perfect. Meet me in room 210 in ten minutes," I say.

Banks cups my cheek, soft this time, gentle. He presses a tender kiss to my lips. "I'm counting down."

Then, he gives me the kiss I was expecting at first. A slow, heady kiss. A kiss that makes my mind feel hazy and my body warm. I'm melting into it and into him. He's the most alluring mix of rough and tender, and I'm dying to experience more of him.

Maybe more of my own untested wishes tonight.

He breaks the kiss, leaving me wanting him even more, then runs his knuckles along my jawline possessively. "Whatever you want tonight, it's yours."

I want to explore my desires. "I'll tell you when I see you in ten minutes."

"You better," he says. That dark look has returned, and he maneuvers a hand down my back, smacking my ass lightly but sending a message. *There's more where that came from.* "Nine minutes and forty-five seconds now. Better get moving, Ripley."

I hustle out of there so fast. I can't wait for my night to really begin.

CHAPTER 4
MY LUCKY NIGHT
BANKS

My dick hasn't even had a chance to deflate when my phone rings thirty seconds later.

Annoyed at the interruption, I reach for the device in my back pocket where I've been happily ignoring it since I met the most interesting woman I've encountered in ages. I don't want to deal with a phone call right now while my mind is lasered in on room 210 and all the ways I want to make Ripley come tonight.

But you never know who's calling. Could be Mom, or my sister Emily, or my landlord telling me a pipe's burst. I guess pipes bursting are on my mind. I adjust myself surreptitiously in the booth, even though no one else is in this back corner of the bar. The phone bleats again as I wrestle it from my pocket.

It's…

It's a 415 number.

My heart sprints.

It's the number of the San Francisco referral agency I met with a couple hours ago right here in this hotel where they conducted interviews with a few key candidates about a highly specialized contract job for a hush-hush client, they said. I flew up from Los Angeles for the meeting. Signed an NDA in advance, even though they didn't share details of the client. But that's par for the course in my field, where discretion and subtlety are mission critical. When the meeting ended, the guy told me they'd get back to me soon about the opportunity.

I figured that meant *when the fuck ever, so hurry up and wait.*

But a call mere hours later has got to be good. I try to tamp my excitement, but already I'm feeling damn good. Meeting a sexy-as-sin woman I vibe with *and* scoring a plum gig for our new firm in one night?

I'm not a guy who believes in luck. But maybe I should. I answer it. "Banks here," I say, cool and professional.

"Hello, Banks. It's Liam Halperin," the man says. "We met earlier."

I laugh lightly. "Yes, I remember."

"Of course." He clears his throat. "Listen, our client was impressed with your credentials, and they're moving quickly on the project. Everything has come together quicker than expected. You know how it goes."

In the booth, I sit up straighter, zeroing in on the call as my hard-on vanishes. It's business time now. "I do."

"We need to move fast and provide a full suite of services. And they'd like to hire your firm," he says, then rattles off the parameters of the job and drops a key detail at the end. "And it's a high-profile assignment."

No surprise. Most of them are. That's the nature of my business. "You'll have our utmost discretion."

"Excellent. Let me send you some more details over email. Then, we can connect you with the folks in the Los Angeles offices who handle logistics."

"Perfect," I say.

We hang up, and I pump a fist quietly.

This is fantastic. Dean is going to lose his mind. We set up shop a year or so ago after working for others for years and have been eager to land some marquee clients. But I'll tell him later. For now, I've got five minutes to grab a condom and get to Ripley's room. Then I've got all night to take care of her before my early morning flight.

As I slide out of the booth, snagging my tablet and the butterfly, my email pings. Love a quick-moving client. As I'm walking through the bar to the front desk, I click open the email.

I read the name of the client. Ruby Horizons Film Productions. The work is on an upcoming movie.

Sweet.

We've been making inroads in the entertainment business, but this will help us make further strides for sure. A perfect area for Dean and me.

I scan the email as I stride across the plush carpet but set it aside before I can finish reading. I'm at the front desk now and a cheery man with red hair and redder freckles smiles my way from behind the gleaming marble counter. "Good evening. What can I do for you?"

I scan his name tag. "Evening, Spencer. Any chance you have condoms behind the desk, or anywhere nearby?"

He gives a crisp nod. "Yes, we do. One minute."

Guess this isn't his first time at the *didn't-bring-protection* rodeo. As he steps away from the desk and disappears behind an open door into a small office, I return to the email, reading the rest of the details. The film shoots in Darling Springs. Production starts in a month. The lead actress is Haven Addison.

There's a picture attached. I download it right as Spencer returns from the office with a condom. Actually, three. Well, someone has a lot of faith in me. He hands me the trio. "Just in case."

I flash him the smile that a perfect wingman deserves. "Thank you, brother."

I pocket the condoms as the photo opens and the floor falls out from under me.

In a heartbeat, all the evidence of tonight adds up as the name Ripley reverberates in my skull.

Ripley's Believe It or Not! Ripley from *Alien*. *The Talented Mr. Ripley.*

Ripley's gotta be the fake name that Haven uses. Because I'm staring at the image of the woman upstairs. The one expecting me to throw her onto the bed in less than thirty seconds.

And she's my new client.

CHAPTER 5
CRUMPLE-WORTHY
RIPLEY

There.

Not only have I cleaned up the pile of clothes, the laptop, and the farm merch from the bed, but I've spritzed on some lavender and vanilla body mist.

In the en suite, I fluff out my hair, then take a breath. It's been a long while. As in, a little over a year since my ex sliced my heart and broke my romance confidence when he moved across the country to open a new restaurant, giving me a quick goodbye, and saying, *Thanks for the small-town memories and fun times.*

Um, hello, it was a fucking relationship.

But I do not want to think about Eric Patrick, of the two first names, blindsiding me. Since he took off, I've been all work, work, work, and I can't help but wonder: Does sex still go the same? Has there been a new position, a new style, new kinks since I last had it oh, say, several epochs ago?

Well, let's hope there are new kinks.

That'd be nice.

I take one last look at my reflection. I ditched the hoodie because what's the point? It's all coming off anyway. My ink is on full display now, birds soaring down my upper arm.

I leave the bathroom, my gaze catching briefly on the origami bird Banks made for me. I'd set it on the nightstand when I swung open the door nine minutes and thirty seconds ago.

Except.

No. That looks like I'm clingy. Like it's a keepsake I'll treasure forever when this is just a one-night stand. I hurry over to grab it when there's a knock on the door. My heart clatters around in my chest, my stomach swooping in excitement. Well, that man can kiss. I bet he can fuck.

"Just a second," I call out.

"Of course," a muffled voice answers as I grab the bird and drop it into—what do I do with it? It's so cute, and I don't want to crush it. Thinking fast, I rush to my suitcase, flip it open, and find an empty blue box. Haven brought me salted caramels from Elodie's Chocolates, and we devoured them last night. Perfect. I put the bird inside so it doesn't get crushed.

Well, I like birds. That's all.

I stand and smooth a hand down my shirt, settling my nerves and my excitement, and head to the door.

When I pass the clock, it vaguely occurs to me he's two minutes late. Huh. Banks hardly seems like a man who'd ever be behind schedule. But I'll have fun with that. I unlock the door, yanking it open while saying, "You're late, but I'll let you make it up to me if you put me on my hands and knees and give me a good, hard spanking."

Then, my dignity flies out the window as I come face-to-face with a man with red hair and a *hospitality first* smile. He's holding a folded sheet of paper. Crisp. White.

"I have a letter for you, ma'am."

I cringe, embarrassment gripping me in a tight noose. "I'm so sorry… I thought you were… I was expecting…"

His smile never wavers. "No worries." He dangles the letter. I wince, and like it contains anthrax, I take it while I search for an escape pod to hurl me through the black hole of dating and hook-ups and return me to Darling Springs.

"Thanks," I say, the word tasting like sour milk.

"Please let me know if there's anything else I can do for you. Champagne on the house?"

So it's that obvious I've been stood up. And that I was expecting a spanking, no less.

But no one, not a damn soul, gets to feel sorry for me. I dealt with enough of that when I was in high school.

I straighten my shoulders, lift my chin, and say, "Actually, if you could tell the valet to bring my car around." I flash an apologetic smile, then improvise. "I was called home, so I have to leave right away." I wave the paper airily, like I don't care about his excuse, whatever it is. "Poor guy. He was so devastated when I told him I had to go early. But business calls."

The smile never leaves the man's face. "Of course."

"Feel free to send that champagne to Banks…" I shrug, laughing off the fact I don't know his last name or room number. "He'll probably need it more than I do."

Then I shut the door, slump against it, and let out the world's most frustrated sigh.

I wish I could say I crumple up the note. But I don't. I'm not that tough. I open it, dreading the words but reading them anyway.

Three lines.

Three lines that feel like lies. Because the truth? The truth is that somewhere between then and now, Banks lost interest in me. Could be the way I kissed. Could be something I said. Or it could be that I wanted him too much.

My stomach roils.

Whatever the reason, he ditched me, and these excuses—these three little sentences—don't change how foolish I feel.

They're crumple-worthy. I ball up the paper and toss it across the room. Then I pack my things at rocket speed, grab my bags, turn off the lights, and go.

Less than two hours later, I'm driving along a winding road, nearing a wooden sign rising up in the hills, lit up at night and declaring: *You're entering Darling Springs.*

It's bright and beckoning even in the starlight. I turn into town, leaving San Francisco, lying men, and failed one-night stands far behind.

CHAPTER 6
MS. FIX IT
RIPLEY

A week later, Hudson trundles through the emerald hills covered in lavender bushes, a used and abused tennis ball in his mouth. I'm carefully snipping sprigs of Otto Quast lavender under the midmorning sun, phone pressed to my ear as the fast-talking, high-strung location scout at Ruby Horizons Productions rattles off not her schedule, but her *sked*, as if the two-syllable version takes too much time to say. "I have a Zoom; then I review some photos from another location. And I seriously need to find a kale smoothie with oat milk, not almond milk," she says, like that last one won't be possible here in Darling Springs.

Oh, ye of little faith.

"Go to The Oasis. It's a cute little smoothie shop just past the community center. Get the Kale Yeah. It's exactly what you're looking for, and you can add honey or hold the honey—whatever works for you," I say as I take the gift of the slobbery tennis ball and lob it down the hill for my Manchester-terrier-meets-cattle-dog mix with *maybe* some lab thrown in, but who really knows? He shoots off chasing it, all floppy ears, wagging tail, and endless drive.

"They do?" It's asked with utter astonishment.

Yes, and we have Wi-Fi and electric cars here too. "Yup. And, fun fact—the kale comes straight from the Simmon family gardens on the outskirts of town. It's run by the Darling Springs sheriff's husband. He supplies some of the best restaurants in the city."

"Oh!"

I've got Juniper's attention now—now that she knows Darling Springs exports things to the big city of San Francisco.

"And where is The Oasis?" She stops herself. "No worries. I'll just plug it into my GPS. That works here."

Technology *is* truly amazing. But her this-town-is-Podunk-USA attitude aside, I'm happy to help the gal from Los Angeles. "I can take you on the way to our tour," I offer.

"That'd be great. Haven said you were helpful, but that's above and beyond."

Today, I feel above and beyond, having smashed my to-do list. I've already fixed the floorboard in the farmhouse where key members of the cast and crew will stay (no falling through the boards here, thank you very much), emailed security and property specs to the logistics producer on the film, prepped the Loddon Blue bunches for the farmers market this afternoon, and updated the spreadsheets for Ramona to work on later when she reviews the books to see what we can't keep in stock in the cute little on-site shop she runs, and what else is dragging us down.

Like the lavender maze off in a corner of the farm. Hardly anyone comes to that, which needs to change. I could add fairy lights at night and make it a fun date destination. It's a twisty, curly series of hedges, with dead ends and paths that lead to a clearing in the middle. We seriously need to get more tourism going to keep this place afloat when it's not summertime. I also want to start promoting have-your-own-picnics here. Some of my lavender farm friends in Washington State have been making extra money by charging a few bucks for folks who want a nice place to enjoy a picnic lunch—in this case, in the lavender fields. It's an easy way to make money off our best asset—the flowers in bloom.

For now though, best I stay focused on the film prep. The crew arrives in three weeks. Only twenty-one more days. Today's tour is yet another item on my get-ready-in-record-time list. I've been busier than ever since Mister Ditch-a-Girl-in-Seconds-Flat sent the desk clerk to do his bidding last week. I've been nothing but nonstop energy. I haven't even thought about the ghoster. I don't have time. Not when the climactic wedding scene in *Someone Else's Ring* is going to be shot here on the farm, as well as, oh, about ten others.

Today's goal? Keep Juniper happy. She's my main contact with the production company. If she's happy, she'll—I hope—say nice things to Tabitha, the logistics producer, then Vega, the director, about this town. If the director's in a good mood, that'll help the shoot. If the shoot goes well, my sister's happy. When my sister's happy, she can pour her big squishy heart into her role.

Not to mention what it'll do for the farm. But Haven first.

As Hudson artfully lopes through the blue and purple flowers that form the world's prettiest outdoor carpet—he's learned to run through the bushes like it's an obstacle course for big mutts—I tell Juniper I'll be there soon. I finish clipping the Otto Quast and take it to Cyrus in the shop, who's rocking out to something from the looks of it, his shaggy head of hair bobbing. He's got sunscreen streaks all across his pale arms. He's as religious about applying it as he is about worshipping the sun.

When I reach him, he turns down his music. He's listening to the *Bob's Burgers* soundtrack. *Again.* "Thanks, bro," he says, since he calls everyone *bro*, regardless of gender. "I'll add it to the herb stash. But not my personal herb stash."

"Appreciate that," I say dryly, hoping he's not seriously considering smoking the product.

I peel off my purple gardening gloves and head inside the farmhouse, lured by the yummy scent of butter and dough, and a cheery voice echoing from the kitchen.

"On n'est pas des robots."

My grandmother repeats the French phrase in her warm, husky tone as she rolls out dough for croissants. "*On n'est pas des robots.* We are not robots."

I arch a dubious brow. "Do you really think you're going to vouch for your humanity in Paris someday?"

She looks up from her rolling pin, giving a *you never know* shrug. "It's possible, love."

"I don't know if you're open-minded or prepared for anything," I say as I head to the big sink to wash my hands.

"Both," she says, and that is my grandmother in a nutshell.

"Je suis un docteur," the app singsongs.

Over my shoulder, I side-eye her phone. "I am a doctor?"

"Some doctors might be using this app to learn French too," she says.

I turn off the water and dry my hands. "Even if you were a doctor, would you be spouting that phrase in Paris?" I raise an arm grandly, like I'm marching through town. "Attention! Je suis un docteur." I come around, squeeze her shoulders. "Maybe time for a new French app, Grandma?"

But the robotic voice chatters on, saying, "Je mange du beurre."

My grandma's blue eyes brighten, crinkling at the corners. "Ooh! I knew it. That one is useful. I *am* eating butter."

I use the diversion to pinch off a sliver of the dough and pop it in my mouth. "Me too."

She waves a blue-and-white-striped kitchen towel my way, shooing me out of there. "You were never able to wait, Ripley," she tuts.

"Why should I?"

"It tastes better when it's, you know, done."

"I guess I just like to live dangerously," I say.

"And the gray hairs on my head are proof."

"You don't have any gray hairs!"

She shakes her head of platinum-blond hair like a shampoo model. "Only my stylist knows the truth."

I bring a finger to my lips. "And Kyle never tells."

"Exactly." She points to the door. "Now go, you croissant thief."

I flash her a *gotcha* smile. "Bet you'll need to say that in French."

She rolls her eyes. "Au revoir!"

"Bye, Grandma," I say, shifting to practical mode now. "I need to take Juniper around town, but I'll be back in a few hours. Also, when you see Ramona, remind her we need more bottles of lotion for—"

"The Slippery Dipper," she supplies. "I know. I used to run this place."

She ran Lavender Bliss Farms for years, before my parents died, and after too. Much longer than she planned to. Now, she takes care of the bees. She loves bees, and bees are cool. Also, they get along great with flowers, so we like to give bees a good home.

"And now you get to make croissants and study French and possibly go to Paris," I say, hoping she hears the gratitude in my voice for all she's done.

"Peut-être," she says. I've learned by osmosis that means both *perhaps* and *maybe*. I prefer *perhaps* since that's more hopeful. Grandma wants to spend the fall in Paris with her boyfriend, Laurent, a handsome Frenchman she met on a cruise last year.

And dammit, she will. As long as I can keep this place in the black. The film should help that if everything goes as planned. After grabbing a canvas bag, I stuff it with some lavender goodies, then head out to the garage. I hop into my pickup truck—*electric, Juniper, imagine that*—and drive off to the inn a couple of miles away.

I trot up the steps and dart into the lobby, ready to say hello to Bridget, one of my besties and inn owner extraordinaire, but my plans are thwarted when the businesslike-during-the-day brunette is chatting amiably with a guest. "Of course we'll make sure you have hot towels in your room every morning," Bridget tells the man.

I walk behind the guest, furrowing my brow and mouthing, "Hot towels? WTF?" at Bridget, but she keeps smiling, masterful at ignoring my shenanigans.

I beeline to the lobby library, where a woman with bright-blue hair, a porcelain complexion, black glasses, and a camera slung around her neck stands against a tall bookshelf. She's bent over a phone, swiping across the screen. "Ready for some Kale Yeah?" I ask Juniper.

She smiles. At least, I think it's a smile. The corner of her lips moves maybe a millimeter. "Yes. Just checking my Helios Pro," she says, her brow creased with worry.

"Cool," I say, because I have no clue what that is.

"It's an app that tracks the sun at different locations," she adds, like she needs to justify what she's up to. Maybe she's under a lot of pressure for this film shoot too. That makes sense.

"Glad you have it then," I say, and she tells me more about it as we head to my truck. How she needs to make absolutely certain what the light's like at different places and times, and yup, she's stressed. Who isn't these days? I listen to her as she goes on about permits next, since I suspect that's what she needs—an ear.

We hit the smoothie shop, and she seems a touch calmer once she's sucking green liquid through a straw. We walk to the community center a block away. After a quick pit stop there, where we meet my friend Chloe's mom and Juniper asks her about using some of the local community theater actors to play extras in the film since Chloe's mom's the director, we head to Josiah's Hardware.

Once we arrive, I snag a small pot of the Loddon Blue from the bed of the truck and go inside. I spot the affable owner offering a

Churu to a fluffy orange cat, who saunters across the counter like he's going to take the cat treat, but then snaps his furry head toward me, eyes bugging out before he flies off the wood, racing who the hell knows where.

Josiah shrugs when he sees me, apologizing for the feline. "Cats."

"Cats," I second.

I know Josiah well. His family is from Haiti, but he doesn't speak with an accent since he was born here. He was a friend of my father's, and they went fishing together on weekends.

A warm smile coasts across his weathered face. "I've told Sheldon you're friendly. I've told him you've always been friendly, but…"

"But cats," I say, handing him the pot, then gesture to the blue-haired woman with me. "And I believe you know Juniper Claire from Ruby Horizons."

"Sure do. Met the other week. Sheldon likes you," he says to Juniper.

"I'm a cat person," she says, and I file that detail away.

Especially since it just tracks.

Juniper quickly shifts gears, noting she needs to double-check the power supply options in the store for the shoot. As they chat, I grab some of the paint he'd told me he'd set aside for me as part of our regular trades, and I load the tins up in the truck.

On the way back into town, we drive past the local university, an enclave of learning and cherry blossom trees. Both are quiet during the summer, but I point out the quad where the trees bloom gloriously each April, then the small art museum just beyond, which recently hosted a pop art exhibit that brought new crowds to the town.

We pull over on Main Street to pay a visit to The Slippery Dipper, where a key scene in the film will take place. Outside the lotions-and-potions shop hangs a cheeky awning with a black-and-white illustration of a cartoon woman in an old-fashioned bathtub, taking a sudsy shower. Juniper stops under it, swiping on her screen, perhaps recording sunlight amounts, or I dunno, checking to see if her kale levels have slipped too low.

When she's done, I grab the handle of the door, but then pause before opening it. "I swear this guy here—his name is Noah—is like some kind of romance soothsayer."

That seems to perk her interest. She cocks her head. "Really? In what way?"

"He seems to know exactly what every dude in town needs," I say, then an irksome thought lands in my head. Banks could have used Noah's help. He would definitely have benefitted from some serious guidance because ghosting a one-night stand before the deed is not okay.

But then I dismiss the thought.

There's no help for that man I met in San Francisco. Some guys just aren't worth the trouble. Like the ones who kiss you breathless then disappear without a trace, leaving you feeling like a complete and utter fool.

I'd never have had time for romance anyway. Fine, fine, it was only going to be a one-night stand, but even that would have occupied too much space in my head. It's a good thing the night with Banks didn't happen.

It really, *really* is.

A few hours later, after I drop off Juniper at The BookHouse, I've crossed another item off my to-do list. "I should go recharge now," she says, and briefly I picture her plugging herself into a wall socket so she can handle her job tomorrow.

Once I'm home, I grab my gloves, ready to hit the farm chores again, but I stop on my way through the kitchen. There's a package from Haven waiting on the kitchen counter. Grandma must have brought it in and left it for me.

I open it, grabbing the card on top of the gift.

You're the best. I don't know what I'd do without you. I can't wait to see you soon.

Then, there's a packet of biodegradable tennis balls for my dog. My heart warms. Haven knows the way to my heart.

I show Hudson and he wags his tail, ready again, no recharge necessary.

I spend the next few weeks prepping, then finally catching my breath at Prohibition Spirit with my best girlfriends—Chloe and Bridget—a few nights before my sister and the crew arrive.

Inside the whiskey bar with the rich deep-red upholstery and high windows, we order old-fashioneds. "Coming right up," the bartender-owner says in a honey voice worthy of a torch singer as jazz music plays faintly overhead.

When she plunks them down a few minutes later, she locks her big eyes with mine. Tiny silver skull earrings line both ears from lobe to top. Matching skulls snake across her arms, and a silver stud is parked in the side of her nose. "All right, Addison. Who do I need to fuck around here to get my bar on the location list?"

For a few seconds, I draw a blank. I didn't know Esmeralda Polanco was so…blunt. "I…"

She points at my chest. "Oh, you?" She's so deadpan I don't know if she means it.

"I swear it's not up to me," I say, holding up my hands in surrender. "I was just helping the location scout."

But Esmeralda cracks a smile, then slaps the counter. "Just giving you a hard time, girl. I don't want my bar in the film. Earlier today this place was crawling with amateur photogs. I swear I had to swat 'em out of here with my extra-large broom." Then she wiggles her eyebrows. "The one I fly on at night."

Relieved she's not annoyed, I laugh too. "Oh good. I mean, it's not good that you're…but it's good…"

Bridget sets a hand on my shoulder. "What Ripley means is *tell us every dirty detail*."

"Yes, and leave nothing out," Chloe adds.

Esmeralda leans in, tips her forehead to the door, and says, "There was a tour group trying to get in before I even opened. Some local guide from the city is offering tours of Darling Springs. *A Hollywood hot spot*," she says.

"Oh, wow. Already?" I ask.

"Evidently. With the book having been such a hit, the new game is guessing which local spots represent which places from the book. But that's not even the big news." She leans closer.

"I heard today the male lead was recast. Now, Chris Carlisle is playing him."

"The...New Chris?" I ask, a little starstruck. Haven didn't mention this—and surely she'd have mentioned the sexy superstar who pretty much guarantees box office success. He's the *it* guy in Hollywood these days after *Bangable*, his sleeper rom-com hit, became a global phenom last year thanks to word of mouth and word of abs. Chris's, of course.

"And if you see me wearing more makeup when he arrives, you'll know why," Esmeralda says, then pantomimes fishing and reeling in a big one. When she catches the imaginary fish—it's gotta be fifty pounds at least—she nods to a group of new customers who just grabbed stools. "I'll catch you chickies later."

I turn to my friends. "Chris Carlisle?"

"I'm asking Haven right now!" Chloe taps out a text message, since she was friends with Haven when we were in school too. But Haven doesn't reply right away, and all they find on the internet are rumors, so we table the hunt, lifting our drinks instead and toasting.

"Here's to prepping a farmhouse, a farm, and a cottage for a whole damn crew," Bridget says to me.

Chloe lifts her glass too. "That was an impressive feat, Mrs. Fix It. Even for you."

I blow on my nails, unpolished. I borrowed Chloe's polish remover the day after I returned from San Francisco and scrubbed that color right off, going back to me as quickly as I could. As I take a drink, I think of Grandma and her dreams, the ones she set aside when our parents died. I think of my sister and her hopes. The one

I feared she'd never realize during those dark days when she was younger. When I made it my mission to look out for her. Always. To fix whatever I could for her since I could never fix the hole in her heart from losing our mom and dad.

Finally, their dreams are close to coming true.

That night as I crawl into bed next to Hudson, a message blinks up on my phone. Finally, it's Haven. I click it open instantly.

> **Haven:** I was doing some interviews for *Vanity Fair* about the new guard in Hollywood. Is this my life?
> **Ripley:** Yes, and you're the new guard!
> **Haven:** THIS IS SO WEIRD! And Yes, New Chris is on the movie, and I'm trying not to freak out. The producers want to make some last-minute changes.

My stomach sinks. Are they recasting her? I don't even want to touch that, but I have to.

> **Ripley:** Like what? Everything OK with you?
> **Haven:** I'm great! And they're just adding a few more people. I'll call you tomorrow. But don't worry.

That sounds ominous, but I tell myself not to let it bother me. I'm not sure I listen though.

CHAPTER 7
A STANDARD RAISER
BANKS

With my jaw ticking tightly like the clock as it moves closer to the inevitable, I thumb through a shelf in the etiquette section at An Open Book in San Francisco on a Thursday morning. My notorious nerves of steel feel like they're made of spaghetti as I think about seeing her again. There's got to be a book here to help me. I scan for something, *anything*, to guide me through this terrible mess I haven't figured out how to undo for the last twenty-six days. As I'm searching futilely, a woman with red hair and red glasses comes over to me. "Is there anything I can get for you?"

A do-over? A time machine? A better plan than leaving a fucking letter for a woman I wanted to spend the whole damn night with?

"I'm all good, thanks," I say, then think the better of it. "Actually, I need a new book for my sister. She likes, um…" I hesitate, thinking about what Emily calls her favorite romances. "A standard raiser?"

The woman smiles. "Haven't heard that one before. But it's a good term. Now let's see." She rattles off options: "Rom-com? Dark romance? Mafia romance? Romantasy? Billionaire?"

I snap my fingers. "The last one."

She finds me a book with a black and gold cover, and I grab it, then pick up a celebrity memoir for Mom, and a new Stephen King for me. After I buy them, I take off, heading over the bridge to Sausalito. I'm meeting my mom and sister for a quick lunch before the drive to Darling Springs today, where I'll have to face Haven again. I still have no clue how to handle it. I could ask the ladies in my life, but once we settle in at an outdoor table at a café overlooking Richardson Bay, they're updating me on the latest in their worlds, so I keep my focus on them. As it should be. Just like my focus was on them when our lives capsized back when I was in high school, thanks to my dad. I don't want to be like him. *Ever.*

But near the end of the meal, Mom puts on her *very concerned about her son* face. "You seem distracted, Banks."

Distraction is bad in my line of business. No, it's the kiss of death. "I'm all good."

"Is it the new business?" she asks, clearly not buying my lie.

Ah, hell.

Best to deal with the distraction right now so I can do my job later. I can't risk the company Dean and I are building. Well, any more than I might already have. "How do I apologize? For fucking something up badly?"

"Language," Mom says.

"For messing something up badly," I quickly correct.

"How badly?" Emily asks, parking her chin in her hand, like she's ready to break out the popcorn.

I drag a hand through my hair and sigh heavily. "Pretty badly," I say, but then shut the hell up. There's not much more I *can* say. I signed an NDA. I can't tell them who I'm working for even if it gets out soon. I'll just have to...

Do better this time around.

"I'll figure it out," I say, then pay for the meal when we're done and head on my way.

As I drive to Darling Springs blasting Beethoven's Symphony No. 5 since it suits my angsty mood, I mentally prep to see Haven again.

When she finds out I'm on the team that's been hired, she'll likely either one, fire my ass into next year; two, call me all kinds of names then slay me with her sexy eyes (if she doesn't knee me in the balls); or three, kiss her co-star, since she's already forgotten all about me.

I growl, unbidden, at the thought of option three. But one is most likely. I just have to hope Dean is around to cover for me if she does pull the *it's him or me* card.

Facts are facts—I kissed the lead actress and was making plans to fuck her. I'm man enough to handle the consequences now. I hope Dean will understand when he finds out.

That night though, I didn't know who Haven Addison even was. I definitely didn't know she'd been cast on the film, or that it was a film client since the referral firm hadn't shared the details with me.

But on my flight home to Los Angeles—I switched it to that night and got the hell out of there—I googled Haven Addison and learned she's a twin. Learned, too, that her identical twin sister, Ripley, runs a lavender farm in Darling Springs.

Doesn't take a genius to put two and two together. Haven must use her sister's name when she's out and about. No wonder she was so emphatic about the name Ripley. Haven really wanted me to think she wasn't Haven, understandably.

But when I googled pics of the two of them, I noticed a few key details. Haven always polishes her nails. Ripley never does. Yet that night, Haven-posing-as-Ripley had cotton-candy-pink nails.

Haven-posing-as-Ripley also dropped that bit about mulch into the convo, maybe to underscore she wasn't Haven.

But c'mon.

Nails aside, of course it was Haven-posing-as-Ripley. The woman was in the same damn hotel where I'd had a meeting about the film Haven's starring in. The same night the film got the green light. Plus, there's what she said when I made her the origami bird.

I just got some wild news. Then, she added, *It's a huge project.*

And of course it makes perfect sense that an actress would use a fake name when she's at a bar and meeting a guy, *especially* after a jackass hit on her.

The evidence added up.

I wasn't going to take a chance at risking a reputation our firm has just started to build. One wrong step and all our work could go down the drain. I learned the hard way from my liar of a father how precious your reputation is. So I walked away rather than risking it.

I chose the careful path.

With Haven's star rising, she'll need to be even more careful when she's out in public, when she meets random guys. I can help her with that. That's what I do. I can give her some tips and strategies.

If she doesn't kick me in the balls, that is. Like I probably deserve.

I take the exit for Darling Springs, hoping my balls stay intact. Once I'm driving down Main Street, my phone rings. I turn off the fourth movement when I see it's the logistics producer with Ruby Horizons.

"Banks here," I say.

Tabitha wastes no time. "Change of plans. We need to get you started, stat. There's a situation."

CHAPTER 8
GOOD-ISH
RIPLEY

I'm riding toward Main Street on my purple beach cruiser, with a bike basket of lavender bouquets slated for the gourmet market. I told Salma, the owner, I'd have this delivery to her by 2:00 p.m.—fresh and on time—for the early Thursday evening wave of *what's for dinner* shoppers.

Ordinarily, I'd send Cyrus with the delivery, but he took a mental health day. Which is fine. I'm all for mental health days. It's a little annoying when he *also* posts pics on social about how great the waves are at the nearest beach.

Which I only know he posted about because Ramona stomped out of the shop earlier, waggling her phone, her curls wild, her dark eyes determined to get her due, declaring she wanted to go surfing too, like Cyrus and his boyfriend. But like a good girl, she was waiting for her day off.

"And I appreciate you coming to work," I told Ramona.

"Thank you," she said with a proud lift of her chin.

"I'll get you a treat," I said.

"That would be great," she said, and I gave myself a mental note to thank Chloe for that tip since she's a self-proclaimed practitioner of treat culture, getting herself rewards when she finishes errands and such.

As I near The Sweet Spot, the scent of cinnamon banana bread wafts out the open door of the white storefront that's decorated with pink polka dots. I'll snag some for Ramona on my return.

I'm nearly past the shop when someone shouts: "Ripley!"

I slam on the brakes, then turn toward Katrina, the makeup-free and ever-so-casual owner of the bakery. Except, now she's the owner of the longest lashes and reddest lips I've seen. But the change in her makeup routine aside, maybe she sensed I was entering the treat zone. She races to the curb, where I stopped my bike.

"Hi, Katrina. I was just inhaling the banana bread," I say, tipping my forehead to the storefront.

"Great. Awesome. So good. That's fantastic," she says at the speed of a locomotive as she brushes her hands over her white apron with, you guessed it, pink polka dots all over it. "I'll get you some right away. But first, is he here? Is it true? Is he with her?" She flaps a hand in front of her face and takes a deep breath, settling her obvious excitement. "Because if he's not, I think it might be my chance."

But what the heck is she talking about? "I'm not sure what you mean."

"Chris Carlisle," she says reverently, her voice breaking.

Suddenly, the makeover makes all the sense in the world. "I don't think he's in town yet."

"Does he like banana bread? Will you take some to him? Tell him it's from me. I think he'll like it. I went to Tell Me Your Tarot and she said the man of my dreams was coming to town soon. And I am sure it's him. But if he's involved with your sister, I take it all back," she says, then holds up her flour-covered hands in surrender. "I would never go after your or her guy or anyone's guy."

This is more info than I expected at 1:45 in the afternoon. But everything comes into focus now—why she burst out when she saw me. Like I'm the keeper of all the intel. "I have no idea if he likes banana bread, but who doesn't like it? Also, I don't think he's involved with Haven."

She squeaks. That's the only way to describe the high-pitched sound that exits her mouth. "Be right back." She flies into her shop and returns with a white paper bag seconds later, thrusting it at me. "Take it. In case you see him. Tell him it's from Katrina Goldstein, owner of The Sweet Spot."

"But what if I don't see him?"

"Then it's yours, and I'll make you more tomorrow for him."

It does smell good. Maybe Ramona's not the only one who deserves a treat. "Okay, thanks." I take the bag and set it in the basket next to the bouquets of Grosso, a type of French lavender that's among the most popular.

I thank her, then shake my head in amusement as I leave. Is this the town's new norm—obsessing over New Chris?

After I pedal across the street, I pull over by a parklet for the breakfast café that's now closed for the rest of the day. Jamming a hand into my back pocket, I grab my phone right as it rings with Haven's ringtone.

"Hey. Is there something you've been meaning to tell me?" I ask playfully.

"As a matter of fact, there is," she says.

Not the answer I expected, so I straighten, on alert as I switch to AirPods and Bluetooth. "So you *are* involved with New Chris?"

She snort-laughs. "Oh god no." She takes a pause. Blows out a breath. "Buuuut." She says it like it has five syllables. "Everyone thinks we are because we had lunch the other day."

"Haven, haven't I told you? Lunch means you're engaged."

"I'm sure they'll say that next. It's all over a bunch of celebrity sites—the photo from lunch. *Page Six* and *VIP Vibes* and a bunch of others. We were talking about the movie, and I was showing him a picture of the farm on my phone. I leaned close to him, and he leaned into me…"

Of course. "And that's the shot they got?"

"Yes," she says with remorse.

I hate to do this, but it's best to be prepared, so I google Chris. And holy shit. The first thing that pops up is the image of them at a white wooden table at a sidewalk café, surrounded by tall potted plants, looking like a couple, all close and snuggly, his hand on her arm.

"It's only his hand on your arm," I say. I still feel queasy because *I* know that, but others won't see just a hand on an arm. They'll see the start of a new celebrity romance.

"And now," she continues, "the gossip sites are saying he *asked* to be on the movie so he could be with me."

"Oh." I process this twist. "Is that good or bad?"

"It's good-ish. Good adjacent," she says, like she's hedging her bets.

"Elaborate." I check the time. I told Salma I'd be at the market in five minutes.

"Well, it's great because the movie is getting more buzz, and so is the farm and the town here." She seems to be laying out all the good news before she gets to the bad bits. "But Ruby Horizons is increasing security for the film."

My shoulders relax. That's not bad news at all. "That's great, actually." I check the street and continue down the bike lane, chatting as I ride slowly. "You can't be too careful in this day and age. Seems like a normal thing on a film shoot, right?"

I can actually hear her gulp as I pedal.

"Haven," I press. "What is it?"

"It's not just more security *in general*. I mean, this is Chris Carlisle. He has photogs following him everywhere."

"Paparazzi still exist?"

She laughs, but not cruelly. "They do. There's this idea that they don't because of the rise of cell phones, but there's a big difference between a photo taken by someone with a long-range lens and a photo taken with a cell phone camera by just anyone."

That's fair. "Sure, they have skills."

"Exactly."

"But with social media and celebs posting their own stuff, there's still value?"

"Yes. Because sometimes the public only wants an unposed photo. The uncurated moment. Like right now. Everyone's supposedly dying to get a picture of us kissing. Something that would make it *official*." She sounds annoyed, and that's not her usual MO.

"And you're definitely not involved with him?" I ask.

"Ripley! No. I'd tell you. I'm not involved with him."

"Why doesn't he deny you're a couple then?"

"Because denial would look *even more* like we're involved."

My head spins. "It would?"

"Yes. There's a long history of actors and celebrities denying they're in a relationship, especially when they're filming, then admitting it later. And often it comes out later that they *were* together during the film but then split up afterward. Which means if they admit it too early, then break up during the film—as, let's be honest, often happens—you have a PR mess."

Forget spinning. I have whiplash. "But you're not even involved with him."

"I know! But that's my point. If you deny a rumor, you look like a couple that's, well, trying to hide a relationship, so that makes the paparazzi even more hungry for a picture. It's like feeding a troll."

Ahh. I suppose that does make sense. Hollywood sense. "Got it."

"Which is why it's better to ignore it or not comment on it till it dies down," she adds.

"So what does all this Hollywood logic mean?"

"Well, Chris travels with his own security and he's arriving in Darling Springs today."

"Why is he here earlier than you?"

"It's part of his process," she says.

"Method actor?"

"I guess." She pauses, a weighty beat that's a sign she's about to tell me something I might not like. "They've always been planning on getting me a bodyguard for the shoot. Because of the book's success and all."

"And yours," I point out. "Don't forget you were on a very successful streaming show."

I can hear her smile, then turn serious again. "I've never had a bodyguard before, but Ruby Horizons is a very cautious company, and they take safety seriously. They think it's a wise idea."

"But again, that's not bad news. That's good news," I say.

She sighs happily. "I'm so glad you said that because—"

There's a siren on her end, and I can't hear the next thing she says as I near the market, which has a line outside the door. Good for Salma. I'm glad her place is becoming more popular.

"Sorry, Haven. I didn't hear you," I say as I slow near the bike racks.

"I said I'm so glad you said that because now they've decided they're sending one for you too."

I always thought it was just a saying—I stop in my tracks. I thought it was along the lines of an *I did a double take* or *I spat out my drink*.

But I literally stop in my bike tracks like I've hit an invisible wall. "Why the hell are they sending a bodyguard for me?"

Then I catch my reflection in the window of The Slippery Dipper, next to the market, and have my answer. Except for the ink flying down my right arm—visible in my white tank top—I'm the spitting image of the woman rumored to be dating a bona fide known-around-the-world movie star.

Still. I don't want or need a goon following me around my hometown all day.

"Because we look alike," Haven says apologetically.

"Right, but a bodyguard is a hundred percent unnecessary. I know literally everyone in Darling Springs. And they know me. No one here confuses me for you."

"But there are so many new people coming to town. Tourists, the crew, the press, and so on. It'll only be for the next few days, and then for the shoot itself. It's a good idea, like you said. Mace can only do so much," she says, all upbeat as she sells me something I definitely don't want.

I have enough happening in my life and business right now—managing the farm, the employees, and the deliveries, not to mention the freaking location shoot at my home *and* place of business.

"It sounds like a terrible idea," I correct her. "I live a normal life in a small town. I'm not a celebrity. I'm a farmer, for bee's sake."

But Haven's already making the case. "This firm is great though. It's run by a couple former Marines and—"

I lose the rest when a pale stocky man in jeans, a backward baseball cap, and a black T-shirt appears out of nowhere. He trots beside the bike, gets in my face, a camera around his neck.

Holy shit. Haven was right. These guys are good at staying hidden. I didn't even see him coming.

"How's Chris?" the man barks. "Is he here yet? Is everything good with him?"

What?

"Are you two going out tonight? Bet you're excited to see him."

I'm so flustered by the bizarrely mundane way he asks the questions as he snaps pictures of me that my tire smacks into the bike rack, knocking me off-kilter.

I wobble on the bicycle, the bouquets and banana bread toppling out of the basket. I slam a sneaker on the sidewalk and hop off the bike as it's falling.

Haven's tinny voice grows faint in my ear. "He's already on his way to handle advance security."

A man made only of muscle swoops in between me and the photog, catching my shoulder, then wrapping an arm around me while steadying the bike in one smooth motion. "I've got you," he says. Then, to the guy, he says, "That's enough."

Two words. Stern. Commanding. Clear.

The photographer backs off, and before I can process what just happened, the sturdy man scoops the bouquets and the bag of banana bread from the sidewalk, slides my bike into the rack, and then whisks me away, an arm wrapped protectively around my shoulder.

My skin is buzzing.

My heart is hammering.

And my mind is whirling with brand-new fantasies of a wildly protective man who saves the day. A hero with thick thighs, flat abs, and sturdy pecs. A man with a trim beard on his chiseled jaw, and tattoos on his arms of steel.

Tattoos with geometric shapes that tickle my memory.

I steal another glance at this tall, ripped body next to mine, enjoying the view, *thank you very much*, up until my gaze lands squarely on a very familiar face.

My new bodyguard is none other than The One Who Ran Away.

CHAPTER 9
HELL-FIERY
BANKS

"Are you kidding me?"

With fire in her blue eyes, she rips away from me at the corner of Main Street. I don't grab Ripley since that'd defeat the purpose of my help. The last thing *we* need is a scene. The last thing *I* need is to get in trouble for putting hands on a client.

Even an angry one.

I'd been warned on my call with the logistics producer moments ago that the twin sister probably wouldn't want security. But a lot of *regular people* don't. Calming someone down is part of the job. "I'm your new bodyguard. I'm only here to make sure you're safe, Ripley," I say, trying to appeal like it's a basic human need.

Safety is important to emphasize. It's something we all want. Food, shelter, safety, love—things many people don't get in life.

She rolls those pretty blue eyes next. "Right. Sure. That's

your goal." She reaches for the bouquets of lavender I'm holding. Probably a half dozen.

Ah, my trump card while I manage a client who doesn't want to be a client—a good game of keep-away. I wrap an arm tighter around the flowers, keeping a grip on the bag of baked goods too, in case that's what she's angling for the most.

"Oh, c'mon. Give me my things," she says. "I want to make my delivery and get my bike."

"In a minute, of course. Let's chat first," I say, trying to let her know I'm on her side.

She huffs, staring me down fiercely. "What is your deal?"

Fiery doesn't really cut it with this one. More like hell-fiery.

"I'm part of the team working on the film. I've been assigned to you," I say. *Just a few minutes ago, in fact.* I glance around, checking behind us, down the street, across from it. Sure, there are townspeople and tourists milling about. A block away, a woman pushing a jogging stroller turns into a white-and-pink bakery. Down the road, a man stops outside a tattoo shop, checking out the designs in the window. Most importantly though, we're out of sight of the photogs who stalk Chris Carlisle incessantly. Still, I really don't want to have this conversation on the street.

Near the end of the block, a pack of women in varying shades of pastel yoga attire streams into a yoga studio. Next to that is a coffee shop, and on the sidewalk outside sits a chalkboard sign with a peach-colored coffee-cup drawing. Steam curls from the top of the cup, beckoning.

"Let's duck into Pick Me Up."

"Yes, Banks. That sounds great. I *really* want to get coffee with you," she says dryly.

This is going to be so fun. Both sisters probably hate me. But at least Ripley knows my name. That has to be a good sign. When my firm first landed the gig with the film last month, the plan was to provide security for the shoot itself. Now, with Chris Carlisle on the movie, coupled with the rumors about Haven and him, the key players are getting close protection officers. Tabitha asked me to personally handle security for Ripley when she called a few minutes ago. That call was brief, but Tabitha said she'd given my name to Haven, so Haven must have passed it on to her sister. At least Haven hasn't canned me yet, but it seems she's definitely given Ripley the lowdown on our almost rendezvous.

"We should get away from crowds," I say, keeping my tone so goddamn calm and relaxed, like I've been trained to do.

"No." She's emphatic as she wiggles her fingers at the bouquets in my hand. "Gimme my flowers and we can go. Like I told my sister, I don't need a babysitter."

Ah, hell.

They both definitely hate me. Of course they hate me. Fuck my life.

"I'm sure you don't, but let's chat in the shop, and I'll give you your things," I say, trying to wrest control of a difficult client.

She folds her arms over her chest, sneering at me. "You're actually holding my Grosso bouquets hostage?"

"Gross? That seems a little harsh. I think they're okay." I take a deep inhale of the pretty flowers.

"Grosso, and they're more than okay. They're some of my customers' favorites." Ripley sighs. "And you're sniffing all over them. Real nice."

"I'm not the enemy here," I say, frustrated, pointing toward the door.

She stares at the flowers even harder. "But *you* have my flowers."

For a few seconds, I'm not sure who's going to cave because this woman is staring at me like she's the zombie slayer and I'm the undead she's been waiting to obliterate. But after a tense face-off, she relents, marching ahead to the shop. Fast. Like *she's going to race-walk in the Olympics* fast. Like she thinks she'll lose me with her pace.

That's cute.

But my long legs eat up the sidewalk and in seconds I'm ahead of her, reaching for the door, holding it open.

"Aww, you are a gentleman after all," she says.

I wince but try not to let it show at the particular use of that word.

"Hey, Ripley," a woman with a fair complexion and big black glasses calls out as she works the espresso machine.

"Hey, Callie," Ripley says, all friendly, the polar opposite of the tone she's taken with me.

"The usual?"

"Later. I have to deal with"—she tosses a careless glance my way—"a hiccup in my schedule."

The woman smiles. "Hiccups are the worst."

"Don't I know it."

She storms to the back of the shop, then stops by an empty table in the corner next to a worn leather couch with cracks in it. Across from the couch is a scratched wooden table, covered with stacks of vintage board games and coffee-table art books.

Ripley parks her hands on her hips. "I'd like my things. I need to take them to the store. I'm late for my delivery. That's where I was going, you know."

"Yes, when the paparazzo showed up. That guy with the ball cap? That's Silas. He gives no fucks. He works a lot for *Page Six*. He's been on Carlisle since *Bangable* took off. I'm sure that photo of you is going to be on the internet any minute," I tell her, then shrug. "Until they realize you're the twin."

She slow claps. "Bravo. You can observe. So impressive. But observe this, buddy." She strides away from the corner, pointing wildly to the front of the store. "No one followed us down the street. Or in here. So someone took a pic of *the twin*. Big deal. Whatever." Then she holds her arms out wide, like she's saying *no harm, no foul*. "I'm fine. Just fine. Let me be."

At least I haven't been fired yet. At least I haven't screwed over Dean yet.

I try to take solace in those facts. "And it's my job to make sure you continue to be just fine. There are going to be a ton of new people in town. Camera crews and the press. Tourists. Not to mention more paps. But that's only the start of it. Regular people have become the paps. Everyone is a photographer. They're going to be looking at you because you look—"

"Just like my sister." She stares hard at me. "Dude, I know." She gestures emphatically to her chest, her stomach, her thighs. "I've lived in this body for thirty years. I am well aware I look just like her. You don't need to mansplain it to me."

"It wasn't mansplaining," I say, defensively, except...shit. I was. I nod, taking that one on the chin. "You're right. That was patronizing, and I'm sorry. I understand you don't want a close protection officer, but the film company approved one for Haven, and they want one for you too. I promise I'll do my best to be unobtrusive and stay out of the way."

She snorts. "Your best? I mean, it shouldn't be that hard. You're pretty good at staying out of the way, *Banks*." She spits out my name like it tastes bad, and...hold on.

Her voice. The sass in it. The fire.

Also, the sheer specificity.

My brow pinches.

Like the high-speed rewind when the movie guy realizes he's been played all along, that night at the hotel flashes before my eyes in sharp, clear detail.

I add in the biggest clue—the one standing in front of me.

It's not the tattoos covering her right arm, which I expected from the pics of her on the farm.

It's not the ease with which she sails through town, chatting with shop owners, which I'd expect from a local.

It's not the nails, unpolished, which I expected too.

It's the *attitude* of Ripley.

All *take no prisoners*.

Like the woman I met that night at the bar.

Like the way she said *gentleman*.

The way she said my name.

The way she doesn't suffer fools.

Shock isn't useful in my line of work. But my jaw comes unhinged. "You're…Ripley?" My voice sounds like it's coming from another man, on another night.

Then Ripley-Ripley, not Haven-posing-as-Ripley—because Haven was never posing as Ripley—flashes me a *fuck you* smile. "Just like I said."

CHAPTER 10
AISLE TEN
RIPLEY

"I had no idea. But I can totally explain," he says, sounding desperate to right things.

Spare me. Seriously. Just spare me. I'm not in the mood for his song-and-dance routine. Especially when he acted like it was nothing to see me again.

But then, that fits his MO. Fine. Whatever. I've had twenty-six days to get over the embarrassment of asking a hotel clerk to spank me, so yeah, I'm so over Banks, I don't care what he wants to explain. Even though, fine… I didn't like the way that photog invaded my space. It made my pulse spike, and not just because I don't love being photographed.

Still, the encounter was only with one person and nothing bad came of it. I definitely don't need *this guy* shadowing me around my hometown. "Cool. Now I believe we had a deal. Can I please have my bouquets and we can go? Salma's expecting this. French lavender is her favorite."

For a second, he feints, like he's going to hand them to me. But then he hugs them closer. "I'll carry them."

This guy. But I try again. "Or how about I take them, and you can stay, say, fifty feet behind me?"

I can manage that. *I think.*

Banks smiles and…damn him. The fucker has a dimple. Does the universe hate me? Giving me a bodyguard who rushes out on me before the banging, then giving him a freaking dimple? If that isn't evidence of the universe's disdain, I don't know what is. "I'll walk with you, Ripley. There's a lot I need to say."

"There's a statute of limitations and it's passed, so no need."

"I'd like to," he says. His tone is firm, sturdy, but there's a bit of a plea in it, like this is important.

But I have things to do. "As fascinating as I'm sure your explanation is, I have to make a delivery. Pretty sure it'd look bad for your"—I flap a hand at his brick wall of a big strong frame—"bodyguarding if your client falls behind on her work, right?"

I'm winging it, making up things as I go along. But logic and all—a bodyguard should help you not hinder you.

His face is stoic for a minute; then he nods tightly. "Fine, but I'm going with you."

"I can find the store myself." Maybe the more I irritate him, the more I can scare him off. Hell, it worked once already, and I wasn't even trying.

No one ever warns you what it does to your relationship

self-esteem to run into a hookup who ran out on you. I already have a speckled history of men leaving me. Like Eric Patrick Waterstone—he of the two first names—from San Francisco. A chef, he romanced me through my stomach, making mouthwatering dishes in his San Francisco apartment when I came down to visit him on weekends. He took amazing pics of his food too, for social media, and created quite the following that he then used as a springboard for the next step in his career. "Darling Springs is just too small for me, baby," he'd say. But I was in love—or so I'd thought—so I kept driving to the city every weekend to see him. He even said he was thinking of opening a place in Darling Springs, but then he changed his mind, took off for New York to start a fusion café, and never looked back.

Leaving me standing like a fool in the dust.

But I don't want to linger on the guys who can't stick around. Especially ones who can't even stick around for one night.

"I know you can find it, but I'm going with you, and I'm going to make sure no one knocks into you again, so get used to it."

I scoff. "*Get used to it?*" Does he think that line works?

"I'm here to protect you. You're mine," he says, his voice calm, deep, reassuring. "It's that simple."

I hate that my stupid pulse surges from those two possessive words. *You're mine.*

Why do I have a thing for men swooping in and saving me? But that's a topic for another day. For now, I don't bother to stare him down. I give a careless shrug. "Let's go then, babysitter boy."

The corner of his mouth twitches, but not for long. He's

stony-faced. As we head out of the shop, I smile as I pass Callie at the counter. "Hiccups not quite gone yet, but I'm trying to shake them," I say.

"Try biting on a lemon."

I smile brighter at her. "Pretty sure that's what I am doing," I say, then toss a sour smile at Banks.

Once we're out on the sidewalk, he says dryly, "I like lemons."

"Of course you do."

Clearing his throat, he turns to me as we walk. "Listen. I'm sorry about that night. I wanted to explain."

"No worries. I didn't think twice about it," I say breezily, chin up, armor on. Like I'll let him think I was stewing on it.

No way he is getting the better of me.

Not this man in his jeans that hug a firm ass I could bounce a quarter off, those arms made of rocks, that face chiseled from a sculptor's tool.

"Still, it's been weighing on me," he says, but then his attention shoots elsewhere. He jerks his gaze across the street, then up the block. The guy in the hat is turning down the street, I think. Maybe heading toward The Ladybug Inn. Hmm. I bet New Chris is staying there.

Banks turns back to me, like he's ready to resume this convo. But as we near The Slippery Dipper, I spy my chance to dodge this topic again.

Noah's outside, spraying the window with cleaner and wiping it down. He wears a blue polo and jeans—his dad outfit, he told me, and it's pretty much become his uniform since he became one a couple years ago. He catches my eye, then spots the bouquets Banks is holding. "New employee?"

That gives me an idea. If this goon is going to stick around, maybe I can use him to pick up some slack at the farm. Like moving the rototiller. Or pushing the wheelbarrow. Spreading the weed barrier cloth. I mean, if he has to be so close to me, he might as well help. "Something like that. He's carrying heavy things for me. Boulders. Tractors, that kind of stuff."

"And bouquets?" Noah asks, clearly amused, eyes straying toward the nearly weightless flowers in Banks's arms.

"Training wheels," Banks deadpans.

Noah nods to him. "Welcome to the Lavender Bliss team."

"Thanks," he says. Once we resume our path to the store a few feet ahead, he says, "You don't have tractors."

True. But do facts matter? "Are you a lavender farmer *and* a bodyguard?"

His gaze slides down to the pretty purple flowers in his arms, then back to The Slippery Dipper. "Evidently, I just became one."

I head into the market, Banks next to me the whole time as I head toward Salma, who waits at the floral counter, a little impatiently. She's always punctual in opening and closing her store and has been for the decade she's been running it, so I know she likes me to be on time too. Her steady green eyes crinkle at the corners as she adjusts her hijab, making sure it's snug, which it always is.

"I thought you were going to miss the delivery," she says when I reach her.

"Me too. I'm sorry to leave you hanging," I say genuinely.

"It's fine. You made it." She tips her chin toward the man by my side. "Who's this?"

I could say he's my new employee, maintaining the joke, but I think I'll keep him on his toes. "My guard dog. Banks."

Salma snorts. "Perhaps you need a collar then. Aisle ten is for pet supplies."

And I'm forgiven for being late. She takes the bouquets and brings them to the front of the store.

When I catch Banks's gaze, he's rolling his eyes.

"Well, if the shoe fits," I say.

His dark eyes level me. "Sweetheart, I've been called so much worse."

And I guess we're over the explanation phase. I tilt my head. I don't blink as I say, "Guess your desire to *explain* didn't last long."

"No, I listened to you."

Please. Like he's the mature one. Like he's the adult.

Two can play at his game. When we exit, I spot my bike right where Banks left it, resting in the bike rack.

Safe and unharmed. Like a beacon.

I don't map out a plan. I just grab it from the rack. Like I'm escaping from a robbery, I hop on and pedal at the same time, then ride as fast as I can down the sidewalk and far away from my guard dog.

Take that.

CHAPTER 11
THAT KIND OF FINE
BANKS

So this is how we're doing it.

Fine by me. It's not as if I can't follow her easily on foot. Or, hey, by car. I did bring wheels, and I walk to them across the street.

But I let her get a head start so she can think she's gotten the better of me. I'm sure a wicked thrill is rushing through Ripley's veins right now as she looks right, then left, then rides across the street, the wind in her hair, clearly figuring she's escaped me.

Resting my elbow on the roof of the car, I watch her, a smile tipping my lips. It's so damn cute the way she thinks she's lost me. Once her purple beach cruiser whizzes down the next block, I hop in my car, turn it on, and follow her.

People are creatures of habit. They like routine. They stick to the familiar.

Someone like Ripley, who runs a farm that's a fixture in Darling Springs—a tourist destination at that—isn't likely to ditch town, let alone work. *Maybe* she'll visit a friend. *Possibly* she'll ride out to the beach.

But I'll take my chances. My gut tells me she's heading to home base, so I drive slowly, letting her ride ahead. I follow the GPS directions there, passing the sign for the local university on the edge of town, and a few minutes later, I cut the engine outside Lavender Bliss Farms at the top of a hill. I take off my shades, smiling victoriously when I catch a glimpse of a woman in a white tank and jeans cutting across the gorgeous front lawn teeming with purple flowers.

There's a spring in her step. No, it's more like a victory dance. But we'll see how long that lasts.

I swing open the car door, then sigh deeply, breathing in the floral, powdery scent, letting it fill my lungs, before I shift into business mode. Peering around, I scan the expansive property for points of vulnerability.

I've researched this place online since it'll be the site for a handful of movie scenes, so already I know it's a six-acre flower farm, focusing on lavender of course. The land houses bees too, for noncommercial honey production, so I'm guessing those wooden boxes stacked behind the cottage are where the honey-makers hang out. The white clapboard cottage at the top of the hill is a studio, while the farmhouse itself is large enough for a big family and can be used for renting out as an Airbnb. It has six bedrooms, a spacious kitchen, a living room, a den, an attic, and an attached garage. There's a garden-level suite too. The property also has an alarm system; Tabitha checked on that and sent me the info, so that's good. Between the two structures sits a shed, likely for tools and fertilizer. Finally, there's the little shop with a wide-open door and one small room, plus windows everywhere.

The entire farm is fenced in, but it's a white picket fence, so that won't keep out anyone who's truly determined to penetrate the place. But that's where our security team will come into play. We'll have round-the-clock guards on the property when the shoot is underway. We'll also add some temporary exterior lights along the fence. Never underestimate the benefit of floodlights in keeping intruders away and giving our team a heads-up about potential photographers milling around. I'll have to make sure Ripley and everyone else here is debriefed on best practices.

I walk past the open gates, cruising by the wooden sandwich board sign advertising the hours. I head straight for the gift shop. Behind the counter, a woman with curly black hair and bronze skin is bent over her phone, nibbling on what looks and smells like banana bread. My footsteps catch her attention, and when I enter the open-air shop, she scrambles to put it away and sets down the bread.

"Hi there! Welcome to Lavender Bliss Farms. How can I help you?"

"This place is beautiful, Ramona," I say, reading her name tag. "And I'd love your help. I'm looking for Ripley."

"She's—"

A harrumph of defeat comes from behind me, then Ripley's voice. "Right here."

I turn around. Ripley sighs again, but it says *well played*. "Fine. You found me. Let's do this."

By *this* I presume she means negotiate the terms of our detente, so I follow her inside the farmhouse. A sturdy black-and-white mutt trots alongside us. He drops a tennis ball at my feet, then nudges it with his snout in a hopeful canine demand.

"Hudson, don't be a traitor," she says to the dog.

"It's okay. Dogs like me," I say.

"Well, you are a guard—"

But she must think better of calling me her guard dog. Clearly, she likes dogs, so that isn't quite the insult she once intended.

Inside the farmhouse kitchen, she tells the dog to lie down. Once he obeys, I commandeer the convo because I owe her a proper explanation. "Look, here's what happened that night—"

"There's no need," she says, shaking her head.

But there is a need. We're working together, and I want her to trust me. That starts with helping her to understand that I was trying to do the right thing that evening. "I'm Banks Kendrick. I live in Los Angeles. My friend Dean and I started Apex Solutions a year or so ago. Last month, I flew up to San Francisco for a meeting with a referral agency about a possible job. They didn't tell us who the job was for. I honestly didn't know who Haven was till that night. When I met you at the bar, I definitely didn't know a damn thing about the movie or that I'd be working on it," I say, and her expression is stoic, but at least she's listening.

Ripley gives a small nod, the gesture saying *go on*. That's promising, her being willing to listen.

"And then when you went to your room, that's when I got a call from the agency I'd met with, telling me my partner and I had landed the job with Ruby Horizons. A few minutes later, they sent me Haven's pic, and since I didn't know she was a twin, I had no way of knowing she *wasn't* you. I thought I was about to sleep with a client," I say, a little imploring now. She's got to understand the bind I was in.

Ripley side-eyes me, her gaze dubious, but terribly intrigued. Like she hates how intrigued she is. "You thought I was my sister that night? Even though I told you my name?"

"But you emphasized your name so many times that it felt deliberate. Like an actress giving a bar name. And you were in the hotel at the same time as I was. The hotel is where I'd had the meeting about the job. Ergo…"

She blows out a breath, long and full of frustration, but chased with amusement perhaps. There's a smile at the end of it. Like she's realized it was all a silly mistake and we'll just move on.

A man can hope. A man can fucking dream.

"So you really thought I was your new client?" she confirms, like she's keeping track of the details I just shared.

Relieved, I nod, hoping we're finally getting somewhere. "I did."

"And you figured it'd be wise not to get involved with someone you're working with?"

"Yes," I say, though really, that's a big yes. Reputation is everything. I can't risk it by sleeping with a client. I know what happens when a man's word is dirt. Like my father's.

She's quiet for a beat, as if she's absorbing all the details. "Everything about that makes a lot of sense."

A weight I've been carrying for twenty-six days starts to slide off my shoulders. No, it doesn't slide. It crumbles, and good riddance.

"Except," she adds slowly, like the word has ten syllables, and I groan inside, "your solution *wasn't* to knock on my door and explain all that like a guy who felt really bad? It was to send the desk clerk with a three-sentence apology letter that sure seemed like its own form of ghosting? Polite ghosting, but ghosting nonetheless." She clears her throat, then adopts a masculine voice. *"Maybe in another world tonight would have ended differently, and I'll explain what I mean when I see you again. I'm trying desperately to do the gentlemanly thing. Also, please don't kick me in the balls when you see me."*

When she puts it like that, I feel like an un-gentleman. "But I had an NDA and everything," I say, and dammit. That doesn't sound much better.

"But you had an NDA and yet you're explaining right now. So you could have then."

Fact is, she's right. I *should* have said something that night. I'd thought I was being gentlemanly sending a letter, but now that I'm hearing how it sounded from her POV, I chose badly. Plus, I ended the letter trying to protect myself rather than her.

I did the opposite of what I vow to do in my job—protect my clients and keep them safe. But no time like the present. I clear my throat, ready to tell her she's right, and I could have done better, when her phone trills.

After grabbing it from her pocket, she checks the screen, holds up a finger, then answers, saying brightly, "Hi, Haven."

A pause. "Everything's great."

Another pause. "He's…great."

One more pause. "It'll be fabulous. No, it'll be fun having a bodyguard." There's a whole cheer squad on the other line, it seems. "Yep. Don't you worry about a thing. Everything will be fine."

As she moves to the sink, straightening up while she rolls through a series of *but how are you*s and *I can't wait to see you soon*s, I've learned something key about Ripley.

She desperately wants to make Haven happy. So she probably didn't tell Haven about that night. Because that info wouldn't make Haven happy. That also translates into the fact that Ripley's probably not going to tell her now either. Which means—drum roll—I'm exonerated. With a reprieve in hand, I vow to focus only on doing the best damn job possible.

When Ripley hangs up, she turns around, meeting my gaze. Goddamn, she's gorgeous. Those fiery eyes, those pretty lips, that fearless attitude. Her tough side is my undoing. All the more reason to stay strong.

"Anyway," Ripley says, waving a hand like this entire thing is no big deal. "You know what, Banks? Let's just move on."

Message received and gladly accepted. But there is still the matter of working together to iron out. "So you're not going to try to escape from me again?"

"I make no promises."

"Ripley," I warn her. "You just said let's move on."

"This is you moving on? Making sure I help you do your job?" she asks, but she's sassy now. Not angry. That's a welcome change.

"Yes. This is me moving on. Part of me doing my job is working with you, not against you."

"I'm not going to try to escape from you." She pauses before she adds, "All the time."

"Then I'll just have to stay real close to you…*all the time*."

She narrows her eyes, huffing. "Fine. I won't try to escape, but I can't have you up my ass."

I snort. "I won't be up your ass."

"Or too close," she adds.

"I'll give you space *if* you don't pull a runner."

"So many rules."

I can tell she doesn't want to follow them. I can tell too, she'll try to bend them. But she also needs them to keep her sister safe. "Rule number one is I keep you safe. From paps who think you're Haven. From fans who think the same. From anyone who might cause trouble now that your sister has all this extra attention on her."

"Thanks for spelling it out," she says dryly.

"You're welcome. Rule number two is you don't try to run away from me as I keep you safe."

"What's rule number three? Do I have to do *everything you say?*" It's said tauntingly.

"Sure. I like that rule."

"I bet you do."

"Good. We're in agreement then on the three basic rules," I say, hopeful we can indeed move on even though I know she's not agreeing to the last one.

She scoffs. "If you think I'm doing everything you say, you've got another think coming."

This woman is giving me a run for my money. But this gig is too important for it to go sideways. My job is to hunt for weak spots. I've learned one of hers already, and I'll gladly use it to my advantage. "Haven wants you to be safe, Ripley."

She shoots red flames at me with her eyes. "Fine."

"Fine, as in you're going to let me keep you safe, right? Fine, as in you understand I'll be looking out for you as you go about your day? Fine, as in you won't protest when I watch your back as you go around town and do your thing? That kind of fine?"

She's quiet but unflinching for a few seconds till she says, "Fine. I won't try to run off. But I want something in return."

"What's that?"

She lifts a finger, points it at me. "Don't stay too close. I need to do my job, and I don't want to scare off all my clients. I don't want them to worry that I think Darling Springs is unsafe and that's why I have a guard. I also don't want them to think I think I'm too big for my britches or whatever. I'm not a celebrity. I'm not a movie star. I'm a flower farmer. So just let me do my thing. How's that for my kind of fine?"

That's entirely fair. "I'll give you some space. You'll hardly know I'm there."

"Doubtful." She draws a big breath, the kind that says the conversation is over. Tipping her chin to the lavender fields beyond the farmhouse, she says, "I should get back to work. Are you going to follow me around here?"

I shake my head. "I don't need to. I can do some admin stuff on my laptop," I say, and now's as good a time as any to touch on another important part of the job. "I trust you. If you trust me to keep you safe, I'll trust you not to ride off on your bike again."

She smiles. Devilishly. "That's why you had to drive, right? Only way you could keep up?"

A laugh bursts from me. This woman is some kind of piece of work. "Yes. That's it."

"I thought so," she says, then pulls out a stool at the kitchen counter and pats the wooden seat. "You can work here." She gestures to the living room. "Or there."

"Kitchen counter is fine." I don't tell her why. I don't even let my gaze stray to the big window over the sink that gives me a great view of the lavender fields beyond and the shop too. From this perch, I can keep my eye on her outside as I work inside. I meant it when I said trust *is* important, and I sure as shit don't trust her. "Wi-Fi password?"

"The network is Lavender Haze, and the guest password is don'ttouchadamnthingofmine."

I laugh. "I won't, Ripley. I won't."

"In that case, the guest password is *Melissa*," she relents.

I wonder if that was her late mother's name, but I don't ask. It's not my place to open that wound. "Thanks."

She turns to go, but after a few steps, she spins back around. "Where are you staying? The Ladybug Inn? The BookHouse? An Airbnb?" Her voice pitches up with hope at the last one.

I can't help it. I smile. It's too fun to wind her up. "Sweetheart, I'm protecting you. How would I do that from a hotel?"

"Binoculars sound like a good idea to me."

She says it with such a straight face that I have no choice but to play it even drier as I ask, "Or a telescope?"

Her smile is pleased. "Excellent. Enjoy the stay at your hotel with your telescope."

"Didn't you learn this afternoon that you can't shake me that easily?"

"Is that rule number four? I should try harder to shake you?"

"It wasn't a challenge," I say, with a sigh. "Anyway, I'm staying here."

She scoffs. "That's presumptuous."

"Ripley, I'm here for you. I need to be close to you. You have six bedrooms."

"But the crew will be here soon. The producer. The camera guys," she says, sounding overwhelmed momentarily. Like she did that night when she mentioned a big project.

"I'll sleep in my car if I have to. Or I'll get a tent and sleep in that," I say. She's not getting rid of me that easily.

When her eyes widen, possibly in surprise that I'd be willing to do either of those, she waves a hand, like she's dismissing the options. "There's no need to sleep on the ground or the car. You can stay in the cottage. It's for guests anyway."

That's nicer than I'd thought. I guess she really is moving past that night. I should let her know I've done that too. "Thank you. And listen, we can pretend that night never happened," I say, since I'm pretty sure that's what she wants.

She heads to the kitchen door that leads back outside and stops in the archway, tossing me a carefree smile. "Works for me. You're not my type anyway."

Damn. Talk about knocking me down a peg.

CHAPTER 12
BRAINS AND BRAWN
BANKS

But I can't let her parting shot get to me. There's too much to do. That afternoon, I power through emails and proposals to other clients, including some for our cybersecurity services, an area that's already become mission critical to our business in a short time. Then I check the gossip sites, especially *Page Six* and *VIP Vibes*. Nothing featuring Ripley yet, but that doesn't mean something won't show up later.

That carries me through the next few hours while I keep my eye on the client, who never stops moving. One minute Ripley's pruning flowers; the next she's spraying them; then she's pushing them in a wheelbarrow to the shed. After she unloads the wheelbarrow, she stops, wipes a hand across her brow, then stretches her neck from side to side, like she's working out some tightness. Even from a distance, I can tell she's wincing as she leans her head to the right for several seconds, then the left.

Soon, she resumes her pace through the property, stopping to throw a tennis ball to that dog. That much I can see through the window. Pretty sure she's taking care of customers too, who stop in at the store.

Right now, it looks like she's just left the shop, walking down the stone path next to a man in jeans and a short-sleeve button-down who lifts a finger as if to say he'll be right back.

That catches my full attention.

I stand, head to the big window, then watch him like a motherfucking hawk as he trots to a black bike, resting against the white fence. He grabs something from a saddlebag under the seat. Ah, it's a couple of books. With them in hand, he heads back across the lawn.

The fucker has a chiseled jaw. Light-brown hair with russet tones. A toothpaste-commercial smile.

Is that her boyfriend? Does she have a new dude?

Are you surprised? You're the jerk who ditched her with a vague-as-fuck letter.

I suck in a tight breath through my teeth, hating him on principle as he hands her the books and returns to his bike, strapping on a helmet before he goes.

Which reminds me.

I grab my phone from my pocket and unlock it to google a couple local businesses. I check the hours, then make plans to run an errand later. When that's done, I tell myself to put Ripley's possible romantic life out of my head. It's not my business, no matter how much I once wanted to touch her, kiss her, throw her on the bed.

After I tuck the phone away, I return to the counter right as the soft shuffle of bare feet approaches from the hallway.

A woman, with even blonder hair than Ripley's, turns into the kitchen. Her warm eyes are lined with wrinkles, and while she's clearly much older than her granddaughter, the similarity is uncanny. "Good afternoon," I say.

"You must be the bodyguard," she says with a cheery smile.

"I am," I say, though the preferred term is *close protection officer*. But there's a time and place for corrections. This isn't one of those times or places. "Banks Kendrick."

"I'm Lila Addison. The girls' grandmother," she says.

"Nice to meet you," I say, and extend a hand.

After we shake, she nods to my laptop on the counter in front of a few jars of honey I've no doubt was produced by those little winged workers in the fields. "Hope this won't disturb you, but I have some madeleines I need to make."

My stomach growls, Pavlovian thing. "Those scallop-shaped cookies that taste like heaven?"

Mom used to make them after football practice.

Her smile magnifies as she starts rummaging through the cupboards for baking supplies. "We'll get along just fine, Banks."

Fifteen minutes later, Lila deputizes me for kitchen duty. At her insistence, I wear a white apron decorated with bumblebees while I mix sugar, vanilla, eggs, and melted butter.

"So, Banks," she starts, her tone casual yet probing, "tell me about this bodyguarding gig of yours. How does a young man like you end up doing something like that?"

Translation: *Why do you want to protect others?*

Because I couldn't protect my mother from my liar of a father. While he never hit her, he manipulated her in other ways. He lied about everything. The least I can do is be the opposite of him.

Protect rather than deceive.

But that's not the kind of story I share with everyone I meet. "I spent the last few years in private security, including cyber. Saw the market expanding and took a chance. Now this is a whole new level, running my own firm with my good friend who's my business partner."

She nods thoughtfully, a mischievous spark in her eyes as she folds the flour, baking powder, and salt mixture carefully into the batter. "And how do you plan on keeping my granddaughter safe? Do you have any special skills up your sleeve?"

Unable to resist her charm, I smile. "I spent eight years in the Marines. First in MARSOC," I say, and when she, understandably, tilts her head in question, I add, "Special forces for the Marines."

"Like SEALs?"

I smile. "Well, we're both Navy, but we're Raiders. Which is cooler."

"I don't know. SEALs are pretty cute," she says with a smirk. "The animal, not the special forces guys…although, now that I think about it, they're cute too."

"My point exactly," I say, then add, "and the last few years, I spent in intelligence."

"Brains and brawn," she says approvingly.

"Let's hope so."

She stops folding, fixing me with an intense gaze, not at all unlike her granddaughter's. "Now tell me something. Why can't I have a bodyguard? I'd ideally love a hot, swoony older gentleman who can hold his own in the kitchen."

"Then we should find you one." I tilt my head toward my laptop as if I'm about to make a start on that project.

"Just kidding. I know self-defense, plus I have my own mon cheri across the ocean." Her whole face lights up as she tells me about a man in Paris named Laurent. They FaceTime every day, play trivia games online, and binge TV shows together too. She's hoping to see him there at the end of the summer. "We want to take pastry-making classes together in the sixth arrondissement."

"That sounds lovely, Lila," I say.

She sighs hopefully. "We'll see if it works out for him to be my French bodyguard who bakes." She nods toward the mixing bowl. "Try it. I plan to have pastry competitions with him. I need to beat him."

I take the mixing spoon and sample some of the batter. It's sweet and full of promise. "Delish."

She arches a brow. "You really think so, or are you lying to get me to say nice things to my granddaughter about you?"

And I can see where Ripley gets it from—her skepticism. "Both."

Lila's quiet for a beat. She stares out the window at the fields of purple, the sun dipping low in the sky, Ripley off in the distance working. "She's my fearless girl. Full of energy too. I swear there's nothing she won't try to fix. Nothing she won't try to do. She doesn't stop," she says, her tone full of maternal pride, but something wistful too. Like she wants Ripley to slow down perhaps.

As we watch, I wonder if Ripley needs to keep going all day long for some reason. I wonder what drives her. It'd be good for me to know her more, I reason. It'll help me do my job, so I turn to Lila. "Who was that guy here earlier? The one who brought the books?"

"Are you worried about him? She won't need to break out her self-defense moves for that man."

I laugh. "I was just curious. And I'm glad to hear that—that she knows them and that she won't have to use them."

"He's William O'Connor. He runs A Likely Story in town. Cute little bookshop. Nice young man." Then she smiles, the kind that says she can see right through me. "Jealous?"

Where the hell did my poker face go with Ripley's grandmother? I pride myself on being unreadable when I have to. Valiantly, I try to erase any emotions from my face. "Just curious."

She pats my arm. "Sure. Of course."

As we finish arranging the dough for the madeleines on trays, a voice carries from the other room, growing closer. "There's no way I'm not eating dessert first tonight, Grandma, and you only have yourself to blame."

Ripley strides into the kitchen, nose up in the air, drawing a deep inhale. When her gaze lands on me in the bumblebee apron, sliding a tray into the oven, she sighs like she can't believe it. "And you help grandmas too?"

Not her type, my ass. I flash a smile right back at her. "You bet I do, sweetheart."

CHAPTER 13
APOLOGY ADJACENT
RIPLEY

I still can't believe I said that.

Not the *helping grandmas* comment. But the *You're not my type* zinger I fired off earlier today.

It's been weighing on me all afternoon as I worked, and it weighed on me through dinner with Grandma. Banks helped with the meal, slicing green beans from the garden while I made a salad, and Grandma whipped up a summer squash and quinoa dish. But then he took off to run an errand, reasoning I was safe and sound during dinner in my house.

As I'm cleaning up, scraping the remains of the salad into the compost bucket on the counter, I sigh.

"All right, that's your fifty-ninth sigh tonight," Grandma says as she loads the dishwasher.

"You're counting my sighs?"

"Actually, I lost track somewhere between the salad and the madeleines. My point is—out with it."

I wash my hands free of compost, then check the window. After I confirm Banks hasn't yet returned, I meet Grandma's kind eyes as she leans against the counter, patiently waiting.

But I'm not sure where to start. Yes, the comment's been weighing on me. I'm not a mean person. I was just frazzled but also still embarrassed. The way he stood me up hurt so much. Even though I understand his reasoning, it's taken me a while to forget the embarrassment of opening the door and saying *spank me* to a stranger.

Especially when I thought I was saying it to a man who understood me. A man who liked my humor, my mouth, the things I said. A man I could *finally* share some of those secret bedroom desires with.

I've never said *spank me* to anyone. Not to Eric Patrick, certainly. I'm not sure why. Maybe because it never seemed like his thing? But that night, I wanted to say it to Banks. Because I wanted it. Because I felt *his* want. Because I felt both safe with him and turned on.

The irony.

I haven't told a soul what happened that night, not even Bridget or Chloe. But if I don't tell someone, it's going to eat away at me the next few weeks during the shoot. I won't be able to focus on work, or running this place, or making sure Haven has everything she needs.

"Grandma," I begin, readying myself to speak plainly to the woman who took over the task of being my parent when my own died one night on a snowy road when I was only fifteen. "I met him before."

She sets down her towel and leans against the counter. "The baking bodyguard?"

"Yes," I say, my voice wobbly. "And it was a total mess."

"Oh, sweetie. Why?"

"We met at a bar," I say, then I tell her the whole story. Well, I give her the PG version. "And then we were going up to my room, and he never showed." She blinks, eyes big and full of surprise. "But the clerk brought me a letter Banks left, saying he'd explain, and I felt so stupid. All I could think was it was something I'd said. For close to a month, that's what I thought. He'd lost interest in me. Or he'd been lying to me. Or he was playing me. Or he was looking for an excuse all along and he found one. But it all came down to the same thing—he didn't like me after all," I say, my *I can handle the world* attitude sliding off my shoulders like a coat shed at the end of the day. "Because how could he truly be into me if he'd leave like that?"

"Oh hon, why would you think someone wouldn't be into you?" she asks.

I give her a look. "Have you seen my track record, Grandma?"

"We all have track records."

"But mine's kind of a pattern," I say, folding and unfolding the stack of cloth napkins on the counter. My ex isn't the first man to go poof in a cloud of smoke. This guy I was seeing five years ago turned out to have been cheating on me the entire time before I found out when an alarm went off on Chad's phone—pick up flowers for Samantha. His name was Chad though, so it served me right.

"A pattern's only a pattern *till* you break it. I had such a thing for bad boys in leather jackets when I was younger," Grandma says, a little wistful, shaking her head in amusement.

"What's wrong with leather jackets?"

"Nothing, but they were all bad men who didn't know how to treat a woman till I met your grandfather," she says with a fond smile for the man she loved madly for many years till he died of a heart attack when I was ten. "Didn't mean something was wrong with me. I didn't know what I wanted and what I deserved till I met Russ. So why do you even think it's you?"

"I don't know."

"You do know," she says.

I dip my face so she can't see me. "Because I'm bossy and difficult," I grumble.

"You're not difficult."

I latch on to what's unsaid as I lift my face. "But I am bossy?"

"You are the boss. You run a business."

I'm the girl who knows how to *get things done*. The person who *doesn't back down from a challenge*. Banks said as much the night I met him. But maybe he didn't like those things after all. "I'm not the sweet sister like Haven. I'm the know-it-all. I'm the *too independent* one. I'm the pushy one."

"And I love you both madly," she says.

I believe that with my whole heart, but I'm on a roll, dammit, and nothing is stopping me. "And then I think I was kind of mean this afternoon," I admit.

"Why? What did you do?"

I wince. "I said to his face that he wasn't my type."

She gives me the look—the look that says *you didn't do your best.* "Apologize then," she says.

"I don't want to." I pout.

"You do have to work with him over the next few weeks," she points out.

This whole situation gets messier by the minute. "I just want to move past that night."

"And why can't you? Is it because…he's exactly your type?"

Way to see inside my soul, Grandma.

I close my eyes, a whoosh rushing through my body. That man drives me wild and turns me inside out. "It's hard to be around him."

"Because you want him to swoop you up and carry you up the stairs?"

My eyes fly open. "Grandma!"

"I'm seventy-five. I'm not dead."

"I'm shocked."

"Why do you think I'm trying to go to Paris to see Laurent?"

"To make croissants," I say immediately. Innocently.

The saucy minx winks. "Sure, if that's what you call it these days."

I cover my face. She comes in for a hug, and I breathe it in, letting her comfort me. Maybe I needed this. No, I'm sure I did. I'm glad I got the truth off my chest.

After we finish cleaning up, Banks's car crunches on the gravel driveway, and a few minutes later, he knocks on the door, then strides in.

"How's it going?" His dark eyes find me immediately, roaming up and down like he's assessing me. They linger on me a little longer than is necessary, and my stomach doesn't just flip. It cartwheels.

Attraction is such a pesky thing. Especially when it's written all over your face, and I'm sure mine is a billboard.

"It's all good. I'll show you to the cottage," I say, because at least I can be a good hostess, even if I'm having a hard time apologizing.

The bed's already made up in the cottage, so there's not much to do. It's a big one-room cottage—a studio essentially. But I bring him an extra blanket, another pillow, and some fresh towels.

After I set the towels on the bathroom counter, it's probably time to leave. Instead, I point to the shower door. "You need to let the water run for a few minutes to heat up," I say.

"Good to know."

"If you want a hot shower, that is," I add. I really should go.

He crosses his arms. His broad chest somehow looks broader. "I love a hot shower," he says, his voice a little lower than usual.

"Me too," I say.

His eyes darken as he adds, "I'll probably take one in a few minutes."

I swallow roughly, grabbing on to the counter so I don't melt into a puddle of hormones. I'm picturing this man stripping down to nothing, the water sliding over his strong body and down his pecs, his abs, his thighs.

How far does his ink go? Does it extend up his arms, over his biceps, across his chest? I try to undress him with my eyes, but unfortunately, they don't have X-ray powers yet.

"So, yeah. Enjoy," I say, and it's late. The stars are winking in the sky. It's been a long day. I need to give him some space now.

"I will," he says. "Enjoy it, that is."

Just say you're sorry, then go. "I should go," I say.

"See you in the morning. Let me know what's on the agenda tomorrow, Ripley," he says as he walks me to the door. My gaze strays to the tablet on the nightstand. A sheet of paper pokes out from it, like it did the night I met him. Looks like he's still doing origami. This time he's made a cat.

It's my last chance to do the right thing. I reach for the knob, then try. I swear I try to say *sorry about what I said earlier.*

But instead, the words that fly out sound a lot like, "You're good with your hands."

I mean, it's close to an apology.

The farmhouse is quiet as I get out of the shower a little later and pull on sleep shorts and a cami. My grandmother lives in the garden-level suite—her own apartment in the house.

I'm up on the top floor with my dog. When I slide into bed, Hudson sits dutifully on the floor, wags his tail, asking to join me. I pat the mattress. He jumps, springing onto the bed, ready to slumber.

I settle into bed, grabbing my phone to text my besties. I see Bridget and Chloe pretty often, so I don't want to run into them on the street with my hot, hulking, too-handsome-for-words bodyguard without letting them know I have one. They'd give me a hard time about not telling them first. Best to warn them. Besides, I'm still feeling all twisted up about...everything.

> **Ripley:** Things I didn't have on my bingo card for today—getting a bodyguard.
> **Chloe:** WHAT?????
> **Bridget:** Details!

I grumble as I type out a quick explanation about Haven, and Chris, and the film.

> **Chloe:** So basically, you're living the dream.
> **Ripley:** What dream?
> **Chloe:** The regular-girl-gets-a-bodyguard dream.
> **Ripley:** I don't think that's a dream.
> **Bridget:** You're wrong, Ripley. You're just wrong.
> **Ripley:** So much for getting any sympathy from you two.
> **Chloe:** I'll see if I can bring you a cup of sympathy tomorrow. Ideally, when he's striding next to you, wearing aviator shades, a snug T-shirt, and a broody expression.
> **Ripley:** Are you seriously already having fantasies about my bodyguard? You haven't even met him.
> **Bridget:** Irrelevant. Also, yes. She is and I am.
> **Ripley:** Regular girls with bodyguards get no sympathy.
> **Chloe:** You got that right.

After I thank Chloe for her treat-culture tips, explaining how it helped with Ramona, I say good night, put my phone down, then grab a book from the two William gave me. One is for my sister, and then there's this one for me—a thriller that promises to keep me turning pages well past my bedtime.

But I can't focus on the story even as the hero races down the city block, hunting for the one spot where he can possibly lose the guy who's chasing him.

I'm too busy thinking of tomorrow. And the next day and the next. How the hell am I supposed to spend all this time with my sexy bodyguard, who even my besties are drooling over from a distance? I'm not sure there's enough room on my farm for him, my attraction, and me.

Then, I devise a plan to shake him. And I can't wait for tomorrow to come.

CHAPTER 14
SILENT CHICKEN
RIPLEY

Not many people wake up earlier than farmers.

On weekdays, I need to get everything ready in the fields before my employees come to work. Today I will use my early birdness to my advantage. Before the sun is even poking above the horizon on Friday morning, I'm up and out of bed, twisting my hair into a long ponytail, then pulling on shorts and a sports tank.

I smile evilly, then pat Hudson on the flank where he's stretched out on the floor. "You ready to see how brilliant your mom is?"

He lifts his snout in curiosity.

"I say *brilliant*..." I hold up my palms like scales. "You say *nefarious*. What's the difference?"

I grab socks and quietly pad downstairs. Hudson isn't so quiet as he follows me, but Banks is in the cottage, so no way can he hear him. The floorboards creak as I make my way to the front door. In the foyer, I grab dog bags from the shelves, then tug on my sneakers and tie them quickly. Hudson's leash is on a hook, so I slip that on my boy, then inch by quiet inch, I open the door.

I'm holding my breath the entire time.

When I survey the property for signs of the tattooed hottie and find none, I let out a huge sigh of relief. I look to the east. The pale light of dawn is starting to fade away as the morning's first light brightens the edge of the world. At least I can get a walk in without that tempting man by my side. I'll use the time to enjoy the sounds of the day beginning—a bird, the rustle of grass, the chewing of the horse at a pasture down the road. I hustle along the path toward the gate twenty feet away. My escape hatch.

Ten feet away.

Five feet.

Freedom is nigh! I'll get thirty minutes, maybe an hour of alone time where I'm not amped up from being near that man.

I hazard a glance at the cottage.

Yes!

The lights aren't even on. Ha. Someone likes to sleep in. And… it's not my bodyguard. Because I jump, startled, since Banks is suddenly right beside me, wearing shorts, sneakers, and a workout tank, looking like he's been up for an hour at least, waiting to ambush me.

Banks smiles, all crooked and cheerful. "You forgot to send me the agenda," he says, but then shrugs happily. "But no worries. I took a guess you'd be up early with my new best friend." He scratches Hudson's ears, then rises to his full height—six foot three, I'm guessing. He's all towering and strapping, and yes, those tattoos do climb across his pecs since I just got a peek through his muscle tank. My mouth waters. Stupid mouth. "And I guess I was right," he adds annoyingly, and annoying me.

"Yes, you were right, Banks. I do walk my dog in the morning," I say, as I turn down the quiet road. "But I don't like to talk at this hour."

"No worries. I've got music to listen to," he says, brandishing his earbuds from his pocket. My chest burns with irritation. I should have brought mine.

I wave to the gate. "How did you do that? Just appear out of nowhere?"

"It's my special skill. Especially since I had a feeling you were going to break rule number one and rule number two."

"There's plenty of time for me to try again," I say.

"I have no doubt." He bends to pet my dog on the chin this time.

The traitor wags his tail and asks for more scratches. "Aww, such a good boy," Banks says as Hudson bounces in response. "Guess I am good with my hands."

I snap my gaze to him. "I wouldn't know."

Then I look ahead and try not to check out his arms, his legs, and his whole stupidly handsome body as we walk my dog in a silent game of chicken.

Forty-five minutes later, we're back, and I'm seriously going to have to work harder to lose him.

But there's more to my plan than my thwarted dog walk. It's still early, but I know Grandma can cover for me for a couple hours.

When we near the porch, he says, "So, what's on the agenda?"

I smile. "You want to be my shadow? Guess what? We're doing yoga."

I lift my chin. How's that for brilliant? Plenty of guys do yoga. But I'm guessing a bodyguard isn't the yoga type. Banks's muscles will probably atrophy if he doesn't find a weight bench soon to recharge his muscle cells. A man like him survives on protein powder and weight plates, not sun salutations and shavasanas.

"Sounds great. I'll drive," he says.

"Actually, we can walk," I say, cheery and upbeat—all part of the plan.

"That works too," he says. "Meet you in…?"

"Fifteen minutes," I supply, then bound up the steps before a smidge of guilt hits me again. He's really going to hate me soon. Might as well just clear the air for the sake of doing the right thing. I spin around. "Banks?"

He turns around. "Yes?"

My chest twinges. Or maybe that's my pride acting up. Either way, I meet his gaze straight on, and I woman up. "SorryIsaidyou'renotmytype. Thatwasn'tnice."

There. Done.

But he stares at me, brow furrowed, confused. "Excuse me?"

Did I really say it that quickly? I draw a breath, square my shoulders, then try again. Slower this time. Or really, normal speed. "Sorry I said you're not my type. That wasn't nice."

"Ah," he says, nodding. "I thought that's what you said, but I wanted to be sure."

My jaw drops. "You knew and made me repeat it?"

"It's good to be certain, right?"

"And you want me to trust you?"

"I need to trust my ears, Ripley," he says with a smile. "But don't think twice about it. We're all good."

"Good."

I turn to open the door when he adds, "Besides, I knew you didn't mean it."

This man. I seethe. I have no regrets for what I'm about to do.

Five minutes later, I'm out the door again, grabbing my bike from where I left it by the fence and hopping on.

Let him run after me. I don't care. Let him take his freaking car. That's fine too.

I fly down the hill on two wheels, lift my left hand to show I'm turning right, then turn, when the sound of tires against asphalt grows louder. I peek behind me and groan. "Are you kidding me?"

Banks is wearing a black helmet and riding a mint-green beach cruiser, and in seconds he's pedaling by my side. "I figured it'd just be easier if I got one too," he says, calm and too amused for my taste. "Don't you think?"

"Where did you get a bike?" I ask, annoyed and impressed at the same time. But then it hits me. When I had dinner last night and he went to run errands, he must have gone into town, or to a nearby town, to pick one up. "Forget it. I don't even want to know."

"Too bad mint was the only color," he says, glancing briefly down at the pretty frame. "I'd have preferred we have matching bikes. But the shop didn't have a purple one."

"Such a shame," I mutter as I slow at the upcoming stop sign.

"But hold on. One more thing," he says.

At the sign, I set my feet down on the road. He reaches into the basket on his handlebars and retrieves another helmet. "You really should wear one of these things."

He leans across the space between us and sets the most adorable pink helmet on my head. "I usually wear one," I grumble.

"I'm sure you do, sweetheart. But, like I said, it's my job to keep you safe."

His midnight eyes stay on me as he adjusts the pink helmet, then tucks some loose strands of hair behind my ear, his finger whisking over the shell.

His touch lasts a little longer than I'd expect.

His fingers slide along my jawline; then he snaps the buckle under my chin. He takes a beat, then fiddles with it some more, moving it just so.

Then just so again. His breath hitches. Quietly, but I hear it. A quick, sharp intake.

When he lifts his face, he meets my eyes, and I see that same dark desire from the night we met. Raw. Primal. A flash of heat too.

"There. How's that?" His voice is lower than before, raspier.

Holy shit.

He meant everything he said then. He was into me. And now, all this proximity is as hard for him as it is for me.

Guess I am *his* type.

"It's good," I say, answering him at last, even though it's not good. It's bad, how dangerously attracted I am to my bodyguard. Especially since he keeps up with me the whole way to the Downward Dog All Day yoga studio.

After we lock up the bikes on a rack and go inside, a pink-haired woman behind the check-in counter says to me, "Ripley, you're finally taking a class."

I wince and paste on a smile.

Yeah, maybe it wasn't the brightest idea to play chicken here. Since I've never done yoga before.

CHAPTER 15

UPSIDE DOWN

BANKS

B et she thinks I don't know my *utkatasana* from my *uttanasana*. But when the instructor—a guest teacher from San Francisco—calls out the first instruction, I bend my knees, lower my hips, and move into the chair pose easily.

I peer to the right as Ripley stands awkwardly and jerks her gaze to the right too, avoiding me to check out the woman next to her, then does something vaguely resembling a squat.

Since this is a vinyasa flow class, the teacher's already moving into *uttanasana,* a forward fold. She's using the English words for the poses too, but she calls those out a few seconds after the Sanskrit now, so Ripley's moving on a five-second delay. "And now, if you want, take a flow into your *chaturanga* or go straight into *urdhva mukha svanasana.*"

Once again Ripley cheats to the right, watching the woman

next to her fluidly shift from plank to an upward cobra as the instructor adds, "And we all meet in downward dog."

But Ripley—oh, sassy Ripley who tried to ditch me with yoga—doesn't know her cat from her cow, and I am here for it.

I smother a smile as she's a few steps out of sync, but her jaw is set, her gaze is focused, and her determination is screwed to the sticking post.

As the instructor guides us into a mountain pose, she must see that Ripley's lagging behind, since she stops at the very obvious newcomer and offers some tips. My yoga companion breathes a noticeable sigh of relief, then rises into a standing pose with the rest of the class. Did Ripley even read the schedule online? If she knew this was an intermediate class, would she still have taken it? Or did she just want to scare me off that badly?

Well, she's going to have to work a lot harder to give me the slip, especially given what's on *Page Six* today.

A little later, when the instructor guides us through a twisting chair pose, I'm vaguely tempted to tell Ripley she doesn't need to sit so low. That she might risk overextending something.

But why bother? She'd bite my head off.

And you'd like it.

Yeah, I would.

After forty-five minutes of Miss Stubborn white-knuckling it through the class, the teacher gracefully pads to the front of the studio again. "And now we'll start to slow down. It's easy to focus on strength and balance. We spend all day going, going, going. We check things off our lists. We *do* all day. And so we often are drawn to the strength poses, the balance ones, the ones we feel like we *should* do, but slowing down is just as important."

Out of the corner of my eye, I notice Ripley's expression soften. It's like tension melts away as the instructor gives her maybe something she doesn't often give herself—permission.

"Let's take a child's pose now," the instructor says.

In a heartbeat, Ripley sits on her knees and leans forward with a contented sigh as she rests her forehead against the mat, stretching, easing, then letting out a long breath.

Then another.

Soon, all that tension she holds seems to slough off her shoulders.

When we move into the final resting pose, flat on our backs on our mats, Ripley's like a happy dog, settling in at night in bed, before she closes her eyes.

I should close my eyes too. Really, I should. Since I'm not technically worried about her safety during a yoga class, it would be no big deal to do it.

But I can't close my eyes. I just…can't.

So I lie there as I stare at the ceiling. Wishing this painful part of the class would go faster. Willing the second hand to tick by at a higher speed. C'mon. It's taking forever. Pretty sure the old dude a few mats away is snoozing. The young woman on my other side looks so serene. Ripley's practically murmuring as she just…lies there.

Me? I'm trying not to bolt up, roll away my mat, get the hell out.

After a few laboriously long moments, the instructor speaks again, leading us out of that pose as she sits cross-legged at the front of the classroom. "Thank you for coming to this intermediate flow class here at Downward Dog All Day. I'm Briar Delaney. I live and work in San Francisco, but occasionally get the chance to lead special classes like this. If you want more yoga classes from me, try my Flow and Flex Fitness app. And I hope you all have a beautiful day."

I really shouldn't rib Ripley about her lack of research in trying to give me the slip as we clean our mats and return them to their baskets.

Truly, I shouldn't, as we say goodbye to the instructor, then grab our shoes in the lobby.

I absolutely should refrain from teasing her as I head outside first, scanning the street for photographers or anything out of the norm. The coast is clear, so I hold open the door for her.

Then, fuck it. "So, you were thinking you'd give me the slip, but you wound up in a yoga class a little tougher than you were expecting?"

She digs her heels in. "I knew that was an intermediate class," she says, lying through her teeth. It's cute, the way she tries so hard to be so tough.

As we pass a tourist shop peddling sunglasses and beach hats, I check behind us once more, then look at my watch. It's eight-fifteen. "What's next? Are you planning on face masks? A spa day? Taking me to a salon? Oh, I know! Should we get a blowout?" I stop to run both hands through my hair, like I've got a luxurious mane.

With a confused look, she stops too, asking, "What was that?"

"What was what?"

She twirls a finger around my face. "That thing you just did with your hands in your hair."

Was it not clear? "Like I'm a shampoo model."

She gives a long nod. "My bad. I thought you were doing a stripper move."

I huff. "I was not doing a stripper move."

"Looked like a stripper move."

I set my hands on my hips, then punch them forward. Add in a little gyration. "How's that for a stripper move?"

Her eyes pop, but she holds her own with a comeback. "I didn't know your bodyguard services included a free show."

"Who said it was free?" I counter.

"I guess I could go get some dollar bills and make it rain." She snaps her fingers. "Better idea. Maybe we should sign up for a pole dancing class!" She bats her lashes. "Would that work for you? We could learn together." Then she pauses, tapping her chin. "But you probably know how to pole dance already. Like you know yoga. And when I'd be up. And that I'd ride my bike."

"If you can find a place that teaches pole dancing, I'm there." Just let her try to call my bluff. She has no idea I don't have a bluff to call.

She lifts her chin. "Bet you think we don't have dance studios in small towns."

"Bet you think I wasn't raised in one."

She blinks. "Oh." There's a furrow in her brow—a momentary truce in our zings as she asks earnestly, "You were? Which town?"

"Lucky Falls," I say.

At the mention of the little town thirty or so minutes away, a genuine smile tips her lips. "That place is so cute. I love the bookstore there. And there's a great wine shop."

"It's not a bad place." Too bad we couldn't stay there after my father's lies were exposed. After everyone stared at Mom, my sister, and me, whispering about our family.

"There's not actually a dance studio here though," she says, flapping a hand toward the street, as if to indicate all of Darling Springs. "But the community center has been adding some fun new classes. Candle-making and pottery and stuff. Maybe pole dancing will be next. You never know," she says, then her gaze strays longingly toward the end of the block, landing on the chalkboard sign with the coffee cup on it.

Pick Me Up.

She lifts her nose slightly skyward, like she's trying to catch the faint scent of freshly brewed beans. I know a caffeine hankering when I see one, especially since I'm feeling it myself.

"Want a coffee? It's on me," I add.

Her eyes widen in surprise. Possibly delight. Then, she's all sarcasm once more as she says, "In that case, I'll have a dozen coffees."

"I wouldn't be surprised in the least if that was what you ordered."

We turn toward Pick Me Up, and as we walk, I set a hand on the small of her back. The second I touch her, a small shudder runs down her body.

Same here.

Same fucking here.

She looks down at my arm. "Is that…to keep me safe?"

She asks only with curiosity. Maybe a hint of hope.

The coffee shop is a few feet away. She's safe. I don't want to worry her. But I don't want to admit the truth either.

I'm touching you because I want to.

"It's just…a good idea." That sounds true enough. But really, it's a bad idea, and I'm doing it anyway.

CHAPTER 16
NAP TIME
BANKS

After I grab coffees for both of us, we snag a table in the back in a quiet nook, away from morning crowds. She lifts her cup and takes a sip, her eyes going thoughtful, her tone open. "I didn't think you'd be such a yoga pro."

"I've done it for a few years now," I say.

"So I gathered from your upside-downward-dog-snake-in-the-chair pose."

I smile as I lift my cup. "Wait till you see my crow pose."

"I don't even want to know what that is," she says, stretching her neck from side to side, something she did yesterday at the farm. "Unless it can make my neck not hurt."

"Probably not. It's just an arm balance thing," I say.

"And I'm guessing like the yoga, and sensing my whereabouts at any second of the day, it's just another thing you can do obscenely well?"

"Glad you've noticed some of my skills."

She sets her chin in her hand. "What are you *not* good at?"

Relaxing. Letting go. Unwinding.

I smirk. "Not much really." But since she asked the question not with sarcasm but real interest, I try to answer her in kind. "Except… communication." I offer a sympathetic smile.

She gives me one in return—a forgiving one, and I'm damn grateful for that.

"It's all good, Banks," she says, then takes another sip of her coffee, her guard still down as she says, "I guess it was obvious it was my first yoga class?"

I'm a little surprised she relented and admitted something that's hard for her. But it's a good surprise. I hold up my thumb and forefinger. "Just a little." Because it was hard for her, the last thing I want is for her to feel embarrassed or foolish. "But you did great. Seriously."

She scoffs. "I barely could figure out the poses. I was twenty steps behind. Honestly, I was just making it up most of the time."

I lift my cup in a toast to her. "Even so, you burst into an intermediate class guns blazing and didn't fall on your ass. That's impressive."

"Or stupid," she says, and hell, this is cute too—this self-deprecating side of her, this forthright side.

"Sometimes they're the same," I say with a shrug.

She sighs, like she's letting go of the running act she tried to pull this morning. "Look, I don't love being…babysat," she says, but it's not a sassy retort. It's more a quiet admission.

"I know," I say gently. She's not my first client who didn't want close protection.

"And I get it's for my own good and everything," she says. "It's just…hard for me."

I flash back to her comments the night we met—feeling overwhelmed but wanting something badly too. Then to what Tabitha told me in earlier calls—the sister was taking on a lot of work prepping the farm. Finally, to what Lila said last night—Ripley doesn't stop.

"You're used to calling the shots," I say, hoping to understand her reticence better. The more I understand her, the better the job I can do. At least that's what I tell myself as I get to know her better.

"Yes."

"Now, you feel like I call the shots?"

She gives me a look. "Well, you are, Banks."

"You don't like that? Someone else being in control?" I ask.

She's quiet for a long beat, and in those breath-held seconds, as her eyes lock with mine, it's like she's saying she'd want that in other ways.

Maybe in bed.

Or could be that's my hopeful imagination. My dirty wishes. Since she'd look fantastic taking orders. I'd love to give them to her. To tell her to clasp her wrists behind her back so I could tie them together.

She meets my eyes. "Not in my daily life," she says, and I hear a distinction. Perhaps she likes it at nighttime. *Maybe.* "So I'm just struggling."

Before I can think the better of it, I say, "That makes two of us."

Her brow knits, like she's replaying the words I just said, till she finds the meaning—*it's a struggle for me to work with you when I want you*. But maybe that's expecting her to read too much into something.

With a heavy sigh, she says, "I just feel I need to take care of everyone and everything. The farm, my employees, Grandma, my sister, and her dreams... I want to be able to still do that while you're..."

"By your side every day?"

"More like every second," she says.

"I don't want to get in the way. And I noticed you like that—taking care of everything," I say, but I do wonder...who takes care of her?

"I do," she says with a crisp nod, then takes a long swallow of her coffee. "I like to." There's a pause. "Maybe I need to. And I want the freedom to keep doing that."

"I hear you. I want you to have that freedom too, but I also want you to understand that your life is going to be a little more complicated for the next few weeks," I say, leaning forward. "Your photo did show up this morning."

Nerves flash in her eyes. "It did?"

I take my phone from my pocket to show her. There's the shot of her on the street, and a caption that says, Haven Addison's in town early just like Chris Carlisle. Is there a secret meet-up in the script in Darling Springs? We'll make sure you're the first to know.

Ripley winces. Then shudders. "That's...kind of gross. They don't care if they took my pic or Haven's."

"Exactly. They just wanted the clicks. They'll get in your face for them. Possibly they'll figure out you're Ripley and your sister's Haven, but from a distance, when they're chasing that supposed first-kiss shot of Carlisle and his alleged new girlfriend, they won't care. They'll shoot first and ask questions later."

Her gaze is serious as she nods in understanding. "I get it."

"But I heard you yesterday. You want to run your business and go about your life as best you can," I add, speaking with total sincerity. She asked me to give her space, but we were both still worked up during that conversation. I want her to know I listened to her then, and I'm definitely listening to her now. And I want to prove myself to her. "Let me show you today that you can still do that with me around."

She lifts a doubtful brow. "Yeah?"

"Yes. I promise."

"Okay then." She extends a hand across the table to shake. I take it, and when I let go, she reaches a hand behind her neck and rubs. "My neck is both stiffer and looser at the same time. How is that possible after yoga?"

"Yoga makes us move our bodies in different ways than we're used to," I say, then try to focus on the positive. "You seemed like you enjoyed the end of the class though?"

"Yes. Can I just do the slowing-down part?" she asks with a spark in her voice, and there's that flirty, fun side from the night I met her. "I'd like to go to a class where someone tells me to lie down on a mat and close my eyes, and then bam, I'm asleep."

That sounds awful to me, but I do like that she's talking to me rather than running from me. "So basically, nap time?"

"Yes. I would like a nap class."

"Do they have those too, at the community center? Pole dancing and nap classes?"

"A girl can dream," she says.

I shudder.

She points at me like she's caught me on a technicality. "Ah, so you don't like pole dancing."

"Actually, you have me there. I probably suck at pole dancing. Never done it before, but I'm pretty sure I can*not* rock a pole," I say.

She thrusts her arms in the air. "And he is human after all." After she takes a victorious sip of her coffee, her brow furrows, like she's clearly rewinding something in her head. "Wait. You shuddered when I mentioned naps and pole dancing, but you never did pole dancing. Banks," she says, her voice lowering to a conspiratorial whisper, "do you hate naps?"

"With a deep and ferocious passion."

She looks at me like I'm nuts. "Who are you? A robot? Wait. I might believe that."

"I'll take that as a compliment."

"Of course you would," she says, rolling her eyes, but more playfully this time. Then, she holds up a *wait a second* finger. "Did you not even do the sleepy pose?"

"Shavasana," I supply.

"I saw you didn't close your eyes."

"You were checking me out," I say, deflecting.

"Is there room in the shop for you and your ego?"

I look around the café. "We both seem to fit comfortably. Now tell me more about how you were keeping an eye on me during sleepy pose?"

"Banks," she chides, and it's clear she's trying to understand me rather than trip me up. "You really don't like napping?"

Ah, hell. She opened up to me. The least I can do is give her some of the same. I relent. "I…don't like relaxing."

She flinches, like that does not compute. "That's like not liking sunshine. Or music. Or a night out with friends."

"I like all of the above."

"But not relaxing?"

No, because what if that leads to napping at other times? Like on the job? No way. I won't leave my charges unprotected while I'm on shift, so I won't risk napping. Shavasana is something I don't do. "I don't sleep on planes. Or buses. Or park benches. Or yoga studios. I like…control," I admit, then pick up a paper menu on the table listing the coffee drinks.

"But in the Marines—you were in the Marines, right?"

"Yes." I furrow my brow, folding it into a triangle. "How did you know? Did Lila tell you?"

She laughs, shaking her head. "Just something Haven said, but even if she hadn't, I'd have guessed. Just like you guessed I'd try to ditch you on two wheels."

Damn. She's good. "Impressive."

"So when you were in the Marines, you probably had to sleep anywhere?"

After I fold the bottom right of the paper to the top, I stop and lift a finger. "I *can* sleep anywhere. Now that I don't have to—I choose not to."

"Huh."

I brace myself for a barb as I flip the paper over. That's what we do, after all, this woman and me. We fire sarcasm-dipped arrows at each other. But Ripley is surprisingly quiet, thoughtful even, as she nods. "I can see that—for someone who likes control, that pose would be hard."

"Yes. Exactly," I say.

"Is that why you do origami too? Control?"

I stop before I finish the animal I'm making. "This isn't for control," I say, but I'm not about to tell her folding paper into animals is a habit I picked up long ago. Way back when my father's secrets were unraveling, when the life we lived growing up imploded, when I needed something to keep me busy so I didn't punch the asshole every time I saw him. It calmed me down, and then it became a daily practice.

"What's it for?"

I pause. "Relaxation," I admit as I finish the creation. Then I hand her a small paper fox.

A smile shifts her pretty mouth. "It's cute."

"Keep it," I grumble.

She tilts her head, assessing my offer, then says, "Thank you." She sets it down next to her mug, turns the mug, releases a breath. "I don't like having my picture taken. By random people. Not that I do. Not that it happens to me now," she says, emphasis on the *now*, like a correction. Which means there was a *then*.

Questions pound my mind. Who took her picture *then*? Who made her feel uncomfortable *then*? And where can I find them and hurt them?

"But I think that's one of the things that bugged me about yesterday," she says, a vulnerable admission.

"When the photog thought you were Haven?"

"Yes." She sounds sad but also distressed.

Instinctively, I reach for her. Like I'm going to squeeze her shoulder or brush a strand of hair from her cheek. Something comforting. But I pull back, instead asking, "Why don't you like having your picture taken? Because you can't control the photo?"

"It's not that I'm image-conscious. It's just…well, I grew up here. Everyone knows me. Everyone *knew* my family."

Knew. Past tense. My heart squeezes in sympathy. When I researched the farm, I learned the bare details of her past. Her parents died when she was in high school. That has to be what she means.

"You're cautious then about…image?"

She turns her mug in a circle. The drink's likely getting cold. "Sounds vain, but it's not that. It's just I'm trying to make something of this farm I inherited from my parents. Trying to make it a success. So, in a way, every time I go out of the house, I need to make sure I'm representing Lavender Bliss Farms too, you know what I mean?"

That makes perfect sense but still doesn't give me the entire picture. "I do."

"But it's fine," she says, waving a hand like she can make

the whole conversation vanish. "I should get back to work soon anyway."

I could press, but she's said enough for now. Invited me in some. I nod, taking a final sip of my coffee. "Let's get you home. Don't we have boulders to lift today or something?"

"Exactly," she says, finishing her drink, then setting down the mug. As she does, she turns her face to one side, then the other, stretching her neck again.

If that's not an opening, I don't know what is.

"Let me help," I say, and before she has a chance to protest, I drag my chair closer to hers and curl a hand under her hair and around her neck.

"Ohhhh," she moans at the first touch.

A kernel of pride spreads in me from her reaction. I dig my thumb into her flesh, sliding it up and down the column of her soft neck. Kneading. Trying to help her release some of the tension.

She drops her head forward, giving me more room, savoring it even. "Is this part of keeping me safe?"

"Yes. When your neck doesn't hurt, you're less ornery," I deadpan.

"I'm not ornery."

I scoff. "Then what even is ornery if not you?"

"Not me. More like you."

I dig a thumb into the base of her neck, and she unleashes another moan. "Ripley, you're fiery and feisty, and you keep me on my toes."

"Good," she says, then draws a deep breath and relaxes into my hand as I run my fingers along her neck and under her hair. This close, it's hard not to think about kissing her. Hard not to think about all the other ways I want to touch her given how intimate this is—from the sounds she makes to how close we are. So close she could turn her face, tip her chin, and wait for a kiss. One I desperately want to give her.

Those lips. Those beautiful, lush lips.

Eventually, I let go. She gathers her phone and the paper fox; then we leave.

When we reach the sidewalk in front of the tourist shop, she glances at the time on her phone. "Should we race? See if I can ditch you on two wheels?"

"You can't."

"Let me try."

"Why?" I ask.

"Because I bet I can."

"Just like you thought you'd best me at yoga?"

"Hey, yoga's not a competition," she says.

"Spoken by the woman who tried to turn it into one," I retort.

She flashes me a *please say yes* smile. "It'll be fun. Like bungee-jumping fun."

"Bungee jumping is not fun."

"It's so fun," she says, and I'm ready to counter her when I catch sight of a group of people with one person acting as the leader—likely one of the tour groups frequenting Darling Springs lately—at the end of the block, lifting their phones our way.

No one's rushing Ripley. Still, I go on high alert, but I don't want to alarm her. "Hold on," I say, then I grab a *Such a Darling Town* cap from the rack of sunglasses and hats next to us and turn to Ripley. "This would look good on you."

I put it on her head without a second of hesitation. She flinches, and if flinches could be good, this one sure qualifies. It comes with a hitch in her breath. A parting of her lips.

I inhale, try to center myself and focus on the job—obscuring her. I grab the shades too. "This could be your new disguise." I move her ever so slightly to the right so her back is to the tour group. The look on her face says she understands, and that she wants to be blocked from view. Just to be sure, I take my time adjusting the hat and the shades.

My hands are on her face, cupping her cheeks the way I did at the bar the night I kissed her—like I'd go mad if I didn't taste her lips. That was how I felt then. Now, on the street, early in the morning, that madness returns.

It winds through me, an insistent buzz. A thrum of desire. The deep and potent need to kiss those pretty pink lips, to hold her face, to devour her kisses.

Then, to strip her down to nothing and...*control* her.

Like I think she wants.

I swallow my rough desires, stealing a glance at the group. They're dispersing.

"Do I look like me?" she asks.

What? Oh, right. The disguise. "It's harder to tell," I rasp out.

But I bet it's not hard to tell where my mind went. I bet it's written in my eyes.

That's what I ought to be looking out for—this *lust*. The more I want her, the harder it'll be to do my job without distraction.

Yet, I'm still here, adjusting the cap, touching her hair, wondering if she'd like it if I ran my fingers through it, then curled a fist around and tugged. The image sends a jolt of heat through me. Like a warning.

"We should go," I say.

She stares at me like I'm an oddity.

"Well, we should."

She points to the hat and the glasses. "Did you want me to get these?"

Oh. Shit. Right. "Yes. Good idea."

I've got to get my focus back. I take her into the store and buy them, vowing to fight off all distractions for the rest of the day.

This is going to be the hardest job of my life.

CHAPTER 17
A LAVENDER EYE MASK, PLEASE
BANKS

After we return, she retreats to the house to get ready for the day. I take the opportunity to check in with Dean back in Los Angeles as I walk around the perimeter of the property, chatting with my longtime friend on the phone.

He's the kind of friend who'd bail you out of jail no problem and ask questions later. Fortunately, he's never had to do that for me. Like me, he's also laser-focused on growing this business.

"The crew arrives tomorrow—Saturday," I say, recapping the plans for the upcoming shoot starting this weekend. "Vega, the director, the rest of the cast, and so on. We have our best-practices briefing scheduled then. And everything's a go for securing the location for the first shots on Sunday afternoon, which is pretty basic, no principal cast, just beauty shots."

"Great. And we've got Wanda Rodriguez on Haven," he says.

"It was a lucky break she was available," I say of the former CIA field agent, who's been protecting several high-profile clients since leaving the agency.

"I'd like to think it was my magic touch at convincing her," he says.

He's never been short on confidence. "Yeah. It was you, Dean."

"I know," he deadpans, then shifts to a more serious tone. "But it's a damn good thing. Tabitha was happy to hear we could get a woman on the job."

The logistics producer made it clear that since the film is helmed by a female director, written by a woman, and produced by a woman-owned company, it'd sure be nice to see some women in the security team too.

Done.

We have backup coming in as well, so I'll have some other close protection officers covering Haven and Ripley from time to time, since Wanda and I can't do twenty-four-seven security. After Dean and I cover the prep work, as well as the assignments for our team on site, then cover the projects he's handling in Los Angeles for corporate clients, he clears his throat and says, "How's it going so far? You seemed a little…before you left."

I bristle as I walk past the white fence hemming in row after row of purple flowers with that soft, powdery, woodsy scent that's supposed to be calming. "A little what?"

"A little tense every time the job came up," he says, getting straight to the point now.

How the fuck could he tell? I thought I was playing it cool. I roll my shoulders like I can shrug it off. Maybe I need a lavender eye mask. "Just because it's a big job."

"That's what I meant," he says. Oh. So he thought I was stressed about the importance of the job. Not that I might fuck it up beyond all recognition thanks to this unchecked attraction.

"Hell, I'm a little tense about the job," he continues.

"Yeah?"

"I'm so over working for other people," he says as I reach the corner of the fields, then turn up the street that runs along the back of the farm. "Did that long enough for Stan. Don't want to do it again."

There it is. The reminder. "Same, brother. Same."

He blows out a breath. If a breath could sound hopeful, this one does. "It'll be good," he says, like he's reassuring himself more than me.

"Absolutely," I say, because it fucking will; I'll make sure of it. We won't miss a thing. No one in the whole damn world is more organized than I am. Being a little bit of a control freak goes a long way in my field.

"And how's the sister?" he asks.

It's a standard business question. A normal check-in about the client. A conversation we've had a hundred times before in the last year as we've worked together, running our firm. But also in the years before when we were working for Stan Withers and our *didn't give a shit* boss sent us too-thin briefs without any real research, leaving Dean and me to sink or swim, whether it came to fieldwork or cybersecurity.

Plus side though? We learned by doing, because we had no other choice but to figure out the jobs all on our own.

No job, though, has ever been this tempting.

In all my years in close protection, I've never warred with desire for a client. I think about the answer I can't give to Dean's question.

Ripley Addison is sexy. Fiery. Challenging. All the things she was the night I met her and even more. But I don't say any of that because I don't want Dean to worry. Like it's no big deal, since really, it has to be no big deal, I say, "She's a typical non-celeb client. Doesn't think she needs a bodyguard. But it's fine."

He chuckles. "Know the type well."

"Yup. How are things with the McKellar project?" I ask, shifting gears to a corporate client, since I don't want to dwell on me and these feelings I can't entertain.

He slides into those details easily and when I've rounded the property a third time, we're done. "Keep me posted," he says.

"You know I will."

"I do," he says.

I hang up, wishing I didn't feel like I've lied to my friend and business partner. But when I reach the main gate for Lavender Bliss Farms, I try to shrug off the uncomfortable feelings, vowing to focus on the client's needs—giving her the space she asked for while watching her back.

That I can do without lying.

By the end of the evening, I've finished some admin work, helped pick and prune flowers with Ripley, and accompanied her on some deliveries. I stayed in the background, giving her space to chat with her customers, her employees, her friends. While she talked to Ramona by the lavender maze about something that clearly distressed the woman in the shop, I hung back, out of earshot. When she ran into a woman with heavily pierced ears and a nose ring, I gave them space for the convo.

As we return to the farm, Ripley heads inside the home, and I go to the shop, on a mission. A guy I'm pretty sure is Cyrus is working there today, bobbing his shaggy head of hair to something that sounds like Jack Johnson. He's a white surfer dude with long hair, a deep tan, and an obvious *vibe*—that his life is a vibe.

"Hey, bro," he says with a smile. "What can I do you for?"

"How's it going?" He doesn't have a name tag, but Ripley told me the names of everyone who worked here so I can surmise. And I like to use people's names when I can. That's something my mother taught me. It personalizes interactions. Shows them you care, even if it's someone you'll never see again, she says. "I'm Banks. You must be Cyrus."

He puffs out his chest. "I am. And you're like Kevin Costner, right? I love that movie. I mean it's old, but old movies are so cute, man, aren't they? But hey, no surprise there. Old people are rad. I wonder what it would have been like to be an old person back then?"

Wow. That is quite an *if you give a moose a muffin* train of thought. He seems to be enjoying it since his gaze is drifting off, and perhaps he's picturing himself in the good old days of the nineties.

I wait for him to come back to the present moment.

He shakes his head. "Anyhoo. Talk to me, bro."

I nod toward the lavender eye masks. "I'll take one of those, Cyrus."

"Sweet," he says, then hands me one, not making a move to ask for payment.

My brow knits. "How much?"

"Bro, you're keeping my boss safe. It's on the house."

Pretty sure giving things away is not helping the boss, but this is not my circus nor my monkeys. "I'd like to pay."

He shakes his head. "Your money's no good here."

"I bet it cashes just fine," I say.

"Nope," he says with a pop of his lips.

The fact that he thinks he can win this battle of wills with me is, admittedly, impressive. No wonder Ripley hired him. He has tenacity under this *chill* exterior.

That goes on for about another minute until I stare him down and say in no uncertain terms, "I'm not leaving until I pay."

With a huff, he holds up his hands, relenting. "Have it your way."

I buy the eye mask, thank him, and leave, setting the mask neatly on the nightstand in the cottage. We'll see if it helps relieve all my supposed tension after all.

When it's dinnertime, I don't expect Ripley to feed me. I tell Lila and Ripley that I'll order takeout, but Lila insists, and I'm not one to argue with grandmothers. At dinner we discuss security precautions for the farm, and I review the plan. But I'm pleased that Lila and Ripley are savvy already about best practices.

And, like I promised, I show Ripley that she can take care of everyone and everything while I look out for her. I'll do it again tomorrow and throughout the length of the shoot, respecting her boundaries and the boundaries of the job.

As the day fades and night settles its blanket over the farm, I nod toward the front door, a sign I'm heading off to my quarters for the night.

"See you and Hudson bright and early," I say with a wink as I reach for the doorknob but don't open it.

"Just try to keep up with me," she retorts.

"I'll be up and at 'em."

"Right, because you don't sleep." She cocks her head to the side, lifting her chin. "Hey. Are you a vampire bodyguard?"

"Do you think I am, Ripley?"

"I'm definitely getting that impression. But you're not allergic to sunlight. Hmm."

I roll my eyes, but I'm smiling as I shift back to the practical. "Tomorrow, the crew comes. That's when things will start to get more hectic. It'll be more important—"

"I know. I get why it's important to have you," she says, mimicking my serious tone.

I'd like to have her.

"You're just saying that because you can't shake me," I tease.

She arches an eyebrow. "I can't?"

Fuck. I almost forgot who I was dealing with. I drag a hand down my face. "What have I done?" I mutter.

When I look up, she sure looks like she'll be having the last laugh. "I guess we'll see."

I sure will. But I'll rise to the challenge. "Then, I can't wait to see how you're going to try to shake me tomorrow."

Ripley's smile is too damn pleased. "It is on."

CHAPTER 18
THE TOILET PAPER FAIRY
RIPLEY

Do I have a lot to do at the farm?

You bet.

Am I going to get it all done?

No problem.

But am I still going to find new ways to drive Banks crazy?

Of course I am. A challenge is a challenge is a challenge.

After I walk the dog (with Banks), do the Saturday-morning chores (with Banks), hop on my computer in my makeshift office on the living room couch in the farmhouse to pay some invoices, review production plans, and check in with the stores around the area that carry our lavender oils, soaps, sachets, lotions, and potions (without Banks, who's presumably skulking around the lavender maze, checking for hidden cameras in its coils and twists of hedges), I grab my phone. Make an appointment for this afternoon. Then, I text my girls as I trot upstairs to grab the laundry.

Ripley: Guess who has a plan to drive her bodyguard crazy?

Then, I tell them about the plan and the appointment I made. But Chloe's not interested in my evil genius, evidently.

Chloe: Um, can we hear more about the hot bodyguard instead of your plans?
Bridget: As in, where can I get one?
Chloe: What she said!
Bridget: Honestly, all innkeepers should henceforth have bodyguards. Let's make it a new town ordinance.
Chloe: I'd be all over that vote. Solidarity!
Ripley: Excuse me, can I get a word in edgewise?
Chloe: Better text faster, girl.
Bridget: Yeah, we have town bylaws to pass, Ripley. Hear ye, hear ye—I hereby declare all the women of Darling Springs who want a bodyguard shall have one.
Chloe: Some men might want them too.
Bridget: Good point. Come and get 'em! Hot bodyguards for sale here at my hot bodyguard stand!
Ripley: It's not all it's cracked up to be!
Chloe: La, la, la, la, la. I can't hear you.
Ripley: He follows me everywhere!
Bridget: To the bathroom? To the shower?
Ripley: No, and no.
Chloe: To your...bedroom?

She finishes that text with the wide-open-eyes emoji. I laugh as I dump the clothes and towels in the washing machine, voice texting my reply.

Ripley: No!
Chloe: Then I'm not seeing the problem.
Bridget: Me neither.
Ripley: Why am I cursed with loving you two so much? You never see things my way.
Bridget: Because your way is wrong. And, also, my inn is all booked out for the next month! My bank account is happy!
Chloe: Things I've never said in my life.

I shift gears instantly as I set the timer on the machine. Chloe works at the doggie daycare in town. She loves it since she loves dogs and moonlights as a dog trainer, but money has been a constant struggle for her.

Ripley: I heard Sheriff Simmon's family adopted a new old Chihuahua from Little Friends. The sheriff herself is too busy to train him and he seems to be driving her bananas. Maybe he needs some training lessons from you?
Chloe: Oooh! Because you know what I say—you *can* teach an old dog new tricks.

We chat about potential work for her as I rush through the house, tidying up as I go. They tell me how much they're keen to catch up with Haven again, since it's been so long, as I pop into the kitchen to clean coffee cups—everyone who works here, from Cyrus and Ramona to the farmhands, wander into the kitchen throughout the day to grab a cup or two or three. But the sink is shining and empty. I didn't expect that. I spin around, opening a cupboard. All the mugs are put away. That's a surprise too. But a welcome one. The kitchen is more immaculate than it's ever been. I finish my chat with my friends—finally telling them about my plan for the afternoon—when Grandma breezes in, looking fabulous in linen pants with a tie waist and short-sleeve blouse. Dropping my phone into my shorts pocket, I whirl around, grateful for her magic touch here in the kitchen. "Thank you for cleaning. You didn't have to, but I sure appreciate it," I say. She's retired, and I want her to enjoy her life, not clean up after me.

"Wasn't me. Maybe the kitchen fairy came by."

I laugh, then stop at the counter to meet her gaze across from it. "And the toilet paper fairy is still going strong."

"The toilet paper fairy never misses a beat. She popped by this morning."

Grandma's been stocking all the bathrooms with toilet paper forever. She did it when Haven and I were in high school. When she came home from shopping, she'd drop off rolls in every bathroom. We never once had to hunt for a roll under the cabinet because Grandma was the toilet paper fairy. And often, the bed-making fairy, the laundry fairy, and the *straightened up your desk* fairy. "I don't deserve you," I say.

"You do," she says, then comes around the counter and drops a kiss to my forehead. "Also, I'm going to Petaluma today to see some friends. Translation: *have a long lunch and get day-drunk*."

I wag a finger. "Don't drive."

"Please. Daisy's picking me up in a few minutes. She's our DD and always has been."

"God bless Sober D."

"Indeed."

I shoo her out of the kitchen. "Now go enjoy your wine and girl time. You deserve it."

"I do. But so do you," she says, then waves goodbye.

I check the time on my phone. A zing of anticipation thrums through me. Only twenty more minutes till our appointment. As I grab my canvas bag from a hook in the foyer, a name I haven't seen in more than a year flashes in my texts. My ex, Eric Patrick. Intrigued, I click on it.

Hey, hey! How's everything, Ripley? Looks like Darling Springs is about to become the darling of the movies. Maybe I should open another fusion café there after all! Would love your thoughts on that! You know the town so well.

Um, no.

I stare at the message for a beat longer. The guy ditched me because he was tired of small-town life. Now he wants to profit from it. I do have a terrible track record with men, but I also know how to use the Delete button.

I lift a finger, and with much fanfare, I send his text to the trash, then move on to the next one. I tap out a text to Sheriff Simmon about her new pup, then head to the little shop on the farm. Ramona wanted to talk to me yesterday about how to handle a complicated situation with a friend who lately only ever talks about herself.

I rap on the door even though it's open and she's organizing shelves of lavender lotion. "So how are you feeling today about our chat?"

She blows out a thoughtful breath. "Well, it's just a lot. On the one hand, do I say something the next time we're hanging out? On the other hand, what if she's going through something, and this is her way of coping?"

I nod sympathetically. "You never really know what someone's going through. But maybe you can try and ask that?"

Ramona seems to consider what I've said. "Maybe I will. Thanks, Ripley," she says, then nods to the gate. "Where are you and the sexy warden going?"

I smile at the nickname, then tell her my plans.

"Oh! I want a boyfriend who does that with me," she says, a little impressed.

Better squash that notion, stat. "He's not my boyfriend."

She snickers.

"He's not," I say, more insistent.

"I mean, maybe not yet."

"See if I get you a treat again," I tease; then I turn around and head toward the sexy warden.

He's waiting for me.

At the gates.

With our bikes.

But I like to keep him on his toes. Literally. "Guess what?"

"You signed us up for that pole dancing class after all and you've got spike heels in that bag?" he says, nodding toward my shoulder.

I pat the bag, making sure he can't see it. "Good guess." I mean, he's not far off when it comes to what I'm carrying with me. "But that's not what I was going to say." I gesture toward my pickup, parked down the road. "We can use my truck today."

He holds out his hand, clearly asking for keys. "I'll drive."

"My truck?"

"Presumably it has a steering wheel, brakes, and gas?"

"Yes," I grumble.

"Then I'll drive," he says.

"But it's *my* truck."

"What if there are paps in town and we need to lose them?"

"There's not going to be a high-speed chase."

"You never know." He's not joking.

"Banks," I press.

He sighs, then relents. "Fine," he says, then rolls his shoulders, like he's mentally girding himself for the indignity of being the passenger.

My mind flashes back to yesterday at the coffee shop. To him not liking naps. To him liking control. Then to now—the kitchen being pristine. "Did you clean the kitchen?"

"I did," he says.

"Thank you," I say genuinely. "That was thoughtful."

"Happy to do it."

"You don't like messes, do you?"

"I do not," he says.

But it's more than that. Banks Kendrick likes to be in control of his life, his environment, his job, the premises. He likes to handle things. But people are who they are for a reason. Maybe that's just his nature.

Or maybe once upon a time, he wasn't able to control a damn thing.

I hand him the keys. "You can drive," I say.

He clutches them like they're a precious gift; then we head to my wheels.

CHAPTER 19
THE PERILS OF PEDICURES
RIPLEY

If Banks had taken this detour two days ago, I'd have been pissed that he was trying to make the point he's making. But now I'm damn curious as he drives slowly past The Ladybug Inn. So curious I'm rubbernecking, but it's not for a glimpse of the star supposedly staying there, getting into his small-town character.

I'm checking out the guys waiting outside. A chill slides down my spine, but I try to shake it off. I don't like the invasion of the paps in my hometown, but they're only doing their job. It'll be over soon enough, I hope.

That same stocky guy in the ball cap from the other day is across the street, camera in hand, like he's been staking out the entrance, waiting for New Chris. There's another man next to him, also with a camera. He's short, with a fair complexion, and also sporting a man bun. He's in position too.

"That's Silas, as you know," Banks says, nodding to the first guy.

"He's still here?" I ask, a little amazed at his, well, stamina. "Doesn't he have other work?"

"Sure. But he can do both. He's a former sports journalist, so he's agile with a camera. He does a lot of work in San Francisco since Webflix is shooting some TV shows there. He's always following some of those celebs, and sports stars there too when he's up in Northern California instead of LA."

That makes sense, I suppose. With some reluctance, I nod. "And the other guy? Any idea?"

"Ludwig," Banks says. "He fancies himself an Ansel Adams. Takes moody black-and-white rain shots in Seattle or fog shots in San Francisco. So when there's a big fish, he chases it."

"And Chris is a big fish," I say.

"Yup, and that's why he wants a shot of Chris and Haven. Ludwig has a six-month-old and a four-year-old. He freelances for the highest bidder. Usually to *News Site Ink*, which is a company that buys pics from photographers and sells them to celeb sites."

"You know him too?"

"Do you know all the varieties of lavender?"

"Yes," I say.

"Then I know all these guys."

"How did you know they were here?"

"I did some recon the night I arrived. Figured they'd be camped out at one of the hotels in town. But I've got a friend in LA—guy named Tyler—who works in private security too. Former Marine. We help each other out with intel."

"Why wouldn't Chris stay someplace else? Like another town? Somewhere harder to find."

Banks shrugs as he drives past the inn. "They'd find him there too. Why make it harder for himself?"

That's kind of sad. But also the reality of fame, I suppose. "Fair point."

He comes to a stop at the stop sign. "But let's hope they won't be chasing you." He blows out a breath. "Why don't we make sure there aren't others stationed outside of wherever you're taking me?"

I scoff. "It's not like I dropped hints on the farm's socials about where I'd be going."

"I know. Just let me keep you safe."

"Fine," I say, but *maybe* I do like how intent he is on doing the job. "Just go down Main Street."

He does a drive-by, and the coast is clear. That's a relief. I don't want to spend my days ducking and hiding. Besides, I have a challenge to carry out.

"Ah, this is nice," Banks says ten minutes later, rolling up the cuffs of his jeans and dipping his feet into the bubbling water at Daisy's Nails.

With a whole lot of panache.

Damn him. I can't win.

"I have always wanted to get a pedicure," he says, tossing me one of those dimpled smiles that make my chest flip.

I look away so he can't see the cartoon hearts fluttering over my chest. I'm right next to him in a comfy faux-leather chair too. We're both waiting for our nail techs to return from wherever nail techs go when you soak your feet.

Banks did not balk when we walked through the door of the salon, and I told him we were getting our toes done. He didn't flinch. He simply said, "How did you know this was on my bucket list?" For such a control freak, the man rolls with my one-upmanship.

Though, admittedly, I haven't been able to one-up him. He meets all of my challenges, then exceeds them.

I don't know if I should be irritated or impressed.

As he stretches out his big burly frame in the massage chair, he reaches for the controller on the arm and punches a few buttons. The back of his chair rolls. It bumps him forward, and as it does, he says, "Ahhh," in a choppy rhythm. "This is fun too. You should try it. Want me to turn yours on?"

"I can turn mine on myself, thank you."

With a sly grin, he jumps on the double entendre, asking, "Can you now? Turn yours on?"

"You bet I can," I say, but I don't activate the chair. I've never liked the high intensity of the mechanical pressure.

"You really should try it," Banks says, the words coming out staccato again as the chair bumps him along once more. "Or wait. Should we get a couples massage after this?" He presses his hands together in prayer. "Tell me that's next on your *try to ditch me* list."

He has me there. I don't know how to play chicken with him. "You'll have to wait and see what I have planned," I say, though I'm scrambling mentally to figure it out.

"I'll be ready for the dare," he says, clearly having too much fun with me as he paddles his feet in the pedicure tub. "I might get addicted to pedicures."

A laugh bubbles in my throat. I jerk my gaze forward so I don't give him the satisfaction of seeing my mirth. I'm exasperated with him, not amused, dammit. He's aggravating…and yet I keep wanting to push his buttons. To aggravate him more. Why is it so much fun to press him?

I wish I knew.

"But I will give you credit for a valiant effort today," he adds, poking the massage chair arm with a finger to emphasize his point. "Lesser men would cower at having their feet done. I am not one of those men."

"Of course you're not. I should have known a guy who does origami and listens to Mozart wouldn't be scared off by a pedicure," I say, an admission of sorts.

"I'm evolved," he says.

I stifle a smile.

"I saw that," he mutters.

"Saw what?"

"That little tease of a smile."

"No, you didn't," I say, trying to stay stoic.

"Yes, I did."

"You're impossible," I say, right as Daisy's granddaughter,

Maggie, hustles over to me from the front counter and gives my arm a squeeze. "Hey there, Ripley. I just saw Sarah is handling you today. She's my new girl, and I love her already. You're getting the usual? A standard pedi?"

"That'd be perfect."

As Maggie grabs a towel, Banks looks my way. "So you don't do manicures, but pedicures are your thing?"

I shrug happily. Maybe I threw him for a loop there. "I love pedis. My mom always used to take Haven and me when we were younger," I say, fondly remembering those times when Mom took us out for our girls' trips, her little matching towheads happily following her down the street to this very salon.

"That sounds nice," he says with a warm smile.

"It was. A little treat every few months. I kept it up. But manicures are a waste in my line of work."

"Makes sense."

I pause for a beat, giving him a playful look. "Or maybe I just contain multitudes," I add.

His lips curve up. "You sure do."

Maggie returns and sets up a towel on the footrest. "Here you go."

"And how's little Carson?" I ask Maggie, the friendly, freckled woman who owns the shop now. It's gone from generation to generation, like my farm.

"Aww, he's great. Just started to crawl last week."

"Watch out, Mama," I say with a low whistle.

"Don't I know it," she says, then tells me about her little baby and all the milestones he's hit. When she's done, she squeezes my arm again and takes off as Sarah returns and sets up on a low stool. Another tech parks a stool at Banks's feet.

I turn to my shadow. "My grandma's bestie—Daisy—owned this shop, and then her son ran it, and now her son's daughter runs it. Maggie," I say, nodding toward the front counter, where Maggie's set up on the computer.

"Family business. Nice," he says warmly as the tech scrubs my feet with an exfoliating scrub. "That must be one of the things you like about this town?"

The earnestness of his question catches my full attention. "I do. I love that everyone looks out for each other," I say, thinking of high school, when my parents died. My throat squeezes with emotion. It was fifteen years ago, and I can still remember the aftermath of their death clearly. Not just the day we got the terrible news, but the way the people of Darling Springs took care of Haven, my grandmother, and me.

I must be wearing my emotions on my face since Banks shifts in his chair, almost like he's trying to shield me with his body. He can't, of course. But I can feel it in the gesture. Like he's trying to protect me from anyone listening in on the emotional moment as he asks quietly, "You okay?"

With sadness, I meet his dark-brown gaze, answering first with a sturdy nod. "I am. Just remembering when my parents died. It was like the whole town wanted to take care of us afterward."

His expression is sympathetic, his tone solemn. "I'm sorry for your loss, but I'm glad you had people to comfort you."

"Thank you," I say, then look around toward the door and the street beyond. The businesses I know. The families I see every day. The stories they share. I look back at him. "Even though there are photogs in town for the movie and paparazzi now and tour groups, I don't think I could leave. It's weird, but it's like the whole place became my family. Even when Haven left, I always felt like"—I pause, take a moment to collect my thoughts—"this was where I was supposed to be. I have good friends here," I say, and before I know it, I'm telling him about Chloe and Bridget and even some of my new friends in Darling Springs. "Like this woman named Juliet who moved here recently. Well, she's a part-timer. She lives and works in San Francisco."

"Does that mean she feels like less a part of the town?"

I shake my head. "Oh, she's one of us now. She's brought a lot of business to Darling Springs. She and her hubs started hosting couples retreats here," I say, enthused as I tell him more about the new kids. "They have this podcast all about romance and dating and such, so they host couples retreats at a house they were gifted by a listener who's from here."

"Juliet and Monroe, right?" he asks.

I blink, pull back. "You know them?"

"Not terribly well, but I was passing through town a year or so ago and ran into Monroe. Since then, I've listened to their show a few times."

I smile. "Small world."

He smiles too. "I suppose it is."

"Do you know what they call their house here? The Horny House."

Banks laughs. Big, deep, pleased. "Sounds like my kind of home."

"It's a fun place," I say as the tech rubs hot stones along my calves. I sigh contentedly, enjoying the touch. "And you live in Los Angeles now, you said?"

"I do," he says.

"Even though you grew up in Lucky Falls?"

"I did."

He's a little clipped when I ask about Lucky Falls. I'm not entirely used to that from the king of comebacks. Come to think of it, he didn't say much about Lucky Falls yesterday either, when he told me where he was from, only that *it's not a bad place*. Does that mean he dislikes small towns? He didn't sound that way a few minutes ago. But maybe there's something about that place he doesn't care for. "Are you a city guy?"

"Yes."

"Why?"

His expression darkens, like there's a storm cloud over his head. "Anonymity is a good thing, I've found," he says, a little evasively.

So then it's not a Lucky Falls thing. It's a Banks thing. I press a little more. "In your line of work?"

"Something like that," he says, then looks to his feet.

It's a sign he doesn't want to talk much anymore about where he's from or where he lives now. I respect the boundary he's created and move on. "This is *really* your first pedicure?"

His laugh is instant. "Do I seem like a natural or something?"

"Sort of."

"You're my first, Ripley," Banks reassures me, putting a little extra whiskey and seduction in his voice. It's intended to be playful, I'm sure. But it still sends a zing through me. "But my sister's tried to get me to go many times. I used to drop her and her friends off when she was younger before she could drive. And it became this thing Emily did—trying to convince me to join them."

"She's the one who taught you origami?"

"Good memory."

"I remember a lot of things from that night."

Banks holds my gaze, leveling me with a hot stare that nearly burns my T-shirt from the intensity. "I remember everything."

Lust holds me in its grip for several long seconds before I manage to form words rather than sighs. "Anyway…how old is your sister?"

He reorients to the conversation too. "Twenty-seven. Seven years younger," he says as the tech tells me to put my feet on the towel.

I comply as she grabs some polish. "And you never joined her?"

"Nope. Just stood outside the salon. Read a book. Went for a walk."

"A bodyguard in the making," I tease.

He gives me a stern look. "You don't see me walking around the block here."

"Yes, you're protecting me from the perils of pedicures so well," I say, then return to the why. "Why did you say no to her? You obviously adore her."

"Yeah, I do. Good observation." He sighs deeply, like he's giving the question real thought.

"Is it because you don't like relaxing?"

"Maybe I thought I was too tough for pampering," he says, a little sheepish.

I can see that in him. He has to spend his days being badass. It can be hard to let go. "Big tough Marine and all?"

"Something like that," he says, and his smile is self-deprecating. "Kind of ridiculous now that I think about it."

"Or maybe you'd always wanted one and you finally gave yourself permission to get one with me. Since you had no choice but to follow me into the salon to save me from all the dangers in Darling Springs."

"Damn, look at you psychoanalyzing me."

"Am I wrong? You seem to be enjoying it," I say, gesturing to him relaxing in the chair, resting comfortably, looking like he's having a good time as he gets his feet buffed and beautified. "Just like I unexpectedly enjoyed yoga yesterday," I add.

He studies my face, like he's looking for the answer in my eyes. Then he sighs thoughtfully. "You might not be wrong."

I don't bother to hide a smile whatsoever. Maybe this is my victory after all. "Score one for the farmer girl."

Banks shakes his head, like *not so fast*. "I'm not sure you won. Since you actually wanted to shake me today but didn't."

But he's wrong there. "No. I didn't entirely want that."

"You weren't trying to shake me by taking me on a girlie outing?"

"I was trying to rise to the challenge," I say with a confident lift of my chin. But I don't add *I may have met my match*.

"Have you ever *not* risen to the challenge?"

I tap my chin. "My friend Chloe dared me to bungee jump, so I did it once to prove I could do it. So I'd have to say no. Also, it *was* fun."

Smiling, he leans back in the chair as the tech pats his feet dry. "You," he begins, then shakes his head, as if that's all he can say—just *you*. But it's said with affection, exasperation, and honestly, a little unchecked desire.

Like how I feel.

When we leave the shop a little later, a pretty woman with sleek chestnut hair nearly bumps into me on the street.

She's not a photog though.

It's Bridget. Then, a redhead knocks into me. Chloe.

Gee, it's almost as if they're stalking me since they knew I'd be here at this time. "Fancy meeting you here," I say.

Bridget says, faux innocently, "This must be your hot bodyguard."

The look on Banks's face is pure satisfaction.

I want to kill my friends.

CHAPTER 20
HOT BODYGUARD MOVES
RIPLEY

Since I did serve up the details of my whereabouts with them this morning, I only have myself to blame for their appearance. Still, I can't be responsible for the way I introduce them. "This is Bridget. She's Chief Troublemaker," I say, squeezing her shoulder so hard. Then turning to Chloe and giving her the same treatment. "And Chloe is Number One Pain in the Ass."

Chloe beams, evidently loving the nickname. "What are friends for?" Chloe says, then extends a hand.

Banks shakes it. "Nice to meet you, Chloe," he says, then offers a hand to Bridget. "Pleased to meet you too, Bridget. I've heard so much about both of you."

"I swear none of what she says is true," Bridget says, pointing to me after she lets go of his hand. "Ripley was the one who Saran Wrapped Scott Nelson's truck back in twelfth grade."

I snap my gaze to her. "Dude! That was you, Bridge!"

Chloe bounces on her pink Converse-clad toes. "And Ripley was the one who insisted, too, that we remove the door to the science lab and hide it in the boys' locker room."

"Again, *not* me. That one was you," I point out. "Also, I stopped you from doing that, Chloe."

She frowns. "I know. I'm still sad about it."

After scanning behind us, then across the street, Banks smiles her way. "Tell me more. What was Ripley like in high school, and do you have pics?"

"Of course," Bridget says, then digs into her pants pocket for her phone. I slap her hand away.

"Anyway, as I was saying, we need to go," I say tightly, then try to send them mind messages to *please leave* because I can only imagine what they're going to reveal about me next. Photos of me in braces. That video they took when I tripped on my own sneakers *after* scoring a goal in a soccer game in twelfth grade. My prom hairstyle. (Sadly I was not able to make retro 80s hair come back in.)

But Chloe's brain receiver must be on the fritz since she waves off my protest, saying to Banks, "We have lots of time to hear more about all your hot bodyguarding and to show you Ripley's hairstyles through the years."

"I am going to Saran Wrap your car," I hiss out at her.

Chloe grins evilly. "And please take the passenger door off while you're at it. It's dented so maybe I can claim it was stolen and get a new door."

"And we really need to go, because with friends like these…" I say, exasperated.

If Banks was enjoying himself before, he's having the time of his life now, his amused gaze ping-ponging between my two friends.

They're not even close to done since Bridget clears her throat. "But don't leave until you two share all the on-the-job stories of how this hot-bodyguarding thing works. Don't skimp on a single detail, please." Bridget slides close to me. Actually, it's more like she plasters her body to my left side while Chloe wedges herself to my right. What the hell are they up to?

They're sandwiching me as Bridget looks to Banks, saying, "Like, for instance, what would you do if her two besties crowded her on the street and you needed to tug her close to keep her safe?"

I blink, and then I'm looking at the sky. In no time, Banks has roped one big arm around my back, the other around my hamstrings, and he's lifted me up. He carries me in his arms down the street away from the salon and them.

Bridget and Chloe squeal and clap.

"Again! Do it again," Chloe calls out as we go.

"Best show ever," Bridget hoots.

From all the way across the street, Noah at The Slippery Dipper has stepped out of his shop and is shouting his approval, "Nice move, man."

Even Salma has a front-row ticket to the show. She's outside the market, laughing at my friends' antics.

"You two are in so much trouble," I shout at them as Banks grips me tighter, then turns down the alley behind the salon.

He doesn't set me down. I'm still in his arms, his warm skin against my bare legs in my shorts. He doesn't need to be carrying me. There was no real threat. There weren't even any photographers around. None that I saw at least, and I suspect Banks didn't either since he was scanning the street while my friends were giving me a hard time. And yet, he's still holding me close, striding down the alley, arms wrapped around me like he won't let go anytime soon.

I don't protest either. I let him carry me because I like it. Because his arms feel so good wrapped around me. Because his chest is a strong, safe place, and I can feel his heart beating against my shoulder. Because his arms anchor me to him, almost, *almost* like he wants me close. When we're several feet away from the street, he finally sets me down, away from them, away from everyone.

With my flip-flopped, freshly pedicured feet on the ground, I smooth a hand over my shirt. Try to collect my thoughts. My racing pulse too. It takes a few seconds before I ask, "Were you just…flexing?"

"Maybe I like challenges," he says.

"I knew that about you."

"And maybe I liked *that* challenge." His deep, dark eyes don't look away.

My pulse skitters. "Did you?"

"It was a little," he says, then takes his time before he adds, "irresistible."

He makes no move to leave. He stays a foot away, his fists clenched like he's holding back, his eyes locked on me.

Maybe I'm reading something into nothing, but it sure feels like he's saying I'm irresistible. In this moment, I almost feel that way. It's the opposite of how I felt when I left the hotel the night I met him. I felt rejected then. I feel craved now. For a few tantalizing seconds, I'm holding my breath, hoping he's going to kiss me in an alley behind the nail salon in my hometown.

The sound of a door opening breaks the moment. Someone who works at the salon heads outside, then tosses a bag of trash into a can.

It's enough to send us both back to the street where Chloe and Bridget are waiting, like they've just exited their new favorite theatrical production—the Interactive Wind-Up Ripley Show.

"Dude, that is my new favorite thing ever," Chloe says to Banks.

"Glad to help," Banks says, then the corner of his lips curves up. "It's only one of my many hot bodyguard services, isn't it, Ripley?" He turns to me, eyes glinting, the delight in them reappearing.

The joke's on me. But considering how much I liked him carrying me for a whole block, maybe it's on them too. Trouble is I'm also pretty sure I finally like having a hot bodyguard, and that's a whole other problem.

One that weighs on me as we head to my car, but then I stop in my tracks after a few feet, remembering a return text that landed on my phone during the pedicure. "Chloe!" I shout.

She turns around.

"Sheriff Simmon said she'd love some lessons. Her new dog is a toy guarder."

Chloe's eyes pop. "You're the best, and I won't show anyone your eighties phase now."

I roll my eyes, and we leave.

On the drive back to the farm as the sun dips lower in the afternoon sky, I'm stuck on something—how the man's always a step ahead.

I'm replaying all the moments. Like when he picked me up in a flash, like it didn't even faze him. But before then, he didn't flinch either when I took him for the pedicure. He went along with it, even though he'd never had one. The day before, he anticipated I'd try to ride off on my bike, and he was ready first thing in the morning with a bike of his own.

He doesn't break, and I'm dying to know *why*. As he slows to a stop at the last light downtown, I turn to him, blurting out, "How are you so unflappable?"

He looks my way. "How are you so on top of everything?"

"You think I'm on top of everything?" I ask, a little surprised he's turned my question around.

"I do. You take care of everyone and everything. Like when you talked to Ramona yesterday. Like how you take care of your sister. Like helping Chloe with the dog-lesson thing."

"I guess it's just…my job."

"Same for me," he says as the light changes and he taps the gas.

"But it's part of who you are," I say, curious, so damn curious to know more about him.

He shoots me a look. "Same for you, Ripley. It's not just the job. It's who you are."

There he goes again, deflecting. I turn to the window, twirling a strand of hair.

But Banks sighs, then says, "When my mom left my dad, it was a whole fucking mess, Ripley." I turn back, my attention only on him. "I had to be…*steady*."

I wasn't expecting that kind of admission from him. "For them?" I ask gently.

"Yeah. Things were hard for Mom. Real hard for a while. Someone had to step up," he says, swallowing roughly.

My throat tightens with emotions. I feel deeply for the younger Banks, and I feel like I understand so much more of him. "Like, you looked out for her and your sister?"

He nods. "I did. Still do. Can't help myself."

"It was good they had you then and now," I say, without knowing the details.

"I'm glad I had them. So, yeah, I guess it's in my nature to be unflappable, but also…" He purses his lips, his brow furrowing. He goes quiet as he turns down another road, a quiet one that winds past a small chicken farm, then a pasture with horses. We're cruising past patches of land, hemmed in by white fences and wide-open skies before he finishes the thought: "I have to be."

"To do your job?"

"Yes. But I have to be unflappable with you. I need to be professional with you, Ripley." There's no teasing in his tone this time.

He's all business, almost like he's issuing a directive. Drawing a line in the sand.

"Well, you're good at it, Banks. I can't get you to break," I say, injecting a little levity into the conversation. "And trust me, I'm trying."

"I know you are," he says, then his jaw ticks. He rolls his lips together, and I swear there's some battle going on in his head. Then, with his hands firmly gripping the wheel, he steals a glance my way. "But maybe you didn't try the right thing to get me to break."

"I didn't?" I ask carefully, trying to figure out where he's going.

He shakes his head. "Maybe if you did, then I wouldn't be so unflappable."

Another stolen glance. This time with heat in his eyes. I'm not sure we're talking about our game of chicken anymore.

Or maybe that's all we're talking about, so I push a little more. He's the one who suggested I'm irresistible. He's the one who said he remembers everything from that night we met. He's the one, too, who said he'd be ready for my next dare.

I'm not even sure if I'm daring him. But I am sure I'm goading him as I say, "If you hadn't run that night, there's no way you'd be acting so professional now."

"You think so?"

"I sure do." It comes out flirty on purpose.

There's a heated pause even as he drives. An electrical charge sparking between us. Then, a challenge of his own as he says, "Try me, sweetheart."

My pulse speeds up. With excitement. With danger. "What do you mean?"

"This," he bites out, brusquely. He pulls over to the side of the road, cuts the engine, and says, "You won."

He curls a hand around my head and kisses the breath out of me.

CHAPTER 21
SEEMED LIKE A BAD IDEA AT THE TIME
BANKS

There are bad ideas and then there are spectacularly bad ideas. This would be the latter—messing around with a client I promised to protect—and yet I can't find it in me to stop.

Ripley tastes too good. Smells too intoxicating. Responds too temptingly. Her lips part the second I seal my mouth to hers. She invites my kiss, and I take everything she offers on the side of a quiet road in her pickup truck.

I travel my hand up the back of her neck, cataloging the way she trembles as I touch her. Her murmurs as my fingers glide into her hair. Her sighs as I hold her tight.

The kiss is a little frantic, a lot noisy. Or maybe that's the rub of denim from my jeans against the old leather of the seats, or her thigh against the gearshift as she inches closer, or my arm knocking against the steering wheel as I reach for her.

But I'm not going to let something like limited space stop me now that I've given in. I kiss her harder, like that'll cover up the annoyance of no fucking room. The only space I truly care about is the distance between us, and I'd like to turn that to nothing. Dipping her head back, I capture each plaintive moan of hers with another hungry kiss. She reaches for the collar of my polo, jerking me closer. I nip the corner of her mouth, then kiss her hard again.

Until my elbow scrapes the horn and it bleats. "Fuck," I mutter, wrenching away.

I should stop. This is a sign. This truck is too small. It only has front seats and mine's nearly all the way back. It's late afternoon and the sun is still bright. There's no privacy. But then my gaze lands on her bee-stung lips. Yeah, I'm not unflappable now whatsoever. "Guess you got me to break," I mutter.

Her lips twitch, like she's trying not to show how pleased that makes her. "Guess I did."

I grab her jaw. Her breath hitches. I slide my thumb along her face. Ripley is such a conundrum. A tough-as-nails woman who seems to like being…taken. I glance around the cab, assessing the space quickly, making plans in a second. "Fuck it," I say with a shrug. "Stay there. Don't move."

She gives a dutiful nod. I open my door, shut it, then quickly survey the surroundings as I move to the passenger side. There's no one here on this stretch of road. I open the passenger door. Standing by her seat, I reach across her and unbuckle her seat belt.

The look in her eyes is full of anticipation. Excitement even. That revs me up—I felt the chemistry between us the first night. I feel it even more now. A heady possibility.

"You can move," I tell her. She shifts to the driver's side, and I get in and shut the door.

She swallows noticeably. "Now what?" It's asked with an eagerness that sends a jolt of lust down my spine.

I sigh, both relieved and wildly turned on as I stare at the woman who drives me wild. "Now, get the fuck on me."

She scrambles to climb onto my lap, and I help her along, manhandling her a little as I adjust this gorgeous woman so she's straddling my thighs. Her shorts ride up farther, so her bare thighs bracket mine. She sets her hands on my shoulders, then sinks a little lower, her center grazing the ridge of my erection.

I groan, unbidden.

She smiles. "Better?"

So much, but I'm not letting on yet. Not when I can tease her.

"Let me see if this is better." I roam my eyes up and down her strong body, toned from years of hard work on the farm. Drinking in every detail. Her glittering eyes. Her parted lips. The flush across the top of her chest. Most of all—the way she waits for my answer.

Ripley is a firecracker every second I'm with her, but in moments like this, she's someone else too. She's softer, eager, hopeful.

"Better now?" she asks.

I tilt my head, like I'm giving it real thought.

"A little," I say, then I slide a hand down the soft flesh of her chest, over the tops of her breasts, teasing her before I travel back up to her eager mouth. I trace my thumb along her bottom lip, eliciting a shudder from her. Her eyes flutter closed as she moves slowly with me.

This is the opposite of our first night, when we smashed into each other in the booth in the bar. Now, it's like we're spending a lazy afternoon in the sun, when we have all the time in the world to do the things we want to do.

Even though I don't.

Even though we shouldn't cross this line.

But I do it anyway. "*This* would make it better," I rasp out, then reach for her hands on me. I take the right one from my shoulder, moving it off me, then behind her back. I reach for her other hand, shifting that one behind her back too.

Desire thrums through me, hot and sizzling, and wickedly hopeful too—I fucking hope she likes this. She parts her lips on a gasp, a bit of an answer, as I bind her wrists in one hand, gripping them both tight.

She shudders, a clearer answer.

Yessss.

I dip my face to her neck and blaze a trail of kisses up the hinge of her jaw, kissing her there. She moves with me, stretching her neck as I go. I lift my free hand, cup her jaw, then jerk her gaze to me. Her eyes are blue flames. My body is a furnace. "So much fucking better, sweetheart," I say; then I kiss her lush lips while I hold her in place.

With my free hand, my fingers coast down her throat, and I cover the hollow of it with my palm. "You like this?"

I'm pretty sure she does, but I want to hear it from her. "I do," she murmurs, sounding a little lost in the moment.

"Then show me. Use me," I command.

With a grateful moan, Ripley rocks against my dick. Seeking

out friction, she rides my erection as I keep her wrists bound behind her back, my hand gripping her face, her body under my control.

A rumble works its way up my chest as I stare at the gorgeous sight in front of me. On me. "You look good like this," I say.

"When I can't move?"

I glance down at her hips, swaying. "You're moving."

"You know what I mean," she pants out.

"Do I?" I ask, goading her to say it. To acknowledge that she likes being restrained.

"Banks," she grumbles, annoyed but aroused, as she grinds down against my hard length.

"Answer me, Ripley. What do I mean?" I repeat.

"You're such a dick," she bites out.

I laugh, then bring my mouth down on her collarbone, nipping her there. She tastes so good. The scent goes to my head, fries a few more brain cells, and makes it harder for me to tease the hell out of her. "You taste like lavender."

"What a surprise," she deadpans, but then her retort fades, turning into a sharp hitch in her breath.

I grip her wrists tighter. She moves faster. "Tell me what you like about this," I demand.

"You ass," she mutters.

Fine, she's not too soft when lust takes the wheel. Guess I was a little wrong. She's still all fire. But the thing is, she's also not in control. I am. I let go of her face to grab her hip and lift her off my dick, breaking the contact. "Tell me," I say again, sternly, meeting her eyes.

"Fine. I like where your hands are," she says, a needy admission.

Because I know that was hard for her, I reward her, yanking her back down on my hard-on. Then I punch up my hips, giving her more of what she wants.

"Use me, sweetheart," I say.

She rocks against me faster, her mouth falling open, her eyes squeezing shut. It's so fucking beautiful the way she's chasing release on the side of the road.

I give her what she needs. My lips on her neck, my fingers curled around her wrists, my hand caressing her breast, squeezing a nipple through her shirt and her bra.

"Ohhh," she murmurs; then her head falls forward, resting against the side of my face, giving me another hit of her sweet scent. Maybe it's lavender shampoo.

She's too pretty, too aroused, too needy. And I just can't resist her. "Can you come like this?" I ask, and I'm the desperate one now. I need her orgasm more than anything. "Or do you want fingers?"

"Yes," she says on a staggered breath.

"Which one?" I demand since I may be desperate, but I fucking love to play.

She grinds hard against me. "Fingers. Now."

"Say please."

"Fuck you. Give me your fingers," she says.

"Since you asked so nicely." I let go of her breast, unzip her shorts, and thrust my fingers inside her panties.

She's slick and hot, and her needy clit is so damn eager for attention. The second I touch her, she's shuddering. Then gasping, arching, and falling apart with a long, gorgeous cry that I cover with my mouth. You never know who might hear.

As I kiss her tenderly through her release, a healthy dose of pride floods me from the *instant O, just add fingers*.

When I let go of her lips, she's breathing hard, her shoulders heaving. And I catch the far-off sound of an engine.

Or maybe not so far-off after all. I jerk my gaze behind us.

Holy shit.

Coming our way on this winding, supposedly quiet road is a black town car. There's another one behind it. Then an SUV. Just what I need—a goddamn caravan.

I don't think they belong to photographers. But I can't know for sure. Besides, it could be anyone. Someone she knows. A customer.

Think fast.

"Ripley, get down on your knees."

She blinks, but she's obedient as she slides off me to the floor of the car, her hands reaching for my jeans.

I stifle a laugh as I cover her wrists, stopping her unzip as I lean my head back against the headrest, then close my eyes. "Quiet," I hiss out.

"Are you serious?"

"Shh," I say as the engines rumble louder.

"You're really shushing me after you've asked for a BJ? My mouth would be full anyway."

I laugh harder. I'm not sure I can survive this woman. "Ripley, there's a car coming."

"And you're pretending you're asleep?"

"Yes," I mutter. "So no one thinks twice of me being parked and stops to try to help. No one can see you. I'm protecting you."

A laugh bursts from her. "This better be a bodyguard first."

"Trust me. It is."

As the head of the convoy passes, I peek open an eye. I had a feeling. The woman in the passenger seat sports shaggy brown hair and big glasses—Vega, the director. The car whooshes by. The next car includes someone else I know—Wanda, our expert security hire.

A new, damning thought touches down in my head. What would she think if she knew what I'd done?

As the last vehicle passes, I catch a glimpse of a woman who looks just like the woman on the floor.

When they're gone, I finally turn my gaze back to her mirror. Ripley's cheeks are still pinkened, her lips still bruised, her hair a gorgeous, wild mess.

I'm keenly aware of just how far I've crossed the line, and just how close I came to getting caught because my steady pulse is beating out of control.

Guess I'm not so unflappable after all.

CHAPTER 22
NO BIG DEAL
BANKS

When the coast is officially clear a few seconds later, I offer Ripley a hand. She doesn't take it. Just climbs back up to the passenger seat as I move over to the driver's side.

"I'm sorry," I say, guilt twisting my gut as she settles in. But do I tell her I feel guilty? Do I tell her I shouldn't have done that?

"It's fine. You just caught me off guard. I thought you wanted me to blow you," she says.

Oh, right. She thinks I feel bad about the blow job misunderstanding when that's the least of my worries. But it lightens the mood for a second. "And that bothered you?" I ask her.

She rolls her eyes. "I got down on my knees. Obviously, it didn't bother me until I thought you were trying to shut me up with your dick."

She's so compliant and sassy at the same time. It's too heady. Too tantalizing. I've got to get my act together. I resist playing verbal volleyball with her this time, instead saying, "That was the crew. Everyone's in town now."

She sits ramrod straight. "Haven," she says, as if she's seen a ghost.

"She was in one of the cars."

Ripley yanks the seat belt across her chest, nodding to the road, like we need to step on it. "I thought she was going to the inn. But I should be there when she arrives."

"Why? I mean, I know we were heading there anyway, but..."

"Because I want to see her," she says, like it's obvious. Still, she adds, "She's probably coming to see me and Grandma before she checks into her hotel."

Oh. Right. "Of course," I say, then turn the keys in the ignition.

Why was I ever arguing with her over seeing her sister? Maybe because her sister's arrival is the reminder that I need to focus on *why* I was hired. Because paparazzi are in town. More have probably descended already. No doubt other photogs have figured out that the shot of the pretty blond dismounting a bicycle from two days ago was the twin, even though *Page Six* didn't care. That means more are likely swarming the town. All with the same goal—to catch the big fish: a photo of Chris Carlisle and Haven. Which is why *I'm* here—to personally protect the woman who looks just like the rising star.

I can't do that if I'm trying to tie her up and drive her to the edge of pleasure.

"Ripley," I say, shoving my desire to the side. There's no room for it. "That was a bad idea. I shouldn't have done that."

For a hot second, her eyes flash with something like hurt. But maybe I'm imagining it because a moment later, it's gone. "Agreed," she says, clipped.

I should drive to the farm. Deal with work. Greet the crew. But I failed that first night with Ripley, running off with barely a word. I could have gone to her hotel room. Said something then, like she pointed out in her kitchen the other day.

I can't redo the night we met, but I *can* give her the full truth now. She deserves it. "It's not that I don't want to," I say, a little desperate. "It'll compromise my ability to do my job."

Her lips are a ruler, but she nods. "Sure."

Is that a doubtful *sure* or a genuine one? "I need to protect you," I add. "I can't do that if I'm distracted."

"And I'm a distraction?"

"Yes. A huge one," I say.

She draws a sharp breath, nodding a few times. "I need to focus on the movie—it's a big break for my sister. And it's a huge opportunity for the farm. If it goes well, I can send my grandma to Paris to see her boyfriend. She deserves it. She'll miss the bees, but I can take care of them."

My heart warms, hearing her plans. Of course they involve others, even bees. "Lila definitely deserves it."

"So, it's fine," she says, raising her chin, being all tough girl.

"Good. Then, it won't happen a second time," I say, hating those words but needing to say them. Especially since I'm wrong. "A third time," I correct.

She smiles mirthlessly; then it fades. "It definitely won't," she says as I start the truck.

"We were just getting it out of our systems."

"Exactly," she echoes as I drive toward the lavender fields, the golden glow of the late-afternoon sun making them shimmer.

"And it's in the past," I add, hammering home the point. "We won't do it again."

"We definitely won't," she says as we reach the farm.

Maybe because I need a final reminder I say, "Good. That's good."

She gives me a big smile, then waves her hand in front of her like she's making it disappear. "I've already forgotten all about it."

Then she jumps out of the car, rushes across the front lawn, and throws her arms around her sister.

Yup. She's forgotten it all right.

I wish I could do the same.

CHAPTER 23
JUST MATH
RIPLEY

It's like a clown car.

Or three clown cars, to be precise. The number of people grabbing bags and gear from the two town cars and the SUV is a little overwhelming.

A lanky guy with a freshly shaven bald head and a long beard slings a black bag on his shoulder. He's chatting with a shorter man sporting an undercut and a goatee. They're giving artsy movie vibes. Betting one's the director of photography and the other's an AD—assistant director. More guys lug boom mics while some women grab what I think are light diffusers from the big SUV.

"Did they multiply?" I ask Haven once I finally let go of my baby sister.

"Yes. Right before my eyes on the plane. It was like mitosis in biology class," she says.

I swat her. "You nerd."

She juts out her hip, like she's owning the moment. "Once a nerd, always a nerd."

I drape an arm around her again. "And you're my nerd," I say, breathing in happiness and contentment. It's so good to see her again, even in spite of that totally awkward conversation with Banks moments ago. Banks, who's chatting with someone who just arrived. Come to think of it, I should probably freshen up post *O*. Change the panties and all. Might as well erase the evidence, just like we're forgetting that tryst in the truck ever happened.

"I'll be—"

But before I can say *right back*, a woman with sleek black hair hidden under a fabulous pink sun hat strides over to us across the emerald-green lawn.

"Cute hat," I say to her, and it seems to be doing the trick at keeping the sun far, far away from her.

"Thanks. It doubles as an umbrella," she says, then sticks out a hand. "I'm Tabitha Zhao. Juniper has told me so much about you."

"And I'm sure it's all fabulous," Haven puts in, squeezing my shoulder. It's cute how she's protective of me. I'm the same with her.

Tabitha smiles at Haven. "Yes, all fabulous." Then to me, she says, "And we appreciate you opening your home to the crew. I'm seriously grateful. Everything happened so quickly with the film and the financing. But your flexibility is not going unnoted by my bosses."

It takes me a second to process the double negative, but I nod, and say, "Anything for Haven."

Maybe I should make it seem like I'm doing all this for Ruby Horizons, but what's the point? All this—the invasion of the crew—is for my sister. And I'm thrilled I can do it for her.

Bonus that this interaction with Tabitha is taking my mind and focus off the awkward end to that side-of-the-road session.

Tabitha looks from Haven to me and back, then shakes her head in a familiar kind of amazement. She's processing the matching blond hair, the identical straight nose, the exact same spray of freckles. "It's uncanny." She holds up a hand in apology. "Sorry, I'm sure you get that all the time."

"We do," Haven and I say in unison.

"Which is why we used to play tricks on our parents and grandparents," Haven adds.

"Could they tell you apart?" Tabitha asks with the kind of curiosity that's pretty natural when you meet identical twins.

Haven grabs my right arm, showing off the sparrows that fly across my skin. Then, the one bird she has on her shoulder. "We didn't have these then. So it was seriously hard for them."

Tabitha taps her temple under her hat. "I'll be looking for Ripley's sparrows then." To Haven, she adds, "And yours is being covered up by makeup. I've told the makeup artist—she's local—to bring tattoo cover-up."

"I know, Tabby," Haven says.

"And don't forget your call time," Tabitha says. But Haven's eyes sparkle like she just saw something exciting, and in a second, she's off, rushing over to tackle-hug Hudson, who's racing up the hill with Cyrus, who must have taken my pup for a walk.

I take the moment to say to Tabitha, "When is her call time?"

Tabitha taps her tablet, then tells me it's 7:00 a.m. the day after tomorrow. "She needs to be in makeup then."

I lean in close and whisper, "Why don't you just tell her she has a six thirty call time? It'll be easier to get what you want that way, if you know what I mean. Especially since she needs to come over from the inn." Haven's staying at The BookHouse, Bridget's inn. She and New Chris are deliberately not staying at the same hotel. When we last chatted, my sister said it made more sense as they're trying to defuse the rumors.

Tabitha gives a grateful nod. "I do. And thanks for the tip."

Peering beyond her, I take in the sheer number of people dotting my lawn, which seems more than I'd expected. My chest tightens, and my heart beats a little faster, my thoughts racing.

This is a lot. For bee's sake, what have I signed up for? I feel like I did when Haven first told me about the flick.

How am I going to fit all these people in? Vega's staying at the hotel, along with Haven and some others. But there are still so many people here. I scan the lawn again, catching a glimpse of Banks chatting with a serious-looking woman close to his height. That must be Haven's bodyguard. Wanda Rodriguez, I think he said. She won't stay here. The lighting guys will though. Some added security too. Some PAs, the camera crew...

"Actually, how many are here?" I ask. "I was expecting five crew members staying at the homestead. Though I know The BookHouse and The Ladybug Inn have a lot of rooms reserved for the cast and others."

I mean, I'm good at math. But I'm pretty sure no matter how you add it up, there aren't enough rooms for everyone.

Tabitha tilts her head, that huge hat tilting with her as she taps her chin. "Well, with the added security and some additional crew, we need as many rooms as you have."

Haven returns to my side with Hudson at her heels. She must read the concern in my eyes since she says, "What's wrong, Rip?"

"Nothing." I fasten on a smile. I don't want to worry her.

"Liar." She stares me down as Tabitha takes off to help the guy with the undercut. "What is it?" Haven asks when Tabitha's out of earshot.

"There aren't enough rooms," I whisper.

Haven shrugs happily, then squeezes my hands. "You can stay with me. We'll have sleepovers like we used to. It'll be so fun. We can eat popcorn and watch movies."

And she'll have to get up early. And she'll need her beauty sleep. And my sister has struggled with sleep since our parents died. In the aftermath of her grief, she battled insomnia and depression. The worse she slept, the worse her depression became. We tried everything to help her, from meds to therapy, but it wasn't till we found a combination of meditation and the right therapist that she was able to finally sleep through the night again.

That was the first step on her road to recovery from the depression.

She needs her rest. And I also need to be here to take care of the farm. "No, you need your sleep."

"Ripley," she says, but there's resignation in her voice. She knows I'm right. She sighs but then brightens in excitement. As the sound of shoes crunching on gravel grows louder, she says cheerily, "You can stay with Grandma though."

There's a couch in my grandma's garden suite, true. But I won't use it. I shake my head. "I don't want to bother her," I say, then screw up the corner of my lips, thinking. How can I fix this problem quickly? That's what I do. Solve problems.

And…I know. It's obvious and easy enough. "I'll just sleep on the couch in the living room. Someone else can have my room. It's fine."

"Are you sure?" Haven asks with a frown as the sound of footsteps grows louder.

In seconds, Banks appears by my side. "I couldn't help but overhear. You can stay in the cottage."

His deep, commanding voice sends a hot shiver down my spine.

Or maybe it's the thought of being close to him in such a tiny space that's lighting me up.

CHAPTER 24
ALL MY FRIENDS ARE ASSHOLES
RIPLEY

My stomach is flipping with nerves. This is bad. So bad I can't believe I'm about to do this, but I duck into my en suite bathroom a little later that evening, shut the door, and emergency text Chief Troublemaker and Number One Pain in the Ass.

> **Ripley:** I need to talk, stat. For real.
> **Bridget:** I'm on it. My assistant manager just arrived. Give me one minute to go to my office.
> **Chloe:** I just finished a dog bath! I'm ready, wet shirt and all.

A minute later, we're on a three-way video call, Bridget in her tiny office at the inn, Chloe walking down the quiet alley behind the doggie daycare, hair swept up in a high pony.

"Listen," I say, cutting to the chase. "I need to tell you something, and don't be assholes."

Bridget straightens her shoulders. "Us, assholes? Never."

"Shocking that I'd think you might be."

Chloe adopts a robotic voice to match her robotic arm movements. "Anti-asshole mode activated."

I breathe out, then begin my full confession. "That weekend I went to San Francisco with Haven? A month ago?" They nod. "I almost hooked up with Banks."

Two pairs of eyes widen on the phone screen. I go on to explain what went down in painstaking detail. "And I didn't tell you because…I felt stupid. Because…boys suck and all."

"They can," Bridget says, but she's the diplomatic one, so she adds, "And so can girls."

"But we're talking about boys," Chloe points out.

"Fine. They can suck," Bridget acknowledges, tucking a strand of brown hair behind her ear.

"And I thought he was a jerk at first, so when it turned out he was my bodyguard, I was pissed. But he explained why he ran, and I got it. I did. And now it's just…complicated," I say, wincing because this afternoon made everything more complicated again.

To their credit, they don't tease me this time. "Sounds like it," Bridget says thoughtfully.

I release another big breath. This is hard for me. It's so much easier to focus on someone else, but I feel untethered right now. "And then this afternoon when he drove me home—well, there was a dare, and we made out on the side of the road, and blah, blah, blah."

Chloe holds up a hand. "Do not blah, blah, blah the orgasm."

"Wait," Bridget says, with fresh worry in her tone. "Did you not come? Is that why you're calling? I'm sorry he didn't give you an *O*, hon."

"He gave me an *O*," I say, heat racing all over me again as I picture the scene a few hours ago—my hands pinned behind me, Banks controlling my pleasure. "A fantastic one. But we agreed it was a mistake. He has to focus on his job and honestly, so do I. My job being making sure this shoot happens without a problem. But now there's no room at the house, and he's offered to let me stay in the cottage where he's been staying, and I don't know if I can handle it."

Chloe squeals, then quickly rearranges her expression to a more serious one. "Sorry. I'm totally not excited for you. Why do you think you can't handle it?"

Because I pride myself on handling anything and everything, but this is uncharted terrain. "I don't know what to do. Do I stay with him or sleep on the floor or stay with you?" Escape has its appeal—as in, I need an escape from my libido.

"But if you stay with us, he'll be here too. With you," Bridget points out.

"True, true."

"Also, don't you want and need to be at the farmhouse?" Chloe asks, a helpful reminder.

I drop my head in my hand. "I do." Then I draw a deep breath and raise my face. "It's fine. I'm fine. I can handle some weird sexual tension. It's no big deal. We're adults sharing a small space. It happens all the time. It doesn't mean we're going to sleep together. We made a pact."

"Yes, and pacts were made to be broken," Chloe says, then shakes her head. "I meant honored. No-sex pacts were made to be honored."

"Chloe," I warn her.

She tilts her head, giving me a soft and genuine smile. "I'm teasing. But I know you're going to be able to handle this, Ripley. That's what you do. Even if it's hard, you always find a way."

"And I bet it's going to be very, *very* hard," Bridget deadpans.

Narrowing my eyes, I lift a finger. "Hey, you promised you wouldn't be assholes."

Bridget arches a brow. "You were an asshole first. You didn't tell us."

"I guess we're all assholes then, so we're even," I say, leaning against the vanity.

"And call us if you feel like you're about to cave," Chloe offers.

"And you'll give me a pep talk?" I ask, hopeful, grateful for this lifeline.

"Or encourage you to ride his big D," she says.

I growl. "You're definitely assholes."

"And you love us," Bridget says.

"I really do," I say, and I feel better from talking to them. I needed to get that off my chest.

Now that I have, I'm confident I can do this. They're right. I can handle this new level of awkward. I can manage the sexual tension. It won't be a problem at all.

I say goodbye, then leave the bathroom, and I survey my bedroom. Guess it's time to pack an overnight bag for a few—*gulp*—tempting weeks.

There's a knock on the door. I head over and open it, then startle. It's the sexy man I need to resist. And my pulse is surging.

"I came to help you pack," he says, and it's a thoughtful gesture. Like something a boyfriend would do rather than a bodyguard.

But I can't linger on that thought so I say, "Let's do it."

His gaze snaps to my nightstand, and I follow it. The fox he made at Pick Me Up sits atop my paperback. A smile curves his lips, but he says nothing.

I don't either as I drop two books from my nightstand into a canvas bag, then head to the closet and grab my overnight bag—the one I used when I visited my sister in San Francisco last month. I bring it to the bed and unzip it. "I'll grab some clothes and toiletries," I say, then head to the bathroom again to gather some things.

When I return with a bag of lotions and potions, Banks is staring at me like a cat who's just finished eating a very delicious trout.

"What is it?" I ask, unsure what that wicked grin is about.

His gaze drifts to my bag. Inside it is a small box. I left it open when I put the bag away because I didn't want to throw out the contents.

One origami bird.

"You kept that too."

"It's a nice bird," I say defensively.

"It really is." A pause. A nod of his head toward the nightstand. "So's the fox."

"Oh, shut up."

"It's quite a collection."

"Banks," I warn.

"Don't worry. I'll forget all about it," he says, turning my words back on me. But he's smiling, like he's deliciously pleased with the twin discoveries.

I roll my eyes. "I'm sure you'll never let me forget it."

"I see you understand me finally," he says, then helps me pack.

The thing is, I think I do understand him, and I like it too much.

Or him.

CHAPTER 25
ONE-BED-NESS
RIPLEY

B ut I don't make it to the cottage right away because there's too much to deal with on the farm. Finally, after I check off a few more items on my to-do list, but don't finish it, because what even is finishing a to-do list, I close my laptop and set it down on the couch in the living room.

Grandma's back from her day with Daisy and friends, but I play the toilet paper fairy anyway since she's hanging out with Haven. While they catch up, I make sure all the bathrooms are stocked, checking with the guests to see who needs towels and who forgot toothpaste. I've learned the guy with the undercut is Arjun; he's the director of photography, and he's from New Jersey. He forgot floss, so I give him some and then give him points for excellent dental care. I have extras on hand of everything, so next up I give some of my favorite cruelty-free Tom's toothpaste to the bearded, bald guy who said he forgot to bring some. His name is Sam, he's Australian, and he's the AD.

"Thanks so much. Really appreciate this," Sam says, standing in front of his first-floor room as he clutches the tube to his chest like it's a prize.

"Happy brushing."

"I'll be the happiest," he replies, but makes no move to leave.

"Do you need a toothbrush too?"

He taps his chin, his smile a little flirty. "Think I remembered to bring that. I'm good to go, but I'll see if I can forget something else."

Okaaaay.

"Just let me know," I say, keeping it friendly. I point to the kitchen. "I have a few more things to do."

"Have fun," he says.

I return to the kitchen, where Banks is leaning against the counter with one eyebrow raised—he likely saw that interaction. He's finishing takeout from a cardboard bowl, something with kale and sweet potatoes and fresh chicken, as he chats with Wanda and Haven and Grandma.

I pass them, grabbing my laptop from the sofa to finalize one more order for new pruners. They debate the best way to make macarons while Banks straightens up. When I'm done, I say good night to Grandma and Haven.

"Don't stay up too late chatting," I warn, but it's a moot point. They will. They've always been late-night chatters.

"We'll behave," Grandma says with a smirk.

"We'll be sooo good," Haven adds.

Yup, moot point. But there's nothing I can do about it, so I grab my phone and head over to the cottage as the stars flicker in the sky. An antsy feeling chases me as I cross the lawn with Banks. Like we're walking toward the inevitable—the inevitable tension.

Banks opens the door, and I go inside. He brought my shoulder bag and my overnight bag here earlier, and I stop in the doorway. I have never seen the cottage like this.

It's immaculate. The bed is crisply made, each corner of the white comforter smoothed over, and the blue-and-white-striped pillows arranged like the room's going to be featured in a photo shoot.

On the nightstand there's just the lamp and what looks like a black eye mask, folded over. The kind we sell in the little shop.

I pull my gaze away from the bed, taking in the rest of the room I know well as he shuts the door, sealing us into this small space. That restless feeling in me amps up.

The one-room cottage is big enough for a king-size bed, a couch, a coffee table, a small fridge, and a little sink, as well as a bathroom. The couch looks out on the deck overlooking the lavender fields.

On the coffee table across from the dove-gray couch is a paperback—a big book. Stephen King, I think. It sits atop a sleek silver laptop.

That's it.

There's no messy array of items strewn across the wooden tabletop. No T-shirt, no sunglasses, or lip balm, or keys. There's not a banana left there from when someone thought they wanted a snack but never ate. There's no water bottle. We should deal with the sleeping arrangements, but I'm too surprised by the unusually spotless state of the cottage to think about the bigger issue.

"Have you been living here at all?" I ask, confused by the neatness. His suitcase isn't even open. It's closed and placed on the floor by the wardrobe beside the bed. My overnight bag is stacked neatly there too, but I forgot to bring my canvas bag with my books. I'll grab it before bedtime though.

"Yes," he says, his brow pinched, perhaps confused by my question.

I try to explain better. "It's never looked this nice. It's neater than when you arrived."

He drags a hand through his thick hair, then dips his face for a second, maybe embarrassed. When he raises it, he says, "I'm just neat."

"A little," I say, then set my phone on the table. I feel instantly guilty for messing up the table's feng shui.

The neatness is, admittedly, taking my mind off other things. Like the one-bed-ness of it all. One bed against the wall, with a pulse, a heartbeat, and a voice whispering low and smoky, *What are you going to do about me?*

I shift my focus back to Banks. "Is it the military training?" I ask since this is easier than dealing with the voice in my head.

"Probably," he says, then pauses like he's reconsidering. "Maybe."

He doesn't sound evasive so much as uncomfortable, so I say, "Well, I like what you've done with it. It's hardly good enough for me now."

He wrinkles his nose, then groans. "You're a slob, right?"

"No!" I say with over-the-top indignation. But then I wince. "I mean, compared to you, yeah. I'm not like this."

"Admit it. You're a pig. I'll be cleaning up after you."

I arch a brow. "I believe we already established you did that this morning with the coffee cups."

"And I have no regrets," he says, then stage-whispers, "slob."

"Stop it," I say, but the teasing is working. It's defusing some of the obvious tension from the obvious issue. The one we can't avoid much longer. I stroll over to his side of the bed and pick up the lavender mask—a distraction. "You like my store," I tease.

With a one-shouldered shrug, he says, "It's okay."

"Please. It's amazing," I say.

"It is," he says from the other side of the room.

I'm just making small talk. That's all this is. Someone needs to deal with the bed. The space. The problem.

But we're both deathly silent for another long, weighty beat till Banks squares his shoulders. "I'll take the couch."

He is a gentleman in a lot of ways. But there's no way he can sleep on the couch. The sofa's not long. But Banks *is*. "I can take it," I offer.

He shakes his head. "Nope. I'll take it or the floor."

I scoff. "You can't sleep on the floor."

A brow lifts in challenge. "Wanna bet, sweetheart?"

"Sure," I say, squaring my shoulders too.

"Really? You really think I won't sleep on the floor? After the yoga and the pedicure?"

He doesn't mention the other challenge—the *try me* one from earlier. I don't want him sleeping on the floor no matter what, but I know he'd do it to prove a point. He'll be uncomfortable, but he's so tough he won't let on, and he's so stubborn he'll do it. "Fine. You can couch it," I say, sort of giving in, but I prefer to think I'm being strategically nice. "Unless you want to sleep in the gardening shed."

"Would you bring me a pillow and a blanket?"

I cross my arms. "I would."

"Sounds kind of nice," he says, then eyes the couch, lifting one palm, then the other. "Couch? Shed? Shed? Couch?"

It's asked like he's on *Jeopardy!*, and he tilts his head back and forth, weighing the options.

Both are ridiculous. He should just sleep in the bed. It's big enough for two. "Banks," I say, when my phone trills.

I grab it from my back pocket, grateful for the distraction. It's Haven.

"Hey, what's going on?" I ask. "Are you at the hotel already? Want me to virtually tuck you in and read you a book?"

"You know I do."

She used to ask me to do that—read a book to her when we were much younger. She'd say, *I just like hearing the story better than reading it, and you're so good at character voices.*

I wasn't good at character voices. She just liked the company.

"But, no I'm not at the hotel. I'm still at the house and your dog is wandering around here like a lost soul."

"Hudson!" I shriek. "I'll come get him. Also, you need to get to the hotel and get your sleep."

"I will."

I end the call, then meet Banks's eyes. "Can the dog sleep here?"

"Of course."

I rush across the lawn, into the house, and to the living room. Hudson leaps up from the floor, greeting me with the waggiest tail I've ever seen.

"He's been whimpering at the door," Haven says as she stands and stretches, phone and a pair of pink heart-shaped sunglasses in hand. "He *wuvs* you."

I kneel and cup his soft snout. "I *wuv* him too."

He happy-whimpers against my face, then I stand and pat his side. "You can come with me, buddy." Then I turn to her. "Are you taking off?"

She nods. "Just said good night to Grandma and Wanda's at the door." She steps closer and flashes a smile. "She's hilarious. She's like a standup comic. She has the funniest stories about her kids and her wife."

"I'm glad your bodyguard doubles as entertainment," I say.

"Me too."

Before I say goodbye, my gaze strays to the coffee table. Ah, there's the canvas bag with my books, one of which is for Haven. I grab it and reach inside for the one William brought over the other day for her. The cover is light blue with a photo of an inviting beach house overlooking the ocean. *That Summer with You* is the title. "I almost forgot. William brought this over for you when he brought my book," I say, then hand her the paperback.

"Oh fun!"

A note slips out. It's folded in half so I can't see it, but I grab it before it falls to the floor. I hand the cream piece of paper to her, along with the book. "What's up with the note?"

"I bet he marked his favorite pages," she says with a friendly smile.

"Does he normally?" I ask. "And do you normally get books from him?"

"I do. I always try to order from the hometown store. You know how it goes. Support a local business and all. So he leaves notes on his favorite scenes. Such a book guy," she says with a shrug, then takes the note and the book.

I arch a brow. That sounds like more than bookishness. "He probably has a crush on you."

She scoffs. "Doubtful."

"Not doubtful. You're kind of a movie star," I stage-whisper. "Also, look at you. You're gorgeous."

She stares right back at me, then clears her throat. "Ahem. Pot. Kettle. *Literally.*"

"That's not what I meant."

"And speaking of crushes, is your bodyguard hot for you?" she whispers.

A flush spreads like wildfire up my chest. "No," I say immediately. "He just stays close to me."

"That's not what I meant, Ripley."

But I don't want to talk about Banks with her. Because nothing more can happen with him, and she doesn't need to worry about me. She especially doesn't need to play matchmaker when she should be playing Lucy Snow, the heroine in *Someone Else's Ring*.

"Enjoy the book from the *not-crush*," I say.

"Enjoy the cottage with the *not-crush*."

We leave together, with Wanda mentioning that her son thinks there's a dinosaur named Asparagus Rex.

"Honestly, that'd be a good name for a dino," I admit.

"Or a new variety of asparagus," she says.

"I'd eat that asparagus," Haven puts in.

"Just grill it with a little olive oil and it'll be delish," Wanda says as they head to the car.

A few minutes later, Hudson and I are back at the cottage. I knock on the door, and Banks swings it open.

"You didn't follow me to the house," I point out.

"I figured you weren't going to run tonight. Plus, I was holding your origami menagerie hostage."

He's set the bird and the fox on the coffee table. The damning evidence is now home decor. He must have snuck the fox out of my room without me noticing. He is stealthy. I head inside, Hudson trotting behind me, giving a lick hello to his new friend.

In the few minutes I've been gone, Banks has already set a pillow on the couch and spread out the blanket that had been on the foot of the bed.

Shame. I was hoping he'd talked himself into sharing.

The pillows are stacked against the headboard, and I'm under the covers in my cami and sleep shorts, the dog snoozing at my feet,

Banks reading on the couch. He's wearing shorts and a T-shirt, the ink on his arms on full display. His knees are tucked up.

Since he doesn't fit.

I sigh from the bed.

He turns a page.

I flip another page in my book.

He slides a little lower on the couch, knees jutting higher.

I read another page.

He flips to the next one in his book.

I slap my book down on the cover. "This is stupid. If you're not going to sleep with the gardening equipment, just share the bed."

Slowly, he turns his head, meeting my gaze, his lips quirking up. "Is that your way of telling me to hit the shed?"

"No. Just come here. I won't bite."

He puts the book down on the coffee table. "What if I like biting?"

A whoosh of heat rushes through me. "Do you?" I ask in a low voice, then shake my head. I don't want to know. Only because I do want to know. "Forget I asked."

"Okay."

"Banks," I say with a sigh.

"Yes, Ripley?"

"We can handle this," I say.

His stoic expression fades. There's real concern in his eyes. "You think so?"

"Yes," I say, emphatic. "I have faith in us."

With a heavy sigh, he stares back at the couch with disdain. "Good, because this couch sucks."

He grabs his pillow, comes around to the bed, and sets it down. Then he slides under the covers, patting them on his chest.

We're like two sticks in a bed.

I try to come up with a topic to relieve the tension, when he says, "Sam wants you."

I scoff. "He does not."

Banks shifts to his side, giving me a look. "He was checking you out."

"Then he wants Haven too," I say.

His brow knits. "Just because you look alike doesn't mean someone is attracted to both of you."

I know this to be true, but it's rare to hear from someone else. "You think so?"

"Yes. I know so," he says. "Case in point—me."

My chest warms dangerously, so naturally I push back. "But you thought I was Haven the night we met."

"Correction: I thought you were Ripley; then I thought you were Haven pretending to be Ripley. Then I met you again. It was always Ripley I was attracted to."

The temperature in me shoots up. I should leave this topic alone, but I don't. "Glad you're not into both twins."

"I can tell you apart."

"You couldn't at first."

He levels me with a dark gaze. "I can now. I can tell here," he says, tapping his chest. "Only one of you turns me on."

It's official—I'm on fire. I can't even speak.

"And Sam was definitely flirting with you," he says, a little irked.

I can't resist. "Did that bother you?"

The tension in his forehead says it did. The tightness in his jaw is another sign. "What do you think?"

"A little," I say, smiling.

A laugh bursts from him. "You love to fuck with me."

"*You* love to fuck with *me*."

There's a weighted pause, then Banks nods at the book I brought. The cover is midnight blue, with a stark-white serif font for the title. "That bookstore guy brought that for you." There's still some jealousy in his tone.

"I ordered it from his store."

"Does he hand-deliver books to all his customers?"

"He's one of my customers! He has lavender bouquets at the counter in A Likely Story." I take a moment, then add, "And when he brought the book I purchased, he brought one for Haven too. It was marked up with favorite lines and stuff."

"Ah." Banks nods, his shoulders relaxing like that settles that issue for him.

"I guess they're friends," I add. But I don't want to talk about my sister or other guys. I glance around the cottage. "You don't like messes, do you?"

"I hate them," he says, then scrubs a hand through his hair, messing it up—an incongruous move.

"Why?" I ask softly.

"I just like order. I like things the way I like them. I like to be able to control my environment."

Earlier he said the situation with his parents splitting up was messy. That he had to step up. "Is that because there was a time when you couldn't?"

He's quiet at first, then sighs. But it's not a frustrated sound. It's more thoughtful, and so is his gaze as he says, "Definitely. The thing I told you earlier? In your truck?"

"Yes?"

"We had to move. Well, my mom wanted to, as well. But she definitely felt like she had to—to start over."

"That must have been hard."

"It was. For her."

"And for you and your sister."

Silence fills the space, but it's not uncomfortable. It's necessary. He nods. "Yeah, for everyone. Guess that's why I like things the way I like them."

"I won't tease you about being a neat freak then," I say genuinely.

He stares me down. "But if you didn't tease me, maybe I wouldn't know it was you."

There's nowhere for this fizzy feeling to go, so I bottle it up. "What's the eye mask for?"

"Tension," he says with some vulnerability. "I was feeling it the other day.'"

"With me?"

He's quiet for a beat, then sighs and nods. "Yeah. I was."

That makes me happy, but it's a futile happiness. "Did it help?"

"It did." A pause. "Be sure to tell the owner that lavender works."

"I'll let her know," I say, but I don't want him to feel more tense.

He already seems to carry a lot on his shoulders. "Good night, Banks. Don't try to cuddle me while we sleep."

"Don't you try to cuddle me," he fires back.

"I mean it."

"You mean it like a challenge?"

"I dare you not to cuddle me."

After he sheds his shorts, so he's down to boxer briefs and a T-shirt, he flips to his other side, his big back to me. "Done."

We turn off our bedside lamps. The cottage goes dark. Eventually, sometime later, we fall asleep.

I wake to his arms wrapped around me, his breathing steady against my neck, his body unbearably close to mine.

CHAPTER 26
THE BIG EXUBERANT SPOON
BANKS

Mmm, this is nice. Soft, warm skin. Sheets of silky hair. The first rays of sunlight drifting over our bodies. The last remnants of sleep fading away. Before I open my eyes, I drink in this floaty moment one more time. I breathe in—long and leisurely.

Yeah, this is better than nice. She smells like lavender and vanilla, and fresh laundry, and all my dirty dreams. There were a lot of them. A round-the-clock movie house playing in my brain all night long as she snuggled up against me. Wedged her body to mine. Murmured in the dark.

I burrow my face in the crook of her neck and wrap my arms a little tighter around her. This lovely, sexy, feisty woman is in my bed, out here in a cottage, far away from everyone else. Just us.

Except…whoa.

There's a tongue on my face.

Lapping me from chin to cheekbone. Then a rattle of tags, and a needy whimper. A thumping tail, a rustle of sheets, then a quiet, "Good morning."

My eyes fly open.

Fuckity, fuck, fuck, double fuck! I wrench away from Ripley and Hudson. Goddamn bed, goddamn dreams, goddamn hazy morning with this woman too close to me.

"I'll take the dog out," I blurt, then bolt out of bed in my boxer briefs and T-shirt and hustle to the door, the dog at my side, and my…

Great. Just great.

My morning wood is pointing the way.

Ripley chuckles from the bed. "Have fun walking him like that."

"It's fine," I mumble, then spin around and head to my suitcase to grab a pair of workout shorts. I tug them on at the speed of sound as Ripley pushes herself up to her elbows, eyeing me with too much amusement.

"You sure it won't be too hard?" she deadpans. "Walking him and all, I mean?"

"Won't be," I say but my dick is a traitor. He won't stand down. Rude.

"True. If you get lost though, just use your internal compass. Looks like it'll point you back."

I grit my teeth. "Built-in GPS."

"Handy," she says with a smile like she's eating this up. "Just don't bump into anything. You might break it."

"I'll be careful."

"You do that. Flagpoles can be seriously dangerous."

"Thanks for the warning."

I grab the leash from the floor, then open the door. Hudson bounds ahead of me. As he waters a nearby patch of grass, I close my eyes, pretend I'm in yoga class, and find a mantra to deal with this situation.

I am letting go of the things that don't serve me.

Like this annoying erection. Which, finally, after a few deep breaths, settles the fuck down.

With that matter settled, I leash up the dog and take him for a walk around the property, passing the maze that looks perfect for kids to play in. "You like that maze?"

He pants.

"Bet you know it perfectly," I say.

As we walk, I flash back to last night in bed with Ripley. Sometime in the middle of the night, I must have curled up next to her. Tugged her close. Held her tight. An image flickers before my eyes. Me roping an arm around her stomach. Her wriggling near to me, her sweet ass pressed against my dick.

I groan audibly as I replay the moment. We can't keep cuddling each other in our sleep. Cuddling leads to morning wood that needs to be talked down.

I'll apologize to Ripley when I return, and we'll agree to move on. I'll do better tonight. Hell, that shed sounds good right about now.

I reach for my phone to turn on some Brahms to distract me but come up empty in my pocket. Right. I'm the idiot who ran out the door without a phone, without even brushing my teeth.

Gross. Morning breath sucks. I hope I don't run into anyone I need to talk to.

Like I've summoned her, there's Tabitha coming my way wearing a baseball cap, a tank top, and a pair of running shorts. She's racing toward me, arms tucked by her sides in a runner's stride, legs moving fast. When she nears me, she slows and pops out an earbud. "How's it going, Banks? Did you sleep well?"

Like I was in an OnlyFans waiting room all night long. "Great," I say, making sure I don't expose my dragon breath to her.

With a deep sigh, she glances around, gesturing to the long country road stretching in front of her, then to the violet blooms forming a blanket across the property beside me. "I haven't slept that well in ages. It must be the quiet out here in a small town. Not a single siren, or argument on the street, or even traffic at three in the morning. You know how it is in Los Angeles. There's always traffic."

"Sure is," I say.

She points toward the fields just past me. "That's pretty, whatever it is."

"Grosso," I say immediately.

She shoots me a quizzical look. "You know the kind of lavender?"

"Well, I've been here a few days," I say, nonchalant. "I picked up a few things."

Which is true, but I also researched varieties of lavender after Ripley said these were one of her customers' favorites. I was curious. Or, okay, fine. Maybe I wanted to know more about Ripley and her business. "It's used for drying and in cooking," I add.

An eyebrow arches. "Well, if a scene calls for a lavender expert and I can't find Ripley, I'll look for you."

Note to self: shut the fuck up. I don't want to let on to the producer that I'm too interested in all things related to my client.

"I was just...curious," I add. I can't follow my own orders this morning. Jesus, if sleeping next to a beautiful woman turns me into a blabbermouth, that shed is looking better by the minute. "Anyway," I say, suddenly at a loss for words.

Tabitha's wristwatch beeps a warning, and she snaps her gaze to it, then closes the alert.

"I'd ask about the other varieties, but I'll lose my cardio bennies if I don't take off," she says, tapping her device.

"Don't want to lose those bennies. Have a good run," I say.

She gives a wave, then trots off.

Relieved to see her go, I circle the farm, giving the dog a chance to stretch his morning legs and myself some space from an unexpectedly spoon-y kind of night.

Fifteen or so minutes later, I return to the cottage, the dog bounding to the door. As I follow, I review the plan. I'll apologize for my overexuberant spooning, and then we'll move on. At least I have the day off, since Marcus, one of my backups, will look out for Ripley. The space will be good. Hell, it's necessary.

I jerk open the door and Hudson rushes inside, racing to his favorite person, who's coming around the corner from the bathroom.

She's wearing only a towel cinched around her breasts and coming down to her midthighs. Her wet hair is sleek against her shoulders, and a drop of water slides down her chest between the valley of her breasts.

So much for the disappearance of my hard-on.

"Oh. I just got out of the shower," she says, a little flustered.

"I figured as much," I say dryly. Mostly to cover up the heat flaring in my bones.

"I'll get out of your way." She gestures to the bathroom.

I shake my head, waving to the door I just walked through. "No, I'll get out of your way."

"Banks, I really don't want to put you out. You're my guest. Let me grab my clothes and I'll change in there." She scurries over to her suitcase, and I stand stock-still by the door. If I leave, I'll look like I can't handle this close proximity.

If I can't handle this, I can't handle the job. I'm only three days in. I've got to get a handle on this…lust.

"Yeah, no problem," I say, all cool and casual as I finally move, heading to the couch, looking elsewhere. Looking anywhere but at Ripley. Even when she walks past me again, clutching some clothes to her chest. Those lucky clothes.

Fine, I looked.

Once she's snicked the door shut to the bathroom, I sink down on the couch, drop my head in my hands, and sigh heavily. "How the hell am I going to make it through the next few weeks?"

The universe doesn't answer. Nor do I.

A couple minutes later, she emerges, fresh-faced and dressed in a…*kill me now.*

She's wearing a sundress.

Also known as the world's most appealing item of clothing a woman can wear. It's peach and it swishes against her tanned legs, with little straps that hug her bare shoulders.

"Thanks for taking out the dog," she says, then heads to the coffeepot, waggling it. "Want coffee?"

"Always," I say, and as she brews it, I dart into the bathroom to brush my teeth. As I brush, I check out the vanity. She's set a few items on it—a vanilla and lavender body mist, a lotion that purportedly smells like satsuma oranges, a small makeup bag with cartoon dogs on it and the words *Sorry I'm late, I saw a dog*, then a toothbrush.

She's placed them all neatly on the counter next to my aftershave and deodorant. Their organization is a contrast to how she had them arranged on her own bathroom counter yesterday when she scooped them all up and stuffed them into her overnight bag.

In the shower, she's set down lavender shampoo. Ah, that explains her twin scents—the lavender is in her hair. The citrus on her body.

When I finish brushing and return to the tiny space we're sharing, my gaze lands on the coffee table. She's set a small vase of lavender there, next to the origami bird and fox. There are stacks of brown paper next to it, along with some ribbon. But the flowers catch my eye the most.

"Is that Provence?" I ask as she hands me a mug of hot coffee.

A smile spreads like pure delight on her face. "How did you know?"

"I looked up lavender the other night," I admit, taking a drink of the morning brew. She does the same with her coffee. When I set down the cup, I lift the vase and sniff the flowers.

"I just grabbed some this morning when you were out. And—spoiler alert: I'm turning this cottage into a workshop today. I need to prep some big bundles of flowers for an event at the art museum this afternoon. But don't worry. Your replacement will take me, and I'll clean up everything here in the room before I go. I just thought a vase would be nice in here."

They're a homey touch. A thoughtful one. Like her.

"They are," I say, inhaling the perfume-y scent, then meeting her eyes and taking a beat before I say, "They're quite pretty."

She holds my gaze for a few seconds, then looks down at the flowers. "I love this one," she says with a contented sigh.

"Is it your favorite?"

She shakes her head. "No, Melissa is."

That name tickles my brain. "Your password?"

"Yes."

"I thought it was your mom's name," I say, intrigued.

"Her name was Sydney. My dad's name was Henry. I just always liked Melissa the best. My mom used to cut bouquets of it and put them in my room and Haven's," she says as she takes another inhale, closing her eyes, looking a little lost in a memory. A fond one it seems, but a sad one too.

I want to hug her, but I'm not sure it would lead anywhere good. When she opens her eyes, I say, "I'm sorry about this morning."

"What do you mean?"

I scrub a hand along my neck. "I got a little too cuddly in bed."

She rolls her eyes. "We survived."

Barely. At least, I barely survived. "True," I say, then take another drink of the coffee as I swing my gaze to her bare arms. I can't help myself. With my free hand, I run my fingers down her sparrows, watching as goose bumps rise. "Why do you have a flock of birds on your arm and Haven has only one?"

"We got them together. Here in town. When we turned eighteen. We both really wanted tattoos, but she wanted to be an actress too, so she didn't want too many. As for me, I wanted something that represented freedom and a happy life," she says, a little sad, but a little hopeful too. "It was my greatest dream after my parents died. Especially since it was even harder for Haven."

"Their death?"

"Yes," she says.

"Why?"

"I don't know. Some people just grieve differently. So I tried to help her through the dark days. She had a lot of them, and I tried to take care of her." Some people do grieve differently, but I suspect Ripley was resilient in ways she had to be. "And Haven wanted something that matched mine, so she got one," she adds.

"They're beautiful," I say, my voice a little hoarse as I stare too long at the lovely ink on her arm.

"Thanks," she says, then nods to my tattoos—the visible ones, at least. Geometric circles and shapes along my right biceps. "And yours?"

It's natural she'd ask. And while I don't often share personal stuff, we're not going to sleep together. I'm not going to touch her again. I swear I'm not. The least I can do is be friendly with my client. Be open. She deserves it, and hell, it'll make it easier for us to work together. So as she runs her finger over the lines on my arm, I answer her, meeting her blue eyes. "The triangles are for ambition, growth, and moving on. Like we all—my mom, sister, and I—had to move on when my parents split up."

She nods, her gaze thoughtful, open. "I can see that."

I point to the squares they intersect with. "Those are for a new foundation."

"After that?" she asks.

"Yes," I say, then take her hand and set it on a hexagon. "This is for balance."

She spreads her palm, warm and steady, over it, curling it around my arm. "They're beautiful too. I love that they mean something important to you."

"They do," I say, voice strained, heart beating faster, enjoying her touch too much. "Like I said, it was a real mess when my dad left. We couldn't stay in town." My gut twists. That's enough. I take a steadying breath. "Since I have the day off, I'm going to see my mom and Emily for lunch."

"Nice," she says, and I'm almost tempted to invite her.

I nod toward the bathroom instead. "I get a little wound up about things being neat. I'll try not to be an ass about it though."

"I can be neat," she says.

"I saw that you were. And I appreciate it." I hesitate, not wanting to break the moment. But I should. "I need to…shower."

"Oh. Of course. Let me just grab my makeup bag."

"Sure."

She rushes into the bathroom, and I quickly straighten up the table. When she comes out, her gaze strays to it. "Banks. You didn't have to."

I shrug. "I know. I wanted to help."

"Thank you."

Then, so I don't take her into my arms and kiss her like it's all I'm thinking about, I head to the shower.

I take a speedy one and head off, needing the space so I can make it through another night with her in the same bed.

CHAPTER 27
THE DIFFERENCE BETWEEN *SHOULD* AND *WILL*
BANKS

Later that morning, as I walk along the Sausalito streets to meet Mom and Emily for lunch, I try not to relive every moment of that conversation with Ripley or the way her finger traced the intricate lines of my tattoos. Did that already on the drive down. But still, a mixture of longing and guilt rushes through me. I do my best to shove it aside when I reach the café overlooking the clear blue waters of Richardson Bay.

As I open the door to the café, I try to reset. Best to focus on family today, and when I return, to somehow keep my distance from Ripley, who's become more than a client.

And that's a big problem.

Especially since I'm sharing a bed with her that isn't big enough for me and my desire.

But now it's time for salad and chicken sandwiches, since this place has the best. Walking into Gigi's Café—named after the owner's dog, Gigi McDoodle—I find Mom right away, her curly hair framing her face, her smile as warm as ever. She's earlier than I am. No surprise since she hates surprises. She'd had enough of those. After setting down her phone, where no doubt she was texting with her girlfriends, she hops up quickly, and I give her a big hug.

"So good to see you. You need a haircut," she says, then ruffles my hair.

"Maybe I do."

"Or maybe your new girlfriend likes it messy?" Mom asks with a lift of an eyebrow when she lets go.

"One, I know that was your not-so-subtle way of asking me if I have a girlfriend. And two, I do not," I say.

"Can't fault a mom for trying."

Emily joins us a few minutes later at the small table on the deck, and after we order, the conversation immediately turns to me again.

"So, spill the tea. I heard the crew arrived yesterday," Emily says, parking her chin in her hand, her eager eyes ready to eat up any details I can serve.

"They did," I say.

She huffs. "Tell me something. Anything. What is New Chris like? Is Haven as cool as she seems? And was she buying flowers for him at the grocery store the other day?"

"Emily," Mom chides.

I shake my head. "No, she wasn't, and that wasn't Haven," I say, a little frustrated. "That was her sister, Ripley."

"Oh," Emily says, frowning. Then she seems to refocus. "Still... how's Chris?"

"I wouldn't know," I say, then give her a stern look. "And it's bad to feed bread to ducks. Like you."

She rolls her eyes.

"And you think the job will help you get more work?" Mom asks, diverting.

"Definitely," I say. "Dean and I have some inquiries, and we're putting together proposals for new jobs. Which means," I say, nodding toward my troublemaking sister, "we can put more aside in the retirement fund we started for you."

"Banks," she says gently. "You don't need to do that. I do have one, and it's fine."

"I know, but we want to," I say.

"We do, Mom," Emily seconds.

"You don't have to," Mom says, but her throat tightens.

She's a physical therapist, and while she's had a steady job her whole life, her life and her finances were upended by my father's lies years ago, when she took time off. Emily and I want to do what we can for her because she did everything for us.

"It's the least we can do," I say.

Mom shakes her head, like she's exonerating us from supporting her. "No, all I want is for you two to be happy and to be good people, so I have everything I could want," she says, then pats my hand. "Now tell us about your client."

"And ideally your woman problems," Emily adds, batting her lashes like the troublemaker she is.

But I love her madly.

And it's clear Mom is done with the attention. "It's good. It's all great," I say, since it will be. Truly it will be. Even if I have to sleep on the floor.

Which I will.

Probably.

After lunch, we wander through the touristy city, and when Mom pops into a shop selling cute aprons and cooking utensils, coasters, mugs, and little trays with irreverent sayings on them, Emily touches my arm and pulls me aside by a coaster with the words *A fun thing to do in the morning is not talk to me.*

"Things are going well with Brandon," she says, a cautious sort of optimism in her tone as she nods toward Mom, who's checking out the counter displays. "She took him to a co-worker's birthday party the other night."

"That's promising."

"Seems that way."

Emily's eyes dart around; then she says, "You don't think she'd…"

A throat clears. "Marry again?"

It's my mom, and she must have heard us talking about her boyfriend.

Emily smiles like *oops*. "Um, yeah."

Mom pats Emily's shoulder. "I'm not sure I want or need to. But Brandon is a nice guy and he's honest, so that seems enough for now."

Enough for now.

Sometimes that's all you can hope for.

I don't go back to the farm right away. I pop into Mister Fox, the Darling Springs watering hole—the non-fancy-pants one.

It's a standard-order bar, with pool tables, rock music, and wooden counters that reek of beer and stories.

"What can I get for you?" the guy behind the counter asks. "The usual?"

It's the owner, a guy named, well, Fox. Met him when I was first in town a year or so ago while passing through on the way to another job.

I shake my head. "Just an iced tea."

He nods knowingly. "It's that kind of night?"

"I suppose it is," I say, feeling a little contemplative after that time with Mom and Emily.

"I got you," he says, then fills a glass and slides it to me, gesturing to a pool table. "The good doc is in town."

I turn around, spotting Monroe, the guy I met on my last trip here—and who Ripley evidently knows too. Or she knows his wife, anyhow.

Will everything remind me of her?

I shake the thought away and focus on my friend, who's not here with his wife tonight, but with a friend. When Monroe catches my gaze, he waves me over and I join the two of them. Monroe makes a quick intro to the dark-haired guy next to him, who's wearing a button-down shirt like he had business meetings then came straight here. "This is Sawyer. He's *maybe* moving to town," Monroe says of his friend.

"That so?" I ask as I shake Sawyer's hand.

"It's a definite maybe," he says dryly.

"Hope that *maybe* is for all the right reasons," I say.

"I've been checking out property for my business expansion, so we'll see. It's not a bad place," Sawyer adds, then frowns. "I've got some stuff to figure out though."

And the way he says that—heavily, but thoughtfully too—makes me think it's romantic stuff to figure out.

"Who doesn't?"

"Truth," Monroe seconds, then hands me a pool cue.

I take it and issue a warning when it's my turn. "Be prepared for me to lock this game up."

Monroe rolls his eyes. "Yeah, right."

I point my cue at him. "Fighting words from a guy who apparently owns a place called The Horny House."

Monroe gives a laid-back shrug. "Don't be jealous."

But I'm not. His words remind me I've got my own horny problems in a cottage less than ten minutes away.

"Let's just play pool," I mutter, and I give it my all, sinking every ball, then flashing a cocky smile.

Sawyer looks to Monroe, like *what gives*. "Thanks for the warning that we've got a pool shark in the house. Why the hell are we playing with him?"

Monroe lifts his glass of scotch. "Don't worry. Banks once told me he only ever comes in here when he's working through some shit in his head. Which means he'll be off his game in no time."

"Hey! I take issue with that," I say.

Monroe points the cue to me. "Speaking of—what's the issue?"

I huff.

"There's definitely an issue then," Sawyer adds with a smirk.

I sigh, then shrug. "There's this woman. And I can't get her out of my head."

"Talk to us," Monroe says.

I do, giving them the bare minimum; then I say, "I really should resist her."

"You should," Sawyer says. "But *should* and *will* are two entirely different things."

They are, and they're probably the reason I do lose the next couple games.

When I'm back at the cottage that night, and Ripley's sliding into bed in a tank top, the difference between the two feels worlds apart.

I don't bother with my earlier plan to sleep on the floor. Or the couch. I go straight to the bed and grab a sheet of white paper from the inside of my tablet, which is set on the nightstand. I lie down on the covers, with her under them; then I start folding the paper as her dog curls into a ball at the foot of the bed.

Ripley sets down the thriller she's reading and nods to the paper in my hand. "Do you need to relax?"

I need to not touch her. I need to resist her. I need to find the line between *should* and *will*, so I don't cross it. This paper is it. "Mostly I need a distraction," I grit out.

She's quiet for a beat, then says, "Me too. Teach me origami."

"Now?"

"Why not? You're awake. I'm awake. Can't think of anything else we could be doing at night."

It's said dryly. A clear acknowledgment.

For a hot second, I meet her gaze. Bright, glittering, and full of memories of yesterday. Her words from that afternoon echo in my mind. *I've already forgotten all about it.*

They're a beautiful lie. She hasn't. I haven't. So I do the next best thing. I give her the paper so I can show her how to make a dog. "Make a triangle so there's a crease down the middle," I tell her.

She makes that move, then waits.

"Now fold the bottom point to the middle crease," I say.

"Like this?" she asks when she's done it.

"Yes. Do that till it's a diamond shape. Now you're going to turn it and repeat it," I say, but her brow knits, and she pauses, clearly unsure where to turn it.

With a shrug and a laugh, she says, "Help."

I slide closer, the distance between us shrinking. But at least there's a comforter here separating her from me. This blanket is doing a lot of work in this room tonight. "Like this," I say, then cover her hands.

Her breath hitches. My pulse surges.

We go quiet as I move her fingers, flipping over the shape. "Turn it so the largest diamond is on top and the smallest points toward you," I say.

She complies, then looks at me with wide eyes that spark with anticipation. She lifts her chin, like she's waiting for an order. Images flicker temptingly before my eyes in the stretched-out silence till she asks, "What do I do now?"

I swallow roughly, fighting off the desire building strength and steam inside me. Expanding, shoving all the *should*s further away.

But still, I curl my fingers over hers. "Now, open the triangle and fold along the crease to create a new shape. Press down. That'll help," I rasp out as she works on a clean, strong fold with my hands guiding hers.

The faint scent of satsuma oranges drifts past my nose. Her lotion? Yeah, I think so. She must have taken a shower tonight. I draw a furtive inhale, catching more of that heady, intoxicating scent. From lavender to oranges, whatever she wears does me in.

"How's this?"

Focus, man. Focus on the origami dog. She's showing me the paper, and I have to blink away my thoughts and check her progress.

I stare down at our creation, at the way the paper becomes something new in our hands. Something other than what it was minutes ago.

It was a flat, two-dimensional thing. Now it's evolved, and sure, it's chaste enough, making origami. But as I slide my thumb over the space between her thumb and her forefinger, this craft is not so chaste anymore.

Not when a gust of breath crosses her pretty lips.

Not when her chest flushes.

Not when a tremble runs down her body.

And not when my body is made of lava, and it's melting my will right into the ocean.

"Like that?" she asks, her voice feathery.

I coast my thumb along her finger, slow and sensual, taking my time, then spreading my right hand over hers. All my fingers cover hers, then curl over them.

"Just like that," I say as our gazes lock.

The air between us crackles. An electric charge sparks and sizzles. Her dog must sense it too, since he jumps off the bed, settling in on the floor.

What a wingman.

"What do I do next?" she asks, and we're not looking at the paper in our hands.

I don't say a word for several weighty seconds. I just flip through possibilities. Choices. Consequences. Then, fuck origami. "You take the paper, toss it, and tell me to pin you to the bed and kiss you like it's all I've thought about all day long, every single goddamn second."

She crumples it into a ball and tosses it over her shoulder. "Take me."

CHAPTER 28
A LOVE BITE
RIPLEY

Banks pins me down in a flash, my arms above my head, my wrists in his hands, his body covering mine. There's a duvet between us, but I can feel him, thick, hard, insistent between my thighs.

His chest, strong and sturdy against me.

His stubble, scratchy and just the right amount of whiskery, against my face as he seals his mouth to mine in the world's most necessary kiss.

It hardly feels like it was only yesterday afternoon when we kissed feverishly on the side of the road. That seems like ages ago. Like it's taken Herculean strength to get through the last day and a half since we touched.

His teeth are hard against my lips. His hands wind around my wrists. His hips roll into mine.

And I melt into the kiss. I melt into the bed. Into the moment where I'm trapped under him. I'm arching my hips, frantically seeking friction, seeking heat. With each dizzying kiss, I grow hotter, needier.

His hands grip tighter as his kisses turn more passionate. I drown in them willingly as his mouth explores mine, and my body begs for him.

Getting closer to him is a terrible risk. Touching like this is a bad idea. It will only cause problems during the movie shoot. Yet this insistent ache thrumming in my bones has grabbed hold of all my senses. It's owning my body and my voice.

When he breaks the kiss and catches his breath, I say the only words I can manage. "I want you. Please."

His eyes squeeze shut. His jaw clenches. He's still for a few dangerously long seconds, like this is the tipping point. But when he opens those deep, dark eyes, he's clearly lost too—to this feeling.

"I can't stop thinking about you." He lets go of one of my wrists and grabs my chin, making sure I'm looking at him. As if I could look away. "I can't stop wanting you. Tell me you feel the same."

It's a demand, but it's more like a desperate plea. "Same," I say, reaching for him with my body.

He lets go of my other wrist, moves like a cheetah off me, and yanks the covers off too. Then he climbs back over me, our hips flush. This time I wrap my arms around his neck, tugging him close.

He finds the pulse at the base of my throat and kisses me there. I arch, moaning as wicked sensations radiate through me from my core all the way to my toes.

His mouth skims over my neck; then he moves down my chest, kissing me here, there, everywhere—my shoulders, the tops of my breasts, my arms.

He tugs at my cami. "Need this off."

In a flash it's gone, and his mouth comes down on my right breast, his teeth grazing my nipple.

"God," I gasp, my fingers lacing through his thick, messy hair. I want to hold on to this hair. Grab it hard as he goes down on me. I want to rake my fingers through it as he fucks me. But I want something else first.

As the idea takes shape in my head, Banks travels down my body till his mouth is on my stomach and he's lighting me up with hungry, needy kisses. "Need to taste you before I fuck you."

That sounds amazing. Truly, it does. But first, I push up to my elbows, breathing hard, frantically. "There's something I want."

He stops, his eyes blazing with heat. "What is it, Ripley?"

My gaze strays to his hands. "You're good with your hands," I begin, then swallow, my desire spreading like liquid inside me.

A vein pulses in his neck. "I am."

I picture yesterday in the front seat of the truck. How he held me. "Do you want me to…?" This shouldn't be hard to say, and truly, it's not. But I'm taking my time since I'm loving his reaction. The anticipation in his irises. The quiet gust of his breath. The rise and fall of his chest. My gaze drifts up toward the slats of the headboard. "…Hold on to the headboard?"

His eyes darken and he licks his lips. But he's quiet for a beat, like the thought is almost too much to bear. Like he needs time to process. Or maybe not too much time, since a second later, one word flies out of his mouth. "Yes."

"Great. That's great. Really. Because yesterday in the car…when you held my wrists…that was good. Really good. I liked it." I'm talking too much. Too fast. Too pointlessly. But I can't stop. "It seemed like you did too."

I'm babbling. Holy fuck. I'm definitely babbling. But I want this so much, even though he's already said yes.

"Fucking loved it." Banks's smile is filthy as he grabs the waistband of my panties, then tugs them off. "But first, I really need to taste you."

He spreads my legs and buries his face between my thighs. He eats me like I'm the meal he desperately needs at the end of the day. There's no hesitation, no teasing, just a hungry man craving sustenance. In no time, I'm grabbing his hair and jerking him close. Panting and gasping.

Lifting my hips.

Pleading.

Wanting.

But when my breath comes faster, he stops, denying me. Then rises. Wipes a hand across his mouth. "Patience," he says, smooth and controlling. *Patience*, like he said to me the first night.

"Goddamn you," I mutter as he moves to the edge of the bed.

"That's right. Curse me, sweetheart. You know I like it."

"You're really going to make me wait?"

"Yes, I'm going to make you wait. And beg. And call my name."

I grab a pillow and throw it at him as he walks to the table. "You jackass, Banks."

He tosses me a smug smile. "I was right. You called my name."

"You're the worst," I mutter, feeling a little silly since I'm naked in bed, and wet and horny.

And yet I'm totally intrigued as he pops out of bed. He's still dressed in a gray T-shirt and shorts. They're tented beyond my wildest dreams. The compass of his erection is bigger than it was this morning, I swear.

He strides across the room to the vase and snags a sprig of Provence lavender. When he returns to me, he runs a big hand down my hair, a tender, caring gesture. "I promise I'll give you everything you asked for."

Heat sparks in me from the promise. He drops his mouth to my ear, tugs on the lobe with his teeth. "But let me try something first."

Anticipation rushes through as I nod against him. "Anything."

He rises up, holding the lavender, then lowering the flower end to my neck. He coasts the tiny blooms down the side of my throat. I gasp. He sweeps it along my collarbone. I moan. Then he slowly, deliciously, dusts it down my chest, between my breasts, and along my belly.

I shudder as wild sensations whip through me. This man is touching me in brand-new ways. In ways I never dreamed of. He's turning me on with my own flowers, and as he travels down my legs, tracing my thighs, my calves, my ankles with the lavender buds, I grow hotter, needier, and more aroused.

"Banks, please," I gasp as he brushes the flowers back up me, then over my belly button.

"Please what?" he asks, innocently.

I can't even taunt him, I'm so needy right now. So achy. "Now. I want you *now*."

With a wicked smile, he tosses the lavender onto the nightstand. "I thought you'd never ask."

I roll my eyes. "Yes, I've been the one holding out."

He runs the back of his knuckles against my cheek. "You're even sexier like this. When you want it more. When you're hungrier for my cock every single second."

My breath comes in a rush. "Then, stop taking so long."

But he doesn't match my tease. His expression is serious. Seconds later, my arms are above my head, and my hands are gripping the slats. "Don't let go," he says, a warning.

"I won't."

He runs his palms down my body. I'm spread out before him.

Correction: he's spreading me out.

He's kneeling between my legs, adjusting my hips, then he slides down between my thighs, pressing them open. An appreciative rumble falls from his lips. I smile in heady anticipation, waiting for his next move. And he makes it as he reaches a hand to the back of his shirt, then tugs it off. "Now, where were we?"

I roll my eyes. "Gee, I wonder."

"If memory serves," he says, and right when I think he's going to slide between my thighs again, he straddles me instead. He pushes down his shorts halfway, runs his palm over his hard cock, then shoves his shorts down, his dick springing free.

It's hard, thick, and hungry for me, with a drop of liquid beading at the tip.

My mouth waters. "Please," I breathe out hard, staring at his cock, then his hungry eyes.

"Love the way you beg for it," he says, then climbs off me, sheds his shorts, and grabs a condom from the nightstand.

"Did you just have those handy?"

"Bought them today," he says.

"So you knew?" I ask as he moves over me again.

"That I couldn't resist you?"

"Yes."

He sets a hand on my chest, then coasts it down my body. "Sweetheart, I've never been able to resist you."

"Same," I say with a shudder.

After he rolls on the protection, he kneels between my thighs and pushes up my legs so my knees are at my chest. I'm not trapped now. I'm not bound. But the vulnerability of this position is all new to me. And it's strangely freeing. From my mind, from my to-do list, from my constant need to take care of everything.

I can't take care of anything right now.

When he nudges the head of his thick cock against my wetness, a breath shudders through my whole body. All my instincts tell me to move, to wrap my arms around him, to thread my hands in his hair.

But I don't let go.

I don't want to do a thing but take him. He grips my hips and pushes in. His eyes are blazing with desire, and they stay locked on my face as he sinks into me more, inch by tantalizing inch.

Till I'm so full I feel stretched.

"Beautiful," he murmurs, inhaling a big breath that seems to spread across his chest as he gazes at me with lust and reverence.

I tremble, then ask, "Because my hands are above my head?"

He shakes his head. "No. You. Just you. Like this. With me."

On his knees, he tugs my hips tighter against him and fucks me. He's not gentle. He's not tender. He fucks me like a man who craves control. Driving into me. Reaching the depths of me.

Pleasure rockets through me as I sink into the sensations. But I'm dying to touch him too. Only, I'm not letting go yet. I like this too much. Banks's hungry gaze snaps to my hands gripping the headboard, then to my face. He growls, then looks back at me with even more heat in his eyes.

"Want more, sweetheart?"

"Yes. All of you." It's a desperate demand.

He eases out, almost all the way. His lips curve up. "You sure?"

"Fuck me," I demand.

His dark eyes drift to my hands. "Beg for it." It's said offhand, almost casual. Like he knows I will.

"You cocky ass," I mutter.

A wicked smile. A slide of his hands up my belly. A squeeze of my nipple. "C'mon. You can do it, Ripley."

I seethe. "Fuck me," I murmur.

He lifts his chin, almost in idle curiosity. "How? How do you want me to fuck you?" His hands cup my breasts as he stays like that, barely inside me.

Making me ache for him.

And I do ache.

Desperately.

"Hard. Fuck me hard. Please. Do it now," I say, and I'm begging, but I'm still me, so I add, "you ass."

With a glint in his eyes, he says, "Since you begged so nicely, sweetheart. But…"

"But what?" I ask, desperate.

His gaze turns needy, as he says, "Let go. Put your hands around my neck, sweetheart. I want to feel you closer."

A blast of pleasure surges through me. Hot, electric, wild. But emotional too, in its own way. Turns out I want to touch him as much as he wants me to. I let go and loop my arms around him, my fingers twisting into his hair instantly.

He groans. Shudders.

I smile, savoring this discovery. Banks loves when I play with his hair. I twine my fingers in those thick strands, running them through his hair as he thrusts deep into me, filling me till there's no room left, then pulling back so the head of his cock teases me.

But I'm racing faster to the edge as he takes me apart, until I'm panting, writhing, then well and truly begging.

His control seems to fray as he drives into me, one hand on my hip, the other sliding between my legs. His thumb teases my clit, and I'm nothing but raw nerves and dirty desires as my bodyguard takes me to the edge of pleasure.

My legs shake. My body tightens. With one powerful thrust, he sends me over.

I'm spinning into bliss, my thoughts breaking apart, my world turning beautifully black as I cry out. He covers me as he drives into me, like he's making sure I feel all of him as I fall apart.

With a deep grunt, he tenses, then groans, coming too, helpless to the pleasure, helpless to me, when he murmurs, "Yes, fuck yes."

A few seconds later, he's saying my name, faint but full of need. "Ripley."

For a minute or ten, who even knows, we gasp and pant together—his body on mine, me under him, my legs wrapped around his waist, my arms wrapped loosely around his neck.

At last, he pushes up on his palms and looks down at me with passion in his eyes. "Thank you."

He eases out, ties off the condom, then pads to the bathroom. He's back seconds later, lying next to me. He takes my palm and kisses my wrist. "You're good with your hands too."

I laugh.

He meets my gaze, shooting me a deadpan look. "Laugh at me when I'm being sweet. Thanks, Ripley."

"Like you'd expect anything less," I tease.

"Yup. That's how I know you're not an imposter. But also for *that*, I think you need this…"

He brings my wrist to his mouth, giving me the swooniest wrist kiss in the world. It's so tender, it makes me gasp softly. That seems to spur him on since he travels up my arm, across my birds, to my neck. I'm murmuring the whole time. Until the fucker chases kisses with a loud, boisterous suck on my neck.

"What the…?"

He pulls back, grinning slyly. "You deserve a hickey."

I swat his chest. "That's so high school."

He narrows his eyes. "Did I fuck you like we're in high school?"

I huff, then grumble, "No." I'm not really mad at him though. Because, once I grab my phone to inspect the mark on my neck using the selfie mode of the camera, I find I like it. I sigh, then say, "Fine. I like the love bite."

He presses a soft kiss to my forehead. "Thought you might."

We're quiet for a few moments, the levity fading, till we're left with reality. The two of us working together. "We were just getting that out of our systems, right?"

"Of course."

"Tomorrow, we go back to…?"

"Yes. We do."

But tonight, he curls around me in bed after he kisses my wrist one more time.

CHAPTER 29
FORGETTING ALL ABOUT IT
RIPLEY

No one's in the cottage when I wake on Monday morning. Not even my dog.

Where is Hudson? I fling off the covers and pad to the windows overlooking the deck, peering out.

In the distance, I spot Banks walking Hudson around the farm.

When I look down, the dog's food bowl is empty. Last night I had measured out his kibble for the morning and set it on the counter. Banks already fed my dog and is walking him now. I didn't even have to ask him to.

A stupid smile tugs at my lips as I get in the shower and savor the hot stream. When I dry off and exit the bathroom, there's a vase of fresh-cut Melissa on the table across from the couch. Sometimes lavender's a sex toy with Banks, sometimes a gift.

My smile is even stupider as I get dressed. It's summer, but sometimes a girl just has to wear a turtleneck. Well, a short-sleeve mock turtleneck, but it's the only summery top I own that'll cover up the very obvious hickey on my neck. And I am not going to parade around town and reveal a love bite from my bodyguard to the world, or my sister.

A few minutes later, Grandma lifts a curious brow when I sail into the kitchen in the farmhouse in my *cover-up clothes*. "It's going to be hot out today," she says, giving me a once-over.

I pluck at the blue shirt, trying to make this odd fashion choice seem like no big deal. "It's laundry day."

And that's believable enough, even though it's a bald-faced lie. I do laundry often enough that I rarely have laundry-day problems.

Her brow knits, but she shrugs, buying my excuse. "Don't say I didn't warn you when you're sweating."

"I won't curse you when I melt on the streets of Darling Springs today," I say, but then I gesture to my shorts. "I'll be fine. Plus, I have a lot of flowers to deliver, so this way my arms won't get as scratched up."

Her brows arch higher.

Oops.

The more you say, the more obvious it is you're hiding something. Like a short-sleeve shirt will save me from scratches. "Let me help you with coffee and stuff for the crew," I say, trying to steer the conversation anywhere else. But seriously, the hard time she'll give me for a hickey. I still remember when Haven was seventeen and came home with a purple splotch on her neck, then tried to finesse her way out of it with a tale about a new moisturizer she'd picked up from The Slippery Dipper, and how eager she'd been to try it out as part of this amazing new skin care routine, but oh my god can you believe it left *this purple mark*?

We teased her for days about her allegedly amazing skin care routine.

"I made croissants too," she adds, then taps me on the nose. "Because—"

We both pause, like, *wait for it*, then say in unison, "Muffins suck."

"Seriously, muffins should be abolished," I add, grateful we've moved on to baked goods and away from my cover-up-a-silly-punishment-for-my-sass attire.

As I help her in the kitchen, images of last night flicker before my eyes, and my stomach flips. I really need to stop thinking about what he did to me in bed. Since it can't happen again.

Then, there's the clearing of a throat, the sound of shoes on hardwood floor, and my body reacts instantly as Banks walks into the kitchen.

"Morning, Lila. Morning, Ripley. Hope you didn't think you could give me the slip," he teases.

I don't even look at him. If I do, the desire will be written on my face for my grandma to see. She already knows I like him. She already knows I'm wildly attracted to him. She'll be able to put two and two together and add it up to *you enjoyed hot sex and naughty uses for lavender with your bodyguard last night*, didn't you?

"I didn't know you were my shadow on the farm too," I toss out.

"I'm not. You're safe here. But I'm good at finding you," Banks says, and something about the confidence in his words makes me nearly swoon.

I grab the coffee bag instead and shake it for no good reason. "Thanks for walking the dog."

"Anytime," he says.

Grandma arches a curious brow, like walking the dog is the only proof she needs to know something's going on between us.

"I'll make more coffee," I quickly add.

My grandma gives me the most side-eye of all side-eyes ever, then says playfully and pointedly to Banks, "Yes, thank you so much for walking my granddaughter's most favorite person."

"You're my favorite person," I counter quickly, speaking to her.

Grandma scoffs. "You can't fool me. That dog has ranked top since you adopted him."

"He's a good dog," Banks says evenly.

"Ripley is crazy about him," Grandma says, and that's true, but I'm not entirely sure she's talking about Hudson.

Still, I'm the woman wearing a mock turtleneck in eighty-degree weather, so I shut the hell up and focus so hard on making coffee.

After the crew leaves bright and early to shoot at The Slippery Dipper today, I work on my usual tasks around the farm until it's time to swing by the art museum to pick up the flowers from last night's event. Banks helps me collect them and put them in the bed of the truck. "What will you do with them now?"

"Take them back to the farm and turn them into soil compost," I say.

Under the sun in the museum parking lot, he stares at me for a beat, his lips curving up.

"What?" I ask breathily.

"That's hot."

"Composting my flowers?"

"Yeah. Being good to the earth."

I laugh. "Makes it even harder to resist me, doesn't it?"

"Yes," he says, and he's intensely serious. He heads over to the passenger door and opens it. The man loves driving.

"You and your control," I mutter.

But before I can get in, he ropes an arm around my waist and jerks me against him, my back to his front, his hand coming down on the thin crocheted floral belt I'm wearing since I'm in my vintage '90s era today, it seems, with my jean shorts too. "And you like it," he rasps out.

"I do."

His arm cinches tighter. I melt more. He slides his other hand up my neck and into my hair. "Me too."

"Is anyone watching?" I whisper, but I know the answer. With the movie shooting in town today, no one's really following me. The photographers—from the Hollywood trade press to the paparazzi—are all on Main Street, hunting for the real action.

"I looked around. We're good," he says huskily, then runs his fingers up and into my hair. "Does your neck hurt today?"

"A little."

"Want me to rub it?"

I want him to rub everything. "Yes."

In the parking lot, with his arm locking me in place at the waist, he rubs my neck. It's a better neck massage than the first one, especially since he sighs, and murmurs, and kisses the shell of my ear.

Eventually, when I've turned into a liquid state, I say, "So we're forgetting last night?"

"Yes, this is forgetting." He kisses my neck once—no hickey this time—and lets go.

Back at the farm, Haven texts me a few times during the shoot, sending little updates like this one.

> **Haven:** OMG, I am pretending I run The Slippery Dipper!
> **Ripley:** Dreams do come true.
> **Haven:** I know. I've always wanted to run a cute shop!
> **Ripley:** It's not all sunshine and roses.
> **Haven:** It is for me!
> **Ripley:** Glad to hear.

After I hit Send on the last text, my phone's quiet for a while as I check in with Ramona on the shop's orders, then with Cyrus on his deliveries for the day. He's bopping his head to a beat as he pushes a wheelbarrow up to the shed but stops and nods when he sees me. "What's cooking, boss lady?"

"Do you have the Otto Quast for Prohibition Spirit? Esmeralda has added lavender specials to her menu. Oh, and I need the delivery for the market too."

He flashes a toothy grin, white teeth sparkling. "Always. I'm on top of it," he says, but as we head to the barn where we prep the flowers, my phone trills.

That's the ringtone I gave to Tabitha. I answer it so fast. "Hey, what's going on?"

"Hi, Ripley. Do you have something...purple-y?"

I blink. "Purple-y?"

"Yes. Vega doesn't like the lavender on the counter here at the shop. It's dried-out lavender," she says, her voice frayed, and it's only day one.

A lot of people *do* like dried lavender. That's why the store sells it. But now's not the time to educate her or anyone on the ins and outs of my business. "What would she prefer?" I ask, refraining myself from recommending Provence as a feather tickler.

"It's too washed-out," Tabitha says. "She wants something brighter for this scene."

Ah, that's an easy fix. "I have Impress Purple and Hidcote. Let me send you pics."

"You're a goddess," she says as I find the photos I keep handy and text them.

Seconds later, she's asking the director, who declares, "That one," with something like utter relief.

"The Impress Purple," Tabitha says to me.

"When do you need it?"

I can hear Tabitha grimace as she answers, "Yesterday."

"I'm on my way."

After she tells me how many, I grab the bunches, plus the ones Cyrus has set aside for the market, then let Banks know I'm heading to the set.

It's a little thrilling to say that—*set*. I can't help it. It's exciting that a movie's being shot in my hometown and with my sister as the star.

"Let's deliver this emergency lavender, stat," Banks says.

That giddy feeling carries over when he opens the door of the truck, casts a furtive glance around the farm, then trails his fingers down my back, whispering, "You'd look good on your knees with your hands tied behind you."

It's not my shirt I'm going to need to change soon. It's my panties.

A security officer lets me past the cordoned-off area of the block on Main Street and ushers me inside with Banks staying outside. My heart is sprinting with excitement. I get to see my sister in her element, and when I catch the first sight of her behind the counter, her hair in braids, her eyes sparkling as she chats with Tabitha, my heart surges with joy.

There she is. Making the art she's always wanted.

"It's my heroine!" Haven calls out when she sees me, then she scurries past the cameras and lights and rushes my way.

"Wow. You look amazing," I say, my throat tightening as I check out her cute T-shirt and jeans, face all flawless and camera-ready, her heart-shaped sunglasses pushing back her mane of blond hair.

"So do you," she says.

I laugh it off, then hand the flowers to Tabitha, who joins us and says, "Thank you. You're the goddess of goddesses."

Off in the corner, Vega is chatting with the lighting guy, but when she sees me, she gives a crisp, businesslike nod, calling out, "Thank you for the lavender save."

"Anytime," I say, then turn back to Haven.

"Where's New Chris?" I whisper.

"He's not in this scene, but he'll be in the next one. Want to stay and meet him?"

I check the time. "I'll see if I can come back. I need to bring Salma her flowers."

"Haven!" the director calls out, and my sister returns to the counter.

I weave through the crew, a little overwhelmed and starry-eyed, and head back to the street, where Banks is waiting for me with the lavender delivery for Salma.

"How was it?" he asks.

"Kind of amazing," I whisper, then we walk along the familiar block with its Hollywood blockade.

As we leave it, Banks scans left and right, then says, "Press over there. I've got you."

"Thanks," I say, grateful for his presence as he ushers me past photographers. There are more than last week. So many more. Understandable since, well, the film's actually shooting today.

"Are they all paparazzi?" I ask, recognizing Silas from last week, and the guy Banks pointed out, Ludwig. But there are others too.

"No. Some are with the entertainment press. They aren't quite...hunters."

"Thank god," I say, relieved for that as he whisks me into Salma's market.

"I'll stay here," he says, nodding to the doorway of the shop. "So you can see your customer by yourself."

I'm touched he remembered I wanted that. But not surprised. I head down the first aisle to find Salma at the florist counter, but instead I walk right toward the movie star himself.

Chris Carlisle is in the store, and he's holding a sandwich.

CHAPTER 30
A GRATITUDE SANDWICH
RIPLEY

Chris Carlisle doesn't look like everyone else in town. With his chiseled jawline, carved cheekbones, wavy golden-brown hair, and crystal-blue eyes, he looks as advertised.

A movie star.

He's also got an entourage. A big burly man walks a few feet behind him, wearing a tight black polo shirt that stretches across his chest. That must be his bodyguard. A petite woman in black pants and leopard flats is next to him, a phone, tablet, and notebook in her arms.

They're all heading my way when Chris's gaze lands on mine, and instantly a smile brightens his face.

It's like a billboard on the side of the highway. A movie marquee you have to look at. He strides right up to me, those blue eyes locked on me. "You must be Ripley."

I'm not usually starstruck, only because I don't usually meet stars, so I don't have a second to stammer or gawk. After all, he's the guy my sister says is *so nice*.

"I am," I say, then take a quick pause, assessing my reaction. Yes, he's a movie star, but he also puts his pants on one leg at a time. So I treat him as I'd treat anyone. With kindness and a little humor. "And I'm guessing you're *maybe, possibly* Chris Carlisle?"

He laughs politely, his gaze staying on me the whole time. "Good guess." Then, his expression turns more serious. "I am so grateful for you." Sandwich in hand, he comes closer, extending his free arm. "Hug?"

Oh.

He's asking for consent to hug. Okay. That's interesting. I shift the flowers awkwardly to my other arm, saying, "Sure."

He wraps his arm around me in a side hug that's quick, friendly, respectful; then he lets go. "What an honor to meet you," he says, both earnest and intense.

"It's my pleasure. How are you finding Darling Springs?"

"It's an incredible place," he says, telling me more about the beach, then the tapas he had at dinner last night, then the innkeeper at The Ladybug Inn. He doesn't once look away. He's all about the eye contact, which is nice, but a little overwhelming. Especially with that sandwich. The woman with him, an assistant I'm guessing, steps forward and takes it from him. "I'll hold this."

He turns to her. "Thank you so much, Natasha," he says in a tone full of gratitude.

His gaze returns to mine. "And Ripley," he says, placing his hands together as if in prayer, "I just want to thank you so much for welcoming our set onto your farm. I put you in my gratitude journal and thanked you in my morning meditation."

Ohhhhh. I get it now.

He's a gratitude guy. Which is lovely. And endearing. And also intense.

"That means a lot to me," I say, since I think that's how you respond to that kind of compliment.

"We drove past your farm earlier today. I wanted to see it from a distance, like the character does the first time he sets eyes on it. As an actor, I rely so much on my set and setting to perform, and I find the atmosphere you have created to be…" He pauses, clearly taking a moment to find just the right word. "Profound. I'm so looking forward to shooting there."

"I'm glad you're enjoying Darling Springs."

"It's extraordinary," Chris says while his bodyguard scans the aisle. He must be satisfied that there aren't any paparazzi nearby. "And I think we'll do it justice in the film," Chris adds.

"That's great to hear," I say.

With another heartfelt smile, he moves a hand to my elbow. "Permission to pat your elbow in thanks?"

My god, he's fucking adorable. "Absolutely."

He squeezes it, smiling. "Thank you, again. And I don't want to keep you from your flower delivery."

"It's no problem. I'm glad we met," I say as Natasha hands me the flowers, and Chris takes the sandwich from Natasha, thanking her as if she's saved a kitten.

As he turns to leave, I go the other way and hand my flowers to Salma, who's wearing a summery scarf over her head. "No guard dog today?" she asks.

"He's outside."

"Ah, did you make sure to give him food and water?"

I cover my mouth as if I made a horrible faux pas. "I knew there was something."

"Next time," she says, then tips her forehead to the door. "Business is good today. The place is packed."

"With paparazzi?"

"Probably some, but mostly tourists. Everyone wants a glimpse, and everyone wants some of my world-famous sandwiches."

"You do make the best sandwiches." That gives me an idea. Banks and I do need to eat later. Maybe I'll make a little picnic dinner in the cottage.

I head to the deli, order some sandwiches for pickup tonight, and a few minutes later, I'm back in my truck with the bodyguard who's worlds sexier to me than a movie star. Yet another reason someone should base the lead in a flick on this man.

I toss him a pleased smile. "I pulled that off without any trouble from the paps."

"Yes, you did," he says.

Except...

"I mean, we did," I add as he pulls away from the curb and turns down a side street.

When we're safely away from the tourists downtown, he lifts a hand and slides a thumb down my jaw. "I'm still forgetting all about last night."

A shiver runs through me. "Me too. Want to forget about it over a picnic dinner?"

His smile is smug, deservedly so. "You like me."

"Shut up."

He laughs. "You really like me."

"You're just being mean now pointing that out."

"You really like me so fucking much."

"Oh my god, just play Beethoven instead," I say.

He hits the button on the console and blasts something with joyful piano and violins as he drives me home.

That evening, I wash my face and scrub off my sunscreen after working on the farm all afternoon. Then, with my hair pushed back in a lavender—naturally—cotton headband, I settle onto the couch with Banks. As we're forgetting all about last night thanks to the dinner I ordered, which he picked up—a chicken sandwich for him and an artichoke and cheese for me—Haven calls.

I lunge for it. Her tone's an apology. "There's a photo of you and Chris going viral."

"What?" I ask, sitting up straight on the couch. Hudson lifts his snout from where he's lounging on the floor. "There weren't photographers in the store."

But Banks drags a hand down his face, grumbling, "Everyone's a photographer."

A minute later, I'm staring at a shot on some random person's social media of New Chris and his "new woman." Since the mock turtleneck with the short sleeves means that Haven doesn't know about my *allegedly amazing new skin care routine* on my neck, but also that no one knows I'm not my sister. The sleeves hit at my elbow, and they hid all my birds.

Because the caption reads: Little did I know who was in the produce aisle! And he looks at her like she's the one!

CHAPTER 31
RULE NUMBER FOUR
BANKS

A dose of red-hot anger courses through me. "I should have been there," I mutter, pacing around the cottage.

"Banks," Ripley says, popping up from the couch. "You couldn't have stopped it."

"But I could," I say, hissing out a sharp breath. "I could have been near you instead of waiting outside."

"It was just a flower delivery. I wanted to be able to do it," she tries to reassure me, reaching for my arm with a calm hand.

I shake my head. "But if I were there, I wouldn't have let that happen."

"What were you going to do? Take some random person's phone?" She waggles the phone she's holding, showing me the shot again of her and Chris hugging. A shot that was clearly taken from a distance. Maybe twenty feet away? Ten? Possibly snapped as someone turned into the aisle and spotted the star and his supposed new love?

"Maybe," I mutter.

She puts her phone back in her shorts pocket. "Banks, you weren't going to take someone's phone."

"I would have if I'd had to," I insist, still fuming.

"Are you really going to make a habit of taking random strangers' things? I feel like maybe that's illegal," she says dryly.

"I should have done something. Could have stopped it. Should have stopped it," I say as I pace away from her toward the sliding glass doors of the deck, stopping at the glass to stare at the night sky and the stars twinkling in it.

Here, I can replay this afternoon. Find the moment when I failed. Then never do that again.

She follows me, sets a hand on my shoulder. "You couldn't have," she says, her voice soothing. "It's no big deal. They didn't hurt me or him or anyone. It's fine. It's only a picture. I wasn't scared in the store, and you couldn't have stopped it."

But those words grate at me. They remind me of years ago. When I was younger.

When I had a feeling—I just fucking had a feeling what my dad was up to. And I didn't follow him. I didn't confront him. I didn't stop him.

"But I could have," I say, my voice quieter, filled with regret now. For the past. For the missed opportunities. For justice back then. I close my eyes, dip my face, sigh heavily.

After a few seconds, a hand comes up the back of my neck into my hair. "Banks, is this about today? Or something else?"

It's about…everything.

I look up, meet her caring gaze. As she strokes my hair, I weigh the decision to tell her. I'm not an impulsive guy with my mouth. I'm not even impulsive with my actions.

For work, I react, I anticipate. I *think*. And it's the same in my personal life too. I haven't even told my past girlfriends about the way my family splintered. It's personal, and it's embarrassing.

But when Ripley looks at me with kind eyes and a big heart, when she senses what I need, maybe even before I realize it, I *want* to tell her. I don't want to keep carrying this by myself.

I take her hand from my neck, clasp her fingers through mine. Like that, we head to the couch, Hudson at our feet. Once we're seated, I say, "You know how I told you it was messy when my parents split?"

"Yes."

I swallow past the shame and the hurt. "I grew up in Lucky Falls. My dad was the football coach for my high school, and I played on the team. I was a tight end," I say, as tainted memories flicker by. The way Dad was everyone's buddy. The way my teammates looked up to him, admired him, honestly, even worshiped him. "He also owned a sporting goods chain. About six stores or so, including one in Lucky Falls. And another in San Jose, about two or two and a half hours away. That was the flagship store."

She nods, encouraging me to keep going.

"He was there a lot. Got a place there. A little apartment. Three days a week or so he stayed overnight. Ostensibly for business," I bite out. "Or so my mom thought."

A quiet gasp crosses her lips. "He had an affair?"

I meet her gaze straight on and rip off the terrible truth. "He had a second family. He had young kids. He raised them with their mom. He owned a home with her. He went there to take care of them. Be someone else's dad, someone else's husband for half the week."

Her lips part, and her eyes widen. "I'm so sorry. I can't imagine what that was like."

But I can because I lived it. "It was awful. It came out on social media, which was still relatively new at the time, but that didn't matter. Someone found out, posted it online in some forum, and one thing led to another. Everyone attacked him. He was beloved and everyone on the team, all the families, all the parents were shocked. There was so much outrage. The photos, the details, our address, her name, their names," I say, shaking my head in disgust as those terrible memories crawl to the surface. "Don't get me wrong—he deserved it. All of it. He's a liar, a cheater, a fraud. But my mom was dragged through the mud. *How did she not know? Was she aware of it? How do you miss the signs?*"

Ripley sets a hand on my arm and rubs sympathetically. "I am so, so sorry. That sounds terrible."

"It was. She was devastated. The life she had, the marriage she had—it was all a lie. And she couldn't work for a while. She was floored. She had to take a break from work, even though he'd drained some of their accounts. She was…depressed. Which is kind of an understatement."

"Of course," Ripley says gently. "It sounds like she went through hell."

My jaw ticks. I clench and unclench my fists, then dig down and ask the question that sometimes plagues me, that often drives me. "But what if I could have stopped it?"

"Oh, Banks. How would you have stopped it?"

"Sometimes he was late coming home. Sometimes it felt like he was spending too much time elsewhere. Sometimes he was on his phone more than he should have been. Ripley," I say, my voice full of cracks and potholes, "I had a feeling. I fucking had a feeling. For a few months there in my junior year. Before it all blew up." I draw a tight breath. "I should have done something sooner."

She squeezes my arm tighter, then gently presses her other palm to my face, and turns me toward her, making me meet her caring gaze. "You couldn't have stopped it. You couldn't have done a thing."

"Maybe I could have prevented it from spiraling," I say, because c'mon. I could have. "Right? Don't you think?" I'm practically imploring her.

"No," she says, firm, emphatic. "His affair was not your responsibility."

"But what if I followed him there? Confronted him? Took his phone?" I ask, tossing out options like a desperate man.

She shakes her head, her eyes welling with sympathy. "People do what they do. You can't control them. You can't stop them," she says, then takes a beat. "He made his choice. And part of that choice was you and your mom and sister bearing the consequences."

I close my eyes. Trying, fucking trying, to let her words sink in. My mom has said the same. My sister too. Mostly I believe them, but sometimes I don't.

I open my eyes. When I look at Ripley, I want to believe she's right. No, I have to. I have to believe the truth that they reminded me of all along. That there was nothing I could have done.

"This is why you do what you do, right?"

"Yes. I want to protect people. Especially, honestly, women."

"I love that. I get it. And you do a great job." She rubs my arm. "It's also why you want control. Because once upon a time, your world spun out of control."

Way to see inside my soul. "Yes. Yes, it did."

She presses her forehead gently to mine, staying like that for several necessary seconds. Like that, with her touch, something tight inside me starts to unknot. "You can't stop a fan from taking a picture of me," she says. "You couldn't stop your dad. I couldn't stop a truck from crashing into my parents. All we can do is move forward." She lets go, looks me square in the eyes, then says, "You have to know that."

I draw a deep breath.

I didn't come to this town, this farm, or this job for exoneration from the last kernels of guilt that had dug roots inside me. But maybe I found it anyway. "You're probably right," I admit quietly.

She flutters her lashes. "Say it again."

I roll my eyes. "You're right."

"Louder for those in the back," she says.

I laugh. "You're definitely right."

She smiles, then cups my cheeks and brings me close. "But thank you for telling me. I know that wasn't easy."

"It wasn't."

She drops a kiss to my lips, then backs up. "I feel like I understand you better. Why you like rules. Why you try to be a gentleman. Why you care so much about doing the right thing."

"I do. A lot."

"Why you like it when I follow rules," she adds, her tone flirty.

Lust stirs inside me. "I fucking love rules," I say.

She nibbles on the corner of her lips. "Remember when you gave me three rules?"

I flash back to my first night here last week. "I do."

She tilts her head, takes her time. "Maybe rule number four should involve putting me on my knees."

My gaze drifts to her thick blond hair, held back in that stretchy headband, which looks perfect for us. "And maybe five should involve other uses for headbands."

CHAPTER 32
ALL KINDS OF TOYS
BANKS

"You're so DIY," she says.

"From flowers to headbands, sweetheart," I tell her as I twist the stretchy fabric around her wrists.

"Everything's a sex toy with you," she says, glancing back at me since I'm behind her, adjusting the soft material around her hands, clasped behind her back.

"And everything should be," I murmur as I tug on the material to make sure the hold is firm enough but not too tight. "How does that feel?"

"It'd be better with your dick in my mouth. Can I have *that* sex toy, please?"

"It better be your favorite toy," I say.

"Guess we'll find out."

Heat charges through me, followed by my own laughter. *This woman*. She's sexy and witty, caring and giving. Strong-willed and submissive at times too. If I'm not careful, I'll fall hard for her.

And that unexpected thought was brought to you by your libido.

Or...was it? Because my heart is tripping fast now. So much faster than I'd expected.

What the hell is going on inside me? But now's not the time for me to analyze that organ in my chest. Other organs need tending to.

I rise and come around to face her while the dog settles quietly into a corner of the cottage.

Ripley's on the floor, kneeling on the area rug in front of the couch. She's wearing panties and a white T-shirt that slopes off her shoulder. The simplicity is even sexier than if she were wearing elegant lingerie. I run a hand down her soft blond hair. She stretches her neck, moving with me.

"You like it when I tell you what to do in bed," I say, adding on to our conversation from moments ago, before I bound her. It's a statement, not a question. Still, I'm dying for her response.

"Seems I do, Banks," she says.

I drag my hand to the back of her head, curling it over her neck. "Because you spend all day taking care of everyone else. At night, you don't want to."

A small wise smile shifts her lips. "Yes, so why don't you shut up and fuck my mouth?"

Yup. That's her. Keeping me on my toes with that defiant attitude. My damn heart surges, making a liar of me once more.

I tug off my T-shirt, but I don't fully comply. Instead, I drop down in front of her. Cup her cheek. Hold her gaze. "Patience," I tell her.

"Why do I have to be patient?"

"Because good things come to good girls who wait. Like this," I say, then I brush my lips to hers—a tender, gentle kiss that has her gasping.

Me too.

I dust my mouth over hers again, the kind of kiss that leaves you wanting.

Teasing her, I graze her lips, kiss her jawline, travel up to the shell of her ear. She's sighing and murmuring as I return to her lush mouth, tip up her chin, and take another sip of a kiss. I drink her kisses like they're whiskey I want to savor. Like each drop needs to be tasted fully on my tongue.

We luxuriate in the kiss till my bones are melting and Ripley's breath is stuttering. I let go. "See? Patience is a good thing."

"It is," she whispers.

I stand and drag my thumb over her bottom lip. Pliantly, she opens for me. Swirls her tongue around my thumb, then draws it into her mouth. With avid eyes, she stares at me as she sucks.

Electricity crackles through my entire body, amplified by her hungry gaze.

When she lets go of my thumb, I push down the waistband of my shorts. "Now take it."

Her eyes flicker with desire. "Give it to me."

The give-and-take with her is scrambling my brain. No one has ever revved my engine like Ripley. I push down my shorts to my thighs, then my briefs, and free my aching cock. Her breath hitches.

I rub the tip against her pretty lips. She sighs as she licks the head.

"Beautiful. So fucking beautiful," I grit out.

She flattens her tongue, sliding it along the underside of my dick, and holy fuck. My cells sizzle. My brain goes offline. She's barely drawn me into her mouth, and I'm already burning up everywhere.

"More," she murmurs, a soft but clear order.

I push in farther, and she wraps her mouth around my shaft. Then she sucks and licks. Flicks and swirls. It's intoxicating to watch her. The way she has to balance on her knees, how she can't use her hands. She opens wide, urging me with her mouth and her body to give her everything.

"You want it all, sweetheart?"

She pushes me out. "Fuck my mouth," she instructs.

And that's it. I'm lost. It won't take long. I guide my dick back into the warm paradise, curl a hand around her head, and thrust.

She nods, murmurs, sighs, and through it all...she watches me.

Her blue eyes gaze up at me with heat, curiosity, intrigue. Something else too. Something more than passion. Something like real affection.

I try to shake it off, but maybe that's what's really frying my brain—the realization that we aren't stopping; we aren't forgetting it happened; we just keep happening.

But once again, I try to stop thinking. To let go. To give in to the sensation of her sucking my aching cock till my thighs are shaking, my balls are tightening, and pleasure is barreling down my spine.

I warn her I'm about to come, asking, "Want me to pull out?"

Shaking her head, she answers loud and clear by sucking harder. I practically black out from the ecstasy of her mouth. My brain blurs as I groan, coming hard down her throat, and she swallows.

I can barely catch my breath or get my bearings as I ease out. When I do, something wild and new hits me—I might have tied her up, but she controlled every second of that blow job.

She set the pace.

She gave the orders.

I drop down to my knees, kiss those beautiful lips once, then say, "My turn."

"You better finish what you started last night," she says, another demand.

It's one I desperately want to meet. "You better fucking believe it."

But I don't ask if she wants to be unbound. I do it because I want her to use her hands. I free them from the headband, scoop her up, and carry her to the bed, setting her on the mattress where I peel off her panties in record time.

"Put your hands in my hair. Fuck my face hard. Do whatever you want, sweetheart," I tell her.

She breathes out hard, excitedly. "Yes, sir."

In seconds, she's pushed me down between her thighs, roped her hands in my hair, and is rocking against my face.

It's glorious the way she owns her pleasure as she discovers what she wants. And I'm so fucking lucky that what she wants is me.

It doesn't take long till she's arching and writhing, panting and moaning, then gasping a long, sensual string of *oh god*s till she's falling apart beneath me.

Eventually, sometime later, we slide under the covers, the sheets rustling, the dog hopping up on the end of the bed and settling into a ball with a contented sigh.

"I guess we're not forgetting so well," she says.

"Definitely not."

She's pensive, staring at the ceiling for a while till she turns to me. "But we should be careful. I know the job's important to you."

Now that's something I haven't heard before—a woman trying to protect me. Until Ripley. "It is. I appreciate that."

It's a good reminder too. If word gets out I'm sleeping with a client, Apex Solutions could bear the brunt of the harm. We could lose business. I saw what happened to my dad, and to my mom as collateral damage when business got mixed with pleasure. Don't want that to happen to Dean and me. This situation isn't the same as my dad's secret second family. Not by any stretch.

Still, I'm not an innocent man. The least I can do is vow to be better. "I'll work even harder to protect you. It's not just the paps. There are fans now. Whoever took that photo didn't get too close, but you never know. The town is full of tourists and press. Everyone needs to be vigilant," I say.

She smiles softly. "I'll ring the town bell and let them know."

"I mean it," I press.

"The town bell?" she asks with an arch of a brow.

"No, but just that everyone should be careful. The influx of people and all. Everyone should be on their guard. And even though you're a beautiful distraction, that means I'll work that much harder so I stay focused."

She sets a hand on my chest. "You're all good, Banks. And don't worry. I don't want to let on about this thing either. To Tabitha. The crew. Everyone. I don't want to become a distraction for anyone. I want the film to go smoothly. The town is benefiting from the tourism. We're going to benefit at the farm. A lot is riding on this."

And *everyone* includes someone in particular. "And *everyone* includes Haven, I'm guessing?"

With a wince, she nods. "I don't like to keep secrets from her, but I don't want her to be distracted. She worries about me already. But I only want her to focus on the job."

Pretty sure it's the other way around—Ripley worries about Haven. But it's not my place to point that out. "I understand."

"She worked so hard for this her whole life," she says, her voice tightening as she shifts closer to me. "I think acting was what got her through the death of our parents."

My heart squeezes again. "I completely get it." I run my knuckles down her cheek. "But I bet you got her through it too, Ripley," I say gently.

She shrugs, maybe not wanting to take credit for it.

"You said you helped her through the dark days. I think it was you, not just acting."

She blows out a breath. "Maybe. But the point is—I want this for her. I want her to have her dreams. I want Grandma to have her dreams."

Impulsively, I say, "What about your dreams?"

She blinks, surprised. "What do you mean?"

"Well, what are yours? Is it this farm?"

She smiles. "It's home. I love it. I want it to be the best it can be. I want families to come here and have picnics, to play in the lavender maze, or couples to go on dates here since I finally set up fairy lights at night."

"That sounds very romantic."

"It is. I just want others to enjoy it too. To fill their homes with flowers, to open a bottle of lotion, or oil, or soap, and inhale it and feel…calm and happy."

"You're doing that, Ripley," I say.

"Some more attention from the film would be nice. More tourists, more business—you know what I mean?"

I nod. "I do."

"That's why I said it—we should keep this on the down-low."

I reach for her, press a kiss to her nose. "I like secrets. You're the best kind of secret there is."

She sighs happily, flips to her side, then closes her eyes.

I don't fall asleep as fast as she does.

My mind is racing forward, thinking about tomorrow, and the next day, and the next week.

When this ends.

CHAPTER 33
THEATER MAGIC
RIPLEY

The picture racks up views overnight, but I do my best to ignore it, and honestly, it's not that hard.

Since, well, it's not really me people are seeing in the picture. Besides, it's not the only picture circulating of "Haven and Chris." The film's PR team releases actual pics of the stars too. Posed ones, outside a trailer, with the caption First day on set for *Someone Else's Ring*!

That's a relief, to see a strategy from the producers. I'm grateful they aren't letting the paparazzi and random fans dictate the story; they're telling one as well—the story of the movie.

I'd like to ignore Eric Patrick's new message too, since one lands in the morning as I'm downing my coffee in the kitchen while Banks is busy on his phone. I read the message again though, because I can't really believe my ex is sending this: I'm thinking the space at Prohibition Spirit would be perf for my new fusion café. What do you think? Can you picture it?

I can hear Haven's voice saying *don't feed a troll*. But sometimes I don't do the right thing. I fire off a quick reply. Nope.

I must be making a sour face though, because as I pocket my phone and set the mug in the sink, Banks gives me a curious look. "Everything okay?"

"Just my ex," I say, my tone making my feelings about him clear.

In a nanosecond, Banks goes from relaxed to ready to rumble. "What does he want?"

"Pretty sure he's trying to get me to put in a good word so he can lease the restaurant that Esmeralda is leasing at Prohibition Spirit."

He nods, eyes saying *go on*. I give Banks the brief overview of that failed romance. "And then he left for New York because Darling Springs *just wasn't his scene*."

"Hypocrite." It's said with acid.

"Seems that way."

"He's insulting you too. And then buttering you up. Like he thinks you can't figure out why he's texting," Banks bites out.

Hmm. He has a good point there. "But then again, if he asked directly, it's not like I'd help."

"Good," Banks says, glancing around the empty kitchen before he steps closer. "You deserve someone who appreciates every single thing about *you* and the place you love."

My heart spins a little faster. Like it did when someone walked my dog again this morning. Then, my brain blurs into a hazy shade of summer as Banks loops an arm around my waist and drops a long, slow, passionate kiss to my lips.

When he breaks it, my head's still a little dizzy, so I blame the endorphins for the next thing I say: "Tell me you're possessive without telling me you're possessive."

He smirks. "I believe I just did."

We take off for Haven's hotel, so I can hang out with her in her room as she gets ready for her afternoon shoot.

"I'm so sorry," Haven says as she's putting lotion on her bare legs. "I know you don't like your pic being taken."

I wave a hand as I sit on the bed. "It's fine."

Really it is. The picture's been taken. It's out there. But one thing nags at me. "You really don't mind that people are this obsessed with you?"

"It's not me. It's all about Chris," she says, deflecting.

But that's not entirely true. "Haven. You're not a nobody. *The Dating Games* did pretty well. Do I need to remind you?"

She smiles kindly, and I flash back to the night I met Banks at the San Francisco hotel, when that rando guy who looked like a douchey boss in a Christmas rom-com hit on me. He couldn't quite place her at the time, but he was getting close to her name. That was one of the first times I was confused for her, but I bet it'll happen more for me soon, and a million times more for her. Which means…the attention's not at all only about New Chris. It's about Haven too. "Remember that night in San Francisco when you found out about the film and had to leave early?"

"Of course," she says as she caps the lotion and sets it down.

"I went to the bar to have a drink and to try to plan everything I'd need to do. To write a to-do list."

"That's very you," she says as she twists her hair up into a knot.

"It is. Anyway, some guy hit on me then. He had this very slick look to him, like he expected women to fall at his feet. Anyway, he said something like *Haven't I seen you in a movie?* But he couldn't figure out what," I say, then shudder. "He was so sleazy. And that's only happened to me once. It's going to happen to you a lot," I say. It's a whole new world she's stepping into with this movie. I worry about her.

"I try not to think about it. And just focus on the work," she says.

"Right. But you never know what might happen. I mean, that guy at the bar was a creep, but what if I'd run into him in a parking lot? What if you run into a guy like that?"

"Hello! I was raised by Grandma too. I can throw a punch."

"Me too," I say, but it's a little scary to think about—what her life might be like. "Maybe you'll need more security when you get back to LA. I could talk to Banks about that for you."

"Maybe. That's not a bad idea."

I'm glad she's open to it, but it's not just the security issue. It's the fame issue. "People are going to be obsessed with you."

She comes over to me, takes my hands. "Which is why I'm so glad I have you and Grandma and our friends from here. Chloe and Bridget. Because at the end of the day, I'm just me. I'm just a girl from Darling Springs."

"You sound pretty grounded about it."

"Well, you did make sure I saw a therapist way back when. Years of therapy since then have helped," she says as she pulls on a tank top over her sports bra. She'll change into costume on set, she said. They're shooting outside The Slippery Dipper today.

"Yay, therapy," I say, upbeat and meaning it, because I've gone too. But something else, besides security and fame, keeps sticking in my brain. "For a while I thought maybe you were seeing New Chris."

Her brow pinches. "And keeping it from you?" She sounds aghast at the suggestion she'd do that.

I shrug, a little embarrassed. "I believed you when you told me you weren't involved with him, but I did wonder if you were just keeping it close to the vest."

"I would tell you."

"I know," I say, chagrined. "But now that I've met him, I can see why you're not dating him."

She jerks her gaze back. "What do you mean?"

"He's not really your type," I say, trying to come up with the words to describe the movie star. "He's very…intense. He's all about eye contact and listening and gratitude."

"Are you saying I don't like nice guys who are grateful, or that I'm not?" she asks, but not meanly. Just curiously.

"Nah. He's nice, but almost unreal."

She nods as she grabs a hair tie from the bureau. "I hear you."

"He seems very…actorly. Nice actorly, but actorly nonetheless."

As she loops her hair into a bun, she asks with some concern, "Am I like that?"

I flash back to the way she squealed yesterday when I met her on set. "I don't think so. I hope you keep that genuine enthusiasm for work. I hope it never gets old for you. I hope it's always magical."

"Me too. But I think it will be, Ripley. I do. I love acting in the way you love the farm."

My heart floods with a burst of happiness. "I do love the farm."

"And I want everyone to come to it after the movie," she says.

"Me too."

She flops next to me. "Ripley," she whispers in a confessional tone, shifting gears.

"Yes?"

She reaches into her canvas bag on the bed and fishes out a lavender envelope, a nervous smile spreading on her face as she hands it to me. "Can you take this to William today? At the bookstore?"

I sit up straight as I take it. "Are you and William together?"

She brings her finger to her lips but doesn't hide the smile that seems to take over her soul. "We're…seeing each other."

I'm giddy with excitement. "You and the bookstore owner?"

"Yes," she says, drawing a deep, hopeful breath, but then shaking off her excitement. "But it's new. It's early. We've mostly written letters and talked on the phone while I was in LA. We've only been able to have a couple secret dates while I've been in town."

I punch the air. "Knew it. Called it."

She sets her head on my shoulder, sighing happily. "You did. You always know. And I know you're hot for your bodyguard."

I tense. Should I tell her the truth? That we're involved? But I promised Banks I'd keep us a secret. Then again, she didn't ask if I was involved with him. Only if I was into him. It's not truly a denial then when I say, "Yes, but it could never go anywhere," then hop up and check the time. "I need to go. I have a to-do list ten miles long."

As I leave, the guilt intensifies. My sister's sharing her heart with me, but I'm lying to her by omission.

Still, it's for the best. My job is to protect her. It always has been.

I find Banks in the lobby, and we head over to A Likely Story. William's chatting with a customer in the celebrity memoirs section. "From the second she tells the story of her early life, it's utterly unputdownable," he says to the man in his soft Irish lilt.

"Then I'd better get it."

"Excellent," he says, and after William rings up the customer, he meets my gaze, his brown eyes hopeful. "Hello, Ripley. What brings you to A Likely Story?"

Like he doesn't know. I do my best to rein in a grin as I say, "Just a little epistolary delivery."

His eyes twinkle more. "You don't say?"

"I do say," I add, then thrust the letter at him. He grabs it, clutching it like a precious thing.

Having finished that task, I'm about to leave when I glance around, then lean closer. "You'd better be good to my sister," I whisper-hiss.

Banks flinches.

William holds up his hands in surrender. "That's all I want to be."

"Good," I say, then drop the mama bear act. For now.

I wave goodbye, and once we leave, Banks whistles low and approvingly. "You're fierce."

I square my shoulders. "I know."

"And if it's any consolation, he seems quite taken with her."

"He'd better be."

"Remind me never to cross you two."

"Don't ever cross us," I say with a smile as we walk along the block to my truck.

"Where to next?" Banks asks as we pass the tattoo shop.

"You said you never went back to Lucky Falls."

He tenses. "Right. But I don't want to go there."

"I get that, but Darling Springs is cool. Can I show you around my town?" My voice pitches up.

His shoulders relax, then his eyes twinkle. "You've shown me a lot of it. Did you forget our yoga and nail salon escapades?"

"The local coffee shop too," I add.

"And the fuel at Pick Me Up is top-notch."

"But there's more to Darling Springs," I say, stopping on the sidewalk. "Want to see it?" I feel like I'm on the edge of my seat waiting for an answer, even though he hardly makes me wait.

"I do." He leans forward on his boots, like he's coming in for a kiss. But he stops short, smirking instead. "Can you show me where you Saran Wrapped Scott Nelson's truck back in twelfth grade?"

My mouth falls open. "You jackass."

The smirk spreads. "So that's a yes?"

"A yes to showing you where *Bridget* did it," I say.

"After you," he says, and gestures toward the truck several feet away.

As we resume walking, I'm so tempted to reach for his hand. Maybe he senses it. Or maybe this is just part of the perks of having a secret romance with a bodyguard, but when he puts his palm on the small of my back, he presses harder, spreads his fingers wider, runs his fingertips across my shirt.

It's like a private gesture in public, and I don't mind at all showing him the site of the Saran Wrapping.

We drive to the beach nearby, the scene of the so-called crime. We hop out of the truck, and I take him to the edge of the dunes, where Scott parked his vehicle one fine day.

"Tomorrow, can you show me where you removed the door from the science lab?"

I roll my eyes. "Chloe did it."

"Right, right." He sketches air quotes. "Where Chloe removed it."

"Maybe I will."

But we both know I'm showing him my high school.

Clearly, I'll have to revise my earlier statement that hardly anyone gets up earlier than a farmer to include bodyguards. Mine is killing it in the up-at-the-crack-of-dawn department. The next morning as the sun peeks above the horizon, I wake to a walked and fed dog, and a fresh vase of flowers on the table. Melissa, of course. My heart clatters happily.

But there's no bodyguard. "Where did Banks go?" I ask Hudson.

My boy just tilts his snout in question. If a dog could shrug, this guy does. "But you know all his secrets," I say, trying to goad the pup.

He settles his snout back onto the rug with a sigh. I scratch his head. "Fine, fine. You are my favorite person."

He leans into the petting, and as I give him all the scratches and love he deserves, my gaze strays to the deck, then beyond. Is Banks jumping rope?

I stand and head to the glass. He's outside, on the path, working out. He has earbuds in, and after a few minutes of jumping, he drops down to a plank then executes more push-ups than I can count.

When he comes back into the cottage—a fine sheen of sweat on his brow, his arms, his chest—I postpone the start of my farm chores and show him just how much I appreciate his workout.

After, we're both sweaty and tangled together in bed. "Thanks for walking my dog," I say.

"You're welcome."

"And for feeding him."

"Well, he is your favorite person."

"He is. And for the fresh-cut flowers," I add.

"That was easy, seeing as we're on a flower farm."

I swat his chest. "Don't make a gift seem like it was nothing. It's perfect for me."

He turns to me, runs a finger gently down my nose. "You like your dog, and you like lavender."

That wasn't hard to figure out, but no one else has done a thing about those two very obvious facts.

Until him.

As the crew shoots at the hardware store that day, between my deliveries, we steal away on our bikes to Sunflower Ridge High School, home of the Wildcats of Darling Springs. We cruise past a colorful array of bungalows with red, purple, and peach front doors till we reach the school at the end of a winding street. We rest our bikes against the bike rack, then wander around the grounds. It's summer and the morning sessions must be finished, because we're the only ones here.

"Did you like high school?" Banks asks.

"Does anyone like high school?" I counter.

He taps his chin. "Fair point."

I show him the outside of the science lab, then the auditorium, small in size but mighty in possibility. "That's where Haven did her first musical. *Beauty and the Beast.*"

He turns to me, brown eyes widening with questions. "Tell me. How did the Beast transform at the end?"

I flinch. Rub my ear. "Wait…did you just—"

"Ask you how the beast became the prince," he says quickly, making a rolling gesture with his hands, speed-it-up style. "Yes, I've been dying to know ever since I saw it."

"You saw *Beauty and the Beast*?"

He gives me a look. "Does this surprise you? I listen to classical music. I bake. I have a sister."

"And she didn't take you? You took her?" I ask, processing this new Banks detail.

"For your information, the three of us all like musicals and theater. And yes, I took my mom and my sister. So…how did it happen?"

My heart gallops. This man is so tough and so tender at the same time. I step closer, curl a hand around his ear, and lean close to whisper, "Magic."

He sighs heavily. "Ripley."

I pull back. "You really want to know?"

"I do."

"Spoiler and all?"

"Bring it on."

I lean in and lower my voice again. "Double cast."

When I step back, the look in his eyes is magic. Then, he shakes his head in disbelief. "Another actor must play him in the Gaston battle scene."

I tap his nose. "Exactly."

"I'm a fool," he says, then smacks his forehead. "I can't believe I missed something so obvious."

"Or maybe the magic worked," I say.

He flashes me a warm smile, holding my gaze meaningfully. "It did."

My heart speeds even faster, and I'm not sure we're talking about stage magic anymore.

Banks swings his gaze around and reaches for my hand, clasping our fingers together as we walk through the quad. As we're leaving it, we pass a bench in the corner, set away from others. I stop, my chest squeezing with painful memories. Banks has opened up to me, so it's fair I do the same. But it's not just about fairness. There's something else, something new—an insistent need to let him in. I haven't felt like this before with a man, and I don't know what to make of these new emotions. Still, I forge ahead into the unknown.

"That's why I don't like having my picture taken," I say, pointing toward the seat.

He tilts his head. "The bench? What happened?"

We sit, and I begin the story that I haven't shared with any other man. "There was one day in our sophomore year, a few weeks after our parents died, when Haven was having a really rough time. It was after school, and she was crying." I pat the wood of the bench, feeling like it was just yesterday. "We sat here, and I hugged her as she cried. A girl we both knew—Katrina, she's a friend and she runs The Sweet Spot now—was working for the yearbook and was going around doing slice-of-life pics, and she snapped a bunch of pictures of students doing their thing at the end of the school day. I don't think she fully realized what was going on till the next day in yearbook class."

Heavy-hearted, I remember that photo. A portrait of grief. My baby sister sobbing in my arms. Me, holding her tight. Us, clinging to each other as our life capsized.

I push past the hurt and finish the story that the town knows, my friends know, my grandma knows. But I haven't told anyone else. I've never shared this with a soul who wasn't there at the time. "But the pictures were up on the computer and that one was there. As soon as she realized it, she deleted it. But people had seen it. Even so, she and the teacher and the other students all said, *We shouldn't run that one*. They were so lovely. They knew it was private. They knew Katrina hadn't meant to take it. And she felt terrible, but in the end, she'd actually protected us." My eyes well with tears.

"Sweetheart," Banks, says softly, then tugs me close, wraps his arms around me, and shields me. No one's here. No one can see us, and yet he knows without me saying it that I don't want anyone to see me cry.

I nestle against his chest as a few rebel tears stream down my cheeks till I wipe them away. I feel lighter. I feel like I let go of something I was holding on to for too long. Something that maybe has held me back.

Deep breath. Then I pull back. He runs a hand down my hair. "I get it. I do."

"Why I don't love having my picture taken without knowing it's happening?" I ask in a broken voice.

"Yes, but also, why you love it here. You all look out for each other."

"We do," I say.

I set my head on his shoulder. We sit quietly for a while, and it's nice not to say a word but still feel so connected.

Later, we visit The Sweet Spot, and I buy banana bread from Katrina, who's dolled up again today. As she hands me the bread, her smile grows bigger with hope. "Would you take some cookies to Chris?"

"I'm not sure I'll see him," I admit.

"Or maybe the whole crew," she says, then reaches under the counter and thrusts a white box of a dozen cookies at me.

Banks takes it before I can, saying a heartfelt, "Thank you."

I don't think he's thanking her for the baked goods.

We leave the shop and continue our ride. When we reach Prohibition Spirit, I stop and point it out to Banks. "I love that place. I go there with Chloe and Bridget, and Haven when she's in town. That's the place that my ex wants," I say, nodding to the expanded section with the *for lease* sign in the window. "For a restaurant."

Banks growls. "He won't get it."

"How do you know?"

"I'll stop him," he says.

I'm not sure he can, but I love that he wants to. His possessiveness makes my chest flip. "How would you do that?" I ask.

It feels a little like foreplay, this question.

His eyes travel up and down me, heating me up. "However I need to do it, Ripley."

I can't stop playing this game. "Why?"

"Don't want him near you. *At all*."

I nibble the corner of my lips. "Then I hope you stop him."

"Me fucking too," he says, and I blink off the fog of lust as I push my sneakered feet on the pedals, riding again.

Once we're past Prohibition Spirit, Banks says into the faint breeze blowing past us, "I like that place, but I like Mister Fox too."

"You've been there?"

"A couple of times. That's where I met Monroe last year."

"You've been holding out on me."

"I was there the other night, debating what to do about you."

At the stop sign, I give him a coy look. "And what did you decide?"

"That you're impossible to resist."

I smile. "That bar is the best place for decisions."

When we stop at the hardware store, Banks brings in the box of baked goods for the crew but makes sure Chris gets a cookie when there's a break in action. "It's from The Sweet Spot," he says. "Katrina is a big fan of yours and wanted you to have one."

The movie star pumps Banks's hand, giving him a heartfelt thank-you, then takes a cookie. I figure he'll set it aside or give it away since he's probably on a kale-and-boiled-chicken-only diet. Instead, he takes a bite and then moans. When he's done chewing, he asks, "Where did you say these are from?"

"The Sweet Spot," Banks answers, and Chris looks like he's filing that data in a very special drawer in his head.

Later that night, Banks tells me again I'm impossible to resist as he lies down on the bed.

"Is that so?" I ask from across the room.

"Yep." He pats the mattress. "Get over here."

"So bossy."

"And you like it."

"I do," I say, joining him.

He sits up and strips me in seconds, then tugs off his own shirt in one smooth, sexy motion. "Want you to ride me, sweetheart. Want to watch you bouncing up and down on my dick."

Well then. "I believe that can be arranged." I undo his shorts, find a condom, and cover him.

As midnight settles over Lavender Bliss Farms, I lower myself onto him, gasping and sighing as he fills me up, arching into the sensations racing through me—the pressure, the sparks, the heat. There are no DIY toys this time. No headbands. No flowers. Nor any hands holding my wrists. This time I press my palms to his chest, bracing myself on him as I set the pace. He grips my hips, and we move together, unbound.

Me over him.

Him under me.

Giving and taking. Till we're both chasing the edge, then falling off it together.

Funny how a week ago he was arriving in town, and I was trying to ditch him. Now I'm trying to soak up as much time as I can get before he leaves.

Since he will.

The shoot the next day is here on the farm. I'm showered and dressed and making coffee in the farmhouse kitchen when an image of last night flashes vividly through my mind.

I shiver just as Tabitha walks into the kitchen. I straighten, shaking off the lingering lust. "Good morning. Want some coffee?"

"I'm going to need it. Haven's in makeup right now, but I just got a call that her stand-in is sick. Any chance you could help us out for an hour?"

Well, I guess you can't get a better stand-in than a twin sister.

CHAPTER 34
SO VERY META
RIPLEY

I don't know what to do with my face.

I stand on a stone pathway edged by Hidcote plants, wearing a wide-brimmed hat like the heroine in *Someone Else's Ring* wears in this scene. Sam and some of the other guys are holding up light meters and diffusers as they check the lighting. Meanwhile, I'm smiling like my cheeks are held up by clothespins.

"Whoa. Are you in the pic now, boss?"

Cyrus walks among the bushes, heading my way, shielding his eyes from the morning sun, his floppy hair falling on his hand.

"No. God no," I say. Do my words sound as awkward as my body looks?

"You sure? Because it looks like you're doing a movie." His tone is playful.

"I am not in the movie," I say crisply.

Sam looks at Cyrus with surprised curiosity. "How did you know it was her and not Haven?"

Cyrus frowns at the AD like *are you really asking the question?* "Dude."

"I mean it, mate," says Sam. "You can't see her tats from where you are."

Cyrus chuckles. "I mean, it's not hard. She looks like the one in awkward family photos who doesn't know how to pose."

I seethe at my employee. "Cyrus, you want to keep your job, I presume?"

He laughs harder. "You like me too much to fire me, Rips. I make you laugh," he says, but then turns serious. "Also, idea. It just came to me. I'm going to need your autograph now, 'kay? Damien can make a screen print of it and put it on a T-shirt. He's gonna start making a new line of tees. *Darling Springs—the Canada of California* shirts."

I blink. "Really?"

"No lie. Because a lot of films are shot in Canada," he says helpfully, but I knew that.

"Right. That's just very, *very* meta."

Cyrus shrugs, smiling. "That's us. My dude and I are very meta. Anyway, you game for it?"

"Maybe." I can't focus on potential T-shirt fame while I'm sweating. Is it the lights making me hot? The sun? The attention? How does Haven handle this? The spotlight is too much. I want to hide in the lavender maze.

I stand like a newborn foal for another few minutes as they

check settings on meters and cameras and Banks watches from a distance. When Tabitha heads down the pathway to the cluster of crew members, I jump on the chance of freedom. "Is Haven's stand-in coming back tomorrow?"

"Let's hope it's only a twenty-four-hour stomach bug," she says.

Uh-oh. That's not good. I steal a glance at the edge of the Hidcote where Banks is watching the scene with some amusement.

But mostly intensity. He keeps turning his focus back to the gates of the farm. Several of his security guys are working. A couple of trailers are set up by the white picket fence—including Chris's, though he's in makeup too. The street is closed today for the shoot, so there aren't any photographers here. At least, none I can see.

This also means my shop is closed to the public for the next little while when they shoot scenes at the farm, but I've still got deliveries going out, and Cyrus and Ramona have plenty to do around the farm. I just have to hope that online interest continues to grow thanks to the buzz from the film.

My gaze lands on Banks again. His arms are crossed. He's wearing aviator shades. His black polo is nice and snug against his chest and abs. Bodyguard couture is seriously hot. Good thing he's twenty feet away. This way, I can ogle him, but the distance makes keeping this secret thing between us pretty easy.

"Almost done," Sam says reassuringly as he adjusts another setting on a camera.

"Happy to help," I say, though what I mean is *thank god*.

"You're a trouper," he says, laid-back and chill until Vega, the director, strides over a few seconds later, her phone pressed to her ear.

"Tell me something. Why on god's great green earth would Carlisle's stand-in have the stomach bug too?" A pause as she holds up a stop-sign hand. "Wait. I don't even want to know. We'll find someone else."

Vega ends the call and scans the group, presumably hunting for a suitable stand-in. She moves past Sam, then Arjun, the guy from New Jersey with the undercut, then a gaffer who's on the short side. She spins in slo-mo, finally finding Banks at the outskirts of the fields.

She cups her hands around her mouth. "You. You're tall," she says. "You're big. You look like you work out too. Can you be our stand-in for five minutes?"

He clears his throat. "I'm security, ma'am."

She gestures wildly to the gates. "And your team is doing a great job, including Wanda," she says, since Haven's bodyguard is patrolling the grounds today as well.

With a reluctant sigh, Banks walks over to me.

So much for keeping our distance in public. My too-sexy bodyguard is standing inches from me. Close enough that the aftershave he wears, soapy and woodsy, is going to my head.

"Next to her. Put an arm around her," Vega says, taking my focus from the scent.

Nope. That's a lie. That scent is going to my panties. So much for not touching. Or letting on. Since the second his arm slides around my waist, I'm trembling. I swear, I need to stop being Silly Putty in his hands.

"Closer," she says. "This is a kissing scene."

I blink. "W-what?"

Vega must realize she sounds pushy since she changes her tune. "Don't worry. You don't have to kiss. We don't make stand-ins kiss."

That's not even the issue, but I can't think about issues when Banks curls his fingers around my waist like he's claiming me. My skin heats up. My shoulders rise and fall. I'm dying here as the man I'm pretending I'm not having a secret, stolen romance with isn't turning me on in front of a whole camera crew.

As they hustle around the lawn, Banks's fingers tease at my waist.

"You're impossible," I mutter out of the side of my mouth, but it's more like a murmur.

"Did you say *irresistible*?"

"Now just turn toward each other," Vega says.

I gulp.

We shift, and those dark-chocolate eyes hold my gaze as he tosses a casual question the director's way. "Like I'm going to kiss her, right?"

"Yes, exactly," she says as Banks leans the slightest bit closer, earning some praise. "You're a natural. You really look like you're about to kiss her."

The corner of his lip twitches. "Guess I'm a good actor."

It's said to her, but he's looking at me with such passion we know he's not taking home the statuette tonight. And we shouldn't be doing this—we are playing with fire—but not being with him while pressing so tightly against him feels impossible.

"Now, can you wrap your arms around his neck?" Vega asks in her good-cop voice.

I comply, my hands circling Banks, my fingers brushing against the ends of his hair. A whimper falls from my lips as I touch the man I want. It's like the rest of the crew disappears, and it's us in the lavender fields, escaping for a stolen kiss—since I'm rising on my tiptoes and brushing my lips to his.

When I let go, everyone's clapping. "That was perfect," Vega says, with a quick clap. "You went the distance, and I'm so appreciative. We have what we need."

They let us go, and I hastily excuse myself, beelining for the cottage, away from everyone.

I shut the door and move to the wall next to it. I try to catch my breath, waving a hand in front of me to cool off. A minute later, Banks is here, opening the door. He doesn't say a word—just hauls me against him and devours my lips.

It's a wild, frantic kiss that will lead to one place only.

Before I know it, I'm up against the wall, shorts off, panties gone. After he grabs a condom, Banks is thrusting into me, fucking me hard and mercilessly, just the way I like it with him.

I'm panting and moaning, my noises growing louder with each pump of his hips.

"Banks," I murmur.

"Quiet, sweetheart. Don't want everyone to know you're fucking the stand-in."

"No. The stand-in is fucking me," I correct.

"Damn right he is," Banks says, then covers my mouth with his big hand. "Quiet."

My eyes widen as I nod, urging him to clamp his hand tighter.

He holds my hip tight too, his fingers leaving marks as he drives into me until I lose my mind, falling apart in his arms. A few seconds later, he follows me there with a bitten-off groan.

We slump against the wall, sweaty and panting.

Fifteen minutes later, I'm grabbing bouquets of flowers for my morning delivery. I like this stand-in life very much.

CHAPTER 35
A GIRLFRIEND QUESTION
RIPLEY

It's working. The number of inquiries about having picnics is up. Sales at the online store of lavender pillows, lotions, oils, and soap are slowly rising. Plus, the Darling Springs mayor herself reached out to see if the town could promote tours of the lavender farm and its maze on its site. Yes, please!

All thanks to the advance buzz from the shoot. Several days later, on Wednesday morning, I mention all this to Grandma as we make breakfast for the crew early in the day. "I'll be able to send you to Paris in no time," I tell her.

"I love that you even think about that. But you really shouldn't worry about me. I can probably find a way to do it on my own."

I meet her gaze straight on, brooking no argument. "I want to. You did so much for us."

"And I wouldn't have had it any other way."

"Which is why I want to do this," I say.

"So stubborn. Just like your mother."

I smile. "I'll take that as a compliment." When I leave the kitchen to tend to farm tasks, she returns to her French app, practicing how to say *I would like a baguette*.

"Now that's useful," I call from the door.

The next day, as the crew shoots in the lavender fields again, I tell Banks about the upticks too, as we visit customers, then stop at Josiah's Hardware to pick up some items I need for the farm. "I guess I don't mind all the photos after all. Even the ones of me. They seem to be helping us. So I can't really complain," I say, waving to Josiah at the counter and to his fickle orange cat.

"Good to see you, Ripley," he says.

"How are the fish? Were they biting this weekend?" I ask.

"Caught a couple trout. Grilled them to perfection," he says, and I smile, remembering the times he did that with my dad when I was younger.

"Bet they were delish," I say, even though I don't eat fish or meat. But I'm glad he enjoyed his meal.

"They were. Henry would have loved them," he says, and I smile.

Then Banks and I turn down an aisle of gardening supplies.

"I'm really happy to hear it's all working out," Banks says as we return to our earlier convo.

"Thanks. Me too," I say as I hunt for a new bulb planter. "I wouldn't exactly say the farm was struggling before, but it wasn't a money tree either."

His lips quirk up. "Can you grow those?"

"I wish," I say, laughing as I spot the planter I want. I grab it, then set it in the red basket Banks has been holding.

"If you find the seeds, let me know. So far, it's hard work and hustle."

"Yes. Yes, it is," I say. "Back when my parents did this, I had no idea what went into running a farm, from the insurance to the equipment, to the management, to the employees."

"Did you ever want to do anything else?" he asks as we turn the corner, passing potting plants and soils.

"Briefly, I toyed with being a florist. Which I still think would be fun. *Maybe* being a dog trainer. When I was in my rebellious era, I thought I'd work for some corporation in human resources, so I earned a business degree with an HR focus in college. Then, when I graduated and came back to the farm for the summer, I saw how hard Grandma was working. And I knew it was time to help."

Tilting his head, Banks seems to give that some thought. "Did you do it out of obligation then, or did you like it?"

"Both," I say, answering with total honesty. "I *wanted* to help because it seemed the right thing to do to carry on the farm, and then the more I got to know the inner workings of Lavender Bliss Farms, the more right it seemed *for me*. Like maybe this is where I was supposed to be all along."

"I get that. It's nice when duty and love can be one and the same."

I never heard it put that way, but I couldn't agree more. "Exactly. Besides, I like being the boss and building on what my parents started. And now, I can't imagine doing anything else."

"And I have to say…human resources is very you."

I shrug, owning it. "You're not wrong. What about you? What did you study? You went to college before you were in the Marines, right?"

"I did. Studied psychology," he says as we pass the lighting aisle.

"That tracks."

"And why's that?"

"Because you clearly like to try to understand people."

He eyes me up and down, like he's enjoying the view. Then he drops his voice to a low rasp. "Like you?"

The mood shifts instantly from the heat behind his words. "Be careful with that whole *seduction in the lighting aisle* thing you're doing," I whisper.

He arches a playful brow. "Or you'll throw yourself at me against the lamps?"

"Yes," I say emphatically, still keeping my voice low. "So behave. Anyone could take a pic and say Haven's banging her bodyguard."

He smiles, his dimple popping again, looking far too pleased. "What's that smile for?"

"What can I say? I like that you're banging your bodyguard."

Butterflies. A stupid flock of them takes flight inside me. I shift gears so I don't look all hearts-and-fluttery in the store in case I run into anyone. "Anyway, I'm glad business is increasing."

Banks rolls with the change-up. "Can you imagine what it'll be like when the movie's out?"

I'm a little giddy thinking about it. "I hope the film is great. But what about you?" The second I ask, I remember my conversation with Haven in her hotel room. "And speaking of, do you think Haven will need security when she returns to Los Angeles?"

My cautious and protective bodyguard tilts his head, clearly giving it some thought. "It's not a bad idea. Will she need round-the-clock? Probably not. But it'd be good for her to do a security checkup at her home. Her car. And online too. She might need a close protection officer from time to time, and even more so when she gets her Oscar."

I smile. "I'll make sure she hires you."

"You'd better."

"Do you think this gig will help you grow your business? Land new contracts?"

There's a part of me that keeps wondering, too, what happens when the job ends in another week. We haven't had that conversation. We haven't even tiptoed around it. Maybe because we made the boundaries so clear from the start that this is a temporary fling. A secret romance on the job.

Ergo—when the job ends, he says goodbye and returns to LA, and I stay here. A wave of sadness wallops me, but I try to swim out of it as he answers me with, "Tabitha has made some referrals in the entertainment business. I'm supposed to chat with Dean soon—he's my partner—about a couple leads."

I'm about to ask what sort of leads when his gaze lands squarely on the shelves we're passing. It's the cleaning section, full of mops, brooms, and...feather dusters. I stop abruptly, eyeing a purple one with a promise on its packaging—Synthetic *feathers soft enough to dust the most delicate glass and porcelain! We dare you to feel anything softer!*

Banks's lips twitch. "Should we take that dare?"

"For all the delicate glass and porcelain you've been dying to clean in the farmhouse?"

"Yes, Ripley. For that," he deadpans.

I reach out and touch the feathers. They're silky. "Mmm. Very soft."

He steps closer, scans the aisle, then runs his fingertips down the front of my shirt, over my belly.

My breath catches. "Are you competing with a synthetic feather duster?"

He shakes his head. "Just thinking of all the other DIY sex toys this great wide world has to offer."

But before I can say *me too*, the skitter of paws snags my attention. Josiah's orange cat scurries past us, chasing something unseen, then skidding at the end of the aisle.

A second later, Josiah calls out, "Sheldon! C'mere kitty, kitty." Josiah rounds the corner of an aisle, shrugging an apology for…cats. "He's in a mood today, Ripley. But can I help you with anything?"

He flashes a warm smile at me, then at Banks.

It takes me a second to reorient, and when I do, I just smile and shake my head. "I'm all good."

We leave the aisle immediately. The last thing I need is the whole town knowing this man can turn me on by talking about cleaning supplies.

Well, I sure like not having to do it myself.

Once we're back in the truck, Banks's phone rings. He checks the screen, then answers it. "Banks here."

There's a pause, and I can vaguely hear a masculine voice on the other line; then Banks says, "Excellent. Any idea when they want to schedule it for?"

Another pause; then he hums appreciatively. "Damn, that's soon."

This call sounds promising, especially when he adds, "Let's set it up. Nice work."

Another pause.

"We did it together. Like a team." A few more seconds. "Excellent. Talk soon."

When the call ends, I'm raring to ask, *What was that about?* But I swallow the words. That's a girlfriend question. We're not there. We're not headed there.

I fiddle with the seat belt, like that's what I meant to be doing all along. Banks clears his throat. "That was Dean."

"Oh?" I try to act nonchalant, though I'm dying to know about the call.

His brown eyes flicker with a familiar emotion—professional excitement. "Tabitha made an intro, and we have a meeting with Webflix."

"You do?" I ask cautiously. I don't want to read anything into what this meeting might mean for *us*. Even though I really do. Webflix is based in San Francisco, but I don't say that. The prospect is too thrilling to voice.

"They shoot a bunch of their shows in San Francisco. They need cybersecurity and set security," Banks says evenly.

"That's fantastic. See? This movie is leading to connections for you too," I say, trying to focus purely on the professional side of this news. Then, so it's clear I get where he's coming from, and I support him, I add, a little jokingly, "I promise I won't distract you anymore during the shoot."

But he doesn't take the bait. He peers out the driver's side window, then cranes his neck to check the lot behind us. Seeming satisfied, he sets a hand on my thigh. "This might sound crazy, but…"

My heart explodes into a gallop. It's racing like a horse. "Yes?"

"Well, San Francisco's pretty close," he says, and his smile is hopeful.

"It is. You might be working there?"

"Yeah," he says, squeezing my thigh, his voice pitching up. "What do you think of that, Ripley?"

I think my chest is tingling. I think my cells are dancing. "I think San Francisco has some nice cafés, and restaurants, and nail salons, and yoga places."

He leans a little closer, almost like he's going to kiss me. "Someday, I'll be able to finish that thought in public."

Maybe someday soon.

CHAPTER 36
TOP SECRET
RIPLEY

A few days later, as I'm working on the back deck and reviewing orders from plant shops in the area that carry our flowers, a voice whispers, *"Psst."*

It's Haven, and I set the laptop down and head to the railing. She's been shooting here all day at the farm, and there's clearly a break right now. Most of the crew is near the rows of Impress Purple and the white bench at the top of the path. New Chris and Haven have been talking on the bench in an important scene since all Very Important Conversations are had on benches.

"What's going on?"

She glances around the vast lawn, checking for eavesdroppers before she mutters, "Check your texts."

This is top-secret level. I spin around and grab my phone from the chair, clicking open her message sent five minutes ago.

Haven: Remember when we played that game with Linc Turner?

With curious eyes, I look up at my troublemaking sister, sensing where she's going. Her eager smile gives her away. I tap out a fast reply.

Ripley: You mean the one where I broke up with him for you because the asshole was a cheater?

The second her phone pings, she nods excitedly. "Yes."
I growl. "Who hurt you and where is he?"
Shaking her head, she replies at the speed of light.

Haven: The opposite! Is there any chance you could, you know, leave my hotel in a sort of noticeable way tonight? So any photogs or fans will think I've left?

My jaw comes unhinged, and I mouth, "You naughty minx."
If a shrug could say *yes, I am*, hers does. Without wasting a second, I write back.

Ripley: Does this mean you want to have a date with William at your hotel or out of your hotel?
Haven: Both, hopefully! We want to go to Duck Falls and do a bookstore blind date—it's where you go to a bookshop and pick a book you think the other person will like.

Then have dinner someplace kind of quiet and out of the way. He sent me flowers this morning to ask me if I wanted to go on a date with him.

That sounds fantastic. I smile so big as I meet her gaze, not even waiting to text back, instead asking quietly, "Are you going to go public?"

"It's so early," she says, a nervous smile twisting her lips. "But would it make it easier for you if I did?"

My brow pinches. "What? No! What do you mean?"

"Do you want me to go public so people know I'm not with Chris? Maybe then you won't have to deal with all the trouble of having a bodyguard."

I blanch for so many reasons. First, she and William have only gone on a few actual dates. I don't want to pressure her to go public to make my little life easier. Plus, what if she and William don't last long? Then she's having to acknowledge a breakup in the public eye. Best they be solid before she does announce a relationship status. Besides, the shoot's over soon, and even if she soft-launched her romance tonight, I'd probably still need a bodyguard for the rest of the shoot given how Haven's star has risen quickly over the last year. I also really, *really* like having a bodyguard, it turns out.

I grab her wrist and squeeze it. "Nope. What I want, though, are all the details of your date with the hot Irish bookstore owner."

"And you'll get them," she says.

Then Tabitha calls out, "Haven Addison."

My sister rushes back to the set, waving to me as she goes.

That night, we prep for the full switcheroo, enlisting our bodyguards in it too, so we can sell the ruse to any photographers hanging around outside The BookHouse. Banks is off tonight, so one of his backups is covering me, a sturdy guy named Marcus who Banks knows from the Marines too.

"This might be all for nothing," Haven says as we settle onto her bed to polish my nails. "Sometimes the press is here at the hotel. Sometimes random tourists are, and they take pics of me."

"It's definitely not for nothing. Did you see those set pics the other day?" The film's PR department released more photos from the shoot.

"I did. It's so surreal," Haven says, then shifts again to the matter at hand. "You really don't mind?"

I scoff. "Not only do I not mind, I insist. Because you're never too old to play twin tricks."

"Truth," she says.

"And besides, Addison girls don't cut corners."

"We go all out."

I paint my nails the same light-pink shade as hers, then grab one of her hoodies. But even as we're having a blast, a kernel of guilt wedges into my chest, like a stone in a shoe. Haven's been open with me about her budding romance. Surely I could do the same about mine. We protect each other. We don't reveal each other's secrets.

On the hotel bed, as I flap my hands around to dry the polish, I weigh the possibility of telling her when her phone rings. She stretches across the mattress to grab it from the nightstand.

"Hi, Michelle," she says.

Ah, it's her agent.

"They do?"

A pause.

"When?"

Another pause.

"Of course I can do it."

One more pause. This one is long and Haven nods with wide eyes, her smile growing bigger by the second. As she listens, I flash back to the last time I was in a hotel. Not with Haven, when I stopped by the other week. But more than a month ago. The night I met Banks. I picture opening the door of the room for our tryst and hoping it'd be him.

Then, I remember my embarrassment when the hotel clerk stood there with an envelope of rejection. I can see the moment so clearly, but I don't feel those emotions anymore. The foolishness has vanished. The shame has faded away. I'm no longer worried about my terrible track record with men and what that might mean. I don't see myself anymore as the know-it-all, the *too independent* one, the pushy one, like I told Grandma I feared I was.

Sure, I am those things, but I'm okay with that, because I let Banks get to know the real me. He's shown me who he is too. My whole heart softens as I think of him.

I want to tell Haven about this unexpected romance. I'm desperate to tell her. Maybe I can soon, since so much has changed over the last few weeks.

When the call ends, I shove away the memory and shelve the

desire as Haven says, "First, *The Madison Marlowe Show* invited me as a guest when I return to LA."

"The late-night talk show?" I squeak out. It's become one of the most popular interview shows on-air.

"Yes, to talk about the movie and everything. Plus, there's some interest in me for a lead on a TV show."

I gasp. TV is the golden goose. "Tell me everything."

She shares the details, telling me Vega is writing a script for TV and potentially wants to work with Haven again. When she's done, there's no time for me to confess my burgeoning romance. Maybe tomorrow. Or another day. "That's awesome," I say.

"I can't wait to tell William tonight."

"Maybe he can go down to LA for the appearance," I suggest, since I'm helpful like that.

"You're such an enabler."

"I'm full of brilliant ideas."

"Like this one," she says, then hands me her purse since I suggested earlier that we trade bags. I give her mine. We swapped the contents earlier.

"And now, the pièce de résistance." Grandly, with much fanfare, she hands me her pair of pink heart-shaped shades.

"Ooh, your signature accessory these days." I put on the sunnies, pushing them through my hair so they act as a headband.

Then, it's showtime.

I yank open the door, greeting the sturdy woman who protects my sister most of the time. "Hi, Wanda! How's everything going?" I ask brightly, imitating Haven.

She blinks, shaking her head in amusement. "It's eerie."

"I know," I say, pleased we're so convincing.

She walks with me down the hall, then the steps, then into the lobby. From behind the desk, Bridget doesn't even bat a lash. She simply smiles. "Do you need help with anything, Haven?"

I drum my fingers on the counter, talking a touch faster than I do usually, a bit peppier. "Is that arcade still open on Main Street?"

"The one we all used to go to in high school?"

"Yes. The retro arcade," I say.

"It is."

"Fabulous. I haven't played Ms. Pac-Man in ages," I say, naming Haven's favorite game.

"Pretty sure you still have the high score."

Well, Haven *was* excellent at that game. "Awesome," I say, then turn around, but like I forgot something, I spin back. "What time is it?"

Bridget smiles kindly, clearly knowing Haven was always rubbish with time. "Seven ten."

"Thanks, Bridge. Don't wait up too late for me, but I'll text you later."

She looks momentarily confused, but I'll explain it to her soon.

When I turn around, I say to Wanda, "Do you like arcade games? I have to show you this fun arcade in my hometown. It's even better than the one in—" I stop, think, then take a wild guess: "Santa Monica."

"That's high praise."

"I know," I say, and we make a show of walking through the

lobby. And I mean *show*. Because I want someone to see me act. I thought I'd hate it, but acting in my own body—so to speak—is surprisingly fun. I'm not me right now. I'm my sister, and I know what to do with my face. Smile. Shine. Beam.

Like Haven did when she faced her demons and took charge of her mental health. When she went to therapy and worked on herself. When she moved forward from grief and the choke hold it had on her.

Like that, I protect my sister as I walk out of the hotel, being the best bodyguard for her so her secret boyfriend can slip upstairs and see her.

"Damn, girl. You're working it," Wanda whispers proudly.

"Thank you."

Yup. I'm pulling it off.

C'mon, photographers. Show up. Take my pic. I dare you.

I'm only mildly disappointed that there are no photographers waiting on the street. But I'm wildly happy when I spot William in a blue Prius, pulling around the side of the hotel to the back door.

I turn to go, having pulled it off when someone clears a throat from behind me. "Just the person I wanted to see."

Oh, shit.

I wince, stopping in my tracks at the sound of Vega's voice. Didn't see that coming. But then, I fasten on my best Haven grin, turning around. Vega strides from inside the inn toward me on the street. I'm a little terrified. She's the most no-nonsense of no-nonsense people I've ever met.

"Hey! What's going on?" I ask brightly.

"The scene tomorrow," she says, tapping her chin. "Your character—I think before the wedding, in order for us to believe she'd run off with her brother's best friend when she finds out her groom is cheating, she needs to be doubting her choices already."

Vega waits.

Oh. Right. This is where I speak. "Cold feet?" I ask, hoping that's what an actor would say not only to a director but to a director who possibly wants to work with her again.

Vega's brow knits, a look of displeasure. "Yes, but ask yourself why, Haven. Why does she have cold feet?"

This feels like one of those dreams when you're back in school and you didn't study for the test. I steal a glance at Wanda, like maybe she keeps a crib sheet of actor answers with her. But she's scanning the streets.

It's up to me to play the actress. Time to improvise. Like the kid who definitely missed all the classes, I try again, suggesting, "Because her groom is cheating?"

"But she doesn't know that." It's a slap on an actor's wrist.

Vega taps her toe. I gulp, then try one more time. "Because she's always wondered if maybe the brother's best friend is the guy for her?"

That earns me a small safe nod; then I'm saved by a voice saying, "Two of my favorite people!"

It's New Chris, striding toward the hotel, his bodyguard by his side. New Chris barely seems to notice that Silas and Ludwig are flanking his security team. The star stops right in front of me, flashing that high-wattage smile, ignoring the hell out of the photographers snapping our picture and shouting questions like, "Big date tonight?" "Where are you having dinner?" "How long have you been together?"

Like he doesn't even hear them, he looks me in the eyes as if I'm the only person in the world and says, "I think I heard you talking about the big opening scene. I'd love to discuss my ideas for it. Vega and I were going to get a drink and really break it down. Goal, motivation, wants. Are you in?"

I draw a big blank when it comes to excuses. I stand like a fish with my mouth open. Shoot. Haven would never do that. Haven would say yes. "Of course."

New Chris turns to the pack of pushy photogs, his grin never faltering as he says, "To answer your question, I'm having a drink with my co-star and my director."

And that is how I wind up pretending to be my sister for another hour. I'll take my Oscar right now, thank you very much.

I sink into a booth in the corner of Prohibition Spirit an hour later, exhausted and utterly relieved. I texted Haven a heads-up so she knows what happened; then I sent an emergency get-your-asses-over-here-stat text to my friends. Chloe and Bridget are here while Wanda watches the door.

First, I confess our twin trick, and Bridget swats my arm. "You fooled me."

I blow on my nails. "When you're good, you're good."

"More like when you have matching DNA with another person, you're good," she corrects.

"That's true too," I say; then I tell them all about how I was corralled by the director and the movie star into a quick drink to discuss where the characters were before the scene, what they want, and who they are. "Mostly I learned I'm terrible at bullshitting."

"I want to feel sorry for you, but this is what you get when you play twin tricks on me," Bridget says.

I pluck at my shirt. "I mean, I was sweating. I think I have pit stains. That acting stuff is hard."

Chloe lifts a glass. "Amen. I'm pretty sure I'm an excellent me, but a terrible someone else."

"Let's all drink to being excellent me's," Bridget offers.

I lift my old-fashioned, and we clink glasses.

Then, I take a deep, fortifying breath and tell them what I couldn't say to my sister. I can't keep it inside any longer. "I think I'm falling for my bodyguard."

They huddle closer, and Chloe goes first. "Really? That's so good, especially because you've been so gun-shy since Eric Patrick."

She's not entirely wrong. But my fear of closeness started long before then, and well before I worried I had a terrible track record with men. "It's not just him—not just my ex. Or exes. It's…" I pause and swallow past the deep-seated fears that have lived in me ever since I was fifteen and my life changed irrevocably. "It's just I don't think people stick around."

"Oh, sweet friend," Chloe says, giving me a side hug.

"We do," Bridget says gently, rubbing my shoulder.

My eyes shine, but I fight off the tears. "I know that. I do. You two always have been there. So has Haven. But it's not about that." I tap my sternum. "It's about *this*. And how it broke when my parents died."

They nod thoughtfully, understanding completely.

"But I have to move past it. I *can* move past it. It's time." I swipe away an errant tear on my cheek. "Dating and romance aren't the same as what happened to my parents. I'm learning that. I need to remember that."

The day I told Banks about the photo helped me to see that I could let go of some of my past hurts. That I can move forward even when it's scary. "I think…maybe I'm ready."

Chloe fights off a grin. Bridget smiles proudly. "What are you going to do about it?" Bridget asks.

"You'd better not move to LA," Chloe chides.

I scoff. "Like I could move."

"So what then?" Bridget presses.

"I really don't know, but I think maybe when the film is over, we can explore…something."

"Sounds like you're already exploring lots of things," Chloe says with an arch of her brow.

I laugh, relieved for the levity, and then I drink to that. I feel better that I was honest with them. But there's someone else I need to speak the truth to as well, and it's not my sister. It's the man himself. "He's got a lot riding on this job, so I'll wait to talk to him about what's next." I smile. "I'm very patient."

We finish our glasses and then leave, with Wanda taking me back to the farm. As I walk to the cottage, I set aside thoughts of the future and focus on the now, assembling a plan.

A redo.

I picture the outfit I'll wear. Well, after I shower since…sweat is gross. I imagine what I'll say. How it might feel.

But when I open the door to get ready for Banks, he's already here. And it looks like he's paid a visit to quite a number of local shops to satisfy our DIY sex toy habit.

CHAPTER 37
A SMORGASBORD
RIPLEY

It's a sex toy buffet. "Can I have one of everything?" I ask as I survey the offerings on the coffee table.

"You can have everything," Banks says, standing by like a proud…charcuterist creator? Potluck purveyor? Who knows, but the man has outdone himself with his selection of unconventional toys. I pick up the first one, inspecting it, then dangling the stick with the stuffed fake blue bird at the end. "You stopped by a pet store?"

"Don't knock it. Those fake feathers look pretty soft," he says.

I run the baby-blue faux feathers over my palm. "Cats have the right idea," I say, but there's one issue. "Though I might feel a little weird using a pet toy in bed."

"Fair enough."

I set it down and pick up the next option. A silky pink ribbon, long and curling. "Paid a visit to the craft store?"

"I was a busy boy."

I rub my fingers against the material, then hum approvingly. "It's silky," I say, then drag it over the top of my chest. "Very silky."

His eyes widen as I demonstrate.

Next, I pick up the synthetic feather duster and run it down my arm. My breath catches. But I frown. "I'm not sure I'm ready to come to terms with getting aroused by a cleaning tool. But I would definitely love to watch you do dishes and fold laundry someday because that sounds unspeakably hot."

He leans in, cups my cheek, and plants a quick, firm kiss to my lips. "Just wait till you see what I can do with fitted sheets."

"You can fold fitted sheets?" I ask breathily, my chest already heaving.

"Perfectly," he says in a husky promise.

I nibble on the corner of my lips. "I'm not sure we need toys then. Knowing that is foreplay enough."

He grabs my ass, then hauls me against him for a deeper kiss. When he breaks it, he says, "Get on the bed, sweetheart."

I have a feeling I know which one's coming. In a flash, I shed my clothes, leaving on my white lace bra and panties.

I settle onto the bed on my back, as he prowls over to me. He's wearing jeans and nothing else. My mouth waters at the sight of him—broad chest, thick shoulders, carved abs, and all that ink on his muscular arm. The symbols of who he is, what he believes in. As he returns to the table, picking up the ribbon, he regards me with wild heat in his dark eyes. Passion too, as he returns to me, his gaze journeying up and down me. He dangles the pink ribbon over my chest, the soft end of it teasing against my left breast, tickling me. "Still want to skip foreplay?"

The rush of heat shooting down my body makes me a liar as I arch into the ribbon's touch. "No."

He stands by the side of the bed, teasing the ribbon down my body, between my breasts, over my belly. It's soft, and I shudder as he drags it over me, like it's a feather.

And yes, apparently I'm into flower ticklers, headband bondage, and now ribbon play. Who knew? Maybe Banks did. Maybe he sensed this about me all along. I stretch my neck, a sign for him to keep going. He takes my cue and runs with it, dangling the silky material over me, then coasting the end down my arm. I'm aching. He's not even touching me with his body, not his hands, not his mouth, not his cock, and still my skin is tingling, my thighs shaking.

He continues his erotic torture, unfurling the ribbon down my body, over my legs, then back up, along the inside of my thighs. I part my legs for him.

He stares wantonly at my white panties. "You look so fucking beautiful," he says, and he sounds filthy and adoring.

He drops the ribbon and bends to run his knuckles along the side of my face, tracing my jawline.

Funny how I thought I'd come back to the cottage and demand a spanking, like I wanted the night I met him, but when he showed me the table of toys, I wanted that more.

Because of how he uses whatever sex toys he MacGyvers—he uses them to turn me on. That's his sole mission—*me*. And with

Banks, I'm learning I don't have to solve a thing. I get to fix…nothing. I don't have to think at all, and I like not having a to-do list.

Or perhaps I like that I'm his to-do list.

Banks takes each item on it very seriously, leaning down and starting with tugging down the cup of the bra on my right breast. Giving me a kiss on my nipple. Then sucking.

I draw a sharp breath.

Next, he bites.

I gasp.

He lifts his face, raises an eyebrow. Asking if that was okay.

"Yes," I murmur.

He rubs his chin against my exposed breast, the stubble from his short beard whisking across my skin. He's sandpaper to my softness, and the contrast makes me squirm. Makes me want him. I reach for his chest, my fingers playing with the wiry hair on his pecs.

A grunt falls from his lips. He looks up, and in a flash he's on the bed, straddling me, pinning my wrists down. "You trying to touch me?" he asks, but it's not aggressive. It's curious. Playful. Like he always is with me.

"I am," I admit.

He lifts his chin. "You can touch me when I fuck you."

I shiver. From ribbons to words. "Now you're really teasing me."

He smirks. "I know."

I exhale into the good feelings, then relax into the bed when he lets go of my wrists, expecting Banks to travel down my body. Instead he moves to the side, lying next to me, kissing my neck. My clavicle. My shoulder.

I shudder, luxuriating in him.

He dusts a soft kiss to the top of my arm, then spends a good long time kissing his way down, turning me soft and liquid everywhere as I realize what he's doing. He's kissing each bird on my skin.

As the strength of that hits me, I turn to him, our chests flush, and kiss his mouth—hard, deep, and passionate. We kiss till we're twisting together, our bodies seeking even more contact.

With some reluctance, he breaks the embrace, then pushes me down to my back. Moving along my body, his lips whisk over each breast, travel down my belly, then to my hips.

I'm gasping and arching, desperately hoping he gets the message, when he looks up at me with a satisfied smirk. "Ask for it."

I'm too turned on to taunt him back. "Go down on me," I plead.

"Beg for it." His lips twitch; then his eyes drift so he's staring between my legs. "Beg for my mouth."

I grow wetter from the demand. "Please. I'm begging you, Banks."

That's all it takes. Scooping me up, he flips me over to all fours. "Ass up," he instructs, and I comply as heat sparks through my whole body.

Moving behind me, he settles, then hauls me up higher and dives in, kissing my pussy without mercy.

The sounds I make are long and carnal. I didn't realize how much I needed this till he put me in this position. "Need you. Want you," I murmur as he kisses my wetness.

Stopping briefly, he mutters, "I know."

"So cocky," I say, but it comes out strangled when he flicks his tongue up and down my aching core.

Soon words and taunts become meaningless. He takes me apart with each delicious flick till I'm shaking. I grab at the sheets, clutching them for dear life as his fingers dig into my flesh and his mouth owns me.

I'm dissolving into the bed, panting, moaning. My breathing turns shallow, and I'm close, so damn close. One more flick of his tongue, then he fastens his mouth to my clit and sucks, and pleasure pulses everywhere inside me—a wave relentlessly heading to the shore. With a final hungry groan from him, the wave crashes.

I break apart into moans and sensations, into lust and emotions, into this endlessly wonderful moment with this man. With my face pressed against the covers, I try to catch my breath. He must move off me, because the sound of a zipper coming undone filters by, then the noise of clothes being shed.

A few seconds later, Banks is back on the bed, a foil packet in hand, and he's gently turning me to my side. He spoons me, kissing my neck, running his hands along my arms. "Want to fuck you like this," he murmurs.

"Do it," I urge.

He nips at my neck harder, biting. "Fuck, Ripley. You're so fucking perfect for me," he mutters.

"Same," I pant out.

"Yeah?" It's asked full of wonder.

I don't answer with words but actions, wriggling against him, trying to get closer. He jerks my body tightly to his, gripping me like he never wants to let go, kissing me madly for a breathless second. Then he stops, rolls on the condom, and nudges the head of his cock against my slickness, letting out a staggered breath. "Need you. Want you," he growls, repeating my words from earlier as he fills me.

With a wicked smile I say, "I know."

He doesn't reply in kind saying *so cocky*, like I did to him moments ago. Instead, he says, gravelly and vulnerably at the same time, "Good. I want you to know how much I want you. How much I need you."

That last verb echoes in the night air. *Need.* As he moves in me, I feel it too. All this need. Words break apart. We're both reduced to gasps. Groans. Heated sighs. He wraps one arm around my shoulders, the other around my waist.

It's not slow and languid, like I expected. It's not a middle-of-the-night tender spooning, with gentle kisses. It's passionate and deep. It's him taking me and showing me how much he needs me.

This kind of sex is not at all what I expected when I walked in the door tonight. But then again, everything about this man has surprised me, from his taste in music, to his smart mouth, to his big and scarred heart.

His arms are like ropes, binding me to him, keeping me in his inescapable grasp as he fucks me, his mouth skimming over my neck the whole time. "Fucking love this," he grits out against my skin.

Flesh slaps against flesh. Sweat-slicked skin slides against sweat-slicked skin. We're hot and sweaty and desperate, and I feel like I'm on the verge of release with every punishing thrust.

But there's one more thing I want. We've tried flowers and headbands and ribbons. The man is good with his hands though. Great, actually. I crane my neck and look back at him, at the restraint in his features, the clench of his jaw coupled with the fire in his eyes. "In San Francisco? When I thought you were at the hotel room door?"

He slows his hips, concern briefly flickering across his irises. "Yes?"

"I opened it and said *spank me*." It feels so good to finally say that. To let him know I wanted to explore my desires with him. "I've never said that to anyone," I blurt out, suddenly confessing the depth of my desires.

His cock slides deeper, and the sound he makes is the hottest thing I've ever heard. "You can have anything with me," he says, sounding as desperate as I feel. "Want it now, sweetheart?"

"So much."

He lifts a hand and slaps it on the outside of my ass. The sharp sting radiates through me, then blurs into pleasure.

"More?"

"Yes. Please," I say.

Another smack. Another cry from me. Then, my world tunnels to these sensations—his hand smacking my ass, the bite that spirals through me, the hot rush of pleasure in my core.

Then this—the giving in, as I fall to pieces in his arms one more time, sinking into blissful oblivion. He follows me there with a powerful thrust, then grunts, growls, murmurs.

And quietly kisses me.

Sometime later, I don't know when, he's kissing my hair, whispering sweet nothings of praise, then saying, "Next time I'm going to use that cat toy on you."

"Only after I watch you fold the sheets *and* make the bed."

"Deal."

I feel shiny inside and out from the words *next time*. From the easy promise in them. From the possibility of all our next times.

A little later, after we straighten up, he pulls on clothes and fetches my dog from the house. Through the window, I spot Banks taking Hudson for a quick midnight stroll through the lavender bushes. The sight of that man walking my pooch makes my heart beat far too fast.

When he returns, he settles Hudson onto the floor and comes back to bed.

"Thank you," I tell him. "I seriously appreciate your dog-walking skills." I pause, then add, "Among others."

"You're welcome." He doesn't ask for anything in return. I get the sense he gives to give. It's in his nature, these little acts of service. Gently, he turns me around so I'm facing away from him. He rubs my neck, kneading the usual sore spots. Yeah, it's definitely in his nature.

"Like this skill too," I say, relaxing into his touch.

"Good." He sounds happy. Maybe that's what he gets out of these little gestures. They make him happy too—to be able to give and know it's received. So I happily take, knowing it's working for both of us.

A few minutes later, he kisses the back of my neck, then stops rubbing. With a sigh, he says, "I still regret not coming to your hotel room."

"Don't," I say.

"But I do. If I had, maybe we could have started sooner."

Started, not stopped.

He wraps his arms around me, like we're not stopping whatever this is becoming—little gestures and big feelings.

CHAPTER 38
HER TURN
RIPLEY

"I knew it wasn't her."

The humble-brag comes from Grandma the next day as the three of us settle into a table at the restaurant at The Ladybug Inn.

Haven's call time isn't till this afternoon, so we stole away for a girls' breakfast like old times, when Grandma used to take us here once a month back when we were in high school. Well, as long as we brought home good grades and excellent attendance.

Haven knits her brow at the older woman. "How did you know there's a pic?"

Amused, Grandma shakes her head. "Send my girls out of the nest, and they forget all about me."

Haven's mouth falls open in awareness. "You're right. I almost forgot about Daisy's penchant for gossip. She told you?"

Grandma nods. Her bestie *loves* gossip, so I'm guessing she showed Grandma the pic of Haven, New Chris, and the director from *Page Six* this morning.

I saw it too—Banks showed it to me as we walked Hudson together. He laughed about it, mostly over our *twin antics*. He said the same thing as Grandma. *I knew it was you.*

Right now, he's waiting outside the restaurant with Wanda. I sort of feel like we should invite them in, but Grandma wanted to have a just-family meal.

"How did you know it was Ripley pretending to be me?" Haven whispers.

Grandma grabs her phone from her purse and swipes up. She clicks on something, then swivels the screen around, tapping on that pic. "Ripley always has this little extra sass in her eyes and her expression."

"Thanks, Grandma," I say dryly. "And Haven's sweeter?"

Haven flashes her good-girl-next-door grin. "I'm sugar. You're salt."

I roll my eyes, but still I say, with a you-got-me-there shrug, "No lies detected."

But before Grandma puts her phone away, something catches my attention on screen. "That's not *Page Six*. I thought that's where the picture ran. But it's on *VIP Vibes* too?"

"Seems so." She pauses. "But why do you ask?"

I'm not sure why it matters. "The angle's just different than the other pic." I study the photo info, but it just says News Site Ink. Banks told me that's the company that buys pics from photographers and sells them to celeb sites. He said the stocky guy—Ludwig—sells to News Site Ink a lot, which supplies to *VIP Vibes*. And Silas sells to *Page Six*. That makes sense, after all. I relax again. "It's nothing. There were two photogs last night, so of course there'd be a couple angles."

"And neither one fooled me," Grandma says, "because you're mine and I've never not been able to tell you two apart. But I do think it's hilarious that you're still doing that. You tricked your parents, but..."

Haven and I look at each other, grinning as we recite Grandma's rallying cry in unison. "We never tricked you."

"You never did," she says, then thumps her reading glasses case against the table. "Let's order."

We order the ladybug pancakes, and when we close our menus, I turn to my sister. "Also, that was close," I say, letting out a belated sigh of relief over last night's fake-out.

"I still can't believe you pulled it off," she says, grinning. "Vega texted me this morning to tell me she loved my ideas and can't wait for the wedding scene."

"That's this afternoon?"

"Yes. It's the first scene in the film but one of the last ones we're shooting. We should go out and celebrate some night before I leave," she says, her voice pitching up. "With Chloe and Bridget."

"Let's do it," I say.

The shoot ends after this weekend. That's a reminder that I should talk to Banks about us. But when Grandma clears her throat and says, "Now, girls. I have something I want to tell you," I drop all thoughts of my own romance.

Is she sick? Is something wrong? I'm not even sure why I go there, except when you open the door to a police officer telling you your parents are dead, sometimes you assume the worst.

"What is it?" I ask, my voice threaded with worry.

She reaches across the table for my hand. "I know you're saving for me to go to cooking school in Paris, but I decided I'm doing it myself. I have money saved," she says.

"No," I say instantly. "I told you I want to. As a gift to you."

"That's not necessary."

"But I want to," I repeat, then rattle off all the reasons. The farm is growing in popularity. Sales are up. Tourism is increasing.

I take a breath, building up a new head of steam, but Haven cuts me off. "Actually, I paid for your school."

Grandma snaps her gaze to Haven. "What?"

"You can go anytime. I did it last night, and I'll email you the info. You've both worked so hard to help me, but it's my turn now. I want to give this to you, Grandma. And I didn't want Ripley to know. So I went ahead and took care of it all on my own."

"Haven," I say quietly, my throat tightening with emotion.

My sister squares her shoulders. "It's my turn to give back."

My little sister. Younger by only five minutes, but she's always seemed like the baby of the family. Now, she's taking care of both of us, and it's beautiful to see because of how far she's come.

Grandma's lip quivers, and she meets Haven's eyes, then mine. She reaches for one of my hands and one of Haven's. "My girls."

It's said with such affection and love that my heart breaks in a whole new way—with happiness for the family we became out of necessity one snowy night, then shaped with this deep and abiding love.

Grandma turns her attention to the hostess stand. "We should get two more place settings."

She rises and heads to the front of the café, motioning for Banks and Wanda to join us. They do, keeping watch the whole time, but—I think—enjoying their ladybug pancakes, nonetheless.

After breakfast, Haven's phone rings with Tabitha's name flashing across it. She chats briefly with the producer as we leave The Ladybug Inn, then says to her, "I'm on it." When she ends the call, she says, "A PA spilled coffee on the wedding dress. It's ruined and we need a new one, stat, so Tabitha tracked one down at Second Time Around. They're doing a quick adjustment to the straps, and I offered to pick it up on our way back."

We hustle over to the consignment shop in town and snag the replacement gown. As we leave, there's a tour group coming down the street that stops and asks my sister for autographs.

"We love *Someone Else's Ring* so much," one woman says.

"And you're Lucy Snow! She's so tough. The way she walked out on her wedding day," another coos.

"And you and Chris are the perfect pair to play them," one more adds.

Haven smiles and thanks them all as she signs and poses for selfies.

Wanda stays close to Haven while Grandma and I stand back, Banks scanning the street, watching over us. Across the road, some passersby slow down, lifting their phones to take pics of the moment.

Cyrus would think that was very meta too. I can't wait to tell him. Better yet, to show him. I grab my phone to snap a pic of it, but once I open the camera the group across the street has moved on. As they walk toward the corner, I spot a profile that feels familiar. But then they turn down the block and out of sight, so I let the déjà vu sensation slip away as I return to the farm.

CHAPTER 39
THE CAUTIOUS ONE
BANKS

Dean calls in the afternoon while I'm in the house setting up some security checks with new corporate clients in Los Angeles—we'll test cameras, handle background checks, and evaluate cybersecurity. I answer the phone right away, and Dean wastes no time on a greeting.

"Can you get away Friday afternoon?"

"Nice to hear from you too. And probably," I say. I've got backup here to cover Ripley when I can't. "What's it for? Did you get first-baseline tickets to the Dragons/Cougars game?"

Dean is a notorious baseball fan and will do just about anything to see a game.

"Yes, Banks. I'm suggesting we skip work to see a ball game," he deadpans, then returns to serious business. "Webflix wants to move quickly. They asked to meet with both of us this Friday."

I give a quick fist pump, then say in the same no-nonsense tone, "I'll be there."

"I'll lock it in for the afternoon and we'll meet with them in San Francisco."

"Is that where you'll stay?"

"Yup. I'll fly in Thursday night. I'll get you all the details."

"We should meet beforehand and go over our game plan," I suggest.

"Let's do it."

I exhale, and it feels like I've been holding my breath for a long time. I sink back into the couch, a little amazed. "Can I just say it? This is impressive. What we're pulling off."

"I hear you, but we're not there yet," he says, playing the cautious one, which is usually my role.

Lately though, not so much.

"Right, but still," I point out, "we started this firm a little over a year ago. We're blasting past all the goals we set."

"That is true," he admits.

"We won't have to work for anyone else again. Knock on wood and all."

"It's a relief, man," he says, then pauses for a beat. "And you're right. It's fucking impressive."

"I knew you'd see it my way," I say, my gaze swinging to the kitchen window. I check out the wedding-scene shoot, then turn to watch Ripley working in the fields.

She's gorgeous there amongst the flowers. She's in her element, doing what she loves, and she's damn good at it.

Dean and I chat briefly about the research and prep we'll both need to do, then we end the call. I sigh happily. But contentment is short-lived. I can't bask in the possibility of this business growth. Soon—very soon—I need to let my business partner know I'm not the cautious one. I'm not the obsessive one. I'm the wild card, the rogue one who fell for a client.

I never wanted to be that guy. I despise messes, especially ones I have to clean up. But this isn't a mess. It's a situation with a clear-enough solution.

But I don't have to tell him yet. I can do that when the shoot ends after this weekend.

Right? Right.

The thought twists my gut. I *should* tell him sooner. It's the responsible thing to do. I'm not sure I will though.

At least, not before I talk to Ripley.

That evening, after the cast and crew pack up and head into town for dinner, I find Ripley tossing a ball to Hudson, who hurtles after it toward the lavender maze, twinkling with fairy lights. I catch up with her quickly as the dog enters the purple hedges, hell-bent on chasing the errant missile.

"Hey," I say.

She turns around, seeming to fight a smile before giving in to it. Oh, hell. Is she feeling this too? If she feels even one-quarter of what I do, I'm a lucky guy. Because I am falling so damn hard for the woman I swore to protect. So hard that my stupid heart tumbles over itself as she says, "Oh, hi."

Emotions climb up my chest, but for several seconds, I don't know what to say. Fear holds me back. What if I can't protect her for the next few days? What if these risky feelings distract me on the job at a critical time? What if I fail her somehow?

On the other hand, what if I don't say a word?

Immediately, I know I can't walk away from her. I can't walk away from the possibility of us. The way I feel isn't wrong. It has to be right. I'm not my father. I'm not doing the same thing he did—not even close. I'm measured and calculating, and I have a plan—tell the woman I'm obsessed with how I feel, then tell my business partner.

Emboldened by my private pep talk, I say, "Ripley. That Webflix meeting is this Friday."

"That's great. I'm happy for you," she says.

"Me too, but that's not why I'm mentioning it." My pulse surges with more excitement than nerves. With anticipation of all the good things. "The movie ends after the weekend."

Nerves flicker across her eyes. "I know."

I step closer, look around, making sure it's only us as the sun dips lower in the sky, pink and purple streaks pulling toward the horizon. The lights on the hedges give this place a romantic glow. But it's not only us here. It's her dog too. He trots toward us from one of the coiled hedges, a ball in his mouth. "I want to keep seeing you when it wraps."

Her smile spreads so fast it makes my heart soar. "Yeah?"

"I do. I want us to try this," I say as Hudson drops the ball at our feet. "Out in public. For real. You and me. However we can make it work. Do you?"

She answers by stepping closer, cupping my cheek, quirking up the corner of her lips. "I suppose you're my type."

Of course. Of course she'd respond like that. So I give it right back to her. "I knew it."

She loops her arms around my neck. "Can rule number five be you kiss me right now?"

"Yes."

I comply, and for once in my life I don't mind feeling a little out of control. When we break the kiss, I pick up the ball and toss it back into the maze for Hudson to chase.

CHAPTER 40
TEMPTING AND DISTRACTING
RIPLEY

The next night, I go to Bridget's house to get ready. Haven's with Tabitha and the publicist doing an interview, and since my house is packed with the crew, I head to my friend's place a couple miles away.

Bridget's bungalow has a bright-red door, matching her usual red lipstick. As I knock, Banks gestures to an Adirondack chair on the deck.

"I'll wait here." He's carrying his tablet with a couple of sheets of paper sticking out of the case.

"You can come inside," I say as Bridget swings open the door.

"Nah. I like it here," he says.

"You're not a dog," Bridget says to him.

"Hey, I'd never leave my dog on the porch," I protest.

"That's true. You let Hudson sleep in the bed," Banks deadpans as he takes the seat.

"Where else would a dog sleep?" Chloe calls from inside.

"Fair point."

I follow my friends inside, and the second the door snicks shut, Chloe grabs my wrist. "So is this like a date for you and him?"

I scoff. "It's a girls' night out. He's just my bodyguard for the evening."

But not for much longer.

Bridget snorts, flicking her chestnut waves. "You can drop the act with us. We know he's not *just* anything."

My insides swirl with a giddiness I may never get over. I don't ever want to. "As a matter of fact, we're going to see each other when the job ends."

Chloe holds out a hand toward Bridget, rubbing her thumb against two fingers, the sign for *pay up*.

Bridget does the same to her. "You pay up."

"No, you," Chloe insists.

"You bet on this?" I ask.

"Yes. But we both bet you would get together with him, so we had to bet when you'd tell us. I predicted now," Bridget says.

"I picked tonight," Chloe says with a frown.

"Wow. Glad I'm so predictable," I say as we head to Bridget's bedroom. "But I do need to tell Haven." I haven't yet. She's been busy every day with the shoot and the publicity.

I guess I also haven't said anything because I feel the need to protect Banks. What if Haven accidentally lets it slip in front of Wanda or the other security team members? I don't want to get my guy in trouble. Telling Chloe and Bridget is different. They don't work with Banks's co-workers or employees.

There's time. There will definitely be time.

I focus instead on getting ready, sliding into a pair of jeans and a strappy tank that reveals a hint of my stomach.

Chloe declares it perfect as she wiggles into a purple dress. "What do you think?"

"It's perfection too."

Bridget pulls on a pair of vegan leather shorts with a sexy black top and cute little boots.

As we put the finishing touches on our makeup, huddling close together in front of Bridget's vintage art deco mirror, I turn to Chloe. "So, how's everything going with the dog training?"

"I started with the Simmons' Chihuahua, and you know how spicy those dogs are."

"Spicy dogs need trainers," I say.

"That's why I love spicy dogs," Chloe says.

"And how's everything at the inn?" I ask Bridget as I slick on lip gloss.

"Overbooked," she says, cool and unfazed. "But I can handle it. Hey, you should turn Lavender Bliss Farms into an inn too."

That sounds truly overwhelming. "I'm just happy business is picking up."

When we're all ready a little later, we take off, with Bridget and Chloe sliding into a Lyft, and me joining Banks in the truck, since there's only room for two.

After he shuts my door, he heads to the driver's side, then eyes me up and down as he clicks on his seat belt. "Gonna be really hard not to have my hands all over you tonight, sweetheart."

"Then consider it a test of your control," I tease.

"It will test all of it," he says. He sets down his tablet and hands me a folded piece of paper. "For your collection."

I stare at the paper butterfly, and my heart saunters around like a show-off. "Thank you."

"I knew you liked me," he says with an easy shrug.

"Oh, shut up and drive," I say.

He smiles the whole way, and it feels good, like this is the start of the next phase of our unexpected romance. When we arrive outside Prohibition Spirit, he pulls into the lot next to it, cuts the engine, and then peers into the rearview window behind us. Satisfied, he returns his focus to me, staring with hungry eyes. He groans, shaking his head. "You are too tempting."

I like being tempting to him. So much. "Better work on that resistance."

"I do, every second I'm with you," he says.

He comes around to the passenger door and swings it open, offering me a hand. I take it. This is something he's done before. It's a normal bodyguard gesture, to offer a hand, but he doesn't let go right away.

Not when I step down. Not when I look at him. Not at all. He holds my gaze, pinning me with his dark stare, clasping my hand tight—a man whose restraint is fraying razor-thin. "Soon, sweetheart. I am going to finish this thought in public so damn soon."

"I guess I'll have to be patient."

"You're very, very good at it," he says, looking like it's the hardest thing in the world to resist me.

Faintly, I register someone walking past us toward the bar entrance. A group of people. Banks blinks, dropping my hand instantly as he turns their way, then looks back, frowning.

"What's wrong? Do you know them?" I ask, worried.

He squints. "Nothing." Then he shakes it off. "I can't get distracted, Ripley. You never know. You just never know."

This man is still so hard on himself. "You didn't get distracted though."

He blows out a heavy breath. "I'd better not."

He doesn't sound like he's forgiven himself, but I'm not sure there was a transgression.

We head inside, and seconds later, Haven arrives with Wanda. Before we know it, we're swept up into the hum and buzz of Prohibition Spirit, busier than usual and full of locals we know and tourists we don't. The scales are tipped toward the latter.

Things are changing here, especially since usually this place is a low-key whiskey bar, but tonight Esmeralda has turned up the volume, and she's playing upbeat pop tunes.

We order champagne and toast to Haven and Darling Springs, then to Lavender Bliss and me, then to Chloe and spicy dogs, and to Bridget and putting out fires. At one point, Banks chats with Esmeralda at the bar, a serious conversation. Soon, we're all tipsy, and when a new Amelia Stone song blasts throughout the bar, with Banks and Wanda watching us, we head to a corner and dance.

We all crowd together, singing out loud and moving to the music, and when the chorus hits, my gaze drifts away from my friends once again to a familiar face at the bar.

But it's not the familiar face I expect.

It's my ex.

And Eric Patrick is taking our picture.

CHAPTER 41
JUST A BOUNCER
BANKS

It's a true shame I can't rip that guy's phone from his hand. Smash it in two. Toss him the fuck out.

I don't know who he is. But one of the golden rules of close protection is *not* to let things escalate. My job is to ward off trouble before it can become a bigger problem.

It's one thing to keep a low profile as a random dude takes pictures of an actress and her friends dancing at a bar. But when Ripley stops dancing, tensing everywhere as she spots the guy, it's another thing entirely.

That's my cue.

The moment her smile vanishes, I push away from the wall, stride over to her, and whisper in her ear, "You okay?"

She turns her face toward me, tucking it close to mine. "That's my ex."

Oh, hell no.

My fists clench, and my shoulders tighten. As the song plays on, I weave past the group of women, heading to the shithead at the bar. He's dressed in a white T-shirt and jeans, sporting too-messy-to-be-bothered sandy-brown hair, looking like he's trying to channel Jeremy Allen White chef energy from *The Bear*.

I get too close to him, nodding at his phone. "Maybe put that down," I tell him.

He barely lowers the device and doesn't look my way at all. He just leans harder against the wood counter, like he's the epitome of cool. "Pretty sure it's not a crime to take pictures."

"Pretty sure it's rude," I counter.

"It's a public place. And who put you in charge?" he shoots back.

"I did," I say, cold and unflinching.

He scoffs, shaking his head. "Okay, *bouncer*."

Seriously? Even if I were the bouncer, this is how he talks to someone who could toss him out the door from here?

He doesn't seem to care though. Still holding up his phone, he walks away from me and right toward Ripley and her friends, who have stopped dancing. "Hey, you," he says to her, pasting on an entirely different personality.

What is wrong with this asshole?

She peels away from her friends, moving closer to me as she folds her arms across her chest and answers him. "What do you want?"

He gives her a friendly almost-nudge that makes me want to throttle him. "So good to see you. Love that you're out having fun in this sweet town. I took some pics of you and your crew. You don't mind, do you?" he asks in the schmooziest voice I've ever heard. "This clown seems to think you'd mind." He hooks his thumb toward me.

Oh, fuck him. I bump up next to him, letting my shoulder knock into him. I tower over him by a good six inches. I easily have sixty pounds on the guy, a chest much broader, arms much stronger, and legs much thicker. And, most importantly, I'm not fucking afraid of him.

Ripley flashes a huge smile I know is fake as she says to her ex, while pointing at me, "Oh, you mean my bodyguard?"

All at once, Eric Patrick stands at attention, his eyes flickering my way now with real worry in them. "Wait. You're not—"

"Some random jackass who didn't want you to take pics at a bar?"

He backs away from me. I move closer. "B-b-but I didn't know you were with her." He gulps; then his expression shifts to a sunny smile. "And wouldn't you know it—you guys are just the people I need to talk to. These pics of Ripley and her friends would be the perfect press for the space. If I can get it."

Are you kidding me? One, he's not getting the space, and I know it for a fact. Two, what a fucking phony.

Ripley's brow furrows. "You took pictures of us for press? For the restaurant you don't even have yet?"

Eric Patrick waves toward Haven in the corner. "Your sister's a star, and you're a Darling Springs institution," he says, desperately trying to defend himself. "It'd be such a help. The space I want is right next door. I can say you were here. It'd be such great pre-buzz on social. You're going to talk to Esmeralda for me, right, Ripley? She's got some others looking at the space, and you putting in a good word would smooth it over."

I want to kill him. Pretty sure my woman does too.

She parks her hands on her hips. "No."

"C'mon," he wheedles. "You were always so helpful. You help everyone. Help a guy out. You like my cooking." His voice rises with hope at the end.

Enough of him. "She said no," I bite out.

He shrugs like an oily salesman. "Yeah, but you know how women are." His tone is all *c'mon, buddy, old pal.*

I burn. "I know she said no. That means she doesn't want you to use the pictures, and she doesn't want to help you."

"You could let her tell me that," he says, clinging to the edge of a sinking life raft.

"I did say that," Ripley says, exasperated. "You never listened, and I'm not helping you."

"But that's your thing, Ripley. You help people. You helped that woman change a tire on the side of the road after dinner once. You helped that dog that got out of its yard get back to its home. You brought a coffee from Pick Me Up to the guy who runs The Slippery Dingle."

"The Slippery Dipper, you asshole," she hisses. "You never cared about me or Darling Springs until you thought you could make money off us. So no, I'm not helping you. And you can't use my pictures on your social media."

He clutches the phone to his chest.

Like that's gonna stop me.

I reach across him and grab it easily. It's like taking candy from a baby.

"What? You can't take my phone," he says, flailing to reach his phone.

"I can and I did."

He tries to grab it, but I press a firm hand to his chest, then delete his camera roll with my other.

Then, I see red.

The dude has been live-streaming this on social media too. With the volume down, but I'm sure that's only because he's been talking shit. He probably wants to add music later and show the women dancing or something. "Seriously? Grow the fuck up," I say, then tap on the live stream, ending it. While it's processing, I go to the profile picture, then hit Archive. Next, I find the live archive and click on the broadcast, deleting it for good. Finally, I return to the camera roll to kill the backup.

"Here you go," I say. He takes the phone with a smug smile that I want to wipe off his face. "When someone says no, fucking listen. Like now. Get the hell out of this bar and this town. No one here wants your business."

"You don't know that," he says, not getting the point. "I'm going to talk to Esmeralda."

What he doesn't know is that I already did. Earlier tonight. And I know she's turning him down. We had a nice chat, and she's already lined up someone else.

Still, I'll let her speak for herself—the curly-haired bar owner with the silver stud in her nose is striding my way. "Feel free to toss him out, Banks."

"With so much pleasure," I say. I clamp my hand on to Eric Patrick's shoulder, hard enough to hurt, strong enough to make a statement.

And I escort his sorry ass to the door, then push him out of the establishment, where he stumbles down to one knee. Turns out I used a little bit of force. Oh well. "What do you know? I guess I am a bouncer too."

I dust one palm against the other, then let out a deep, satisfied breath as he scurries away.

CHAPTER 42
SURPRISE GUEST
BANKS

Ripley is on me the instant the cottage door opens, and I could not be happier. Or more turned on.

She grabs my face, her hands roaming possessively over my beard, her breasts pressing to my chest. Her lips devour mine with an *after-midnight* kind of ferocity.

This is what I want—this kind of connection. This strength in desire—hers matching mine. It's a goddamn gift when you both want each other the same way. And oh hell, do we ever. I'm pent-up and have been all night. She's hungry and determined, her hands traveling down my chest, over my stomach, around to my ass.

"Need you right fucking now," I mutter as I kick the door closed to give us some privacy. I break the kiss, but not for long. I haul her up over my shoulder, carry her to the bed, and toss her onto the mattress. Wasting no time, she kicks off her shoes. I toe off mine, then crawl up her, settling between her legs. Right where I want to be—with hardly any distance between us.

She murmurs approvingly. "You were hot back there."

"That turned you on?" I ask, though I fucking know the answer.

Knew it the second we left Prohibition Spirit. She practically pounced on me in the truck. Ran her hands down my arm as I backed up. Murmured dirty wishes as I drove. *Fast.*

"It did. Can you kick guys out of bars every night?"

"That's what it takes to turn you on now?"

She raises her hips, then wraps her legs around my waist, nice and tight. "No. It just got me going," she says, playing with my hair with eager fingers. "Fuck me now. Please."

My brain fries. It overloads with lust and need and something more. Something intense. A deep and fervent need to make this woman happy in every goddamn way.

I strip her to nothing in seconds, then toss my clothes to the floor too, turning my phone to Do Not Disturb and setting it on the nightstand. Don't need a single thing to take my focus away from my woman.

I reach for a condom, but she curls a hand around my shoulder. "I'm on birth control, and I've been tested. Negative."

A hot bolt of pleasure shoots down my spine. "Same." I draw a staggering breath, knowing the answer, but asking anyway. "You want to feel me bare, sweetheart?"

She shudders beautifully everywhere, her nipples hard, her skin flushed.

Yes, fucking yes. That's why I asked. To witness the rush of pleasure in her body.

"I do, Banks. Please."

"Spread your legs nice and wide," I tell her.

She pushes back on her elbows, lets go of my waist, then parts those beautiful thighs. That done, she looks up at me with big blue eyes full of passion and vulnerability.

And, I'm pretty sure, my future.

Emotion spreads through my chest, a deep sense of rightness. A potent hope for many days to come. I sink inside her, trembling at the feel of her and of us.

We move together in the dark, bodies tangling, skin sweating, hearts thrumming. She hooks her heels around me tight and pulls me deeper, even though I'm already so far gone.

It doesn't take long for either of us; then we're tumbling over the edge.

The next morning, I take the dog out; then I'm in and out of the shower in a flash. Ripley is next, the water pattering as I step over Hudson, who's eagerly waiting for his human. I button my shirt and hunt for my phone. Do Not Disturb is still on from last night, and when I turn it off, a slew of text messages land like coins raining down in a slot machine.

A few from Dean.

A few from my sister asking, What's going on?

One from Tabitha.

Unease rolls down my chest, but I don't have a second to open the messages. As Ripley turns off the shower, there's a knock on the door. With some concern, I head over, peer through the peephole, and tense.

It's my partner. In Darling Springs. A day before our meeting.

CHAPTER 43
TRUST YOUR GUT
BANKS

Ripley utters an *oh* when she sees Dean. She's just come out of the bathroom in a tank top and shorts, rubbing a towel in her wet hair. Hudson barks, but he's wagging his tail too. For all intents and purposes, this is an innocent scene. It's no secret we're sharing the cottage. Naturally, we'd both shower here.

Still, my first instinct is to lie. I can feel the false words climbing up my throat. *She was just showering. That's all.*

The sentence jostles around in my mouth, and it feels all too easy to say. Briefly, I part my lips to utter the cover-up. Because *she was just showering* isn't even a lie.

It's true.

But in those few dangerous seconds where lies seem easy and truth slinks far, far away, I grow ashamed.

This is what my father did.

He lied for years about his nights, his days, his whereabouts.

He built a second house of lies, and he slept in the king-size bed in the center of it all.

I've vowed to never be like him.

The fact that I even considered a lie makes my cheeks heat with red-hot shame as I meet the confused eyes of my business partner.

Dean Ortiz is six three and brawny, with a shaved head and inked vines snaking around the light-brown skin on his arms. He's one of my closest friends, and I've known him for more than a decade—yet I feel like we're worlds apart.

Since I've been fucking around and potentially harming the business we've built.

"Hey," I say on a strangled breath. "What are you doing here?"

My business partner cocks his head, saying nothing, clearly trying to make sense of the scene before his eyes—the very domestic scene of Ripley and me in the morning, casual and comfortable in front of each other.

Ripley clears her throat. "I should go do…um…farm stuff. Yeah. That."

Dean blinks again, then takes another beat, brow knitting, gesturing to the bed.

"I take it you didn't get my text?"

Shit. I wince. "Is the Webflix meeting canceled?"

But why the hell would he come here today to tell me a meeting set for tomorrow had been canceled? Why wouldn't he call?

"No. I texted you to tell you I was coming in early, Banks," he says with an unusual emphasis on my name. "Figured it'd be good to see the movie set, say hi to the Ruby Horizons client, and catch up.

I texted so you'd know I'd switched to an earlier flight." He pauses. "But seems you have company."

He says it pointedly and then waits, giving me an opportunity to explain. There *could* be a reasonable explanation. But there isn't.

I can't avoid it any longer, especially since Ripley says, "I was just leaving."

A minute later, she and her dog hustle out, and it's just me and the friend I've been lying to. Lies always catch up to you.

I shut the door, a pit widening in my stomach at the ominous click of the latch. Dean scratches his jaw as he stares at me like he doesn't even know me. The silence stretches for years.

Time to man up. I meet his eyes and own this problem. "It's what you think it is."

Dean shakes his head, letting out a long, frustrated, "Fuuuuuck."

Trudging to the couch, he sinks down and pinches the bridge of his nose. "Seriously? That is so risky, man."

"I know," I say heavily. I don't really feel better for having admitted it. Owning the truth was necessary, but it doesn't absolve me. Neither does the voice saying, *What's so wrong with falling in love?*

I shut up that voice. Now is not the time for the poets to convince me the heart always wins.

"That's like the golden rule of our business," Dean says. "Don't fall for the person you're protecting."

Like I weigh a ton, I sit next to him, "I know. I should have—"

"Told me the truth before it got this far so I could have taken you off the job."

When he puts it like that, more shame creeps up my neck. "Yes," I mutter.

"You know the deal in our line of work. When you fall for the client, you make mistakes. Get distracted. You think with your heart instead of your gut."

It's ingrained in me, and in him, so we say it together: "Always trust your gut first."

That awful feeling coils tighter in my stomach. "I let you down."

"You did. You let *us* down. But we're in this together," he says, apparently ready to roll up his sleeves and fix the mess I made. "Does anyone know?"

I shake my head. "Just some of her friends."

He blows out an annoyed breath. "I really wish you'd said no one." But then he shakes his head, like he's shaking off his frustration. "We'll tell Ruby Horizons you got pulled to another job, and I'll handle Ripley for the rest of the shoot. No one will have to know."

What did I do to deserve a partner like this? His triage skills are unparalleled. "Thank you," I say, grateful, embarrassed it's come to this, but relieved all the same.

"And then we'll move on, and you'll be more careful. Right?" He asks it like a cop letting you off with a warning.

"Of course," I say, and I'm about to add *falling for a client won't be a problem since I'll be with Ripley* when my phone buzzes again. It's as persistent as someone punching a doorbell over and over. It's my sister again, and I click open the text.

You're seeing Haven Addison's sister?

"The fuck?" I drop the phone like it's on fire, then scramble to get it from the floor. Yup. The same damning text still mocks me.

"What's going on?" Dean asks.

What's going on is a photo on *VIP Vibes* of Haven, Ripley, Bridget, and Chloe dancing at Prohibition Spirit last night. I'm in the background next to Wanda.

Why would my sister assume we're together from this shot?

I also didn't realize Ludwig was there last night. He must have been since he regularly sells to *VIP Vibes*.

Dammit, Dean was right. Falling in love does make you lose focus. I should have paid more attention to the other people in the bar.

But my sister sent another link, this one to a social media feed of hashtags from the movie. And that pit in my gut turns into a gaping maw. *That's* why my sister asked if I'm seeing Haven's sister. Because there's a picture making the rounds of Ripley and me getting out of the car, my hand in hers, our gazes locked.

I hate to admit it, but it's a good shot.

If a photo tells a story, this is the tale of two people fighting like hell to resist each other as they fall hard. This picture doesn't lie at all.

My only hope is that the paparazzi assumed Ripley was Haven again, like they've done before.

But they're not stupid.

Last night, Ripley wore a strappy tank, and her birds were visible, flying down her upper arm. That explains why this photo isn't running in *VIP Vibes*—neither of us are celebrities. *VIP Vibes* wouldn't pay News Site Ink for a shot of the star's sister and her bodyguard. This was just one of many images under the hashtag for *Someone Else's Ring*.

Ripley and I are a sidebar. A footnote. An interesting little scandal with the caption: Better look twice! If you thought Haven Addison was having an affair with her bodyguard, you'd be wrong. Her identical twin sister is though, and was seen canoodling with him before she and her star sibling went dancing at a local hot spot.

It had to have been Eric Patrick who posted this online. No wonder he flashed me that smug smile. He'd probably saved this pic somewhere else on his phone after taking it off his camera roll. "Her fucking ex," I mutter.

"This was taken by her ex?" Dean asks.

"I'm guessing so," I say. "The one inside must have been shot by a pap. This was probably shot by her ex. He's into food photography, so I guess he knows his way around a camera. And then he dropped it online because he was pissed she's not helping him get an intro for his restaurant."

Dean runs a hand over the back of his neck as I tell him about last night's encounter. "This is such a mess."

Then his phone beeps, and he checks it, groaning heavily. "What is it?" I ask, though it feels like putting my finger in the fire.

He waves his phone like he wants to chuck it. "I just got an email from Webflix. The meeting is canceled. They're looking elsewhere for security."

I fucked up everything.

CHAPTER 44
A LITTLE GESTURE
RIPLEY

Think, Ripley, think.

If this had happened to Haven, what would you do?

I'd find a way to fix it. That's what I do—fix problems. I need to focus on that instead of freaking out and pacing the lavender fields, unable to do any of my work. All I can do is stare at these pictures of us on my phone.

As soon as Dean appeared, I left the cottage and rushed to the house, finding my grandma in the kitchen, staring at her phone and the pictures her bestie had sent her. And before Grandma left for her in-person French class, she showed the snaps to me.

My heart sank like an anchor to the ocean floor as I read the captions. I owe so many explanations to so many people—starting with my sister.

But first, I need to deal with the man. With Grandma gone to her class, I head for the store before it opens, Hudson trotting alongside me. Inside the shop, I FaceTime Chloe rather than text. She's up already, walking dogs, and sounds concerned when she answers. When I tell her it's an emergency, she patches in Bridget.

My pulse spikes with worry. Wasting no time, I tell them about the pictures, and then about Banks's partner showing up unexpectedly this morning. "What do I do?"

Bridget's been putting on makeup, and she stops, furrows her brow, foundation brush in hand. "Why do *you* have to do something?"

"Because it's a mess. Because *his* business partner showed up. And, well, Banks never wanted him to know about us while we were working together. While he was protecting me." I feel guilty all over as I admit the full scope of the sneaking around. "Banks was always the one who risked the most. And I feel awful."

"But why do *you* have to fix it?" Bridget asks again.

This seems like a trick question.

"Why do you keep asking me that?" I fire back.

"Just answer," she says, loving but firm.

I huff out a harsh breath. "Because I'm fucking in love with him, okay?" I blurt out and my god, that hurt. Like ripping a jagged stone from my chest.

And my asshole friends just smile. Both of them. "Good," Bridget says, her peach lipstick shiny.

Chloe grins too. "I'm proud of you, Ripley."

Up is down. Black is white. "Why are you smiling? Why are you proud of me? This is awful."

"It is. But it's also amazing that you fell in love. Especially when you were convinced you never would again," Chloe says as the sun rises above her, its light mocking me, like it's bringing all my mistakes into the day.

And they may be right, but what good did falling in love do? "It's a mess. And I need to fix it. I have to," I say, desperation driving me on.

Bridget's smile disappears. Once her expression turns serious, she says, "Well, there's one thing you could do."

She tells me, and it sounds awful. My chest squeezes painfully at her suggestion. But I also know she's probably right.

When I end the call, I sink down to the wooden floor amidst the bottles of butterfly lavender essential oils, the eye masks promising calmness, and the dried sachets offering peace.

I don't feel calm or settled or peaceful. I feel terrible. My heart absolutely bleeds for Banks. For me, but mostly for him. Because I know Banks, and I know how awful he must feel right now. Like he failed. I know, too, that he'll do the right thing.

This means there's only one right thing I can do now, even if it feels like I'm excavating all my insides with a bulldozer.

I push up to my feet, intent on finding him, my curious pup rising too. Only, I don't have to look far—Banks is already knocking on the door.

That's so him. He always knows where to find me. He just does. He has a sense for me.

I wish I could revel in that connection. But I can't. With a bruised heart, I open the door and let him into the tiny store as the sun rises over my farm.

"Hi," I manage, and my voice sounds scratchy and raw.

Hudson trots over and wags his tail, licking Banks's hand. Briefly, Banks pets the dog, then meets my gaze. Pain etches his eyes. His hair sticks up everywhere. He drags a hand through it, like he's been doing that all morning.

"I really fucked up, Ripley," he begins, regret thick in his voice.

"Me too," I say.

He shakes his head as if rejecting that thought. "It was my fault. All mine."

"It was ours," I say.

"No. It was mine," he insists, proving that he *only* blames himself. He scrubs a hand down his face. "Webflix canceled the meeting. Just now."

My heart plummets. This is worse than I'd thought. So much worse with him losing business. "Because of the pictures?"

He breathes out hard through his nostrils. His fists are clenched. Every muscle in his body is taut. "Because I didn't act like a fucking professional. Because I didn't do my job. Because I'm a goddamn liability. I prided myself on protecting you at all costs. I take every job seriously. I looked out for you every second of the day, and what happened? I wound up in the press for falling in love with you." He stabs his chest with his finger. "I'm not supposed to fall in love. I'm supposed to protect you. *Perfectly.*"

My heart aches so much I can't even process the terrible beauty of those words—*falling in love*.

The words come with a cost. And the cost is coming. Still, my impulse to take care of everything is too strong to ignore. "You can't beat yourself up," I say gently, trying to shoulder some of the blame.

"But I can, and I will. This is on me. I'm just like my father."

This poor man. "You're not," I say, emphatic as I shake my head.

He's silent for a beat—a long, thoughtful one that lets me hope he'll see the difference between himself and the man who lied about an entire second family.

"Fine. Maybe I'm not," he says quietly, and a sliver of sunshine warms me. Then it disappears behind a cloud when he adds, "But I still can't get away with this."

I brace myself. I knew this was coming because I know this man. He'll take it all on. He'll think he can control everything. And he'll want to pay the price.

So I have to do the right thing, and I must do it before he can. If he says the next thing he came here to say, he'll hate himself even more than he does now. I won't let that happen.

"Banks," I begin, the word scraping my throat raw. But he's not the only one who knows how to protect the people they love. I can protect him too. *From himself.* I won't make this any harder for him than it already is. I won't fight it. I won't try to convince him he's wrong. Nor will I let him be the one to pull the trigger.

I get the words out first: "I think we should…stop."

The word burns my tongue as I break it off.

But when he nods gratefully, muttering a terribly heavy, "We should," I know, too, that I had to be the one to do it. This way, he won't entirely blame himself. I suppose that's the only gift I can give him right now.

Sometimes you just have to let go of the ones you love.

CHAPTER 45
YOU AND NOTTING HILL
RIPLEY

I should have done this weeks ago. When Haven's finished shooting for the day, she meets me in the kitchen. I texted her earlier, asking if she could talk. Her jaw is set, her gaze wary, but curious.

She peers toward the front door. "This isn't very private. Anyone could come in here."

She sounds…professional. I feel awful. But I'm supposed to feel bad because I fucked up. "Let's go to—"

"The lavender maze."

That's where we used to escape to when we were kids. The fact that she picked it gives me hope that I'm not the worst sister in the world. But Haven shakes her head, dismissing the maze idea. "Actually, I don't want to deal with bodyguards watching us."

"Me neither," I say, and when my gaze drifts to the staircase heading to the garden level, it's clear we're both thinking the same thing.

Grandma's suite. Fitting, since Grandma's is where we've both always felt safest.

We head downstairs and rap on the door. It's perfunctory though, since after her in-person French class, she went out with friends. I go inside, and we sink down on the couch.

I don't mince words. "I should have told you sooner."

"Yeah, like all the times I asked," she says pointedly.

She's right. "I'm sorry," I say, guilt twisting in me. I almost say *I wanted to but didn't,* or *I tried to, but it never felt right.*

But it doesn't matter. She asked, and I denied it.

Her blue eyes hold mine, and I don't see forgiveness yet. "Why didn't you?" she asks gently.

I blow out a big breath. It's such a loaded question. It has too many answers. But there's no need to hold back now. "Because I didn't want to worry you. Because I told him I'd keep it between us. Because I wanted your first big role to go off without a hitch. Because I didn't want to pull focus away from the film and on to me. Because it's such a huge chance to bring attention to the farm that Mom and Dad built, to the town they loved. And I didn't want anything to take away from that. And because I didn't want the relationship to go south and then have you worry about me," I say, my voice choking on the bitter irony. "I never want you to worry about me."

"Oh, Ripley," she says. The staunch professionalism vanishes as she reaches out and wraps her arms around me. "But I do worry about you."

"You do?" I ask, voice breaking.

"You're my twin. You're my friend. You're my person. Of course I do. Why would you think I wouldn't?"

"Because I have enough worry for both of us," I say through tears long overdue.

She strokes my hair. "I know. And I've let you do that for too long. I've let you be my big sister instead of my twin sister."

My throat tightens with more emotion. God, it feels never-ending today. "I love being your big sister."

"But sometimes I can carry the burden. Sometimes I can worry about you." She lets go and meets my gaze. "Just because I was once broken and you fixed me doesn't mean I'm still broken."

"I know that," I say, feeling stupid for even thinking that. After all, she did pull that send-Grandma-to-cooking-school rabbit out of her hat.

"I mean it," Haven says. "I know you took care of me when Mom and Dad died. I know you looked out for me. You made sure I got to auditions. You fixed my car, kept me from falling to pieces, handed me tissues, and dried my tears when I cried through the night. And you got me to therapy." She pauses to let all that soak in. "But I healed. I will always love Mom and Dad, and always miss them. Because of you, I learned how to make it through the grief. Sometimes, you can let me take care of you. Like right now."

She reaches for me again, and I can't do a thing but break down in her arms. It's not only for Banks. Mostly, it's for us—two girls who lost their parents and had to find their own way, who had to forge a new family together. I rain tears I barely shed long ago. I cry for days, till my face is red and splotchy and my nose is snotty.

Then, I breathe out and look up. "I'm so sorry."

Haven smiles, exonerating me once more. "There isn't any real harm done. I wish you told me sooner, but I also understand you in ways you think I don't. I get you. I wanted you to tell me, but I know why you didn't." She reaches for my hands, squeezing them. Then she arches a curious brow. "But remember that day you wore the mock turtleneck to The Slippery Dipper when it was fifty million degrees out?"

Uh oh. I should have known she'd figure that out eventually. Still, I protest feebly with, "It wasn't fifty million degrees, and it had short sleeves."

"Fine. Fine. But now that I think about it, was there some new allegedly amazing skin care routine you'd just tried?"

"Maybe," I mutter.

"The kind that leaves a splotchy mark somewhere," she goads.

"Possibly."

She squeezes my shoulder. "Twin powers."

I smile and rest my head on her shoulder. "Nothing gets past you."

"I don't know if that's true. But I want you to know you can tell me things. I want you to know that you can share with me."

"I do. Especially since you told me about *Notting Hill*."

A questioning laugh bursts from her. "*Notting Hill?*"

"That's what I've been calling William in my head. He's *Notting Hill*. Because he runs a bookstore, and you're the movie star."

She smiles, nodding. "Yeah, I get it. I've seen the movie. It's a good one."

"It is. Will you have a happy ending too?"

"I hope so." She pauses, tilting her head. "And you?"

I tell her what happened this morning, and she frowns. "Ripley," she says, full of sadness. "You took the fall."

"I had to. I wanted to make it easier for him."

"The shoot's over in a few days though," she says, hopeful. "Maybe then?"

I shake my head. "I don't think so. He needs to build his business. It won't look right that he had a fling with a client. Reputation matters to him."

She seems to give that some thought, then nods. "I get it," she says.

That night, when she's leaving, we do another switcheroo. Only it's not me pretending to be her or vice versa. We switch bodyguards.

It's just easier that way.

CHAPTER 46
THE COLLATERAL DAMAGE
BANKS

Before I leave that night, there's one more thing I have to do—apologize to Tabitha.

As I wait for Haven to finish up in the house, I hang out near the gate for Lavender Bliss. Tabitha often goes for a run early in the morning and again when the shooting is done for the day. She's a creature of habit, so I find her returning to the property, trotting past the gate. I've been trying to grab a minute with her all day. This is the first chance I've had.

She slows to a walk, and I give a quick wave, the signal for *got a second*. She takes out her earbuds and joins me where I'm waiting by some Hidcote bushes.

"Good run?" I ask.

"It was great," she says, catching her breath. "I'll miss the lavender when we're gone next week."

Me fucking too. But I don't say that. I cut straight to the chase. "I wanted to apologize."

She arches a curious brow. "For what?"

Is it not obvious? "For being distracted on the job."

"Oh. Okay. Apology accepted." She waggles her phone. "Can we talk more tomorrow? I need to jump on a call with Juniper for our next film."

"Of course," I say, and that's that. She's moving on because *she* didn't mess up.

She heads inside, and I have no idea what that exchange means for the rest of the job. Or, more importantly, for any referrals from them in the future.

A few minutes later, Haven comes out and we get on the road. For the first time in three weeks, I leave the farm for the night. It's like leaving a part of my heart behind.

Or maybe all of it.

I try not to look back as I take Haven to her hotel, then head to Wanda's old room, taking it over. Thankfully, one of the crew members finished up early, freeing up a room for Wanda in the main house.

At least I have a job with Ruby Horizons for another night.

What does it matter when I can't have another night—no, all my nights—with Ripley?

I can't escape the feeling of déjà vu when I leave the hotel with Haven on Friday morning. I swear all eyes are on me as we cross the lobby.

That family at the complimentary coffee? They're whispering about me. That haggard businessman checking out? He's definitely seen the hashtag about my fling with the woman I was protecting.

Okay, fine. Logically I know any double takes are solely for the rising star I'm flanking. But emotionally, I can't shake this familiar feeling. It's like the day my mom, sister, and I went into town after the news of my father's second family had made it to the neighborhood forums.

We walked into the ice cream shop for salted caramel cones, and the teenager with braces behind the counter blinked at us, like, *Is that them?*

When my mom stopped at the grocery store, the cashier gave her curious looks. When she picked up her dry cleaning, the woman at the register asked if she was okay.

But were those people checking in on us the same people who'd posted our names, numbers, and addresses on social media? We were the collateral damage of my father's secret second life.

We never knew who'd been talking about us. Eventually, we left town because it was easier to start over.

What will be easier now though? Will all my potential clients know I'm the guy who fucked a client?

I grit my teeth as I walk Haven out of the hotel, scanning left and right, then behind. When we reach my car, I open the door for her and make sure she gets inside safely.

"I'm sorry about what happened," Haven says once I hop into the driver's side. I miss Ripley's truck. I miss Ripley's voice. I miss every single thing about Ripley.

"I appreciate that, but it's okay," I say to Haven, trying to be tough. Impervious.

"You don't have to be stoic. I know you guys were the real deal."

My heart rips all over again. I swallow roughly, nod my best *thank you*, and then turn on the engine. It was the real deal, and I screwed it up. I should have done what Dean said—stepped back before I made my personal life everyone's business.

I knew better.

"Maybe it doesn't have to be over," Haven adds, and it's sweet that she says that. Truly, it is.

But I'm not about to tell her I didn't only ruin a romance. I might also have damaged the business I run with my friend. Webflix was our best new lead, and we're still waiting for the other new contracts to come through.

If they come through.

Hell, I don't even know how Tabitha and Ruby Horizons feel about us, but I'll probably find out any minute.

When we arrive at the farm, that sense that everyone knows my secrets slams into me again. Sam, the guy who's hot for Ripley, gives me a funny look as I bring Haven to the set. Tabitha barely says a word to me. I swear the director is looking at me like *you're the guy who canoodled with the star's sister, you dipshit.*

All day long, I imagine hearing whispers, and I hate them. I don't know why they haven't kicked me off the job for the few remaining days. Maybe it's because Dean's here, keeping the peace, smiling, chatting, making nice. No wonder he's the front man. He's better with people than I am.

Well, nearly anyone is better with people than I am.

The sun's bright today, so I drop on my shades and cross my arms, focusing on the job.

The way I should have done all along.

If I had, this afternoon I'd be leaving the set in the capable hands of my team and traveling down to San Francisco for a meeting at Webflix with my partner. But because of my lack of professionalism, we lost the client.

That evening at The BookHouse, I escort my client down the hall toward her room. If I'd stuck around to sort out the mistaken identity in San Francisco, I might not be in this mess right now. If only I hadn't taken off that night. My list of regrets is long.

"You need anything else?" I ask Haven when we reach her room.

Shaking her head, she smiles, and it's *almost* a familiar smile. It's close to Ripley's, but not as sassy, or as feisty, or as *Ripley*. Another reminder of my mistakes.

"I'm all good," Haven says, then lowers her voice. "But I'm going to have a visitor later."

I straighten my spine. "What time?"

Her lips twitch. "Soon. Maybe a half hour."

"I'll still be working." But once I'm off, Dean and I will meet with Tabitha at last.

Haven brings her finger to her lips. "Don't tell a soul who it is then."

I don't ask for the man's name. I'm pretty sure I know—the

bookstore guy that Ripley went all mama bear over the other week. A smile tugs at my lips as I picture Ripley giving him hell and telling him to be good to her sister. That's so very her. My heart thumps a little harder at the memory, but I try to shut it down.

I don't get to enjoy those memories anymore.

Haven goes into her room, and a half hour later, I spot the bookstore guy heading down the hall carrying a canvas bag with what looks like books in it, and a bottle of wine. A bouquet of tulips too.

He flashes me a smile. "Hey there. How's it going?"

"Great," I lie. When I'd thought he might have had a thing for Ripley, I'd burned with jealousy. Now I envy him for a different reason.

He stops at Haven's door. "I'm here to see Haven."

"She mentioned it," I say. I'm jealous he gets to see his woman. I'm jealous because he hasn't fucked up his romantic life.

I let him in, and when Marcus, my backup, comes, I head to the lobby where Tabitha and Dean wait for me.

"Let's get out of here," Tabitha says. "This place is teeming with people. Mister Fox? Round of pool?"

I love pool, but I'm hardly in the mood, and it shows in my playing. Despite my track record, I miss the first shot. And the second. The next one too.

"Man, you used to be a pool shark." Dean shakes his head sadly as he chalks the end of his pool cue.

"Easy come, easy go," I say, shrugging, hardly caring.

We play a few more rounds, and Tabitha sinks her final shot, winning the game. Then, since I'm the guy on probation, I let Dean take the lead on the debrief.

"Listen," he says to her, setting down the pool stick. "We wanted to chat about what went down yesterday with security—how it was handled and what we can do differently for you."

Tabitha tilts her head. "I'm not sure what you mean."

Figuring it's best to own it, I skip the preliminaries. "The social media stuff about Ripley and me."

"Oh. Right." She sounds blasé.

"You texted about it in the morning," I prompt when she doesn't go on.

"And you apologized for it yesterday evening. But honestly…" Another pause, then she shrugs. "I don't care."

I'm floored. I was not expecting that. "You don't?"

"I really don't care what you do in your personal life. Half of Hollywood is sleeping with each other. The fact that you had a thing for a client on the set? It just kind of sounds like the stuff we make movies about. With the rumors about Chris and Haven, and now the *behind-the-scenes* romance on the side, even more people are talking about the film…so thanks?"

Dean smiles, and it's the brightest one I've seen from him in a while. "I'm pleased to hear it's not an issue, but it won't happen again."

"Me too," I say. Holy shit, that's a relief. We talk for another half hour about security for the shoot and give her some ideas for best-practice talks she can have with her staff on future projects, then we leave on good terms.

Perhaps a lot of what I felt this morning was all in my head.

But it doesn't solve the problem of what's next for Apex Solutions. I need to focus on business for the rest of the shoot, but thoughts of Ripley are lodged in my brain when I get in bed later.

I reach for her in the middle of the night—but she's not there.

In the morning, I look for the dog to take for a walk, but I'm not with him either. I'm not at all where I want to be.

My mom texts me to check in, offering to drive up and take me to dinner that night. I instantly agree. I need to see her and Emily more than ever.

That day I try like hell to zone in on the job as I safely ferry Haven past the photographers waiting for a shot they'll never get of her and Chris.

The money shot.

A picture like that? It's a hell of a payday. Paparazzi would do whatever it took to get a pic of them touching, kissing, hugging. Something unposed. Something unexpected. Something real.

All day I think of photos. The first one that Silas snapped of Ripley outside the market. The picture a tour group might have tried to take of her the next day. The photo of Ripley and Chris in the produce aisle the day the movie began shooting, captured by some random person we never saw. The actual publicity photos of Chris and Haven, and of course plenty of pics of them separately.

During a break, I scroll through my phone and return to the photo that got me in this mess—the one outside Prohibition Spirit before Ripley and I went in. I study the angle, remembering the group of people outside the bar, trying to place Ripley's ex there the other night. Was he walking past the group? Behind them? And when did the paps arrive who took the inside shot, the one that wound up on *VIP Vibes*? I do some more digging on Eric Patrick Waterstone. Not only do I find endless shot after shot of the dishes he's made—the dude is understandably into food porn—I find pics of him posing with local celebs in New York.

My jaw ticks, and I begrudgingly admit the guy knows how to work it.

When I get a break, I lob in a call to my friend Tyler in Los Angeles, since he keeps close tabs on the comings and goings of paps as well.

"Aww, you must need something," he says when he answers.

"Yeah, a cold beer. I'll owe you one when I return to LA," I say, though the thought of leaving twists my gut.

"Deal. Now what can I do for you?"

I ask him to check on who's working for *VIP Vibes* these days.

"I'm on it," he says, then I hang up and get back to work.

CHAPTER 47
LANGUAGE, YOUNG MAN
BANKS

When the final shot is in the can that afternoon, the whole cast and crew whoops. Haven hugs Sam, Chris hugs Vega, Wanda hugs Tabitha, and on and on and on. I can't hug Ripley because she's off in the fields, busy tending to her lavender and her dog.

I watch Ripley as the cast and crew make plans for an impromptu party at Prohibition Spirit. Vega says she needs to stay at the farm and finish up some work, but she hands Sam her credit card, telling him that drinks are on her.

Haven appears beside me, asking in a low but hopeful voice, "You're off tonight. Want to come?" She nods toward the faraway fields, where her sister works with Cyrus by her side. "We could… plot."

Haven wiggles her brows, and I consider the offer as I stare at Ripley. I can't stop wondering. Can't stop asking *what-ifs*.

But it's over with Ripley, and I don't know what there is to plot with Haven, so I smile and say, "Thanks, but I'm having dinner with my family."

"Have fun."

She returns to the group, chatting with Chris, his hand on her arm, the two of them laughing. It seems so platonic to me, but I'm on the inside. From the outside, it could look like something else, and that's why I've had a job for the last few weeks.

But the job ends when the cast and crew leave tomorrow. So the rumors about Haven and Chris aren't really my problem for much longer.

I leave and hit the gym at The BookHouse. Afterward, I shower and head to meet my mom and sister at the tapas bar in town.

I'm more relieved to see them than I ever thought I'd be.

"Hey," I say, and I can hear the gratitude in my voice as Mom pops up from the table and gives me a hug. Can she hear it too? I wrap my arms around her for longer than usual.

Emily gives me a curious look as she comes in for a hug as well. I take it, finding comfort in family.

When we let go, I pull out their chairs and sit once they're settled.

"Okay, you're a nice man and all," Mom says, cutting to the chase, "but you're not Mister Affectionate. What's going on?"

I sigh, but I don't want to burden her with my situation. "Just glad the job is finally over. It was…a complicated one."

Emily eyes me suspiciously over the menu. "Lies. Tell me sweet little lies."

"I assure you, the job was very, very complicated."

She scoffs. "Complicated by you falling in love with your client."

Mom slaps down the menu. "What happened? Who is she? Can I meet her?"

"I wish," I mutter. "Let's order."

"We'll order; then you'll talk," she says in the most mom tone ever.

The server swings by, and once we're alone again, Mom puts on her very-concerned-about-my-son face. "So, I ask again, what happened?"

Emily bats her lashes. "Yes, I really want to know too."

I roll my eyes. "You always want to know."

"I do, and it sounds like you *finally* have good tea. So spill it."

I could act put upon, like I sometimes do with Emily for fun. But I'm frayed too thin, stretched to the bone. I have no fight left in me. "Emily's right. I fell in love with a client, and it was distracting. I couldn't focus on the job. I wound up on social media, of all fucking things."

"Language," Mom says.

"Sorry," I mutter.

Emily fills her in on the details. "There was a picture of him and Haven Addison's sister going out the other night and looking madly in love." Grabbing her phone, she shows Mom the image.

"Oh, I loved Haven in *The Dating Games*." Mom studies the photo and adds, "Her sister's quite pretty too."

For the first time, I look at the picture and see something besides my damaged reputation and a lost client. I see the last few wonderful, amazing weeks. Warmth fills my cells. A dangerous smile tugs at my lips as images of Ripley flash before my eyes and words fight their way out.

"She's beautiful and smart and fiery and caring and thoughtful," I begin, and once I start, I can't stop. The valve has loosened. "She's bold and kind, and she keeps me on my toes. She loves to knock me down a peg or two or three, and she also tries to protect me. When I first started the job, she tried to give me the slip."

Mom's enrapt at this info. Emily too. I take them back to the first day on the job and how valiantly my woman tried to ditch me.

Soon, they're laughing and asking for more. I tell them about the bike, and about Ripley's friends showing up outside the salon and goading us.

I tell them about how we had to share the cottage.

I don't tell them how we spent our nights, or how utterly, absolutely in sync we are after dark. That's for Ripley and me.

Instead, I tell them her favorite lavender is Melissa. That I set bouquets of it in the cottage for her.

"I walked her dog and made her origami, and she showed me around Darling Springs, and I felt like…" I pause, giving some real thought to how I felt with the woman I fell for. The answer's clear and beautiful. Like freedom and desire all at once. "Like I wasn't chased by the past."

Mom sighs happily.

Emily even drops her usual sarcasm. "That sounds really nice." But then she clears her throat. "So why aren't we meeting her tonight then?"

I groan, and it's full of self-loathing. "Because I ruined it all."

I tell them that part too, finishing the tale right as the food arrives.

"This looks delicious," Mom says of the risotto, but she doesn't pick up her fork to take a bite. Instead, she turns her gaze back to me, her eyes thoughtful. "It sounds like you *are* stuck in the past though, Banks."

I flinch. "Why do you say that?"

"So you fell for a client. I get that you want to be professional, but you're not the first person to fall for a client or an employee, and you won't be the last. But you're beating yourself up because you still think it's somehow your fault that your father lied about his second family. But it's not."

Way to be direct.

Ripley said the same thing the other week. Did I believe her? I tried, but maybe I didn't fully accept it.

Emily's gaze softens too. "It's definitely not your fault, Banks. It's Dad's."

"But…" I begin, but the objection dies. What am I even protesting? I'm not entirely sure.

Mom deals me a tough-love stare. "You think you don't deserve nice things because you've held on to this belief that you have to protect me, and Emily, and any woman in your path at all costs since you *think* you could have protected me from him," she says with a strength of character that comes from her own resilience, from the way she picked up the pieces and moved on. "But you couldn't. He did what he did, and he was the *only* one to blame."

Like Ripley said.

And dammit, it's high time I believe it. Maybe belief is a choice. A line in the sand. A before and after.

Right now, I can choose to believe that I wasn't responsible. And I will.

I feel decades lighter. Something I held on to for years is loosening its grip on me. But what about *my* mistakes over the last few weeks? "I am to blame for my own actions though."

Mom shrugs like that's not a big deal. "Fine. Maybe you should have stepped away from the job sooner. But you didn't. Is it such a crime? And did you actually fail to protect Ripley when you worked with her? As far as I can tell, not a hair on her or her sister's head was harmed." She holds up her forefinger. "You lost one potential client, and that's too bad. But maybe the bigger question is this—is she worth it?"

"Worth losing a client over?"

"Yes," Emily says, seeming exasperated.

It takes nothing to answer from my whole heart. "Yes. She is."

Mom smiles. "Then let go of the past and move into your future. You're worth it, and it sure as hell sounds like she is."

Emily's eyes pop. "Mom! Language!"

Mom points her fork at me. "Well, someone was being stubborn, so I had no choice. Now stop being a perfectionist and start moving past your mistakes."

"And start tonight," Emily adds.

"I will." As we formulate a plan, I dig into my pasta, and it's the best meal I've had in ages.

CHAPTER 48
MIDNIGHT PICNIC
RIPLEY

In the cottage bathroom, I set the lotion on the counter, not even remotely lined up with my toothpaste. I get to be chaotic again. I can leave things where I want them. I can clean coffee cups in the afternoon instead of the morning.

Yay.

But the possibilities bring me no real joy.

After I rub the lotion onto my legs post-shower, I trudge back into the main room of the cottage. The lonely cottage. One more night here; then, when the crew leaves, I can return to my house. I'm counting down.

Hudson perks up, then shakes into a stand from his spot on the floor, trotting my way to lick my leg. "Of course, you lotion hound," I say, petting his head.

Dogs are so weird. Why do they like to lick lotion? I should look it up. It'll keep my mind off other things.

Like, oh say, heartache.

I head to the sliding glass doors, yank them open, and sit down on the Adirondack chair on the deck in my sleep shorts, my dog at my side. I look up at the inky-black sky, stars shimmering light-years away, then down at the lavender fields stretching before me into the maze with its fairy lights.

Next week, a tour group will wander through that maze. Next weekend, a couple booked it for an engagement. The week after that, we'll have more picnics than I can count. The shop will reopen, deliveries will continue, and business will increase.

Somehow, in spite of all the madness, everything's worked out.

Nearly everything.

My bad-romance track record remains intact, but other than that, I didn't distract from the shoot, I didn't pull focus from the town, and I didn't worry my sister.

I draw a deep breath, inhaling lavender and calmness, wishing one more thing had worked out. I look up at the sky again, looking for a shooting star.

But finding none.

Oh well. It's for the best anyway.

I'm the practical one. The independent one. The fix-it one. And yet, my heart still hurts, and I keep wondering.

And wishing.

And stupidly hoping.

Best to go inside. Tomorrow I'll need to work on moving on. That'll be easier once I'm back in my regular space. "C'mon, boy," I say to Hudson, and he heads inside with me once again.

As I shut the door, my phone beeps with Haven's ringtone. I grab it from the table and swipe to answer. "Hey, cutie. Do you miss me already?"

"Obviously," she says. In the background, glasses clink, and music plays at the wrap party. "So much so that I want to come over and hang out. You and me. Does that work for you?"

"Of course."

Some things never change. Her and me—the way we depend on each other, need each other, rely on each other.

"I'll be there in thirty minutes. We can have a midnight picnic." Like we did when we used to sneak out of the house after our parents were asleep and play in the field.

"That sounds perfect." I'm genuinely excited to see her. "I'll get everything ready."

"What did you say?" Haven asks, but from her lowered volume, she's not talking to me. Faintly, I hear Chris Carlisle's familiar voice, but I can't make out the words.

When Haven returns to me, she says, "See you soon."

We end the call, and I change out of sleep shorts and into leggings and a T-shirt. I slide on sandals, twist my hair into a bun, then head to the door, expecting Hudson to follow. But he flops down on the carpet with a beleaguered sigh. "Fine, fine. I get it. It's past your bedtime."

He rolls to his side, obliging me to bestow belly rubs onto his soft fur and good-night kisses on his black-and-white head. When I'm done, I head to the kitchen in the house, grabbing olives and cheese from the fridge, then nectarines from the fruit basket.

Grandma sails in as I'm setting things on the counter next to a cutting board.

"Did I wake you?" I ask.

"No. I was reading. Are you making a midnight picnic?"

"I am."

"I'll help." She slides right in, picking a paring knife for the fruit. "It'll be nice to have you back in the house tomorrow."

Vega's still working in a quiet room. The crew will be back to spend their final night here, so I've got one more night in a cottage full of memories. Wanda is in the house tonight, like she's been since she took over for me, but I've never really needed close protection here on the farm. Tomorrow, when the film crew departs, she'll take off too, and my bodyguard days will be behind me.

So it goes.

"I'm looking forward to my own room," I say, but there's wistfulness in my tone too. Yes, I can't wait to return, but I did love sharing that small space and that one bed with Banks.

"But it'll feel odd with everyone gone." Grandma studies the big kitchen. It's clean and neat, like it was when Banks would stroll by in the morning. He must have cleaned up this afternoon. The thought makes my chest hurt.

"I'll miss the coffee cup fairy," she says, then turns to me. "And you?"

There's no point in denying it after I told her everything that happened in the last few days. "I will."

She sighs thoughtfully. "Maybe tell him before he goes."

I scoff. "But he made it clear it was over."

She lifts a questioning brow. "Did he though?"

"Um. Yes."

She sets down the knife. "Or did you do it for him so he wouldn't have to?"

"Six of one. Half a dozen of the other," I say as I set Marcona almonds on the plate.

"Is it though? He told you he fell in love with you. Did you tell him the same?"

I freeze. She's right. I didn't say I loved him. And now I wonder if I should have.

CHAPTER 49
AN EXTRA PASSENGER
BANKS

Emily helps me, so we're done awfully fast. I say goodbye to Mom and my sister, then hop in my car and turn up Bach's Brandenburg Concerto No. 3. The second movement is fast and furious, and with that adrenaline boost, I drive to Prohibition Spirit.

The scene of my big mistake.

Or maybe it's an opportunity. A do-over. A chance to write my future, moving on from the past.

Inside the club, I quickly find Haven. Marcus too. I head over to the former Marine and clap him on the sturdy shoulder. "Thanks, man. I'll take over now."

"You sure?" he asks, his tone serious since he takes his job seriously. "You need me for anything?"

That's a good question, but I don't want to put the cart before the horse. "I'll let you know if I do."

"You know where to find me," he says, giving a crisp nod. It's good to see he's not treating me any differently now than he has in the past.

I turn to Haven. "I can't thank you enough."

She rubs her palms excitedly, her blue eyes twinkling. "Do I get to plot now? Should we grab a booth in the corner and come up with all the plans?"

"Actually, I have one already."

She frowns, but it's playful. In the privacy of the booth, I let her in on the scheme, and her eyes widen. "We need to go now. We can't wait another second."

As we head to the door though, Chris weaves through the crowd, flanked by his own security detail—a guy named Daveed, who's the size of a tank.

Chris reaches Haven, setting a hand on her arm. "Haven, did you say you're going back to Lavender Bliss tonight? Vega is still there, and I desperately need to chat with her. Can I join you? I'd hate for guests to keep showing up all night long since none of us are staying there. Best for your sister if we all show up at once?"

Ah, hell.

I was looking forward to a quiet farm. But maybe it'll be good, having other people there—a distraction so Ripley doesn't spot me too soon. Yeah, I can make this work.

Haven glances at me, making sure it's okay. "Is that all right, Banks?"

"Absolutely," I say. "I've got room in my car for everyone."

Chris clasps his fingers together in gratitude. "I am in your debt."

He's not really, but it's amusing that he says so.

We leave the party, and I'm not at all surprised that the major paparazzi are gone. They've probably realized by now there's no money shot here. A couple of passersby lift their phones, but all they'll get is two actors leaving a bar with their bodyguards.

Haven and Chris smile and wave like it's another publicity shot of co-workers, nothing more. I'm sure that's how PR has coached them, and it's wise in a world where there's a camera in every pocket. Everyone's the paparazzi now.

Daveed and I quickly usher the actors to my car. Once they're in, we take off.

I check the rearview mirror religiously as I drive. No one seems to be following us. That's good. Ten minutes later, we arrive at Lavender Bliss. My pulse spikes, and my heart clatters as I park.

Chris and Haven go inside the farmhouse while Daveed waits at the gate, keeping watch. I dart around the back of the cottage, where Ripley can't see me, and head quietly toward the cottage's front door. On the way, I steal a glance at the main homestead. Through the kitchen window, I can see the woman I'm madly in love with hugging her sister.

That clattering in my heart? It accelerates.

Once inside the cottage, I shut the door. Just in time—a fifty-pound black-and-white pup charges toward me in excitement. Hudson jumps up and licks my face. He smells a little like satsuma oranges.

"You want to help with my project, boy?"

He whimpers happily in agreement.

I tell him to sit. He complies, and I get to work. I'm nearly done when my phone buzzes with a text from Tyler. He's following up on my questions about who works for News Site Ink and, by extension, *VIP Vibes* these days, and he's found something all right.

CHAPTER 50
TABLES TURNED
RIPLEY

Haven seems distracted. But she's leaving tomorrow, and she's meeting William back at her room later, so I don't make a big deal out of her occasionally shifting her gaze around the farm.

As Chris and Vega chat in the kitchen, Haven and I amble past the Hidcote, me carrying the picnic basket and her carting a blanket. The fairy lights welcome us at the entrance to the maze, and we go inside.

"Can you imagine what it'll be like with schoolkids here? Trying to find their way out? Laughing, having a blast when they reach dead ends?"

"Like we did when we first explored it."

"So many years ago." We were the original lavender maze wanderers. We've known its paths for decades, so we head to our favorite spot. Once we settle on the picnic blanket and spread out the food, I'll ask what she thinks about me talking to Banks and whether maybe I should return with her tonight to her hotel and find him there.

But before we can turn the corner, a voice calls out.

"Haven! Got a second?"

It's Chris, and when we turn around, he's jogging into the maze to meet up with us, that warm smile matching his equally warm voice. When he reaches us, he first turns to me. "Thank you again for all your hospitality. I couldn't have done this without you. It was as profound as I'd expected."

"My pleasure," I say.

Then he focuses his attention squarely on Haven. "I was just talking to Vega, as you know, about some of her future projects," he says. "And I told her I'd love it if she could keep me in mind for the TV show she might be doing with you."

Haven's smile is slow and surprised. "Of course. I'd love to work with you again."

"It would be an honor. Truly." He shifts again toward me. "Permission to hug?"

"Absolutely," I say. As he brings me in for a hug, a twig snaps beneath his foot, breaking the silence of the otherwise still night.

He asks the same of Haven, they exchange a hug, and then Chris takes off. As we head deeper into the maze toward our favorite picnic spot, I whisper, "Did he just ask to be on a project with you?"—even though, of course, that's what he did.

"Yes," she says, then holds out her arm, the hair on it standing on end. "Pinch me."

"How the tables have turned," I say.

A twig snaps again.

That's when it hits me. That first twig wasn't under Chris's foot. It was a few rows of lavender hedge away.

A feeling of unease creeps up my spine. "Haven, we should go," I say.

I reach into my pocket for mace but come up empty. Right. I'm at home, on the farm, where I'm safe.

Except, I don't feel safe.

Time to turn around. But when I do, I walk right into a slab of a man instead. He's holding a camera. His hair is blond and slicked back, and he looks terribly familiar.

He's the guy who hit on me the night I met Banks. And in a heartbeat, he grabs me and yanks me into a choke hold.

CHAPTER 51
MY NEW PARTNER
BANKS

A few minutes ago...

I check the text as Hudson lifts his snout, his ears pricking.

Tyler: Hey. Good thing you checked. There's some new hotshot photographer who's working for News Site Ink and anyone he can sell to. His name is Ian Joseph. Used to be a news photographer but lost his job when a lot of pubs went under. He's upside-down in credit card debt. Now he's making a living as a studio photographer, but evidently, he supplements his income from time to time with celeb shots. What do you need to know?

That's a damn good question. With my project nearly finished, I head to the door. I'm honestly not sure I need to know anything more right this second. Because the hair on the back of my neck stands on end, and my gut is telling me something right now.

But so is Hudson.

Out of nowhere, he's up and racing to the door, barking at it. "What's going on, Hudson?" I ask as I swiftly join him, while googling Ian Joseph.

The second his picture pops up, I nearly crush my phone in my hand.

Are you fucking kidding me? That's the sleazeball who hit on my woman the night I met her. He must have been the one who took the picture of us the other night, not her ex. That smug smile from her ex was just a smug smile. I burn, lava flowing through my veins. As I throw open the door, Hudson tilts his head, his ears pointing up. I track him and spot a shadow slipping into the maze on the far side.

Not on my watch.

Adrenaline rushes through me, bulldozing any remnants of fear right out of the way. I run like hell across the front of the lawn, past the shop, to the fairy lights illuminating the lavender maze. Out of the corner of my eye, I spot Daveed hanging back by my car, then straightening up when I pass like a shot. But I've got no time to assess whether he moves or not.

Haven took Ripley into the maze for a midnight picnic to keep her busy. To get her safely out of the way so I could be in the cottage. And some scum sneaked in on the other side. The shoot's over, so we no longer have round-the-clock guards. Even if we did, the property is huge, and a picket fence is nothing to penetrate despite the floodlights.

When I reach the mouth of the maze, I hurtle in with Hudson, powered only by the need to get to the women right this second. And I nearly run into Chris Carlisle. "What's going on?" he asks, alarmed.

Me fucking too.

But I've got no time to talk. "Someone's here," I mutter, then sidestep around him, following the dog.

Briefly, my mind jumps back in time to the other night when Hudson chased a ball into the maze. Holy shit. He knows the maze perfectly. Knows the dead ends and the pass-throughs. He barks at me urgently.

I follow him, racing around one coil, avoiding paths that go nowhere as the sound of a struggle grows louder.

CHAPTER 52
TWIN TRICKS
RIPLEY

The douchebag locks his arm around my neck, my back to his chest as he breathes on me. He smells like patchouli and sandalwood, like he did that night at the hotel bar.

Then, he was just a jerk, not taking no for an answer. Now, he's a threat.

My pulse is surging, and my brain is racing quickly through escape plans, the ones my grandma taught us. But first…his arm. He's not cutting off my airway, but he's coming far too close.

Before I can knock him down or kick him in the balls, I need to turn my head so he doesn't cut off my air.

"I'll make this real easy for you two," he hisses as he sneers at my sister, and in the distance, I hear the scrabble of paws against grass, then footsteps, moving fast.

I don't know how close they are, and Haven's eyes are wide, etched with terror—and fury too. "Let her go, you jackass," she bites out.

"I will. If you do something for me." As he tries to negotiate whatever the hell he's doing, I'm focused on one thing—getting enough oxygen that I don't pass out. Carefully, I turn into his body to relieve the pressure on my airway. "How about you call Chris over here right now?" he says. "So I can get something this time. Now I want my fucking picture."

Jesus. This guy is desperate.

"No," I spit out.

"I'd be happy to hurt your sister so you can help me," he offers to Haven in a faux sweet voice.

Fear charges through me, but so does rage, and I lift a foot to kick him in the shins, but I only clip the edge of his leg.

He dodges the blow, feinting a bit to the side but still keeping that arm around my neck.

"Let her go," Haven demands as she reaches her hand into her front pocket. *Please let that be her mace.*

As I work out a better angle to kick the guy, I hear Hudson barking somewhere nearby. I don't know what my dog will do if he reaches us. He's a tracker and a lover, but he's not a fighter.

I don't let it distract me. I have to focus on fighting.

"One picture; then I'll let you go," he says. "Because guess what? I'm not missing the chance this time."

This guy is pissed because he didn't *get something* from me that night? So now he's determined to get what he thinks he deserves?

Fuck him.

Haven jerks her arm out of her pocket right as I lift my right foot and put everything I've got into a kick aimed straight at his crotch. Hudson's barks grow louder. As I connect, Banks flies around the corner of the hedge past the dog, lunging for the guy while I kick the bastard in the balls.

Banks grabs the guy's arm right as he tries to reach for his bruised crotch with it. "Fuck, that hurt," the guy whines.

"Good," Banks seethes, then rips him the rest of the way off me. In no time, Banks slams him to the grass, jerks both arms behind him, and pins his wrists.

Oh.

Ohhh.

Banks sinks a knee onto the guy's back.

"Get the fuck off me," the asshole mutters in between gasping breaths.

With anger pouring off his body in waves, Banks fumes at him, "Like I told you before, get away from my girlfriend. And her sister." Hudson jumps in front of the guy, barking right at his face.

"Fucking dogs," the guy grumbles.

Banks jerks the guy's wrists harder, handling him in a whole different way than he handles me. "And don't even think about touching her dog."

The helpless photographer kicks his feet as if he can escape that way. But it's like watching a cartoon character try to free himself from under an anvil. Banks is impassable as Hudson barks angrily at the guy who's trespassed in his maze.

And the man who swore he'd protect me turns to me with passion and fire and love in his deep-brown eyes.

"Are you okay, sweetheart?" he asks with such worry that my heart breaks beautifully.

"I'm okay. I kicked him in the balls!" I bounce on my feet, a surge of post-ball-kick adrenaline coursing through me.

"And I was about to mace him if you hadn't," Haven says, waving a small pink tube.

"Twin tricks," I say, then, flooded with relief, I hug my sister, and I'd really like to fall into Banks's arms too, but he's busy restraining the guy who's clearly so pissed at me for turning him down, at Banks for saving the day, and at himself for failing to take a picture of me in the wild back then, that he followed us into a maze tonight.

Only it's my maze, my farm, my home. As Banks jerks him up from the ground, keeping a firm grip on his hands, I stare at the guy, who does indeed look like the douchey boss in a movie. He's got a fancy dress shirt on tonight too. I guess he thinks he doesn't look like a scumbag photographer, but he does look like a scum.

"Guess you missed the shot a second time, asshole," I say, then smile at the jerk.

And we leave the maze.

CHAPTER 53
ORIGAMI SEA
RIPLEY

Sheriff Simmon flips her notebook closed, then pushes her beige hat farther on her head. "Thanks for all the info, Ripley. That'll be real useful," she says, standing on the farmhouse porch.

"No problem," I say.

"And you too, Haven," she says, nodding to my sister.

"Happy to help," Haven says.

Sheriff Simmon knows us both because she goes way back. She's been the sheriff in Darling Springs for about fifteen years.

"You're taking him in on trespassing?" Banks confirms, his arm locked protectively around my waist. He hasn't let go of me since he handed off that asshole to the authorities. Chris contacted them while we were in the maze, and they arrived quickly.

"Yes, we are. Assault too," the sheriff adds.

"Good. Thanks for coming so quickly," he says.

She nods, then says to me, "We'll be in touch. And thanks again for sending Chloe my way. She's great with Baxter."

"Glad to hear. Spicy Chihuahuas are her specialty."

"He's the spiciest." She and her deputy return to their vehicle, where Ian Joseph stews in the backseat, handcuffed.

While Sheriff Simmon was taking Haven's statement, Banks told me Ian Joseph has been freelancing recently for some online celeb sites, trying to make a fast buck or two to get out of debt. He's the one who snapped the picture of Banks and me outside Prohibition Spirit the other night and set it loose online—not my ex. Guess Ian remembered, too, that Banks had called me his girlfriend once upon a time, and he had a bone to pick.

Ian's also the one who took the shot of Haven and me inside that night. And based on what Banks told the sheriff—a bunch of people had taken Chris and Haven's picture when they left the wrap party—it seems Ian was among them and followed the car unseen to the farm, then parked far away and entered on the other side of my property. Haven was right when she said some photographers are really good at staying hidden to get the shot they want. He must have stayed out of sight earlier this week at the bar, and again tonight.

But that guy is off my property now, cruising into custody.

There are still too many people here though—Chris and Daveed, Haven and Wanda, Grandma and Vega—when I only want to be with the man holding me.

So I can tell him how I feel.

I've hardly had a chance to think about what it means that he's still here. But he called me his girlfriend, and I can't help but love that. Even so, I'm going to say my piece as soon as I get a second alone with him.

Grandma hugs me one more time, making sure I'm okay, then Haven clears her throat and says, "Everyone leave."

I blink. Whoa. "Someone's bossy."

"Yes, that was the whole point of my coming here. Go and enjoy your midnight picnic," she tells me.

Right, the picnic. I'd forgotten about that, but Chris and Daveed picked up the food in the maze that Hudson didn't eat. I'm not hungry though, so Haven thrusts the picnic basket at Grandma, and Banks says to me, "Your sister makes a good point. We should enjoy this."

And I do want to be alone with him desperately, but still, I ask Haven, "What did you mean—why you're here?"

But she waves me off and heads to Wanda's car. Another switcheroo.

I don't bother with the hostess thing and say good night. I just wave and head to the cottage with the man and the dog.

Banks keeps his arm around me the whole time, his fingers running along my arm like he can't bear *not* to touch me.

When we reach the cottage, I say, "There's something I've been meaning to tell you."

"There's something I want to tell you too," he says, reaching for the doorknob.

"You go first," we say in unison, then laugh.

He opens the door, holding it for my dog and me. I'm about

to say *I'm in love with you* when my gaze lands on a sea of origami on the bed.

My hand flies to my mouth. "What is that?" I ask, breathless, full of wonder.

"It's for you." He sounds nervous but hopeful—the opposite of how he was thirty minutes ago in the maze when he was tough and terrifying.

I love all sides of him, including this tender, romantic one.

"I enlisted your sister's help to keep you busy so I could do this," he explains.

So that's what Haven meant.

I walk slowly to the bed, in awe of the gorgeous array of pink, red, and white folded letters of the alphabet.

I pick up the first one. It's the letter *I*. Then I read the others, neatly arranged on the bed.

I'm sorry.

I love you.

Let's try again.

So simple. So…everything.

I can't believe he professed his love to me in origami. Emotions swim up my chest, filling me with joy and happiness, with possibility and soul-deep love. I spin around, my throat tight as I say, "I love you too. So much."

Banks crosses the room in a flash, lifts me in his arms, and holds me close. "I'm so glad you're okay. When I saw that guy with his hands on you, all I could think was I can't let him hurt the love of my life."

The intensity of those words echoes like a loud, bright bell. "The love of your life?" I ask, looking back at him.

He sets me down, cups my cheeks, and nods earnestly. "When you know, you know."

My smile is so wide, it can't be contained. "I know too. I feel the same."

He ropes his arms tighter around me and peppers me with kisses. "I can't let you go. You're worth it. You're worth everything. I can't put work in front of you. You're what I want most in the world."

My eyes shine with tears. "You've got me then."

He pulls back and holds my face, his chocolate eyes filled with promise. "We'll make this work. You're worth it," he repeats as if making sure I've heard him.

But I did. "We're worth it, Banks. We are."

He kisses me again, with an intensity that says he fears he almost lost me tonight. With a passion that says he doesn't want to let go.

I don't either.

I melt into his kisses. I glow under his touch. And I want all of him.

I pull him to the bed, the back of my knees hitting the edge of the mattress.

"Hold on," he says, then sweeps the origami onto the floor.

"It's a mess," I shriek playfully.

"And I don't care," he says, then he peels off my clothes and lays me down. His clothes vanish next, and soon, he's sinking inside me.

I wrap my legs around his waist, my arms around his shoulders, and I pull him close, deep inside me.

It's different this time. It's somehow even better. Once more, we come together in the cottage.

Only this time, we won't be a secret in the morning.

After we wake the next day and shower, we get on our bikes and ride into town. We grab coffee together and hold hands as we walk along Main Street, a road so familiar I could close my eyes and still find every shop.

As we near the crosswalk, Banks peers ahead with curious eyes. I follow his gaze to the end of the block where a man's popping out of a real estate office.

"I think that's...Sawyer," Banks says.

"Is he someone you met on one of your various shopping excursions for toys or bikes?"

With a smile, Banks shakes his head. "All good guesses. Actually, I ran into him at Mister Fox, with Monroe. We played pool one night."

Banks calls out to the dark-haired man who looks a touch out of place in his button-down shirt and charcoal slacks. Sawyer's more business-y than most people I see in town. When he hears his name, he turns around. It takes him a few seconds, then he must recognize my guy since the corner of his lips curve up and he says, "Banks."

We catch up to him on the corner of the street, and Banks makes quick intros, then nods to the real estate office. "Is that *maybe* turning into a definite?"

"Maybe," Sawyer answers, but it's said in a hopeful tone.

"Aren't you elusive?" Banks jokes.

"I don't want to jinx anything," Sawyer says, then turns to me. "I might be opening a business here."

"You should," I say, ready to sing Darling Springs's praises. Except, wait. "It's not a competing lavender farm, is it?"

"Ripley will fight you on that," Banks warns.

"I would never dare. Not when there's a world-class one already here," Sawyer says.

I look to Banks approvingly. "I like him. You may keep him as a friend."

"Thanks," he says dryly.

I turn my focus back to Sawyer. "I hope it works out. This is a great place to live and to run a business. Ideally, one that sells my lavender at checkout."

Sawyer flashes a confident smile. "If the deal comes through, I'll sell your lavender. That's a promise. And hopefully I'll see you both around."

"Yes, and for another round of pool since I like taking your money."

"I don't like that part. But I do need some pool," Sawyer says, then sighs heavily as he meets Banks's gaze. "So much stuff to figure out."

"Then that round should be sooner rather than later."

Sawyer gives a nod, then heads in the opposite direction, passing the dog daycare where Chloe sometimes works. He pauses briefly at the window. For a second, I wonder if she caught his eye, but I probably just have romance on my mind.

I focus on Banks, squeezing his hand. "You look good in Darling Springs."

"Good thing I plan to be here quite a bit."

It sure is.

We start making plans for what happens now that the job is over and our life together is beginning.

EPILOGUE
RIPLEY

I'm not a fashion girlie, but some truths are immutable, and this is one: *Thou shalt show your red-carpet dress to your besties.*

In my Los Angeles hotel room with my phone balanced on the bureau, I do the obligatory twirl for Chloe and Bridget via FaceTime. They're at Bridget's house.

"What do you think?"

Bridget taps her chin. "I mean, it's kind of your color," she deadpans.

Chloe smacks her shoulder, then turns to the screen. "She means it's totally your color, and you look perfect."

"You two are such assholes, and I love you."

"Love you too," Bridget says; then Chloe brings my dog into the frame and adds, "Hudson says hi."

I blow him a kiss; then they sign off.

I take a look in the mirror, and they're right—lavender is my color. The satiny dress is a simple sheath with wide straps, and it hits at the knees. My hair is down, curling over my shoulders, and my fingernails are unpolished.

I feel dressed up, but still...like me.

It's a good feeling. But I feel even better a few minutes later when my escort knocks on the hotel-room door. It's *our* hotel room—we're staying here together, but he stepped out to let me finish getting ready.

When I open the door, his breath hitches. "You look incredible," he rumbles.

I feel incredible too, under his heated gaze. "Maybe I'll let you spank me later."

"A man can dream," he says.

"We share the same dreams," I say as I smooth a hand down his dark-blue dress shirt. He's wearing a charcoal suit tonight, with no tie. The combo is doing things to me. He looks hot and all mine—just the way I like it.

"We better go before I toss you on the bed and have my way with you."

"Later," I say.

He offers me his arm, and I take it. Together, we head to the theater for the premiere of *Someone Else's Ring*, several months after it was shot in my hometown.

The lightbulbs don't flash when I step out of the limo. The cameras don't pop. The entertainment press has figured out—mostly—that I'm not my sister. It took a little time and some strapless dresses for them to learn the difference. But I also know the world is fascinated with identical twins, so sometimes we give them what they want—a shot of us together.

Haven waits for me on the red carpet. We smile for the cameras, and a sea of photogs snap shots of us—the star and the sister who hosted the film crew.

Silas and Ludwig are here behind their lenses. Funny how they were never really the problem. They're just a couple of guys trying to make a living. As for Ian, he was charged with trespassing and simple assault and served a short jail sentence. I also have a restraining order against him, so he can never set foot on my farm again.

It's good to be proactive though, so I took a self-defense refresher course that my boyfriend gave me as a gift. Sometimes, I even practice on him. Well, I don't kick him in the balls. I rather like all his parts.

With the photos done, I step out of the limelight, letting Haven take the spotlight she deserves as she walks the red carpet with her fiancé.

Notting Hill.

William proposed to her a few months ago, and they're getting married in Darling Springs in a couple of weeks. I happen to know the perfect place for their wedding—Lavender Bliss.

They went public as a couple shortly after she returned to LA. Their first public date? A bookstore in Silver Lake where they ordered coffees and kissed over a stack of paperbacks.

New Chris also made his first public appearance recently with his new girlfriend. And wouldn't you know it? She's from Darling

Springs as well. Turns out the fortune teller at Tell Me Your Tarot was spot-on. Chris Carlisle, one of the world's most bankable stars, is seeing Katrina from The Sweet Spot. Cookies were the way to his heart.

They head in next.

Grandma is here too. She flew home from Paris to attend the premiere. She's been having the time of her baking life with Laurent, her Frenchman. I miss her fiercely, but I couldn't be happier that she's getting to enjoy her golden years while I manage the farm, her bees, and often, the lives of Ramona and Cyrus. But I wouldn't have it any other way.

After Grandma and her man sail into the theater, I go inside with my boyfriend. But tonight, he's doubling as my bodyguard.

Banks likes to play that role from time to time when I have public events, and since I've always had a thing for his protective side, I don't mind it one bit.

Oh, who am I kidding?

I love it.

BANKS

Inside the lobby, I stop to say hi to Dean, who wears a black suit and an earpiece.

"Everything good tonight?" I ask my business partner.

"Everything's great," he says, then turns to Ripley. "Glad to see his better half," Dean tells her.

"And I'm happy you're keeping busy," she says.

"Me too." It's said with relief, but also with contentment. Dean claps me on the shoulder. "Get inside, brother. You're off duty. Go enjoy the movie with your woman."

I smile. "I will."

As we weave through the glittery crowds, I set a hand on Ripley's back, as I've always done. I keep a close watch for threats, as I always will. She's not a client anymore, but I'm not a bodyguard most of the time either.

Sure, with Apex Solutions I take the occasional job as a close protection officer, but mostly I've transitioned to training new guards and to management and IT security.

The other benefit? I can do it remotely a lot of the time. Apex Solutions has offices now in Los Angeles and just outside of San Francisco, and I can spend most of my days in the small town I've come to love.

All is well with Dean. My friend understood when I told him I'd put my heart on the line for Ripley. Love happened on the job—I'm not the first, and I won't be the last.

And in the end, our business has grown because we're damn good at what we do. True, we didn't get the Webflix gig, but Tabitha sent us more work, and now we handle any security needs for Ruby Horizons Productions, including red-carpet events like this one. We've picked up other clients too, in the entertainment business and out of it, including Lavender Bliss. The farm has grown in popularity as a tourist destination, and Ripley hosts celebrity events there that require security.

Tonight though, my job is to go on a date with my woman.

We head into the auditorium to watch the movie. I take her hand in mine, and as the love story plays out on the screen, I slip back in time, remembering the way our tale played out behind the scenes.

For a while, I wasn't sure if we were just one of those *it seemed like a good idea at the time* kinds of things.

Now I know exactly what we are. We're the kind of good idea that lasts a lifetime.

Soon, very soon, I'm going to put a ring on her finger, maybe after we return to Darling Springs.

Our home.

BONUS EPILOGUE
RIPLEY

"And do you, William O'Connor, take Haven Addison to be your wife?"

The officiant—Cyrus—asks the question in the middle of the lavender fields, just outside of the maze.

My sister's groom gives what sounds like the easiest answer ever: "I do."

My heart swells, and I steal a glance at the man standing mere feet from me. *My guy.* His gaze holds mine with so much love and affection that another tear slips down my cheek.

Grandma's crying too. She stands on Banks's other side. There are no chairs since the ceremony is short and sweet and will lead to a party right here on the lawn, like Haven wanted.

"Now, you may kiss the bride," Cyrus says.

When William leans in to kiss my sister, my heart thunders,

but this time it's not for her sake. It's for the man who can't stop looking at me.

I swear, ever since the night in the maze, Banks has been unable to take his eyes off me. But I don't think it's fear of loss. I think it's just what he said that night—*when you know, you know.*

That's how I feel about him too.

Later, once the ceremony ends and everyone's dancing at the reception, he takes me in his arms and spins me around.

"Do you want to get married here?" he asks when I stop in front of him.

I'm startled, but not for long. "No."

"But you love it."

"I do. But I work here, so I want to get married someplace else. The beach, a restaurant, a coffee shop. Paris. Anyplace."

He laughs. "Anyplace but here."

Well, it's the groom I care about most. But I'm pretty sure he knows that.

"Yes," I say. "Anyplace but here."

He hasn't asked me yet, but I'm very, very patient.

The next day, we take off to San Francisco for a date. Just like we talked about when he first suggested we see each other beyond the assignment, we escape to the city now and then for dates. He mentioned it one day in my truck, and I said *I think San Francisco has some nice cafés, restaurants, nail salons, and yoga places.*

I give my pup a goodbye kiss, and then Banks and I get into my truck. He drives, and on the way, we stop in Sausalito for a quick cup of coffee with his mom and Emily.

I adore them, their love of books, and his mom's love of cooking, which reminds me of Grandma. I love, too, the way they tease Banks. No one is better at teasing him than I am, but Emily is a close second.

We say goodbyes and cruise over the Golden Gate Bridge, and Banks drives me to Hayes Valley.

We spend the day ducking in and out of cute shops, checking out tulips blooming in the park, and popping into a record store where I find some vinyl, one of his favorite Mozart symphonies, for his collection.

He clutches it to his chest. "Can't wait to blast it."

"I know," I say. The day unwinds, and we head to The Resort, a five-star hotel near Yerba Buena Gardens.

We check in and Banks suggests a drink, so we head to the lobby bar. After we order, the bartender sets down a canvas bag next to Banks.

That's odd. I tilt my head. "Why is he giving you a bag?"

Banks's brow furrows. "Good question. Let me see what's in it."

He fishes around in the canvas, then pulls out...an origami bird. It's lavender and sturdy, with bigger wings than the first one he gave me.

Before I can even ask who made it, Banks is down on one knee, holding the bird in his hand. "Ripley Addison, I've said it before, and I won't ever stop saying it. You're the love of my life, and I want nothing more than to spend the rest of mine with you. Will you marry me?"

He lifts the bird higher, and I gasp. It's no ordinary origami animal. Inside is a ring crowned with a sparkling diamond, brighter than a star. It's surrounded by amethyst stones, the shade of… lavender.

My eyes well with tears as joy floods my entire heart and soul. "I would love to be your wife."

He stands and slides the ring on my finger, then he kisses me like I'm worth everything.

Just like he is to me.

READ ON FOR AN EXCERPT OF LAUREN BLAKELY'S
MOST VALUABLE PLAYBOY

CHAPTER 1

My hair is sticking up.

In my defense, it's always sticking up.

I have what's known as permanent bed head. Which can be awesome, if I want to look like I just strolled out of a most excellent roll in the hay, complete with a sexy stranger running her hands through my dark-brown strands.

It's less awesome for pulling off the part of a classy athlete dressed to the nines. I'm decked out in a tailored charcoal-gray suit and parked in a leather chair in a suite at the Whitney Hotel in the heart of San Francisco, along with a bunch of other guys from the team.

Violet's trying to curb my bed head. Her long fingers thread through my hair, aiming for a reverse roll-in-the-hay effect. "I swear, Cooper, you've had the most stubborn hair your entire life."

I wiggle my eyebrows. "It takes after me. I can't be tamed either."

She rolls her amber eyes, her long chestnut hair spilling over her chest. "That's right. You're a wild mustang. Impossible to domesticate."

I neigh.

She stops, sets her hands on my shoulders, and gives me a sharp stare. "Can you count with your hooves too?"

I drag a wing-tipped foot along the carpeted floor one, two, three times. "I can go all the way to ten."

"You let me know when you make it to twenty, Mister Ed. That's when I'll truly be impressed," she says, with the smile I've seen for the last twenty years. I've been friends with Violet since we were kids and I moved to her hometown, a few blocks away from her house.

I rub my palms together. "Excellent. I have a goal to shoot for. You know I love goals."

She laughs. "I do know that."

Give me a task, and I'm nose-to-the-grindstone focused. I've been that way my whole life. Run a mile in under six minutes? Sure thing. Throw a ball downfield twenty-five yards? Let's do it. Win a scholarship to a top-tier school? Consider it done, and done with a smile.

Violet stretches her arm behind her, silver bracelets jingling as she grabs some hair gel in a black tube from the chrome coffee table. "We need to domesticate your lovely locks, Cooper. I don't have a riding crop with me, but I think this gel will do."

I give the tube a skeptical stare. "You're not going to put a ton of goop in my hair, are you?"

She adopts a serious expression. "Absolutely. It's a brand-new product I've been testing at my salon. It's called Goop for Guys. It's so perfect for you." She lowers her voice to a whisper. "But I won't tell anyone you have to use...*product* to look so pretty."

"More like pretty ugly." A deep voice booms the insult across the suite. Jones is the king of put-downs, and one of my closest friends on the team. At the moment, he's lounging in a chair, scrolling through his phone, and wearing a custom-fitted dark-navy suit.

The team publicist, Jillian, organized the event and chose the tailored suit theme for this year's auction, our annual holiday fundraiser for the San Francisco Children's Hospital. Her exact words were, "Suits are like catnip to women, and to men, too, and I want my team of pretty kitties to raise even more money this year."

That's a tall order, but most of the dough comes from the entrance fee—a donation to simply walk in the door. We've already circulated among the crowd, chatting with fans in the ballroom, finishing the mingling session while the speakers played "It's Raining Men." That song presaged the final event of the night—the auction itself, when the single men on the team strut their stuff.

I glance over at Jones, picking up the insult volley. I eye his midsection suspiciously. "How's your girdle fitting you tonight? Is that why you look so nice and trim?"

He pretends to adjust it. "Yeah, I borrowed yours."

"It's a comfort fit. I can see why you'd need it."

"You can wear it next. A *blushing bride* always needs one."

That's what the guys call me now. *Bride.* But hey, I'll take it over *bridesmaid* since it comes with the starting job after three long years on the sidelines.

Violet shakes her head as she flips open the tube. "The two of you—"

"Are clever, brilliant, and handsome devils? Why thank you," I say, straightening my vest. I went three-piece, all the way. If Jillian wants us to wear suits to rake it in, I'll damn well do my best to bring home a four-peat. I've been the recipient of the highest bid the last three years, and since I love streaks, I want to keep it up this year too.

For the kids.

I want to win for the kids. The hospital does amazing work, and I gladly support it.

Plus, bragging rights do rock.

That's all that will be rocking this year. I need all my focus on the field, which means no full-benefits package with this date, even if the opportunity should present itself. I spent the last three years idle on the bench but busy after hours. This season is a whole different beast now that I have a record and reputation to think about. We're closing in on a wild-card spot in the playoffs, and these days the only scoring I plan to do is on the field.

Violet tips her chin at my attire. "I like the vest. You rarely see anyone wearing a vest here."

We live in casual country, home of the hoodie, and land of the jeans. "Is that your way of telling me you're a vest woman?"

She laughs, then lowers her voice. "I'm an *everything* woman." She lets that comment hang between us, and for a moment, my head is in a fog. *Everything.* What sort of everything does Violet Pierson like? Everything in bed? And why the hell am I thinking these thoughts about her? Violet's not only *my* friend, she's also my best friend's sister. "And you're going to clean up, my friend, since there are few things hotter than an athlete dressed in a suit."

"Yeah?" I ask, meeting her eyes as she squeezes the goop onto her hands, and my mind continues to wander down the *everything* yellow-brick road. Every position, every night—is that her sort of everything?

"Of course. You have a great face, a nice body, and that top-notch suit fits like a glove," she says, listing these attributes like they're hardwood floors, a quiet dishwasher, and a front-loading washing machine. Violet meets my eyes, and her tone is cheery. "Don't worry. I'm only saying *nice body* in an empirical sense."

I put on the brakes, since it's not very sexy to be described like an appliance.

"Right. Of course." I nod, wiping the *everything* thoughts from my brain too. "It's a completely objective compliment."

"Totally clinical."

I adjust the vest anyway. Just in case it *empirically* looks better this way. Or clinically, for that matter.

She runs her gel-covered hands through my hair. "Let's at least try to tame you for the cameras."

The auction is being carried live on local TV, and that's why Violet is here—to give us a little touch-up before we go on air. She's a hairstylist, which happens to be one of my favorite professions in the world.

One afternoon during my sophomore year of high school, the grizzled old dude who'd cut my hair forever was out, and his twenty-two-year-old granddaughter filled in for him at the barbershop. I glimpsed the angels in heaven when she leaned in to cut the front of my hair, and I've been a big fan of haircuts ever since.

But I'm not checking out Violet like that, even though her breasts are precariously close to my face as she styles the mop on my head.

I'm absolutely not thinking of the angels I'm seeing.

I can't think of her that way.

She's Trent's sister, and he's been my best friend for twenty years, all the way back in elementary school. That places her firmly in the not-allowed-to-even-consider-whether-she-might-be-hot category. I've never thought of her as a babe, not once in all the years I've known her. Which is all the more impressive considering she has a rocking body, lush chestnut-brown hair, and big amber eyes. Oh, and she has a wicked sense of humor. But I don't think of her as smoking hot, even tonight when she's wearing those black jeans, the kind that look as if they've been painted on, and that silvery tunic thing that clings to her chest.

Nope.

That's why I talk to her like a friend. Or an appliance, for that matter.

"Just don't make me look like a douche," I say.

Jones chimes in from his post on the couch. "Yeah, he can do that just fine on his own."

Violet glances over at him, then back at me as she finishes. "Yes. *Fine* being the operative word. I'd say Cooper looks quite *fine* indeed." She gives me a wink.

Ha, take that, Jones.

She shifts her gaze to the couch and our kicker, Rick. I'd like to say he's our secret weapon, but everyone knows the broody-eyed Stanford grad has the best foot in the league. That right toe of his has hurled the pigskin more than forty yards when he's needed to, and he's only missed one field goal so far this season. Harlan's here, too, his suit jacket hanging over the back of his chair. He's our star running back, and even though I prefer to throw the ball, I'll hand off to him too. He's escaped hordes of humongous linemen with his quicksilver feet.

These guys have seen a hell of a lot more action than I have, since they surrounded the Renegades' superstar Jeff Grant, who retired last year. Despite the ribbing, they've welcomed me as the new quarterback, due in part to the fact that it's December, we're sporting a 9–4 record, and we have a real chance to clinch a wild-card spot in my first season as the starter.

After she wipes her hands on a nearby towel, Violet parks them on her hips, surveying the guys in the room. "Look at you boys. Such pretty Renegades." She waves a hand dismissively. "Don't mind me. I'm just getting into the spirit of objectification for tonight."

"You want to bid on me, don't you, Vi?" Rick calls out, flashing her a gleaming white smile that contrasts with his dark skin.

"It's all I can think about," she says with an over-the-top purr. She leans close to the chrome table, rooting around in her purse. She finds her wallet, flips it open, and shows him a few tens. "Will that be enough for you?"

"We're running a discount on Einstein," Harlan says, scratching his stubbled jaw. "You can have him for a ten and a six-pack."

ACKNOWLEDGMENTS

Thank you so much for reading this book. It's a story I wanted to tell ever since I visited a lavender farm in Washington state. I was absolutely enchanted by the smells, the sights, and the blissful escape that the farm brought to me. I hope that this story has given you a temporary escape while you've spent time in Darling Springs at Lavender Bliss.

Thank you so much to all the wonderful humans who helped to bring this story together. I am so grateful to Michelle Wolfson for her stewardship and abiding faith, to Deb Werksman for her belief in the story and her insight into exactly what it needed to shine, to Jocelyn Travis for shepherding it over the finish line, to Anthony Colletti for his calm wisdom, and to KP Simmon for walking by my side every day. Big thank you to the entire team at Sourcebooks who brought this story onto shelves. And to my team who helped make it shine—Lauren, Rosemary, Kara, Sandra, Karen, Virginia, Steph, Claudia, Kim, Lo, Rae, and Jill. Endless love to my family—my kids and my husband and my four-legged little loves.

Most of all thank you to *you* for picking up this romance.

ABOUT THE AUTHOR

A #1 *New York Times*, #1 *Wall Street Journal*, and #1 Audible best-selling author, Lauren Blakely is known for her contemporary romance style that's cute but spicy. Lauren likes dogs, cake, and show tunes and is the vegetarian at your dinner party.

Website: LaurenBlakely.com
Facebook: LaurenBlakelyBooks
Instagram: @laurenblakelybooks